LORD

& OTHER
LOST STORIES

ARNOLD BENNETT

Edited and with an Introduction by John Shapcott
University of Keele
www.arnoldbennettsociety.org.uk

CHURNET VALLEY BOOKS
6 Stanley Street, Leek, Staffordshire ST13 5HG 01538 399033

© John Shapcott & Churnet Valley Books 2011
ISBN 9781904546818

Dedicated to Peter Preston
Bennett scholar and valued friend

The cover is a painting by Sally Richardson
after a contemporary poster for the
8 h.p. De Dion Bouton

**One of a series of Arnold Bennett titles, in paperback and a limited and
numbered hardback edition:**

HELEN WITH THE HIGH HAND
LEONORA
THE REGENT
THE PRICE OF LOVE
A MAN FROM THE NORTH
THE OLD WIVES' TALE
THE PRETTY LADY
THE CARD
ARNOLD BENNETT'S UNCOLLECTED SHORT STORIES

CONTENTS

'Lord Dover' was serialised in *Gunter's Magazine* in May, June and July 1905

INTRODUCTION

When editing *Arnold Bennett's Uncollected Short Stories 1892-1932* (2010) I included in my 'Introduction' the cautionary note that '[i]t would be premature to claim that this collection is the definitive complete uncollected short stories' (p.7). Such hesitancy was to prove well founded. Within days of publication I was receiving possible leads for new uncollected stories, all of which were diligently followed-up. In the majority of cases the titles forwarded for consideration proved to be either alternative titles for stories already published - English and American magazines sometimes used different titles for the same story - or factual journalistic pieces appearing under titles that could easily be mistaken for fiction, such as 'The Girl' (*T.P.'s Weekly,* 12 November 1909) or 'The Daily Miracle' (*Evening News*, 6 May 1907).

The most substantial, and frankly intriguing, lead came from Alan John, an enthusiast for the short story form in general. He had carried out an extensive search of various newspaper archives online to find previously overlooked stories. In particular he drew my attention to the Fiction Mags Index at philsp.com, which turned out to be an invaluable guide to magazine fiction, and to the New Zealand Government's National Library website of newspapers and magazines. The previously unexplored New Zealand connection opened an entirely new and fascinating window on Bennett bibliographic studies, locating not only a lost Five Towns story, but also providing clear evidence of any number of Bennett stories and serialisations appearing in New Zealand, either simultaneously with, or indeed prior to, their English and American publication. One of the most notable of these is the story 'Midnight at the Grand Babylon Hotel', which was published in the New Zealand *Star* newspaper on 24 March 1905, with an apparent twelve year gap before it appeared in the expanded Thomas Nelson edition of the story collection *The Loot of Cities* (1917).[1]

Given the large number of periodicals published in the United Kingdom during the period in which Bennett was writing (1891-1930), and without even taking into account the important American market and the rapidly expanding demand for magazine and newspaper material in the British Empire, it is perhaps not surprising that definitively cataloguing all of Bennett's more than 160 stories under their variant titles, and in their range of worldwide publications, continues to offer a major bibliographic challenge. In many respects Bennett was fortunate to begin his professional writing career at precisely the time when the demand for periodical fiction encouraged editors to place an emphasis on commissioning short stories. In his *How To Become an Author* (1903) Bennett writes that not only was there a rapidly increasing demand for magazine stories but that 'of course it remains unaffected by the vicissitudes of trade, the rumours of war, and the preoccupation of politics' (p.109). He proceeds to report on the results of his request to editors for statistics relating to the number of stories published in their well-known magazines over the course of a single year:

Strand Magazine	62
Pall Mall Magazine	63
Pearson's Magazine	67
Harper's Magazine .	88

Bennett adds that the 'fiction-manager of Messrs. Tillotson's syndicate[2] informed me that he bought annually about two hundred

1. Anita Miller's authoritative guide to Bennett's published writing, *Arnold Bennett. An Annotated Bibliography 1887-1932* (1977), does not mention 'Midnight at the Grand Babylon Hotel'. Nicholas Redman includes the story in his recent 'Arnold Bennett's Short Stories. An Alphabetical List' (*The Arnold Bennett Society Newsletter*, Vol.4, No.15, Winter 2010-11), with a question mark against its possible periodical publication.

2. As editor of *Woman* Bennett did most of his business with Tillotson's 'Fiction Bureau', a Bolton-based fiction syndicate with a sound literary and commercial track-record for supplying both the London and provincial press since 1871. Peter Keating believes that the 'success of Tillotson's indicates more graphically than any other single factor the enormous market for fiction in the last two decades of the nineteenth century, with the cheap provincial press reaching many readers who were unaffected by the changes in the circulating libraries or by the metropolitan monthlies and weeklies' (*The Haunted Study*, p.44).

short stories of various lengths' (p.110).

Bennett first entered this growing and financially rewarding market for short story fiction in December 1891 with his *Tit-Bits* prize-winning parody of Grant Allen's own *Tit-Bits* prize-winning serial *What's Bred In The Bone,* published earlier the same year. Bennett's achievement in winning the prize appears all the more remarkable when it is realised that he faced competition from some 20,000 other hopeful entrants, whose now lost manuscripts provide evidence indeed of the number of aspirant writers of the period, all anxious to gain entry into the professional magazine market place. Bennett drily records his moment of triumph in his autobiographical *The Truth About An Author* (1903):

> It happened that the most popular of all popular weeklies had recently given a prize of a thousand pounds for a sensational serial. When the serial had run its course, the editor offered another prize of twenty guineas for the best humorous condensation of it in two thousand words. I thought I might try for that, but I feared that my friends would not consider it 'art.' I was mistaken. They pointed out that caricature was a perfectly legitimate form of art, often leading to much original beauty, and they urged me to enter the lists. They read the novel in order the better to enjoy the caricature of it, and when, after six evenings' labour, my work was done, they fiercely exulted in it. Out of the fullness of technical ignorance they predicted with certainty that I should win the prize. (p.58)

Bennett was evidently concerned still in 1903 to protect his hard-won literary reputation by emphasising that his circle of artistic Chelsea friends saw no inconsistency between caricature and aesthetic value. Whilst readers might be hard-pressed to discern much of 'original beauty' in the piece, they will surely discover a story that reproduces the plot and that imitates the style, tone and sentiments of Grant Allen's original serial with uncanny accuracy, together with an impressive ability to maintain a fast farcical pace which disintegrates into incoherence. To have the story now readily available for the first time since its original publication[3] will, I hope, prove invaluable to future Bennett scholarship, making it possible to trace and explore the source of his undoubted fast-paced narrative skills honed in subsequent years in so many of his own short stories.

The first six of Bennett's articles and stories to be published in a London periodical all appeared in *Tit-Bits* between December 1891 and May 1893.[4] When his story 'The Advanced Woman' appeared in T. P. O'Connor's paper, *The Sun*, it marked an advance for his reputation. O'Connor, a radical journalist and Irish Nationalist M.P., saw his newspapers - the half-penny *Evening Star* (founded 1888), the *Sunday Sun* (1891) and *The Sun* (1893) - as vehicles to combine his political reform agenda with a mission to widen his readers' cultural horizons. Toward this end a typical front page of *The Sun* included two columns of political news, a column of celebrity gossip, a column covering international events, another on literary matters, and a complete short story. O'Connor's criterion for selecting the front page story was that it should have immediate appeal to him 'as a fine piece of literary work - as a human document - as something that suggests a moral or draws a noble picture' ('The Gospel According to "The Sun"', *The Sun* 27 June 1893, quoted in McDonald, *British literary culture and publishing practice 1880-1914*, p.96). Bennett passed the test and 'The Advanced Woman', satirising aspects of the 'New Woman' movement, became the first of several of his early stories to be published in *The Sun*.

Prior to the first three volumes of James Hepburn's edition of Bennett's letters (1966-1970) and the publication of Anita Miller's ground-breaking *Annotated Bibliography* (1977), the great majority of Bennett's 1890s stories, including 'The Advanced Woman', had

---

3 The British Library was unable to permit me to reproduce its archive copy of 'What's Bred In The Bone' because of its extremely fragile condition. Its appearance in this collection is due entirely to Nicholas Redman who kindly provided me with a copy of his own fine original.

4. Whilst still living in the Potteries Bennett had written an article for the *Staffordshire Daily Sentinel* (30 April 1887) and a subsequent set of seven local news notes, under the title 'Knotty Notes', for the *Staffordshire Knot* (17 November - 29 December 1888).

not elicited any critical attention. Where they had been referred to, the information given was often wrong, arousing the suspicion that the writer had not bothered to actually read the original. (Miller's 'Introduction' to her *Bibliography* is coruscating on these defects of Bennett scholarship) Hepburn actually read Bennett's early stories, assessing their merits as 'slight' but nevertheless admitting to their interest to scholars as 'indicative of things to come' and singling out 'The Advanced Woman' as preparing the literary ground 'for future advanced women such as Sophia Baines [*The Old Wives' Tale*] and Gracie Savott [*Imperial Palace*], a preoccupation of Bennett's throughout his career, and one that appears in many essays, notably in *Our Women* (*Letters Vol. I,* p.12). Hepburn also draws attention to the way in which the humorous musings of 'The Advanced Woman', concerning an apparently bogus marriage, re-emerge sixteen years later as a more developed plot line in his play *The Honeymoon*. Re-reading and assessing Bennett's early work in the light of Hepburn's initial assessment can prove a rewarding experience.

Within the seemingly conventional and limiting format of the short story, Bennett's 'The Advanced Woman' demonstrates a readiness to adopt a sophisticated literary technique in the context of a popular mass readership. The story rejects a traditional linear story-line in favour of purporting to offer the reader some accidentally discovered documents, and without the benefit of guidance from an omniscient narrator. Here we first encounter Bennett, the future master of several literary genres, blurring the boundaries between literature (story-telling) and reportage. Media criticism might be expected to centre on questions of truth - whether an event really happened - and the accuracy of reporting. Bennett's narrative practice in 'The Advanced Woman' constructs the illusion of objectivity, aligning the story with the paper's predominantly nonfictional discourse, both through the ostensible truth of found 'documents' and the textual referencing of well-known living personalities and their philosophical works.

Fact and fiction is blurred from the opening paragraph where Bennett summons recent autobiographical material into play in the account of how the 'Human documents' were discovered. When he first moved to London in 1889 to work as a solicitor's clerk, Bennett also operated a postal business in second-hand books from his lodgings. In addition to his commercial interest, he began a life-long obsessional interest in book collecting and cataloguing:

> I had scarcely been in London a year when my friend and I decided to collaborate in a bibliographical dictionary of rare and expensive books in all European languages. Such a scheme sounds farcical, but we were perfectly serious over it; and the proof of our seriousness is that we worked at it every morning before breakfast. I may mention also that we lunched daily at the British Museum, much to the detriment of our official duties. For months we must have been quite mad-obsessed. (*Truth About An Author*, p.47)

With only three published letters surviving and no *Journal* entries prior to the appearance of 'The Advanced Woman', Bennett's early story reference to his emergent bibliophilic interest takes on an added interest, helping to verify the truthfulness of his memoir. During his early days in London, living first in Hornsea and later in Chelsea, Bennett compiled two editions of *A Century of Books for Bibliophiles*, listing rare books he had for sale. The 1936 Sotheby's *Catalogue of The Manuscripts and Correspondence of Arnold Bennett* notes that '[a]lthough most of the [books] are priced below ten shillings, they are described and annotated in a thoroughly professional manner.' (p.20) 'The harmless bibliophile, ferreting among the costers' book-barrows which line Farringdon-road' bears an uncanny likeness to the story's author.

After long hours, in his wife's company, turning over thousands of 1890s newspaper pages in the British Museum Newspaper Library at Colindale, Hepburn finally found 'The Advanced Woman'. He describes it as a moment when the 'brick walls vibrated with the joy of our discovery', although he wonders whether 'Bennett [would] have been grateful to me for turning up that lost story....' ('Foreword', Miller, *Annotated Bibliography*, pp.xi-xii). My considered verdict is that Bennett and his admirers must surely be grateful for Hepburn's retrieval of a lost story that has become part of 'looking beyond the sanitized and simplified version of events embodied in the canon, and rescuing the fractured, mobile figure of the author in the process of making a career' (McDonald, p.117).

In addition to 'The Advanced Woman' and 'In a Hospital' (reprinted in *Uncollected Stories 1892-1932*) Hepburn discovered a third early Bennett story published in *The Sun*, 'Restaurant Spooks' (25 August, 1893). He summarises it as 'a complaint about London restaurants' in which a 'growing young man sitting in a cheap and unappetizing restaurant imagines himself having an interview with the French proprietor of a chain of sixty cheap and appetizing restaurants.' Hepburn concludes his somewhat dismissive précis with the supposition that the 'lavish meals in *The Grand Babylon Hotel* and *Imperial Palace* were doubtless in the young man's mind' (*Letters Vol. I*, p.12). The difficulty that arises here is the confusing, if understandable and certainly interesting, conflation in Hepburn's phrasing of Bennett himself and the fictional narrator, both of whom could lay claim to be the owner of 'the young man's mind'. Bennett's mind as a young clerk was certainly occupied with deliberating on the respective merits and demerits of London restaurants, not being in the habit of cooking for himself. When in 'Restaurant Spooks' the interviewer asks the French proprietor 'But what about vegetarian restaurants?' and receives the reply that 'A few of them are admirable, but among the great body of clerks there seems to be an inseparable objection to a vegetarian diet. They must have flesh', Bennett is fictionalising his early experiences as a clerk. In *A Man From The North* (1898), the two young clerks, Richard Larch (a shadowy alternative autobiographical portrait of the author as a young clerk) and his friend Jenkins eat in both French and vegetarian restaurants, the latter providing a dinner for sixpence:

> Richard once suggested that they should try one of the French restaurants in Soho which Mr. Aked had mentioned.
>
> 'Not me!' said Jenkins, in reply. 'You don't catch me going to those parley-voo shops again. I went once. They give you a lot of little messes, faked up from yesterday's dirty plates, and after you've eaten half a dozen of 'em you don't feel a bit fuller. Give me a steak and a potato. I like to know what I'm eating.'
>
> He had an equal detestation of vegetarian restaurants, but once, during a period of financial depression, he agreed to accompany Richard, who knew the place fairly well, to the 'Crabtree' in Charing Cross Roads, and though he grumbled roundly at the insubstantiality of the three-course dinner *à la carte* which could be obtained for sixpence[5], he made no difficulty, afterwards, about dining there whenever prudence demanded the narrowest economy. (*A Man From The North*, pp. 48-49)

Both men cannot help but notice the predominance of female diners at the 'Crabtree', an observation of Bennett's that throws an interesting social sidelight on a developing minor phenomenon of the public gatherings of 'Advanced Women' in the 1890s, a period which saw ten vegetarian restaurants open and flourish in London. They offered the same type of safe social space for their considerable feminist customer element as did London's tea-rooms for women in general.[6] 'Restaurant Spooks' is, however, of more note than as a bland footnote to social history. As with 'The Advanced Woman' it too blurs reportage and fiction, allowing the former to seep into the

5. This is an example of the minor, but nevertheless interesting, variations that can occur in reprints of Bennett's texts. In the John Lane 1898 first edition of the novel the dinner costs eight pence. In the same edition the restaurant is in Charing Cross Road. The extract above is from the Churnet Valley Books 2007 publication based on Methuen's 1912 new edition. (There was a new American edition in 1911.) I am grateful to Nicholas Redman for drawing my attention to the textual discrepancies.

6. Recollecting this period in an August 1927 *Harper's Bazar* article, 'Editing a Woman's Paper', Bennett writes: 'Girls, even in pairs, did not dash off unprotected to restaurants for a change. They ate at home, and if they ate abroad it was at a tea-shop' (reprinted in *The Savour of Life*, p.141). The *Yoga Journal*, May/June 1993 discusses how the 'Advanced Women' frequenting the handful of vegetarian restaurants were part of an important grouping, including Fabians, socialites and positivists who were literally rejecting the patriarchal roast beef of old England (p.144).

Arnold Bennett became Assistant Editor of *Woman* in late December 1893, and the Editor two years later.

latter by virtue of the subtitle 'An Interview', and raising topical issues on a menu of culinary aesthetics readily familiar to readers of today's quality newspapers. It is also a significant, and to date overlooked, precursor to *A Man From The North*.

'The Renaissance of the Romp' also marks a significant addition to early Bennett scholarship, appearing in *Woman* just weeks after he became the paper's Assistant Editor. During his first eight weeks in the job he contributed an article on children's parties, together with the first eight of his long-running and popular 'Book Chat' columns. 'The Renaissance of the Romp', a dramatic sketch illustrative of Bennett's contemporary interest in the Women's Movement, appeared in the 28 February 1894 issue of the paper, along with a 'Book Chat' piece under his by-line of 'Barbara', and Bennett's own translation from the French of Rémy De Gourmont's 'The Silken Serpent'. It deserves critical attention on its own merits, quite apart from its bibliographical importance as Bennett's first original fictional contribution to *Woman*.

The sketch combines two of Bennett's abiding interests as an editor, namely the Women's Movement and the world of the theatre. *Woman*'s mast-head of 'Forward! But Not Too Fast', whilst something of a *double entendre*, nevertheless accurately reflects the paper's relatively non-aggressive liberal presentation of the New Woman's case for equality, without positively campaigning for the radical political programme necessary to drive reform. Reminiscing about his editorial time at *Woman*, Bennett makes light of its contribution to the feminist agenda:

.... so determined to offend the feelings of nobody that our columns almost never indicated in what direction progress ought to be made. No downright opinion upon any controversial topic affecting the relations of the sexes was ever expressed.... Nevertheless *Woman* did mysteriously acquire a reputation for being in the van of progressive movements, though nobody who now examined its files could possibly conceive why. (*Savour*, pp.143-144)

Whilst amusingly written, there is something disingenuous about Bennett's retrospective disavowal of *Woman*'s progressive appeal for, as I have argued elsewhere, ('Introduction' *Uncollected Stories 1892-1932*, pp.9-12), a significant number of his 1890s stories disseminate a cultural poetics and politics that place him alongside those 'Victorian women's rights activists [who] were realizing many of their objectives with help from periodicals that disseminated their ideas' (Broomfield, p.269), and 'The Renaissance of the Romp' is no exception. Indeed, coming as it does at the start of Bennett's intimate and successful six year involvement with all aspects of *Woman*'s production, the story might be read as setting a progressive feminist agenda from the outset, albeit framed within a satirical style, calculated to disarm his more determinedly traditional conservative readers.

Taken out of the context of any fictional 'romp', Rosaly's opening speech becomes a remarkably succinct and coherent statement on the power of fictional representation as a covert vehicle for feminist advancement: 'I look upon these plays as exquisite prophetic allegories, showing us how we may break through all conventional barriers of sex, and take our proper place with men in the real life and struggle of the world, without losing one gracious quality of womanhood'. Bennett is here engaged in the subtle construction of a model of femininity as both an innate quality of womanhood and literally as a performative act intended to seduce a middle-class audience/readership to feminist ideas of equality. It is entirely appropriate that so many of Bennett's 1890s stories touching on the Advanced Woman contain theatrical references, since the theatrical world of the time presented imagery highlighting the subject of gender, providing an accessible public space where new roles for both sexes were being enacted that both influenced and reflected behavioural shifts occurring within the wider social and political environment. Sir Richard's scepticism that the 'spectacle of Ada Rohan, breeched but bewitching, will help a modern woman to smoke a cigar, command a county council, or ride a bicycle without looking ridiculous' is, as Bennett would have known, particularly ill-judged. Ada Rohan was celebrated in particular for her performance as Rosalind in *As You Like It*, portraying her as one of Shakespeare's strongest heroines, which she played as a kind of New Woman whilst remaining, in Margaret D. Stetz's words, 'witty and winsome and, best of all could be relied upon to burst into a denunciation of men or of British marriage laws, as contemporary feminist stage characters were wont to do' (*Gender and the London Theatre*, p.94). An ideal woman to march under the banner of 'Forward! But Not Too Fast.'

Bennett's fascination with the world of theatre is apparent throughout his writing career, beginning with 'The Renaissance of the Romp' in 1894 through to his novella about a struggling actress, *Venus Rising from the Sea*, written in 1929 and published posthumously in 1932. A story such as 'On Growing Old' (1895), for example, dealing with one of Bennett's signature concerns of the inevitability of ageing and physical decline, makes several references to well-known theatrical celebrities. At the same time as he was referencing theatre in his stories Bennett was also working as a drama critic, making a particularly auspicious entry into the field when, in January 1895, he reviewed the opening night of Henry James's *Guy Domville* for his 'Music and Mummery' column in *Woman*. Between 1908 and 1913 five of Bennett's own plays were in performance on the London stage and in 1913 alone no fewer than 2,700 performances of his plays took place around the world.

'The Train', a Christmas entertainment, reprinted here for the first time since 1897, is significant as Bennett's first recorded serious attempt at combining the momentum of the short story with the immediacy of stage dialogue. The resulting hybrid of a sketch intended for private reading, not performance, is an important precursor to his first published one-act farces, *Polite Farces*,[7] (1899). Bennett's *Journal* entry for 2 March 1899 records the party held to celebrate his first ten years in London: 'And my first play, a little duologue called *The Music Lesson*, was performed.... Intense and genuine enthusiasm about it.' With no known surviving manuscript of that play, 'The Train' assumes an added significance in demonstrating Bennett's early facility with dialogue. Hepburn makes a point of defending the quality of this dialogue, which he says is at its very best in the early exchanges. He does this in a footnote to George Sturt's somewhat damning letter: 'This is not worthy of you, Arnold. I expect I shall have to do a paper on Dialogue, if only for your enlightenment. But then, hang it, you'll think it ingenious and yet want to give the lie to every conclusion I come to' (*Letters II*, p.99). Bennett took Sturt's criticism seriously enough to remind him that he, Bennett, knew his market, worked hard to satisfy its demands, and was successful in doing so:

> Your remarks about my dialogue are beside the mark. I know well enough it was not serious. But, granted the convention & class of work, it was just about as clever & neat as it could be. Remember that. It was the work of a man who knew what he wanted to produce, & produced it exactly. To my own knowledge it made a number of excellent people wriggle with laughter. 'Worthy of me.' Rot! I, at any rate, cannot rely on wheelwrighting for a living, & moreover when my paper wants a certain sort of thing, & I happen to be able to supply that thing at a more reasonable rate than it could be got at elsewhere, it is my business to supply it. I do supply it, & I

7. These, along with other Bennett plays, are neglected by today's theatre managements. Having produced one of the *Polite Farces*, 'A Good Woman', as a post-Conference entertainment for the Arnold Bennett Society in June 2004, and 'The Alarm' - included in this collection - to mark the opening of the permanent Bennett display at the Potteries Museum & Art Gallery in March 2006, I can testify both to his precocious sense of stage craft and to his ready ability to make an audience laugh. The Mint Theater Company's production of Bennett's early play *What The Public Wants* (1909) in New York (January - March 2011) met with critical acclaim and popular approval, but it has to be noted that it was only made possible with public funds from the New York City Department of Cultural Affairs and the New York State Council on the Arts. Despite its continuing topicality in depicting the machinations of the press, the available records show only three UK performances in the past eighty-three years, the last of these being a production by the Peter Cotes Company at the Library Theatre, Manchester during their 1948-1950 Seasons.

reckon that in doing a thing well, whatever it is, I am not being unworthy. (*Letters II*, p.98)

It is also worth drawing attention to Bennett's highly amusing and idiosyncratic equivalent of stage-directions for 'The Train'. These delightful vignettes defy ready stage representation:

> *Darkness. The banjo lies apart on the cruel ground. It realises that the world is hard and forgetful.... [Arthur] wonders vaguely where the moon is, and how in September the weather contrives to be so hot in the daytime and so cold, even unimpassioned, at night.*

Bennett's witty interventionist on-stage/page voice hints here at the multiple and complex levels he will ultimately be capable of writing at in his full maturity. His critical journey from pieces such as 'The Train' to his screenplay for E.A. Dupont's silent movie *Piccadilly* (1929) makes for a unique historical/literary record for any one particular author of the time, spanning as it does the great cultural transition from the popular mass format of the late-Victorian short story to the 20th century's voracious appetite for translating the story-teller's art into the mass entertainment of 1920s cinema. To date, however, there exists no comprehensive study of Bennett's dramatic sketches, plays, and film scenarios.

'Stella's Journey' appears in this collection seemingly for the first time since its original publication in the New Zealand newspaper the *Star* on 9 December 1901. It is probably the only piece of short fiction - indeed, the only fiction - Bennett published in 1901.[8] Bennett himself seems to have become increasingly frustrated with his literary agent, William Morris Collis, for his inability to sell his fiction, and it might be to Collis that we owe this odd fallow period in an otherwise prolific career. Initially impressed

8. An examination of the available bibliographical records of Bennett's published output for 1901 reveals that not a single piece of fiction is listed, although we know that he finished the final manuscript of *Anna of the Five Towns* in May 1901 and was working on two plays, *Her Grace's Secret* and *The Ides of March*, neither of which was ever produced. Miller's *Annotated Bibliography* itemises 128 published pieces, all exclusively non-fiction articles. Bennett's *Journal* itself offers no clues to the non-publication enigma, falling silent on 26 May 1901 and not resuming until 28 September 1903.

by Collis when they met in May 1898, Bennett soon revised his opinion and their few surviving letters suggest a growing acrimonious rift. Hepburn puts the position bluntly: 'Collis failed to acknowledge receipt of stories, failed to sell them, had to be advised by Bennett where to sell them' (*Letters I*, p.22). We know from Hepburn's editing of Bennett's letters that Collis had possession of at least one Bennett story which he was unable to trace and it is possible that 'Stella's Journey' is this lost story. Until now, however, we had no knowledge of a New Zealand connection and the emergence of the *Star* as an important market for early Bennett stories deserves further critical investigation.[9]

The story itself can lay claim to being one of Bennett's earliest published Five Towns tales - 'Tiddy-fol-lol: a Miracle' was published in *Lloyds Weekly*, 30 December 1900 - and is not without intrinsic interest. Bennett begins the story in Bruges where 'Stella Marston was showing her young sister round the picture gallery in the quaint and marvellous old town of Bruges' before cutting short the visit to return to Bursley. Bennett describes Bursley in the story as 'perhaps not more ugly than the average manufacturing town, but it is very ugly. On every side are large manufactories with their long monotonous frontages and tall chimneys and squat ovens throwing up columns of smoke day and night.' This is Bennett's childhood home-town of Burslem, described in his *Journal* as 'nestled in the hollow between several hills, and showing a vague picturesque mass of bricks through its heavy pall of smoke. If it were an old Flemish town.... one would say its situation was ideal'. He goes on to invoke

---

9. There is at present no comprehensive study of New Zealand publishing history - certainly British publishers regarded New Zealand and Australia as a single market area. Ross Harvey's chapter 'Newspapers' in *Books and Print in New Zealand: A Guide to Print Culture in New Zealand* (2002) provides general background material. A search of the digitised records of Australian newspapers on trove.nla.gov.au/newspaper shows that several Bennett short stories appeared in Australia either before or concurrently with their British publication: 'A Dinner at the Louvre', *The Queenslander* (Brisbane) 23 November 1903; 'The Railway Station', *Western Mail* (Perth) 25 December 1904; 'News of the Engagement', *The Queenslander*, 23 March 1907; 'The Long-Lost Uncle', *Western Mail*, 5 October 1907; 'The Cat and Cupid', *Western Mail*, 23 January 1909; 'The Fortune Teller', *Western Mail*, 9 October 1909; 'The Tiger and the Baby', *Western Mail*, 10 September 1910. The history of the publication of Bennett's stories in Australian newspapers - and indeed in British Empire publications in general - is an area awaiting detailed exploration.

a sense of the history of industry and romance which 'permeates the district' and 'is quite as wonderfully inspiring as any historic memory would be' (*Journal*, p.49). 'Stella's Journey' encompasses these sentiments in miniature, offering something of a template for the great sequence of Five Towns novels, beginning with *Anna of the Five Towns*, which will make Bursley/Burslem and the Potteries internationally recognised literary brand names. That this literary journey should have its beginnings in New Zealand is remarkable enough in itself, but the retrieval of 'Stella's Journey' as to date the sole piece of Bennett fiction published anywhere in the world in 1901 gives it an added glamour.

Equally remarkable is the discovery of Bennett's long short story 'Lord Dover. The Strange Adventures Of A Spendthrift Peer as Related by Jack Stout', serialised in the American *Gunter's Magazine* between May and July 1905.[10] The words 'as Related by Jack Stout' are printed in a very much smaller font size than the rest of the title, leaving 'Lord Dover' as the obvious indexical search words.[11] Unfortunately previous scholars have been misled by Bennett's *Journal* references to his 'Jack Stout' story, but without any accompanying mention of 'Lord Dover'. In fact, Bennett makes no fewer than four direct references to the story in his published *Journal*:

My flat is repapered, my books shelved and pictures hung, and today I resumed my normal daily existence. I wrote about 3,000 words of the second story in the comic *Jack Stout* series (5 October 1904).

I wrote the third *Jack Stout* story in 2 days, finishing it last night. It is a bad story well done (12 October 1904).

I got so busy finishing *The Adventures of Jack Stout* before F. and F.'s arrival [Bennett's brother and sister] that I couldn't

10. The magazine was also sold/distributed concurrently in Britain with exactly the same page numbers and American spellings.

11. It is a minor but relevant typographical detail in the context of confusion of the title that when the story's first instalment appears in the May 1905 issue of *Gunter's Magazine*, the phrase 'as Related by Jack Stout' is included as an integral part of the title. In the subsequent June and July serialisations, however, this fictional authorial attribution is relegated to a parenthesis.

trouble to make even the smallest notes in a journal (2 November 1904).

Last year I wrote 282,100 words, exclusive of re-writing. This comprises 2 plays .... the greater part of *A Great Man*, the whole of *Hugo*, and one third of *Sacred and Profane Love*; also a series of facetious short stories entitled *The Adventures of Jack Stout*.... (2 January 1905).

Perhaps unsurprisingly past attempts to locate the story have foundered on the assumption that it would have appeared, if at all, under Bennett's given title of 'The Adventures of Jack Stout'. Commenting upon Bennett's postscript in his letter of 20 August 1904 to his literary agent J.B. Pinker - 'I am glad you like the story. I will do a series. Six, I presume' - Hepburn links it to Bennett's *Journal* entries to conclude: 'The series of stories bore the title *The Adventures of Jack Stout*. [A later letter to Pinker] suggests that they may never have been published serially' (*Letters I*, p.57). And there matters might have remained but for Alan John's email of 7 February 2011, drawing my attention to an advertisement he had found for a forthcoming story in *Gunter's Magazine*:

This exceedingly brilliant story of modern London life depicts the curious fate of a young nobleman, celebrated both for his wealth and his prodigality, who was compelled by his ruinous losses on the turf to seek livelihood as a valet. His peculiar steering of the young commercial man, Jack Stout, who had gained a fortune into the higher ranks of English society, is remarkable from its many bizarre episodes and will be recognized by those who are familiar with the London social gossip.

One can only speculate that Bennett's original title may have been changed as a deliberate marketing ploy intended to appeal to American readers' supposed interest at the time in the social activities of their aristocratic English cousins. Whatever the reason, the advertisement's inclusion of Jack Stout was sufficient incentive to try again to find the story, irrespective of whether it featured lord or commoner. In this search Bennett scholar, Kurt Koenigsberger, was instrumental in helping me locate copies of the story in British and American archive holdings. Reading them was one of those rare Eureka moments in the search for lost documents.

The discovery of a long-lost Bennett story is in itself of considerable bibliographic interest, although in this instance the content is also of some critical interest. Jack Stout is only narrowly beaten to laying claim as Bennett's first fictional 'card' by Josiah Curtenty, the hero of 'His Worship the Goosedriver' (*Windsor Magazine*, January 1904): '....he reflected upon his reputation; he knew he was a cure, a card, a character....' (*Tales of the Five Towns*, p.7). Jack Stout, however, makes a more assured appearance as a 'card', writing self-consciously in the first person and ostentatiously drawing the reader's attention to this aspect of his character as if to arouse interest in the absurdities about to unfold. On the first page alone the narrator makes no fewer than seven references to his reputation as a 'card'. But it is only to Jos Curtenty that Denry Machin, the hero of Bennett's famous comic novel *The Card* (1911), traces his fictional lineage: 'Jos Curtenty was old enough to be his grandfather, and had been a recognised "card" and "character" since before Denry's birth' (*Card*, p.130). Bennett appears to have appropriated the term 'card' as an exclusively Five Towns quality and in the process both he and the world in general seem to have forgotten, or dismissed, Jack Stout's earlier metropolitan claim as Denry's more flamboyant literary forefather.

Bennett's story makes two noteworthy references to his early London novels. First, coming to London, Jack Stout occupies a small suite at the Grand Babylon Hotel - 'The Grand Babylon Hotel' was serialised in *The Golden Penny* 2 February-15 June 1901 - and when his cousin Selina visits him there she tells him 'And I went to Hugo's stores this morning to order some matches.' The serial version of 'Hugo' was published in *To-Day* between 3 May and 19 June 1905 before its novel publication in 1906. It takes only a cursory glance at these dates to realise that the two middle-aged bachelors, Jack Stout and Hugo (Owen), both in love for the first time, bared their souls in print on either side of the Atlantic within two days of each other. The recovery of 'Lord Dover' is testament to Bennett's prolific work-rate in 1905, and to his amazing ability to draft and complete two lengthy and intertextually linked stories at the same time.

The story's initial premise of a lord assuming the position of a valet is both a popular fictional trope of its Edwardian times and an obvious model for Priam Farll assuming the identity of his dead valet in Bennett's *Buried Alive: A Tale of These Days* (1908). George Orwell's essay 'Such, Such Were the Joys' captures the generally accepted myopic mythology of pre-First World War pre-lapsarian Edwardian golden age of socio-economic and political stability: 'This oozing bulging wealth of the English upper and upper-middle class [exists in an idyllic world of] eating strawberry ices on green lawns to the tune of the Eton boating song' (quoted in *The Oxford Companion To Edwardian Fiction*, p.xi). In their own small way, however, both Jack Stout and Lord Dover subvert the notion of Edwardian stability and assert their right to adopt new identities either by a determined entry on to the social ladder by marriage, or by the construction of a new and permanent identity in a deliberate move down the social scale. Such conscious, occasionally enforced, assumption of new roles is explored in a range of Edwardian stories, novels and plays.[12] J.M. Barrie's character Crichton (*The Admirable Crichton*, 1902), for example, accompanies Lord Loam on voyage as his valet but when the party is wrecked on an island assumes the mantle of leader and expects social deference as his due, only to revert to type when rescued. Barrie, in *The Admirable Crichton*, like

12. Early cinema complicated even further the fictional page/stage notion of a convincing identity exchange across the class divide. George Méliés's film *Le Sacre d'Edouard VII* (*The Coronation of Edward VII*), made in 1902, includes footage of the crowning, shot prior to the event, but edited into the final cut as an integral part of a supposedly documentary/news presentation, in which Edward VII is played by a man thought to be either a brewery worker or a washroom attendant. His close physical resemblance to the future king creates a convincing simulacrum.

Michael Holt's costume design for *The Admirable Crichton*,
New Vic Theatre 2011.

Bennett in 'Lord Dover' and *Buried Alive*, explores the 'tension between change and changelessness.... an unresolved contradiction between belief in the fixity of human personality and belief in the multiple possibilities opened up for every individual by roles and role-playing' (Hollindale, p.x). In the end, though, both Barrie and Bennett collude with the status quo, restricting their radicalism to role-playing as a safety valve, thus leaving intact the myth of a contented and stable Edwardian England.

'The Clock' is the third lost story included in this section. It was published in the magazine *Black & White* on 2 September 1905, the same year as 'Lord Dover'. Given the disappearance of both stories for over a century it is salutary to read Bennett's prophetic *Journal* entry for 1 December 1903: 'I wrote my fourth and last Tillotson [Newspaper Syndicate] short story yesterday afternoon, 2,000 words. This year I have written 12 short stories, and as some of my stories are apt to disappear from view absolutely in the files of the periodical press, I will make a list of them.' Among the list is 'The Clock' and, interestingly enough in the light of my comments on Bennett's New Zealand connection, 'Midnight at the Great [sic] Babylon'. The circumstances surrounding the discovery of 'The Clock' are illustrative of the mixture of constant vigilance allied to good luck responsible for retrieving Bennett's periodical publications. Without the dedication of Bennett collector and bibliographer Nicholas Redman, 'The Clock' might well have slipped through the cracks once again[13] It was reprinted in the *Arnold Bennett Society Newsletter* for Winter 2010/11, where the

13. Redman's account of how he found 'The Clock' has itself the fictional ring of romance:
For many years a key source for unusual periodicals and newspapers with Bennett items was George Locke who had a small shop in Cecil Court off Charing Cross Road. He put aside all Bennett items for me and I called in every couple of months or so to see what he had.... I was dismayed when he told me last year that he was finally retiring, and began calling in ever more frequently to make sure I had missed nothing. On my very last visit he said 'I've only got one thing, a copy of Black and White from 1905, with a short story, "The Clock"'. I did not have my master list with me, but decided to buy it anyway. When I got home I checked my catalogue - no I did not have it. Then I looked in Anita Miller [*Arnold Bennett. An Annotated Bibliography 1887-1932*] but could find no mention of it. A few more enquiries and I realised that George's last contribution to my collection, very appropriately, was a Bennett short story that had until that moment escaped notice. (Private correspondence, 6 April 2011)

Editor, Alan Pedley, greeted it as:

> .... without much doubt a Five Towns story, and Aunt Susan could be taken as a prefiguration of Auntie Hamps [*Clayhanger* 1910]. It also offers an early example of the London/Five Towns dichotomy which so often features in Bennett novels and stories written in that decade. The theme of the story is fear, a theme so dear to one of Bennett's early mentors, Guy de Maupassant. (*Newsletter*, p.2)

Pedley's reference to a London/Five Towns dichotomy further extends in a story such as 'Stella's Journey' to an equally marked Five Towns/Continental Europe dichotomy where, for instance, the brief reference to a visit to a Bruges art gallery is a typically understated early example of Bennett's opposition to English cultural insularity.

'The Clock' is also typical in its depiction of the slow rhythm of provincial life and the portrayal of largely uneventful lives, especially the domestic lives of women such as Aunt Susan. Within the format of conventional story-telling, Bennett deftly inserts a sentence of central aesthetic importance in both his Five Towns and metropolitan fiction, concerned as it is with constructing an equivalence of balance between character and space: 'And it occurred to me for the first time in my life what a curious, creepy, mysterious, inexplicably alive sort of thing a human house really was.' This is a neat formulation of Bennett's credo for what Fiona Tomkinson argues in her essay 'Escaping from Madame Foucault's chamber: Arnold Bennett's politics and poetics of space' is his all-important focus on what Gaston Bachelard (*The Poetics of Space,* 1958) calls the sense of the verticality of the house and the polarity, stated explicitly in 'The Clock', of attic and cellar. Tomkinson's essay is also helpful in drawing attention to Bennett's 'fascination with nooks and corners; with the 'dynamic of retreat' (Bachelard, p.91) and with the hidden spaces of secret rooms, and of drawers, chests and caskets' ('Escaping' p.60) and, in 'The Clock', of clock-cases.

The present collection represents a critical forage and retrieval among many 'drawers, chests and caskets' without the certainty even now that every long-neglected or lost Bennett story has finally come to light.[14] What is revealed, however, is a fascinating cultural overview that cuts across the late-Victorian/Edwardian divide, complicating any simple notion of a Manichean binary of Victorian and Modern aesthetics. The stories and sketches are eloquent testament to the extraordinary range of Bennett's interests, from the cultural to the personal - from a teasing deconstruction of the Dickens traditional Christmas story in 'Miss Scrooge' to the surprisingly frank semi-autobiographical exposure of a raw nerve in 'What Men Want' - expressed in a prose style that is both aesthetically aware and commercially sound. It is this combination of qualities that leads Samuel Hynes to state '[n]o other English writer in this [20th] century has come so close to reaching the audience that Bennett aspired to, that great actuality, the public' (*Author's Craft*, p.xix). He would have very much appreciated Hynes's acknowledgement of his ability to appeal to a growing literate public. Bennett himself had some good advice for his reading public: 'Never read a book that you haven't bought....[this] rule forces you to wait, which is excellent discipline, besides providing you with the sensations of the hunter who has glimpsed his prey' (*Things*, Third Series, pp.104-105). And the purchase of *Lord Dover & Other Lost Stories* allows the additional pleasure of vicariously sharing in the even longer deferred gratification of the manuscript hunter who has not only glimpsed his prey but has also succeeded in running it to earth.

JOHN SHAPCOTT
University of Keele

14. The 1936 Sotheby's sale of Bennett's manuscripts and correspondence includes, for example, the following unpublished item: 'The Last Short Story Written by Arnold Bennett ...This amusing story tells in the first person, how the author met at a coffee-stall a man who, from an opposite window, had seen him doing his early morning physical jerks; how he was mistaken for his own valet; how he was induced to accompany the man to his home, and there, clad in pyjamas of priestly magnificence, to repeat the exercises, in the presence of the man's Malayan wife, who believed them to be a religious rite performed against the Demons responsible for London's winter weather.' (*Catalogue*, p.11)

ACKNOWLEDGEMENTS

My initial thanks go to Alan John who contacted me after reading *Arnold Bennett's Uncollected Short Stories 1892-1932* with suggestions for further lines of research for finding other lost or forgotten Bennett stories. I am indebted to him for the discovery of this collection's extended title story, 'Lord Dover', and for leading me to find the early Five Towns tale of 'Stella's Journey'.

Kurt Koenigsberger has once again not hesitated in providing invaluable advice on both the style and content of the book. Kurt's generous and detailed help on this and other volumes is very much appreciated.

Nicholas Redman and Martin Laux have both made painstaking trawls through my 'Notes', with the result they are now both fuller and more accurate. Nick has also made available copies of stories from his private collection, as well as providing additional commentary on my 'Introduction'. Any editor would be glad to have two such dedicated and friendly colleagues to call upon.

It has been a pleasure to continue a newly forged Australian contact with Sharon Crozier-De Rosa. Sharon's suggestions for following up Bennett's publications in New Zealand and Australia have opened up an entirely new field of study extending beyond this present collection.

Michael Holt had no hesitation in lending me his design portfolio for the New Vic Theatre's production of *The Admirable Crichton*, and it is a particular pleasure to be able to reproduce his realisation of Crichton's immaculate appearance as butler and valet.

I am grateful to Jenny Graveson for providing me not only with full performance details of Bennett's *What The Public Wants* but also with a copy of the Library Theatre Programme.

My final thanks to Linda, without whose painstaking transcription and typing of original Bennett manuscripts, and of my own idiosyncratic handwriting, this book would still be only a dream.

BIBLIOGRAPHY

Bennett, Arnold *A Man From the North*. Leek: Churnet Valley Books, 2007.

Anna of the Five Towns. London: J. M. Dent, 1997.

The Truth About An Author. London: Archibald Constance, 1903.

How To Become An Author. London: C. A. Pearson, 1903.

Tales of the Five Towns. London: Chatto & Windus, 1905.

Hugo. A Fantasia on Modern Themes. London: Chatto & Windus. 1906.

The Card. Leek: Churnet Valley Books, 2011.

The Regent. Leek: Churnet Valley Books, 2006.

The Loot of Cities. London: Thomas Nelson, 1917.

Things That Have Interested Me. London: Chatto & Windus, 1926.

The Savour of Life. Essays in Gusto. London: Cassell, 1928.

Dream of Destiny & Venus Rising from the Sea. London: Cassell, 1932.

Arnold Bennett's Uncollected Short Stories 1892-1932. Edited by
 John Shapcott. Leek: Churnet Valley Books, 2010.

The Journal of Arnold Bennett. New York: The Literary Guild, 1933.

Letters of Arnold Bennett. Vol.I. Ed. James Hepburn. London: O.U.P., 1966.

Letters of Arnold Bennett. Vol.II. Ed. James Hepburn. London: O U.P., 1968.

The Author's Craft and Other Critical Writings of Arnold Bennett.
 Edited Samuel Hynes. Lincoln: Nebraska U.P., 1968.

Catalogue of the Manuscripts and Correspondence of Arnold Bennett.
 London: Sotheby & Co., 1936.

Berry, Arthur. *Dandelions. Poems*. Newcastle, Staffordshire: Arthur Berry, 1993.

Broomfield, Olga R.R. *Arnold Bennett*. Boston: Twayne, 1984.

Dickens, Charles. *Bleak House*. Middlesex: Penguin Books, 1971.

Drabble, Margaret. *Arnold Bennett*. London: Weidenfeld and Nicolson, 1974.

Griffith, Penny, Ross Harvey, Keith Maslen. *Book & Print in New Zealand: A Guide to Print
 Culture in New Zealand*. http://etext.virginia. Edu/etcbin/toccer-new2?

Hepburn, James, editor. *Arnold Bennett. The Critical Heritag*e. London: Routledge, Kegan Paul, 1981.

Hollindale, Peter. 'Introduction'. J.M. Barrie. *Peter Pan and Other Plays*. Oxford: O.U.P., 1995.

Holmes, Richard. *Shelley. The Pursuit*. London: Quartet Books, 1976.

Keating, Peter. *The Haunted Study. A Social History of the English Novel 1875-1914*.
 London: Secker & Warburg, 1989.

Kemp, Sandra, Charlotte Mitchell, David Trotter, edited.
 The Oxford Companion to Edwardian Fiction. Oxford: O.U.P., 2002.

Liddinton, Jill and Jill Norris. *One Hand Tied Behind Us. The Rise of the Women's Suffrage
 Movement*. London: Virago, 1978.

McDonald, Peter D. *British literary culture and publishing practice 1880-1914*.
 Cambridge:Cambridge U.P., 1997.

Miller, Anita. *Arnold Bennett. An Annotated Bibliography 1887-1932*.
 New York: Garland Publishing, 1977.

Pedley, Alan. 'Editorial', *The Arnold Bennett Society Newsletter Vol.4, No.15*.
 Ross-On-Wye: Arnold Bennett Society, 2010.

Pound, Reginald.   *Arnold Bennett. A Biography*. London: William Heinemann, 1952.

Redman, Nicholas.   'Arnold Bennett's Short Stories: An Alphabetical List'.
                     Edited Alan Pedley, *The Arnold Bennett Society Newsletter Vol. 4, No.15.*
                     Ross-on-Wye: Arnold Bennett Society, 2010.

Squillace, Robert.   *Modernism, Modernity and Arnold Bennett.* Lewisbury: Bucknell U.P., 1997.

Stetz, Margaret D.   *Gender and the London Theatre 1880-1920.*
                     High Wycombe: Rivendale Press, 2004.

Tomkinson, Fiona.   'Escaping from Madame Foucault's Chamber. Arnold Bennett's Politics and
                     poetics of space.' *Arnold Bennett: New Perspectives.* Stoke-on-Trent:
                     Staffordshire University and Arnold Bennett Society, 2007 (revised).

NOTE ON THE TEXTS

The stories in this collection appeared between 1891 and 1924 and, with one exception, are published in date order. The exception is the title story 'Lord Dover. The Adventures of a Spendthrift Peer as Related by Jack Stout', published in America in 1905 and also distributed in Great Britain at the same time, but lost for over a century.

All but one of the stories are transcribed from their original source magazines and newspapers. The exception is 'The Alarm' which is transcribed from Arnold Bennett's typescript for the magazine *Designer*.

In general the original punctuation and spelling have been retained, although quotation marks have been standardised to single marks, with double for quotes within quotes. In all cases where the text is transcribed from an American publication it appears with the original American spelling. Amendments to the texts include corrections to minor typographical errors, together with the standardisation of punctuation within individual stories. In Part I of 'Lord Dover', for example, the character Gerald is now in danger of meeting an 'untimely' rather than an 'ultimately' end on the scaffold, and in Part V a character now says 'Don't talk rot' rather than 'Don't rot'.

Periodical and newspaper publication details are given in the Endnotes appended to each story.

LORD DOVER[1]

THE STRANGE ADVENTURES OF A SPENDTHRIFT PEER

as Related by Jack Stout.

'Lord Dover' is a novella-length comic tale lost since
Gunter's Magazine published it in 1905.

PART I.
THE REVOLVER.

I.

As I read the telegram signed 'Selina,' I felt quite a card.[2] At the age of thirty-seven I had become almost a card by profession, in my simple way. The thing was forced on me. When I first went out to Algiers[3] in the British Consular Service, my comrades looked on me and saw a young man of some sixty inches, very slim, with very fair hair and a perfectly smooth chin, whose name was John Stout. I tried to carry off my preposterous name with a knowing twinkle in my pale blue eye, and my comrades very naturally said to themselves: 'This man, with such a name and such a figure, *must* be a card.' Hence I became a card; it was expected of me.

My father could not help being called Stout; moreover Stout, though inappropriate in certain cases, is a fine old English name. But he, or at least my mother, might have taken measures to prevent me from going through life as 'Jack Stout.' I should have preferred even Augustus.

It is an easy matter once you are labelled, to be a card. By dint of the twinkle in my eye, of never laughing, of frequently saying what I really thought, and of often giving way gracefully to my instincts, I blossomed into a quite successful card. The united staffs of all the consulates in the Boulevard Carnot frankly recognized my success. And when I suddenly came into £97,687 10s. 0$^1/_2$d., the united staffs saw in the occurrence only another example of my cardishness. I feel sure they went about saying: 'Have you heard of Jack Stout's latest? He's come into £97,687 10s. 0$^1/_2$d. Just like him, isn't it?' They swore I had invented the half-penny; but I had not. I may remark here that this money was very useful to me. I had no talent for the consular service, and no influence. I was still a mere clerk at thirty-seven, and I should have been a mere clerk at one hundred and thirty-seven if some circumstance or other had not intervened. 'I am going to see what society is like in London,' I said to my comrades, when they asked me what I meant to do. And they laughed, as though to imply that society in London was in for a lively time, with little Jack Stout in its midst. I had been exiled from England for sixteen years.

And no sooner had I settled myself temporarily in a small suite at the Grand Babylon Hotel,[4] and found a tailor, and written out an advertisement for a valet, than I received this telegram from my sort-of-cousin, a Mrs. Ashway: 'Do come dine to-night, eight, Selina, 7 St. James's Court.' It was very nice and familiar of Selina to sign herself just 'Selina,' like that to a man she hadn't seen for over twenty years. I saw that I should plunge into the whirlpool of London society without any preliminary shivering on the brink.

I was signing 'Jack' to a reply-telegram when a servant entered the sitting-room and handed me a visiting-card.

'To see you, sir,' said he.

'Mrs. Gerald Ashway,' said the visiting-card.

Not content with asking me to dinner, Selina had asked herself to tea!

'So glad to see you again,' said Selina coming in. And then: 'I thought you were older.'

I noticed her hair at once. It was red; it was distinctly and powerfully red. Which, in a married woman, means that for about five minutes in every day the husband knows acutely what it is to be alive. For the rest, she was an attractive, rather girlish being of thirty, tall, decided in manner, with a frank pleasant face, and excessively stylish.

'I *am* older,' I answered. 'I am a great deal older. So are you. You couldn't have been more than six when we last met.'

'I feel sixty now,' she said. I seemed to observe a break in her voice.

And then she sat down and began to cry into her

creaseless white gloves.

I admit I was startled; frightened at first, and then perhaps pleased.

In Algiers one learns a thing or two about women. There is an oriental quality in it, especially in the upper town, which –well!–teaches. I knew there was only one course to pursue, and I pursued it. I sat still and mute for all I was worth. Presently Selina ceased to cry–no woman can cry forever!–and glanced up at me furtively.

'Is this your usual practice?' I asked her. 'Or is there something about me–?'

She smiled faintly. 'You are funny,' she murmured.

'No, I'm not,' I corrected her. 'I shouldn't dream of being funny to a creature in distress. And I'm sure that a strong-minded, sensible woman wouldn't cry unless she had ample cause, ample cause.'

('Now, you agreeable little minx,' I said within myself. 'Let's know what kind of a mess you're in.')

And I added to her:

'I only meant, was it your usual practice to telegraph, and then jump into a cab and try to beat the telegram? By the way, let me take advantage of this lull to thank you for asking me to dinner.'

'Oh!' she exclaimed gloomily. 'You can't come to dinner.'

'I can,' I said. 'I intend to.'

'There will be no dinner,' she blurted out.

'This is getting serious,' I said. 'No wonder you wept. I ought to have wept too.'

'There will never be any more dinners; never any more.'

'What!' I cried. 'End of the World? Judgment Day?'

'It's all over between me and Gerald,' she explained.

'Tell me. Confide in me,' I entreated her, leaning on a table that was close to her chair, and clasping my hands–not hers. 'I shall be sympathetic.'

I don't know whether Selina was my second cousin, or

something nearer and dearer–my first cousin once removed; I have never understood cousinship. All I know is that her father was my first cousin–and my last, too, my sole cousin.

'Yes,' she said. 'That's why I've come. I seemed to feel instinctively that although we were in a sense perfect strangers, yet you would–'

'Exactly,' I agreed, 'Well, about Gerald?'

'It's my birthday to-morrow,' she began. 'And I went to Hugo's stores[5] this morning to order some matches.'

'For your birthday?'

'No. I merely went to order some matches. We buy everything at the Stores. And this afternoon–about an hour ago–there came a revolver and some cartridges from Hugo's. Gerald was just waking up.'

'He works at night?'

'He never works. He never has worked. It isn't his line. He's just a nice English gentleman who dresses perfectly, and goes to his club, and does the correct thing, and is always, always calm. That's why I married him. You've noticed my hair?'

'Not specially,' I said. 'What about it?'

'It's rather auburn, isn't it?' she explained. 'That means temper. My temper's fiery, you know. I admit it is fiery.'

'Better a fiery temper than none at all,' I said.

'You think so? she smiled. 'When Gerald wants to annoy me he calls me his revolver, because I am continually "going off bang! " You see? A poor joke, but Gerald is not very good at jokes. Well, Gerald always dozes between lunch and tea, and he was just waking up when that revolver came. I asked him if he had bought a revolver at Hugo's, and if so, why. "Let's have a look at it," he said. He understands revolvers. He began to load it. I asked him again why he had bought a revolver. He said, "Sweets to the sweet. It's your birthday to-morrow." Now *I* thought it was very bad taste on his part to buy *me* a revolver for a birthday present. A silly, practical joke.

But Gerald's idea of humor is so peculiar! I snatched the revolver out of his hands, and I told him he was horrid and unkind. He merely said again, "Sweets to the sweet." He added that perhaps if I kept the revolver on my dressing table, it might remind me of my fiery temper and help me to cure it. And he laughed all the time. "But, I'll unload it first," he said. I was furious. I can't control myself, you know, when once I'm started. I pointed the revolver at him, and I told him I felt like killing. He just said: "Sweets to the sweet." I said if he said that again, I would shoot him. And of course he just said: "Sweets to the sweet." Then the trigger seemed to touch my finger, and the revolver went off.'

'You've killed your husband!' I exclaimed. 'And you want me to get you out of the country?'

She nodded.

'I do want you to get me out of the country,' she said. 'But I've not killed him. The ball went through the shoulder–'

'Blade? Shattered it?'

'Shoulder-padding of his coat! He was unhurt.'

'Ah!' I breathed.

'But how angry he was! I have never seen him angry before. He said I might have killed him and got myself into a fearful scrape. And he called me the most dreadful names. And then I lost my temper again, and said I would leave him forever. And he said that perhaps that would be safer in the end. So I've come. I want you to take me to Paris. I've decided to live there in the future. My explosiveness won't be so noticeable in Paris.'

'Charmed!' I remarked. 'But why have you selected me for this honor?'

'Well,' she said. 'You know French. You're a consul, or you were a consul.'

'Never,' I asserted.

'Then a vice-consul.'

'No. Only a clerk in the consulate.'

'Anyhow, you're a sort of official person that a woman can travel with.'

'Something between a man and a guardian-angel?'

'And you're a relative–distant, but still a relative.'

I liked Selina. She was a most likable woman. But I didn't exactly see myself escorting her and her red hair and her temper to Paris.

'Did you bring the revolver with you?' I asked her.

'No,' she said. 'Why?'

'Oh, nothing,' I said. 'I only wanted to make sure.'

'Make sure of what?'

'My life,' I explained. And then I proceeded to try to get out of going with her to Paris. 'I'm afraid, Mrs. Ashway,' I said solemnly, 'that you are mistaking me for *the* Jack Stout.'

'Why?' she cried. 'Aren't you Jack Stout?'

'My name is John Stout. But Stout is quite a common name in the consular service. I remember now that *the* Jack Stout used to mention his cousin Selina sometimes.'

'You aren't the Jack Stout who has just come into a fortune?'

'That's *the* Jack Stout,' I said. '*I* am in London on important consular business.'

'And does the government allow the consular clerks to take suites at the Grand Babylon?'

'It doesn't allow,' I said firmly. 'It insists. The dignity of the Empire–'

'Why did you let me run on with my affairs like that?' she demanded.

'Madam,' I said. 'I had not the heart to stop you. Please remember that you began with tears. Moreover–'

What further inventions I should have invented I don't know, but just then the door opened and the servant handed me a visiting-card.

'To see you, sir,' said he.

'Mr. Gerald Ashway,' said the visiting-card.

I passed it to Selina. She gave a little shriek.

'You must pretend to be my cousin, at all events, Mr. Stout,' she informed with a fearful calm. 'Imagine me in the rooms of a complete stranger, who is not even my distant cousin! I should be lost, absolutely lost! You must pretend to be *the* Jack Stout for a few moments. I'll leave you to exercise your discretion with my husband, and I'll run in here till he's gone.'

Before I could protest, she had vanished through a doorway. It happened to lead to the bathroom.

Mr. Gerald Ashway entered, and I was left with the curious task of pretending to be myself to Mr. Gerald Ashway. It is a nice metaphysical question: Can a man pretend to be himself?

II.

I could plainly see the orifice in the shoulder of his coat; it opened its mouth and spoke of perils just past. Nevertheless Mr. Gerald Ashway's demeanor was perfectly calm; his wrath had cooled.

'Be seated, sir,' I said.

And he sat down as though sitting for his portrait.

'Is my wife here?' he demanded.

'She has been here,' I replied.

'And left?'

'And left.'

I was very stern and staccato.

'Where has she gone to? Did she say?'

'Yes,' I said. 'She said she was going to Paris.'

'Alone?'

'No, sir. With a friend–indeed more than a friend.'

'Ah!' Mr. Ashway reflected. 'Who might that be?'

'I know not,' I said, 'whether I have the right to disclose a secret confided to me by a charming and intelligent woman. But I will stretch a point in your favor, Mr. Ashway. The friend in question, the more than friend, is myself.'

'The devil!' exclaimed Mr. Ashway lazily, and then he gave vent to: 'Aha!'

And he tapped his stick reflectively against his boot. He seemed to pump up all his mental force from his boots.

Of course, as a débutant in London society, I deemed it my duty to observe narrowly this individual, whom even his angered wife had admitted to be the mirror of all gentlemanly correctness. He was a tall and broad man with heavy lips, heavy eyes, and a mustache heavy with the riddle of the universe. And I gathered that it was the correct thing in London for a male being to be thoroughly well chained and metalled. A heavy gold chain sprang from one waistcoat-pocket up to a button-hole and down from the button-hole to the other waist-pocket. At one end of this cable was a gold watch which protected the heart, and at the other a gold contraption holding a cigarette-holder, which protected his right breast.

He looked at the time and asked if he might smoke, and from a third waistcoat-pocket he drew a large gold cigarette case which protected some other organ.

I perceived that Selina had shot him in the only vulnerable place, his shoulder-padding; all else was armour-clad.

Another clanking chain (silver) came down from under his waistcoat and curved out of sight towards his coat-tails. His wristbands were firmly linked by chains, and his scarf-pin was also held fast by a chain. Another peculiarity which I noticed was the careful and complete manner in which he had labelled himself. His cigarette case was initialled, 'G.A.' in chiselled letters which the wear of centuries would not efface; so was his watch; so was his match-box (at the end of the silver cable); so was his scarf-pin; so were his cuff-links. And when he raised his boot to strike a match on the sole thereof I saw that his socks (whose pattern was stratified in a sort of geological formation) were also very clearly labelled in white thread. In case this man had one of those sad lapses of memory, which put people in the awkward position of no longer knowing who they are, all he had to do was to hitch his trousers, or take a cigarette, and the desired information would immediately be forthcoming.

'Yes,' I cried, refusing a cigarette. 'I have heard the miserable story of your married life, Mr. Ashway. Selina has told me all. Selina has trusted me. She has found in me a spiritual affinity, a soul that understands her own. I do not blame you for your treatment of her. Nor, on the other hand, do I sympathize with you in the lonely fate which awaits you. Evidently you are devoid of the finer feelings so necessary to the successful management of a wife. That is not your fault. You are as Heaven made you. I merely state the fact in order to justify Selina's future conduct. Selina had determined to leave you for ever. She is going to settle in Paris, and I am going to settle with her.'

Here I heard a movement of the knob on the bathroom side of the bathroom door. But I was fairly started on the enterprise of pretending to be myself, and I continued, especially as Mr. Gerald Ashway coldly but firmly begged me to continue.

'As you are doubtless aware,' I proceeded, 'I am a very near relative of Selina's; we were friends in childhood. I am also a consul of the British Empire, and therefore an official personage. Further I am tolerably wealthy. Selina too is wealthy. Our life will be an idyll. No doubt suitable provision will be made for you; at any rate your club subscriptions and your tailor's bills, and your blacksmith and chainmaker's—'

The bathroom door burst open.

'Oh! Jerry!' Selina sobbed, rushing forward and tumbling against that mass of metal. 'Don't listen to him. It isn't true. He isn't my relative at all, and we aren't going to Paris. I–take me home, Jerry!'

'You had imprisoned my wife in that room, sir!' said Mr.

Ashway, sternly.

This was my reward for obeying Selina in the spirit and in the letter.

'Ah! *Les rosses*! *Les rosses*!' as the second clerk at the French consulate used always to say when we discussed women.

III.

You may be surprised to learn that even when I had explained that I had been merely giving full expression to my natural gaiety of mind, neither Gerald nor Selina would be satisfied. They would not believe that I was myself.

'Why did you act as if you were *our* Jack Stout?' Selina demanded.

'Because I am!' I replied.

'Then why did you deny to my wife that you were her relative?' Gerald demanded.

'Because–' There I stopped. I did not want to say that I shirked the task of escorting Selina and her temper to Paris; I did not want to give Selina away; the pair were evidently reconciled. 'Oh! Just for fun!' I finished.

This explanation did not appear to please the protected cruiser. He looked as if he was in a mind to throw me out of the window or stuff me into the fireplace, and I could not tolerate such operations.

'How can we tell,' asked Selina, 'whether you were lying then or whether you are lying now?'

'But,' I said, 'don't you remember how, when you first came in, I referred quite naturally to our meeting in infancy?'

'That's all very well,' Gerald put in. 'You must give me proof, sir, that you are not an imposter.'

Of course my thoughts turned instantly to birthmarks and other evidences of identity. But the only birthmark I possessed was in the small of my back, and I could not recollect ever hearing that Selina had any birthmarks at all.

'Proof, sir!' reiterated Gerald, swinging his cigarette-holder contraption menacingly on its cable.

At last I pulled myself together.

'Well,' I said, addressing Selina, 'perhaps I can convince you by my knowledge of family history. Your father, my lamented cousin, compounded with his creditors, four and sixpence in the pound, before he made that *coup* in petroleum shares. Your great-aunt Anne always said–'

Here the pair glanced at each other.

'–always said that your Uncle Joe would be hanged. However, he was accidentally saved from that by looking for an escape of gas with a lighted candle. You aren't old enough to call to mind how your grandfather was sued as a widower, aged seventy for breach of promise by that milliner's assistant in Bond Street. Perhaps you may have heard that your parents scandalized all their relatives, including me, by getting themselves married at a registry office off the Strand. Then I needn't rake up the unpleasant business of the quarrel between your mother and the vicar's wife which ended in your father being sued for slander. Nor will I refer too particularly to your brother Edward's exploits at baccarat, near Newmarket. As for yourself, Selina, the excellent postal service between Algiers and England is responsible for my acquaintance with most of the details of your brief engagement to Captain–'

'That will do, Jack, thank you,' said Selina primly. 'There is no doubt that you are *you*; but don't be yourself too humorously in the future.'

'Upon my word, you are a witty woman, Selina!' I exclaimed, charmed. 'We will now have tea, and perhaps the invitation to dinner still stands, eh?'

'I followed my wife here to tell her something,' said Gerald Ashway. 'And I must tell her. And since you are so deucedly in the family now, Mr. Stout, you may as well hear this. All the world will hear it within the next hour.'

The man had remained throughout extremely gloomy.

'Why, Gerald, whatever's the matter,' cried Selina. 'That's the worst of Gerald,' she turned to me. 'He's nearly always got something up his sleeve.'

The only thing that I could perceive up there was his handkerchief; I usually keep mine in my pocket.

'It's that ball,' said Gerald.

'What ball?'

'That bullet–out of that confounded revolver.'

'Well?' Selina urged him on.

'After going through me, it went through the wall into the next flat.'

'Gracious heavens!' said Selina. 'And broke something, no doubt.'

'It slightly wounded the parrot,' said Gerald impressively.

'What! *Her* parrot? The old lady's parrot?'

Gerald nodded.

'Whatever will she say?' Selina speculated.

'She won't say anything,' said Gerald. 'After going through me and the wall and wounding the parrot, it killed the old lady.'

'You're joking,' said I.

'No, he isn't,' Selina asserted. 'That isn't Gerald's kind of joke. He means it. So she's dead! Gerald, how horridly calm you are!' She wept for the second time that afternoon.

'I can't help being calm,' Gerald retorted calmly. 'If you had always been as calm we shouldn't be practically murderers at this moment.'

'Sad as this event is,' I interpolated, 'and I hope it may be a lesson to us all–it is ridiculous to talk of murder! "Death by misadventure" is the phrase to use. The inquest will certainly be an ordeal. But let us hope that the old lady was very, very old, and prepared to die.'

'You don't know the circumstances,' said Gerald.

'No you don't,' said Selina through her tears.

'Or,' Gerald continued, 'you wouldn't talk like that. There

was a regular feud between us and that woman. And her servants, and especially her nephew, the architect, are capable of swearing, and proving, too, that we calculated the distances and deliberately meant to kill her. As a matter of fact, I *had* threatened to kill the parrot, and she had said that I might just as well threaten to kill her, and I had said that I might. I know nothing of law, but I'm ready to lay a monkey they bring it in culpable homicide.'

'Tut–tut!' I said. 'Call this a civilized country–and so much fuss over an old maid! I gather she was a maid from the parrot.'

'However,' Gerald added, glancing at Selina, 'I shall take the matter in my own hands.'

'How?' asked Selina. 'How can you take the matter in your own hands, you dear stupid darling?'

'I mean that I shall tell the police that it was I who fired the revolver.'

She fell on his neck in a paroxysm of marital affection.

'Oh, no you won't, dearest!' she cried. 'I couldn't allow such a thing.'

'Recollect that you are my wife,' said Gerald sternly. 'Do you imagine for an instant that I could permit my wife to appear in the dock of a criminal court? It's unthinkable.'

'Nevertheless,' said Selina, sticking her chin out, 'I fired the revolver, and I shall take the consequences. Besides, you are a gentleman and you couldn't tell a lie on your oath.'

'Prisoners aren't put on their oath,' said Gerald.

'Then I shall insist on giving evidence in your favor.'

'I said I knew nothing about law, but I do know that a wife can't give evidence either for or against her husband.'

'Then I shall give myself up,' said Selina, pouting, and she retreated from his neck.

'I forbid you to do so,' said Gerald.

When the temperature had risen a little higher, and Gerald had grown sullen and Selina's chin was still more pronounced, they appealed to me.

'It's a very pretty argumentative point,' I said. 'But I give my verdict in favor of your husband, Selina. If anyone is to suffer the final penalty, it should be he. In the first place, he loaded the revolver–don't forget that. In the second place, it really wouldn't be at all nice for a member of our family to be hung, or even to get ten years. We've gone far enough. And in the third place, what does it matter if Gerald does come to an untimely end on the scaffold?[6] The world will consider him a criminal, but you and I will know that he was to the last a brave and unspotted English Gentleman. And his life–what is that? The soul is immortal, indestructible. The executioner will merely dispatch it into a new avatar, a new activity. There is no such thing as death, if you look at it philosophically. Moreover, your fortune is your own. The dread sentence of the law will not deprive you of your breadwinner. Fourthly–'

A noise at the door interrupted my discourse.

'The police!' gasped Selina.

IV.

'Now, let everyone clearly understand, once for all, that I and no other person whatever fired the revolver,' whispered Gerald.

And we waited with blanched faces.

However, it was only one of those tame manikins dressed mainly in buttons who appear to be kept in all modern hotels for the purpose of lending vivacity to the corridors.

The freak handed me a sealed envelope.

'Is it right, sir?' he enquired.

I gazed at the superscription.

'Yes,' I said.

'An answer, sir,' he informed me.

'Wait outside,' I commanded, and he vanished.

The letter was addressed: 'Mr. or Mrs. Gerald Ashway, care of J. Stout, Esq., Grand Babylon Hotel.'

'This is evidently for the murderer,' I said. 'Read it.' And I gave it to Gerald, who broke the seal, and then carefully cut the envelope with a paper-knife of Bessemer steel[7] which he produced from yet another waistcoat-pocket.

'Read it aloud, Jerry,' Selina panted.

And he read:

'This morning I went to Hugo's stores to buy a revolver and some cartridges to protect myself and parrot and dog against the epidemic of burglars at present raging in London. The parcel was to be delivered this afternoon. I have, however, received nothing from Hugo's but a large parcel of Swedish matches[8] –'

'That's my parcel,' Selina interrupted. 'I always buy Swedish matches,' she explained to me, 'on principle. I hate to be told to be patriotic by omnibus advertisements.'

'She must have written this before you killed her,' said Gerald to Selina.

'Before *you* killed her,' I corrected him. He bowed.

'Evidently,' said Selina drily. 'Go on.'

He went on reading:

'Clearly Hugo's carman confused the two packages at the doors–'

'Then you didn't buy any revolver to tease me?' Selina suddenly discovered.

'Shut up!' Gerald stopped her rudely. 'Of course I didn't. Haven't I got plenty of revolvers on the premises?'

'Well, go on,' said Selina.

And he went on reading:

'Clearly, also you have perceived the error, since you have already sent me one bullet. I shall be glad if you will let me have the remaining twenty-three cartridges, and also the revolver; but not through the wall. Please hand them to my butler. Your singular method of correcting the mistakes of Hugo's carman has, up to the present, resulted in the death of my dear parrot–sad that my poor pet and lifelong companion should have been extinguished by the very instrument, destined for its protection!–and in the loss of an important curl on the left side of my forehead and a slight abrasion of my skin. It will result further in an action for damages which I shall be compelled to bring against you. My butler will hand you your matches, which I observe, with regret, are not of British manufacture. Yours, etc.'

'Then she isn't dead!' said Selina.

'Obviously not!' said I.

'Would you mind ringing for a whiskey and soda?' said Gerald. 'And if the butler's here we might have him in.'

So through the agency of the manikin, we had in the butler, who deposited a large consignment of Swedish matches on my table.

'Clapton,' Gerald interrogated him. 'Why the devil did you tell me that your mistress was dead and the parrot wounded, when, as a matter of fact, it was exactly the other way about?'

'Did I say that, sir?'

'You said it twice.'

'If I did, sir, it was because I was that flustered I didn't rightly know which of 'em *was* dead, sir.'

'And how did you find your way here, my friend?' Gerald pursued inquisitively.

'The porter at the Court, sir, said he had heard Mrs. Ashway tell her cabman to drive to the Grand Babylon, and that you had gone after her. My mistress said at once you must have gone to see Mr. Stout.'

'Well,' said Gerald, pulling a revolver from his hip-pocket. 'Give this revolver to your mistress with my compliments, and tell her that the cartridges shall be handed over shortly, not through the wall. I suppose the dog wasn't hurt?'

'No, sir. Finette is quite well, thanks, except for a touch of indigestion.'

'More's the pity!' murmured Gerald, when the butler had departed.

'She's a dashed clever woman, this old lady!' I remarked. 'She's got a vein of irony that you don't often meet with. Who is she? And how did she know about me?'

There was a pause.

'As a matter of fact,' said Gerald, 'it's Selina's great-aunt Anne. Doubtless she is aware of your arrival in London. We never let on that she's a relative, because we hate people to think we quarrel with our connections.

'And we can't help quarrelling with her,' said Selina, 'because of her dog that always rushes out and bites you as you pass her door, and your guests, too. And she regularly enjoys it. Oh! She's terrible!'

'Great-aunt Anne!' I cried, I must go and see her at once, terrible or not! She used to give me castor-oil,[9] and in spite of that I've always admired her.'

'Better keep away,' Gerald advised.

I shook my head.

'I'll see her first, and then come in to your dinner at eight o'clock and report. Perhaps I shall bring you a free pardon. Who knows? My manner with great-aunts has always been considered immense.'

Here the whiskey and soda arrived.

I felt that I was fairly launched on the sea of London.

PART II.
MY VALET.[10]

I.

I had just recovered from the adventure of my cousin Selina and her revolver, and was making ready to pay a call upon my great-aunt Anne, when another of those hotel-manikins, who I am sure had more silver buttons to the linear inch than any other page-boy in Europe, burst into my sitting-room and curtly ejaculated:

'Mr. Hatteras!'

For an instant I thought it was a conundrum, or a 'catch' in geography.

'*Cape* Hatteras?' I enquired.

The manikin put his head into the corridor.

'Cape Hatteras?' I heard his head whisper in the corridor, and then he brought his head back again into my sitting-room, and said: 'No, sir.'

'Ah!' I breathed a certain relief. 'In that case, show him in, whoever he is.'

Mr. Hatteras proved to be a perfect gentleman in a blue serge suit; age about thirty; tint blond; gloves slate; hat bowler; physiognomy frank; boots brown; height lofty.

'Good-day,' I said. 'To what am I indebted for the honor–' And then as he did nothing but smile candidly, I added: 'Pray take a seat.'

'The fact is, sir,' murmured Mr. Hatteras, 'you are advertising for a valet.'

'I am,' I admitted. 'But how the deuce do you know that, Mr. Hatteras, seeing that it's barely an hour since I sent the advertisement across to the *Morning Post*?' [11]

'I beg your pardon, sir,' said Mr. Hatteras, 'I have friends on the staff of the *Morning Post*, and I happened to be in there when the advertisement arrived.'

'I see,' said I. 'And am I to understand that you are personally applying for the situation?'

'Precisely, sir.'

'Well,' I insinuated. 'That needn't prevent you from accepting the chair which I offered you, Mr. Hatteras, need it?'

And he sat down gracefully, with a graceful acknowledgement.

His manners were remarkably good, even fine. He was obviously a little timid, but he could combine punctilious deference with profound self-respect in a fashion that I have never seen equalled. I liked him; I was favorably impressed.

'I like you, Mr. Hatteras,' I said with my brutal veracity. 'I am favorably impressed. I make no secret of the fact. May I inquire without indiscretion as to your last place?'

'I have been with Lord Dover.'

'Whew!' I whistled. 'Not *the* Lord Dover?'

He flushed slightly.

'*The* Lord Dover,' he said.

'Then I needn't ask how you came to lose your situation.'

He shook his head sadly.

Lord Dover's name had flamed in the forehead of the half-penny press for months past, as even I knew, for the splendor of his fall had dazzled even North Africa. The young nobleman had squandered a very tidy patrimony on the turf and fine linen, particularly on fine linen; his creditors had taken possession of everything except his title and his skill at cards; and the sensational Dover sale-by-auction was drawing to a close that very week. The half-penny press had it that Lord Dover meant to earn an honest livelihood as a professor of bridge and kindred excitements.

'His lordship's wardrobe is being sold the day after to-morrow, is it not?' I inquired.

'Yes, sir,' said Mr. Hatteras, and then he added: 'It is a thousand pities that his lordship's height was somewhat above the average.'

'Why?' I demanded, curiously.

'His lordship had the finest collection of fancy waistcoats ever seen since the death of the memorable Count D'Orsay.'[12]

'Yes?' I persuaded him to continue. He was evidently beginning to feel his feet, to lose his nervousness.

'You might have bought a few of the choicest, sir, had not the inscrutable decrees of nature ruled otherwise.'

He regarded me meditatively.

No more delicate allusion to my five-feet-nothing could possibly have been made.

'You think these unrivalled waistcoats would be too large for me?' I said.

'I fear it, sir,' Mr. Hatteras murmured. 'I fear the contingency–And they will go for a song, for a song!'

'Could I not buy a few and use them as dressing-gowns?' I suggested gaily.

I thought this would break through the shell of his magnificent formality. But it didn't.

'You forget, sir,' he meekly said, 'that sleeves, which are essential to a dressing-gown, form no part of a waistcoat. Otherwise–'

He regarded me steadfastly. I fancied that his left eyelid quivered for the hundredth part of a second; but perhaps I was mistaken.

'Of course, of course,' I agreed hurriedly. 'I ought to have remembered. Excuse me.'

I said to myself that at no matter what cost I must have Mr. Hatteras for a valet. His personality was astounding. And moreover, a valet fresh from the service of such a flyer as Lord Dover would surely be a flyer himself.

'Have you been long with Lord Dover?' I asked, shattering a silence which had ensued.

'Many years,' said Mr. Hatteras.

'How many? Ten?'

'More, sir.'

'Twelve? Twenty? Fifty?'

'I have had no other master,' said Mr. Hatteras. 'Such as I am Lord Dover made me.'

'He ought to be congratulated,' I cried. 'I will engage you on the spot, Mr. Hatteras, if you think I shall be likely to suit you.'

'I beg your pardon, sir?'

'You heard what I said, Mr. Hatteras. This is a democratic age. Good valets are rare. Valets trained by Lord Dover are unique. You know your worth. You have your own little ways, which you would allow no master to interfere with. You would make certain demands from any master. Is it not well that I should know them? Would it not be annoying for both of us if within a fortnight you reluctantly discovered I was not the master you took me for? Formulate your requirements. I speak not of salary; that is a detail. I refer to more fundamental things. Am I to be allowed to choose my own clothes and part my hair where I like? What would be your attitude to the lady's-maids of my friends' wives? Will it be agreeable to you always to laugh at my jokes? Can I safely refrain from laughing at yours? Do you travel second or third? Do you mind me being a pronounced Radical? On steamers should you feel justified in permitting seasickness to interfere with the performance of your duties? Are you easily shocked? Should you expect a servant to bring tea to your bedside before you brought tea to mine? Do you insist on leading the conversation while I am dressing? Are you an optimist or a pessimist? Have you a liver, and if so, does it need sympathy? Does your Christian name come nice and crisp off the tongue? Or do you make it a condition that I address you as Hatteras? When I am inclined to swear, is the full glorious vocabulary of the Englishman open to me, or do you bar any particular words? And if so, which?-You can whisper them if you prefer not to utter them aloud, or you may write them.'

I paused, breathless.

'Without going into details, sir,' Mr. Hatteras replied with a charming smile, 'I am happy to inform you that I can answer all your questions in a favorable sense.'

'Good!' I said. 'I may mention that I have been out of England for sixteen or seventeen years, and that I am perhaps not very well versed in the latest manifestations of English social life. In such matters I should be glad of all the assistance you are able to give me.'

Mr. Hatteras bowed.

'At present I am living here at the Grand Babylon, but I propose as soon as convenient to take a flat–a flat suitable to your position and mine, Mr. Hatteras–in St. James's street.'

'Nothing could be better, sir,' said Mr. Hatteras.

'I bask in the sunshine of your approval, Mr. Hatteras,' I remarked. 'And now, perhaps, you wouldn't mind stepping into my dressing-room and giving me your professional opinion of my clothes?'

'With pleasure, sir,' said the majestic blond.

And we adjourned.

He gave me to understand that my *clothes* weren't quite too impossibly bad, but that the way they were looked after was painful to him to see.

I had hung my coats up by their loops (what in the name of sense were the loops for?) whereas they ought to have been suspended on shoulder-sticks! And my trouser-stretchers, it appeared, were mediæval! These truths and other similar ones, Mr. Hatteras imparted to me with all his characteristic delicacy of touch.

'I fear that your last man, sir,' said he at length, 'could not have been–'

'Stop right there!' I burst out bravely, 'I cannot and will not act a living lie, Mr. Hatteras. Know, Mr. Hatteras, that there never was a "last man!" You will be my first valet. You will sow the seeds of true dandyism and correctness in virgin soil. I am rich, but I have not always been rich. As I hinted to you in the other room, I want to learn.'

'You shall learn, sir, by all means,' said Mr. Hatteras.

And again I fancied that his left eyelid quivered for the hundredth part of a second.

'You might fold all these trousers as they ought to be folded,' I said. 'Hello! What on earth's that?'

Singular sounds came from the sitting-room.

II.

I discovered that the sounds were due to a certain confusion which had arisen at the door of my sitting-room between the page-boy, an old lady with grey side-curls, and a black-and-tan toy-terrier. The page-boy, who was being beaten off with great loss, vanished as soon as he saw me.

'Wanted to make me wait in the corridor!' the old lady soliloquized. She had not yet noticed me; neither had the dog.

'Madam?' I respectfully drew her attention to myself.

She turned round; so did the dog. For the dog it was the work of a moment to cut a piece out of the extremity of my trousers; I regretted the loss, inasmuch as the trousers, *inter alia*, had but just received the expert approval of Mr. Hatteras. However, the old lady gave me no chance to murmur.

'Well, Jack Stout,' she observed heartily. 'I should have known you anywhere!'

'Not Great-Aunt Anne!' I exclaimed, knowing perfectly well that it was.

I must omit the scene of recognition and osculation; these things are too sacred and too tedious for the stranger's eye. In a few moments we were talking quite naturally and simply, just as though it was not centuries since we last met, just as though I had not spent sixteen years of exile in Algeria, just as though I was a child again to whom she was in the habit of administering castor oil. (It was her dog now who, metaphorically, gave me castor oil.)

'As soon as I heard that your cousin Selina and her

husband had been here,' said my great-aunt, 'I thought I'd come along and see if they'd been slandering me. You know they live in the next flat to mine. We don't get on. I'm a woman of strong character, Jack–'

'I know that, great-auntie,' said I.

'And they're too feeble to stand it. I'm told they decidedly object to this dear old creature.'

She indicated the toy-terrier, which, fortified and refreshed by my raiment, was now resting calmly on its mistress's lap.

'Because it likes to nourish itself on their clothes, I suppose,' I suggested.

'Look here, Jack,' said my great-aunt. 'I may as well warn you at once that I cannot appreciate humor, even the least subtle, when it is directed against Finette.'

'Finette! Is that the fair creature's name? My dear great-auntie, I was quite serious. I am incapable of jesting at the expense of a dumb animal, and especially a dumb lady-animal. Of course, I learnt from Selina all about the sad death of your parrot. And Finette is now your all-in-all.'

'Yes,' said my great-auntie, but rather doubtfully.

'Better that you should keep dogs, even wild ones, than curates, even tame ones. At least such is my opinion, great-auntie. The danger with dogs that live on a diet of trousers and skirts and things is, of course, that accidents are likely to happen to them–mysterious and fatal accidents.'

'No accident will happen to Finette,' said my great-aunt with conviction. '*I* shall take care of that. I'm glad you like Finette, Jack.'

'Our affection is mutual,' I said. At that moment, Mr. Hatteras, having accomplished his task, came gently into the room.

'Oh! I beg pardon!' he exclaimed, seeing that I was engaged.

Finette growled.

'Come in, Mr. Hatteras,' I begged him. 'Great-auntie, permit me to present to you Mr. Hatteras, my new valet.'

But when the eyes of my great-aunt met the eyes of my new valet considerable emotion was aroused.

'Mr. Hatteras, your new valet?' stammered my great-aunt, astounded.

'I really beg pardon!' stammered Mr. Hatteras, much confused, and seeking to retire.

III.

'Mr. Pinder,' cried my great-aunt, evidently meaning Mr. Hatteras, 'why did you leave off coming to see me so suddenly?'

'I regret, I regret deeply, Miss Stout,' was my valet's pained answer, 'that circumstances compelled me to abandon the course –I wrote you to that effect, if I remember rightly.'

'You did, Mr. Pinder. But, regarded as an excuse for your conduct, "circumstances" seem to me to be rather vague and wholly unsatisfactory. And is it pertinent to ask what you are doing here disguised as a valet of the name of Hatteras?'

'My friend,' I observed to the discomfited Hatteras, 'I felt all the time that that name of yours was either invented or borrowed. It has the sound of romance.'

'You are evidently a wicked person, Mr. Pinder,' pursued my great-aunt. 'You might have played some swindling trick upon my poor, dear, innocent great-nephew, so unused, as he is, to the dangers of London, had I not fortunately arrived to protect him.'

'I shall be ever grateful to you for this,' I assured her. 'You shall teach me more of London. But what I want to know at the present moment is the precise object of Mr. Pinder's visits to you at your flat, great-auntie, you, a spinster! As your nearest male relative I have certainly the right to demand this information, dearest.'

'Don't call me "dearest," Jack,' said my great-aunt sharply.

'I won't have it. Mr. Pinder came to me to give me a course of lessons in bridge, which is the comfort and delight of my old age. He gave me two lessons, out of ten bargained for, and then "circumstances compelled" him to give me no more. However, I haven't paid him a penny yet, and I won't.'

My new valet remained speechless. I could see he was unnerved.

'Come now,' I soothed and stimulated him. 'Come, Mr. Hatteras. (I call you by that name because it is such a beautiful name.) Sit down. Pull yourself together and tell us all about it. That will be much the simplest way. We're bound to have it out of you, either here or elsewhere. Let it be here, in decency and decorum.'

So he sat down and pulled himself together.

'My story is a strange one,' he began softly. 'In fact it probably stands by itself.'

'It will only stand by itself if it is true, sir,' said my great-aunt, severely.

Mr. Pinder-Hatteras smiled. The toy-terrier showed her teeth.

'It is true enough,' the penitent said. 'My name is not Pinder and my name is not Hatteras. And yet, although I have assumed an alias, I have harmed no one but myself. I am not in fear of justice. I have neither murdered nor robbed–'

'You have robbed me of eight lessons in bridge,' said my great-aunt.

'I am sorry you should regard the episode in that light, madam,' he laughed easily. He was warming up to his narration. 'To proceed. I was born rich, and with a happy, rather careless disposition. I went to Eton and to Oxford. From the age of twenty-one I was my own master. I decided to open the oyster of life, and I opened it. If I cut myself in opening it, what matter? After a year or two of indecision I definitely chose sport as a career. I determined to win the Derby! I won it.'

'But very few men win the Derby!' my great-aunt put in.

'Quite few,' I agreed. 'In the last ten years only ten men have won it.'

'Then you are one of the ten, Mr. Whatever-your-name is?' my great-aunt discovered to him.

'I am,' he admitted.

'You must be able to ride extremely well to win a race like that!' said my great-aunt.

The man's politeness was equal to the occasion.

'Please do not flatter me,' he protested modestly. 'After I had won the Derby, I found that I was in debt to the extent of some seventy thousand pounds, and that I had practically nothing in the world but the Derby winner, my mortgaged estates, a considerable reputation as a card player—I had given my nights to cards—and an equally considerable reputation for being well-dressed. I sold the Derby winner for twenty thousand pounds, and began to gamble on a large scale in the hope of retrieving my fortunes. I gambled both on the turf and at cards. I lost, lost, lost. I might have pacified my creditors a little by means of cards if I had confined myself to games of skill, but I took a fatal fancy to poker. At poker the finest intellect alive could not be trusted to beat a pork butcher—in the result I was obliged to own defeat in the battle of life—'

'Battle of life indeed!' sniffed my great-aunt.

'If you prefer another phrase, in the struggle for existence, then.'

'Struggle for existence!' sniffed my great-aunt.

I jumped up from my chair.

'Why!' I exclaimed, 'you are—'

'I am the fifth Baron Dover,' said the penitent quietly.

'And you have folded my trousers!' said I, quietly.

'How are we to know that you are the fifth Baron Dover?' asked my great-aunt querulously. 'And where are the other four, anyhow?'

'Madam,' said the baron, 'if you will come with me to the

Turf Club,[13] or to White's,[14] or to the Carlton,[15] a hundred men shall testify to my identity. As to the whereabouts of the other four barons Dover, I can give no positive information. I can guess, I have fears—but no certainty.'

'So I have taken lessons in bridge from a lord!' my great-aunt meditated aloud. 'Well, *that* didn't do me much good. I suppose you turned to card tricks for a living because you couldn't turn to anything else?' she demanded of him coldly.

He paused and coughed.

'I resolved to begin a new life, to have done with all the old frivolities and to take myself seriously. Besides, I was confronted with the problem of earning my daily bread. I took myself very seriously. From the gay, larkish, and irresponsible young man, with his nose always turned towards Newmarket,[16] I became by an effort of the will, the being whom you now see before you, grave, melancholy, and perhaps slightly pompous. "You can do nothing," said my old self, "there is nothing for you but the music halls." "Yes, you can do something," said my new, brave self, "you can play cards as well as any honest man may. Why not take advantage of the present craze, and try to earn a modest income by professing bridge." I abandoned all my friends and acquaintances and haunts, and I trusted to the immensity of London. I disappeared as Lord Dover, and reappeared as Professor Pinder, whose advertisements were to be seen in the *Field*[17] and the *Queen*[18] and the *Pink 'Un.'*[19]

'*I* saw your advertisement in the *Queen*,' snapped my great-aunt.

'I do not doubt it,' said Lord Dover.

'And was I your first pupil?' asked my great-aunt.

'You were,' said Lord Dover, adding: 'And a most apt one.'

'If I was so frightfully apt, why did you abandon me?' demanded the dame.

'Because, madam, I found that cards were having a bad

effect on my fixity of purpose. They reminded me of old and forbidden delights. And I discovered also that bridge circles had a tendency to be frivolous circles—'

'Oh, indeed!' said my great-aunt.

'I speak quite impersonally,' said the fifth baron, and resumed: 'Of course, the least suspicion of frivolity was like poison to my moral nature. Moreover, I was detected by a friend.'

'Ah! So that was it!' my great-aunt reflected, absently stroking Finette.

'Therefore I abandoned the profession of bridge,' the baron pursued. 'The idea struck me that I had indeed another accomplishment besides cards. I really did understand men's clothes and valeting. I had trained several valets. So I decided to sink all false pride and become a valet. I said to myself that there could be no shame, but only honor and self-respect in pursuing with dignity the vocation of a valet. I said to myself that the rank was but the guinea stamp, and that honest hearts were more than coronets and a regular monthly wage than Norman blood. I disappeared as Professor Pinder, bought some mediocre garments, and reappeared as Mr. Hatteras. I hoped to meet with an employer at once wealthy and austere, intelligent and simple, old and young—'

'And you met with this Phœnix of a master in my grand-nephew, Jack!' said my great-aunt. 'Um! Well, fortunately for Jack, I found you out just in time, my lord!'

'Great-auntie,' I expostulated, 'you mustn't talk like that!'

'Why not, child?'

'Because Lord Dover is so obviously an honorable man, and what is more, a man of much force of character, if he will excuse me saying these things in his presence. To be able to withstand the seductions of bridge, after having once yielded to them! Fancy that! For myself I have always preferred whist, but I know the power which bridge at present wields over the intellect of London.'

'My dear Jack,' said my great-aunt, condescendingly, and somewhat ruffled, 'bridge is a far superior game to whist. There can be no question as to that, can there, Mr–Lord Dover?'

'None whatever,' said the fifth baron, piously and positively.

'Possibly in Algiers we never arrived at the higher subtleties of the game. You might initiate me, great-auntie.'

'Some day I certainly will,' said she.

It happened that there were several packs of cards lying on a side table.

'Why not now?' I suggested. I picked up the cards and fingered them invitingly.

'Oh, not now!'

'But why not?'

'Finette would be jealous. She hates cards. She knows they are her rivals in my affection–she is so intelligent, the little dear!'

'We can put the little dear to sleep in the dressing-room,' I proposed.

'So we could! But his lordship–his lordship has conscientious objections to bridge.'

'Only as a serious pursuit. I feel sure that Lord Dover will not in this instance put too strict an interpretation on his maxims of conduct.'

I spread the tempting cards abroad, and Lord Dover fell.

Then I seized a pair of stout driving-gloves and put them on.

'What are you doing, child?' asked my great-aunt.

'I am going to carry Finette into the dressing-room for you,' I replied.

It took the three of us to hush Finette to slumber in the dressing-room, but we did it.

'You know the rules, I suppose?' my great-aunt queried as we sat down to play.

'Yes, I think I know the rules,' I answered.

IV.

At the end of some time, when Great-Aunt Anne had lost £2 16s. 4d. and Lord Dover £1 7s. 1d., and I had won £4 3s. 6d.,[20] the spinster called me names, asserted that the fifth baron and I had conspired to rook her, and departed from the table, declining to play any more.

'Where are you going to, 'great-auntie?' I asked, as she purposefully crossed the room.

'I'm going to fetch Finette,' she said. 'The afternoon has been delightful, but we must tear ourselves away.' I seemed to notice a certain irony in her voice.

What happened next happened very swiftly. Finette had vanished from the dressing-room! The extreme importance of Finette to my great-aunt loomed up like a mountain. Previously I had been intellectually aware that my great-aunt doted on Finette. The fact was now brought home to my heart; Anne Stout lost her head, while pretending to be perfectly calm.

'Was Finette asleep when you went into the dressing-room to look at her?' she questioned Lord Dover.

In the middle of our game Lord Dover, fancying that he heard the voice of Finette uplifted in grief, had crept for a moment into the dressing-room to see.

'The dear creature appeared to be dozing,' replied the baron sympathetically.

Now the door leading from the dressing-room to the corridor was ajar, and my great-aunt announced with a great air of assurance that Finette must have waked up and left the hotel in order to find her way home, and that she was decidedly at St. James's Court at that moment (the so intelligent little thing) unless she had been stolen en route.

'I shall drive back at once, and if she isn't there, I shall drive to Scotland Yard. But she is sure to be there. No, thanks, I need *no* assistance. I have conducted my own affairs for something like half a century.'

So she left, and no sooner had she gone than the reformed baron turned to me and remarked:

'The detestable little animal is in the drawer where your waistcoats are; I put her there.'

'Indeed!' said I.

'Yes,' he proceeded. 'I may confide to you that one reason, perhaps the chief, why I did not continue to profess bridge to your esteemed aunt, was Finette. Finette's attitude towards me was such that I determined that Finette should go to a better world at the earliest opportunity, and the earliest opportunity came this afternoon. Of course, I shall do nothing without your sanction. The animal awaits your decision, Mr. Stout.'

'I share your ideas,' I said, and I indicated the hiatus in my trousers.

'I had already observed it,' said he, sadly.

'You think the aged beast ought to be put out of its misery at once?' I ventured.

'Roughly speaking, that is what I think.'

'The feeling is mutual,' I said. 'But perhaps we should consider a little the susceptibilities of my beloved relative. We ought to break the shock to her gently. Suppose we take Finette and call at a chemist's on the way, and give the animal some slow and painless poison. Then we can inform Miss Stout that we found Finette in the Strand, evidently suffering from nervous strain. We can hint that she must not expect the poor thing to live very long. In a few days the world will be well rid of Finette, but not before my great-aunt has somewhat accustomed herself to the idea of a world without Finette.

'Pardon the remark,' said Lord Dover, 'but you are a genius.'

However, when we opened the drawer in the dressing-room a shock awaited us. Finette was still and cold and stark. Clearly Lord Dover had not allowed for necessary ventilation.

'This is unfortunate,' I observed, as we eyed each other,

alarmed, across the corpse. 'Finette was perhaps more sinned against than sinning, and these aren't my *best* trousers.'

V.

'I suppose we had better bury the whole thing in oblivion,' said the baron.

'Oblivion isn't much to bury a dead dog in,' I replied. 'We should probably have the Inspector of Nuisances after us in a day or two. No, we will get as much *kudos* out of the business as we can. I will manage it. But perhaps you won't mind coming with me.'

I put on my latest Newmarket overcoat, and interred what remained of the toy-terrier in its large inner pocket.

When we arrived at my great-aunt's flat, the butler informed us that my great-aunt had been there and on finding that the dog had not arrived she had gone on to Scotland Yard.

'We will wait,' I said. 'We have grave news.'

And the butler hung up my Newmarket and the canine relics in the hall.

And soon afterwards my great-aunt stumbled in.

She was nearly ill.

'They knew nothing at Scotland Yard,' she told us, without even asking us to explain our presence.

'And they are not likely to,' I said. 'Great-auntie, nerve yourself for a trial. Finette has been found. Our dear baron was determined to leave no handle unturned in the search for that sublime and subtle animal, and ultimately by means of her hairs and her tears he traced her as far as the basement of the Grand Babylon. She had reached the famous kitchens of the hotel. When he arrived she had already eaten a meringue, a *pâté de foie gras*, two tomato *farcies*, and a part of Rocco,[21] the famous chef, which modesty forbids me to particularize. Our dear baron, amid a scene of indescribable confusion, intrepidly seized her, and she bit him–and fell back dead.'

'Fell back dead!'

'Yes. Whether it was the meringue or Rocco that had disagreed with her, or whether she expired from disgust at discovering that in eating Lord Dover she had eaten valet, I cannot say. The fact remains–'

At this very instant there was a prodigious row and clatter in the hall. It appeared that the hat and coat stand had fallen down! And then Finette calmly tottered into the room! She was not dead after all. She had recovered consciousness in my Newmarket and in leaping from the pocket had upset not only the hat and coat stand, but the august butler.

'Oh, Jack! What a tease you are!' cried my great-aunt, when she had recovered from the speechlessness of her joy.

As for the baron and myself, we pretended not to be surprised.

'Hatteras,' I said, 'the incident is closed. You can go on first and put out my things.'

'Yes, sir,' said he, and went.

'Jack!' exclaimed my aunt, as soon as we were alone, 'you don't mean to say–you surely don't mean to say-'

'What?'

'That you're going to employ him as your valet, now that you know–'

'My dear great-aunt,' I said fatigued, 'is not this a democratic country? Are not all people equal in it? If so, it would certainly be ridiculous that I should deprive any capable person of a livelihood merely because he was a lord and had won the Derby. The handicap of a peerage is heavy enough, goodness knows, and I for one, could not find it in my heart to say even to a duke: "No, you shall not earn my money, because you are in the House of Lords," Be charitable, great-auntie; Providence has seen fit to preserve your terrier. Be charitable.'

'Well,' said she, 'I wish you joy of your valet, that's all.'

'I anticipate joy,' I answered.

PART III.
MY DINNER PARTY.

I.

I could plume myself on one thing–that I was the sole man in England who had a lord for a valet. What remarkable vicissitudes occur to the French noblesse I do not know, though I have heard tell, but of the English peerage it could be positively asserted that only a single member of it was following the profession of a valet. All the rest were accounted for. Lord Dover made a good valet. In fact my experience has been such that I should advise every man-about-town who desires to be utterly and absolutely smart to get a lord for a valet, if he can. I warmly recommend lords. And now-a-days there are so many lords who come to grief and smash (as Lord Dover did), who seriously wish to turn over a new leaf (as Lord Dover did), who are forced to earn a living somehow (as Lord Dover was), and who don't mind what they do, so long as they don't run the risk of imprisonment for false pretences while directing a wild-cat company (as Lord Dover didn't), that the chances of obtaining ever a viscount for a valet may not after all be as remote as they seem.

And it is so nice and comforting to feel that while your 'man' is tying your necktie or giving you really expert advice as to braces, he is at the same time turning over a new leaf, learning to be a useful member of society, and building up his moral character.

Lord Dover (it was agreed that I should call him Hatteras, the name by which he had introduced himself to me) proved invaluable in the matter of taking and furnishing a flat in St. James's Street. He was also a perfect fountain of advice on all questions of form. He kept himself to himself, was sober and industrious, had no followers, went to bed after me and rose before me, and never asked for a day off.

'Hatteras.' I said to him one morning, 'I want to give a dinner party, now that we are settled.'

'Certainly sir,' said he. 'But you don't intend to give it *here*?'

'Why not?'

'Such things aren't *done* nowadays, sir,' said he. 'Your long absence from England perhaps accounts for your being unaware of the fact that hospitality is never exercised at home. It upsets the house or the flat, and embitters the servants (not that *I* mind, sir); and, besides, it isn't public enough.'

'You indicate a restaurant for this affair, Hatteras?'

'I do, sir. People don't care to eat nowadays unless they can see hundreds of other people eating at the same time and thus be sure that they are eating the correct thing in the correct way. Moreover, at a high-class restaurant there is invariably a very loud band, which drowns the cries of the martyrized stomach.'

'I am much obliged to you, Hatteras, for this tip,' I answered. 'You are serving me well, and as a mark of my gratitude, I wish that in the future you should not address me as "sir." After all, Hatteras, we are equals in the great lap of Mother Nature, are we not?'

'I suppose we are, sir–I mean I suppose we are,' said Hatteras. 'And since you are distributing favors, may I remind you that next Friday I shall have been with you a month? It would suit me if you could let me have one evening a month. I do not ask for a whole day. I know how inconvenient that would be for you.'

'You would like Friday evening off, Hatteras?'

'I should, s–.'

'It is yours,' said I, 'and, of course, there will be your wages, too.'

II.

Now this dinner party was a philanthropic device of mine. Its purpose was a reconciliation between members of a certain family, my own, in whose history reconciliations had occurred far less frequently than quarrels. Although I had been too busy spending money on the exquisite nothings for my new flat, to see much of either Great-Aunt Anne or my Cousin Selina Ashway and her husband, I knew that the sanguinary vendetta between these near neighbors and relatives still existed and that since the unfortunate episode of the Revolver and the Shot Parrot they had not spoken. I determined that this painful state of affairs should terminate, and my scheme was to invite the Ashways and my great-aunt to dine, without telling my great-aunt that I had invited the Ashways and without telling the Ashways that I had invited my great-aunt. They would at least be compelled to address each other in terms of politeness. And, once I had set their tongues going, I trusted to my wit and my luck for the rest. Moreover (I thought) even if the worst comes to the worst and they fight it out across the fish, I shall at any rate have a front seat at the altercation and the consciousness of my good intentions.

I chose the Louvre for the scene of the peace-making; partly because it was advertising itself then as *the* restaurant de luxe, partly because the Louvre orchestra is renowned for its fervency and fury, and partly because I had heard that they served ices at the Louvre in the form of doves. I thought if I ordered a dove-ice, and secreted in my waistcoat pocket an olive from the earlier portion of the repast, and then stuck the olive in the bird's mouth at the psychological moment, the effect would be magnificent and sublime.

My Great-Aunt Anne was the first to arrive. As she greeted me in the dazzling foyer of the Louvre under the haughty gaze of a legion of silvered officials, I thought she looked triumphant in her imperial purple robe with the large white shawl over her shoulders. But she looked tired, too, and I noticed that her voice was hoarse.

'Naturally, I'm hoarse with talking so much,' she said.

'Are you?' I replied, at a loss. 'And how is Finette?' I

wanted to be polite.

'Oh! I've brought her with me, the little dear!' said my great-aunt.

And sure enough the bright eyes of that destructive and indestructible dog, the real origin of the vendetta, peered out from the interstices of the shawl. I was genuinely shocked. The chances of a reconciliation had vanished almost to zero in a moment!

'Really!' I observed, trying delicately to make my great-aunt perceive that I had not invited the dog.

'Yes,' she added vivaciously, 'of course, she's been alone all day. And besides it's her birthday, and she must have a treat. She's thirteen.'

'What an unfortunate age!' I exclaimed.

'Unfortunate?'

'Unlucky, I mean,' I explained.

'Oh!' said my great-aunt. 'By the way, will you order a couple of meringues for Finette. She will lie on a footstool at my feet and enjoy herself like a little lady, won't you, sweetheart? When's the rest of the company coming? You said there would be two others. Who are they?'

'Here they are,' I answered, seeing Selina and her husband approach.

'Well, Jack!' said Selina with an air of fatigue. 'Gerald's got a bilious attack, but he's come. Will you order some dry toast for him?'

Then she saw Great-Aunt Anne.

'Seen you before to-day!' she murmured carelessly, to Great-Aunt Anne, after a somewhat trying silence had occurred.

'Rather!' agreed the old spinster, with a curious intensification of her air of triumph.

Gerald Ashway was using up all his strength in looking miserable; he spake no word.

'Now we're all going to dine together nicely,' I said with

gaiety, 'and have a friendly chat. We won't stand on ceremony. Come along, great-auntie.' And I bundled them blithely towards the *salles à manger*.

At the further end of the large gold dining-room at the Louvre there is a smaller apartment containing about a dozen tables. I had secured one of these tables. We could see through the agate archway into the main apartment.

We had scarcely arranged ourselves in a *partie carrée*, Selina opposite me, and my great-aunt opposite Gerald, when a boy put a note into my hands. I read these words, scribbled in pencil: *'Please do not give me away. I shall rely on you. Dover.'*

And immediately afterwards the writer of the note, faultlessly garbed, with a vastly pretty and stylish little woman by his side, came through the archway, and took a table in a corner next to ours. Fortunately, my great-aunt did not catch sight of him. I discreetly averted my eyes. The Ashways had never seen my valet.

I threw the note away.

'Bad news?' inquired Selina.

'That depends,' said I.

I reflected upon the remarkableness of my noble valet. Barely an hour ago, clad in his blue reefer suit,[22] he had been engaged in tying my necktie and arranging the curve of my watch-chain. Now he was the peer of the realm, *noli me tangere*[23] in every inch of him. Indeed, he might easily have passed for a duke. And the charming creature by his side–well, she might be anything, from a duchess upwards. (After all, then, he had followers.) You could see the aristocrat all over him. The waiters saw it instantly. And yet this man had not spoken a word, during a whole month of service, to indicate that he had ever been anything else but a valet!

'Still,' I thought, 'it's a bit stiff, him coming the duke over me at the very next table to mine! In future, I shall pay his wages *after* his night out.'

'Iced soup?' asked our waiter.

'Yes, please,' said my great-aunt.

'Yes, please,' said Cousin Selina.

'It's been a very warm day,' I remarked, pleasantly.

'It *has*,' said Gerald Ashway, who was already toying with his toast.

The iced soup was brought. The two women consumed it icily. The atmosphere of the table, despite strenuous efforts on my part, was becoming more arctic every minute.

'What's *up*?' I murmured, inwardly. 'The least they can do is to talk.'

'Come, now,' I said aloud, 'the least you can do is to talk. This is Finette's birthday. Let us talk freely, frankly, as relations should. Gerald, rouse yourself. Have some fizz.'

'Well, Jack Stout,' began my great-aunt, 'as you ask for frankness, all I can say is that, if this dinner is your idea of a joke–!'

'I quite agree with Miss Stout,' said Selina, primly.

'Oh, Lor'!' breathed Gerald.

'Joke?' I cried. 'What do you mean?'

'And to-night of all nights!' Selina said.

'To-night of all nights?' I cried. 'What on earth *do* you mean?'

Just then the laughing voice of Lord Dover's feminine companion grew audible. She was glancing over the *Pall Mall Gazette*.[24] 'Have you read this amusing county court action at Westminster?' she said. 'It's the most screaming thing. Fancy the old lady conducting her own case! When she interrupted the barrister on the other side, and he told her not to teach him his business, she said that she'd no intention of doing so–it would be far too laborious a task! Wasn't that lovely?'

Lord Dover whispered something to his friend, and she shut the paper up hastily.

We had all been listening.

'Jack,' said Selina, who had been gazing hard at me, 'you certainly have got a nerve. You haven't turned a hair.'

'Why should I?' I asked.

'You don't mean to say, old man,' Gerald put in, 'that you haven't heard about the action–our action–I mean Miss Stout's action?'

'Not a word,' I said. 'What action?'

They all three looked at each other.

'Great-aunt's action against us for damages!' burst out Selina. 'It's been tried to-day at the Westminster County Court!'

I seemed suddenly to see a great and blinding light. I stamped my foot, and stamped on Finette's tail. When that affair was smoothed over, I said:

'Tell me about it. Tell me all about it. Why has it been kept a secret from me? We've got to get through this dinner somehow, and so we may as well have the action in full. I meant to try to reconcile you, in my innocence! I must have something to divert my thoughts. Selina, begin.'

III.

'Oh!' said Selina, with a rather hard laugh. 'It's the simplest thing in the world. Great-aunt merely brought an action against us; that's all–an action for damages.'

'I warned you I should!' cried Anne.

'I know you did. But that doesn't make it any nicer of you,' said Selina.

'Damages for what?' I inquired.

'You know perfectly well for what!' said the pugnacious old spinster. 'A revolver bullet comes from their flat through the wall into my flat, scratches my forehead, takes off my best curl, and ushers into eternity a parrot that was over sixty years old and could repeat the Lord's Prayer backwards. And all this without warning! What they were doing, letting off revolvers in their flat, I don't know–'

'That was a private affair,' Selina interpolated, blushing.

'Nor do I seek to inquire,' pursued Great-aunt, 'and,

seeing that it was so private, you might have kept it a little more private. The bullet wasn't very private. And, in any case, you might have apologized.'

'Oh, Great-aunt, we did,' Selina protested. 'We apologized to your butler.'

'What use apologizing to my butler? It wasn't his curl and it wasn't his parrot.'

'You refused to see us,' said Selina, warmly. That red hair of hers was lighting up for an explosion.

'Well, never mind these piquant recriminations,' I suggested. 'And please don't talk so loud. The band is coming to the end of its piece, and if it stops suddenly, while you are in the middle of a sentence, Selina, the dining public may hear things it was not intended to hear. And, let me say, candidly, Selina and Gerald, since this is a family dinner, that it was a pity you fought the action. To avoid a scandal, and out of respect for Great-aunt's advanced age, you ought to have allowed it to go by default.'

'My dear chap,' said Gerald, 'it's all very well you playing Solomon like that. But do you know how much your great-aunt claimed? Only £150! No more! Five shillings for the curl, fifty pounds for the parrot, half a guinea for the scratch, sixteen shillings for damage to wall, and £98 8s. 6d. for nervous shock.

'I ought really to have claimed more for the shock,' said Great-aunt Anne. 'But I fixed that sum to make it level money.'

'Anyhow,' said Gerald, 'we can't afford to avoid scandals at the rate of £150 and costs per scandal.'

'So, naturally, we made a counterclaim,' Selina went on with the story. 'It was Gerald's idea, the counterclaim. Don't you think it was a good one?'

'Ye–e–' I caught my great-aunt's eye. 'I don't know,' I said.

'Of course, you know, child,' my great-aunt corrected me. 'You know it was a monstrous idea.'

'How much did you claim, and what for?' I asked Gerald.

'I'll tell you how much they claimed, and what for!' cried Great-aunt Anne. 'They went back into the past. And they said that Finette had bitten either one or the other of them in the corridor, twenty-one times, and ruined fourteen pairs of trousers at thirty shillings a pair; one pair of kid boots at two guineas, and six skirts at five guineas each. And they also claimed £95 8s. for twenty-one nervous shocks, at the rate of £4 11s. a shock.'

' We ought to have claimed more for the shocks,' said Selina. 'But we compromised at that to make it level money– £150 altogether.'

'I see,' said I.

And, as a matter of fact, I *did* see. I saw one more manifestation of the incurable pugnacity of the Stout blood–in the female line.

'As this is a family dinner, and we are speaking candidly,' said Gerald, 'I may say that I wish you clearly to understand that we were forced into the fight by the tactics of the plaintiff. We wanted peace, and nothing else.'

'I suppose that was why you engaged a solicitor and a barrister!' Great-aunt Anne commented.

There was a pause, while the waiter served beans *à la Waterloo.*

'And so this interesting action was fought out to-day!' I observed. 'Does it not occur to any of you that I am simply dying to hear the result?'

'The judge reserved judgment till tomorrow morning,' said Gerald.

'But he is strongly in my favor,' Great-aunt Anne added.

'Not he!' said Selina. 'He was polite to you because you conducted your own case and kept on squashing our barrister. But that won't affect his judgment. Our barrister says we are certain to win.'

'If you win I shall appeal!' cried my great-aunt.

'And vice-versa!' said Gerald.

'If necessary, we shall carry it to the House of Lords,' Selina stated, impressively.

'You can carry it to Jericho, if you like,' said my great-aunt. 'Waiter, more beans. But I shall win.'

'I foresee the ruin of two branches of our family,' I began, solemnly, 'unless some decisive step is taken by an impartial third party. Now, why not regard me as the House of Lords? I can bring to the case a knowledge of details which the House of Lords could not hope to rival. And as for impartiality, do I not love you all with an equal affection? And, of course, my consular experiences have been quasi-judicial. *** Well, what do you say?'

'I am quite willing,' moaned Gerald, as he reluctantly abandoned a piece of toast, half-eaten.

'I would leave it to you,' said Great-aunt Anne, 'if I thought you had any sense. But I don't think you have.'

'Remember, a series of appeals ending in the House of Lords will cost you thousands, whereas an appeal to me will cost you nothing.'

While uttering this truth I winked knowingly at my great-aunt. She winked back.

'Oh, very well, then,' she agreed, hastily.

'But how soon shall you decide?' Selina asked.

'I can't say,' I replied. 'I shall have to meditate on the facts.'

'Within a week?'

'Yes; within a week, certainly.'

Thus it was agreed by all parties that my verdict should be final, and should override the judgment of the County Court, unless His Honor's happened to coincide with mine.

The middle part of the dinner languished. Gerald Ashway looked as if he was crossing from Dover to Calais in a choppy sea. The women looked their ages, and more. Finette had had one meringue, and was uneasily chewing the cud under the table. Lord Dover and his pretty little friend seemed well satisfied with each other. The orchestra, after a brief rest, was drowning every other racket with renewed vigor; and, although some hundreds of people were dining too well within earshot, we could hear nothing whatever except what passed at our own table and 'Violets.'

I said, cheerfully:

'I have meditated on your case, my dear friends and relatives, and I will deliver judgment.'

'What! Here?' asked Selina.

'Here,' I replied. 'And first, I must express my regret that you should have chosen this particular day for the trial of your County Court action. You had all the days of the year on which to fight out the battle, and you selected the very day on which I had asked you to dinner. You must have known, or you ought to have known, that it would cast gloom over my dinner –my dinner, that I meant to be so gay and amicable. Look at Gerald there, or, rather, look at what once was Gerald, and observe the sad results of undue indulgence in the atmosphere of County Courts!'

'I say, old chap,' Gerald murmured, 'give us the judgment first and the fireworks afterwards.'

'Well,' I proceeded, winking at my great-aunt, who again winked back, 'whereas, the plaintiff hath well proven that she hath suffered damage in the walls of her habitation, and in the hairs of her gray head, and in her aged and religious parrot; and, whereas, she hath suffered a nervous shock, the like of which she hath not suffered since Anno Domini, 1890, to wit, fourteen years past, when she entered the Tivoli in mistake for Exeter Hall;[25] and, whereas, she is my great-aunt, and I am judicially impartial, I give judgment for the said plaintiff for the sum of one hundred and fifty pounds.'

'I told you so!' said my great-aunt, gleefully, to Selina. 'There! You owe me a hundred and fifty pounds.'

'Jack, you are ridiculous!' said Selina, furious.

'Judges often are,' I retorted. 'But they've got to be obeyed.

And, whereas, the defendants hath well proven–I should say "have" well proven–that they have suffered damage in various articles of clothing, too numerous and delicate to mention, at the teeth of a certain terrible wild French beast; and, whereas, they have, collectively and individually, suffered nervous shocks to the number of a score shocks and one shock; and, whereas, nothing before had ever shocked them; and, whereas, they are either my first cousins once removed, or my second cousins, I don't know which, and I am judicially impartial, I give judgment for the said defendants on the counterclaim for the sum of one hundred and fifty pounds. God save the King.'

'Jack, your name ought to have been Daniel,' said Selina.'And what about costs?' Gerald demanded.

'No costs,' I said. 'No costs on any account. I have a moral objection to costs. Each party to this deplorable county court action must pay his own.'

Great-aunt Anne maintained an awful silence. To hide her feelings, she bent down and gave Finette the second meringue. I had timed my judgment very well; the waiter opportunely appeared with the dove-ice, whereupon I took an olive from my waistcoat pocket and jammed it into the bird's mouth. However, the icy beak was not very pliant, and I rather spoilt the shape of the animal, which under the heat of the room began to melt.

'Are you giving that bird a pill?' Gerald inquired.

'No,' I said. 'It's a dove, and this is an olive. See?' I endeavored to look as much like the Brothers Cheerible[26] as I could.

The olive fell out and rolled on the table.

'How stupid you are, child!' Great-aunt exclaimed. 'Of course, I shall abide by your decision; but if you think I'm going to make friends with my stupid relatives, on the top of that, you're in error!'

And Selina said: 'Yes, I think any *friendship* is out of the question, Jack.'

I deemed the moment for firmness had arrived.

'Listen,' I said. 'I am thirty-seven, and I am worth about a hundred thousand pounds. I may die any time. I have made my will and duly remembered you all in it. But I swear by Saturn that, unless you instantly become friends, and the best of friends, I will make a new will tomorrow, and leave every cent to the Home for Decayed County Court Judges. So, there!'

'I *want* to be friends,' said Gerald.

'I am not to be bribed into friendship,' said Great-aunt Anne, pale.

'It's all very well for you to talk like that, Great-aunt,' said Selina, 'because you know you'll die long before Jack does, and so it doesn't matter to you what sort of a will he makes. But we're young, aren't we, Gerald–?'

'Girl!' cried my great-aunt, in loud tones.

At that very second the band finished 'Violets,' and you could hear the subdued rumor of hundreds of people dining too well.

But my great-aunt broke out none the less into a harangue directed against Selina, in which her aim was evidently to make it perfectly clear to Selina what she thought of Selina.

V.

My party was attracting too much attention.

I do not positively assert that my great-aunt was creating a larger volume of sound than people often do create towards the end of a Louvre dinner; but I do assert that she had the air of being too much in earnest over her performance. And the proof that she was too much in earnest is that she did not even hear the sudden barking of Finette. Finette had strayed from the protecting skirts of her mistress and was at Lord Dover's table. My noble valet had bent down to the dog, but I could not see what he was doing. Finette barked more loudly, and then began to prance about the floor.

I jumped up and faced the room.

'Ladies and gentlemen,' I announced as rapidly and distinctly as possible, 'kindly excuse this unconventional address, but I think you will be interested to know that there is a mad dog in the room. She is small, but vicious, and she is at large on the floor. At the present instant she is foaming at the mouth.' (It was the creamy remains of the meringue on her chops.) 'I regret to say that she was introduced into England illegally in a lady's reticule. Perhaps you may consider it advisable to retire temporarily while measures are taken for her destruction.'

Save for ourselves, and Lord Dover and his pretty little friend, the room was emptied in ten seconds.

'Jack!' Selina whispered, aghast. 'What mad prank will you play next?'

'No mad prank at all!' said I. 'Great-auntie and you were on the verge of making a spectacle of yourselves for the benefit of the dining public, and I was obliged to get the room emptied somehow to save you from disgrace. I fancy I have succeeded. Besides, look at the dog!'

Lord Dover had bravely picked up the animal, regardless of the fatal foam, and was apparently trying to soothe her. Great-aunt sprang from her chair. The objurgatory harangue was effectually dammed. The recognition between Great-aunt and Lord Dover was mutual. And, moreover, his manner towards Finette was so sympathetic that my great-aunt softened towards him at once. They collaborated in various enterprises to calm the unfortunate beast, but without success. After making several insertions in Lord Dover's coat and my great-aunt's lace, Finette crossed the bar, and lay still. Finette had caused us to believe that she was dead once before, but this time there could be no mistake.

'Poor little thing!' murmured Selina, involuntarily, gazing at the corpse on my great-aunt's lap.

'So unexpected!' murmured Lord Dover.

But Lord Dover's eyelid quivered humorously as he

caught my glance over Great-aunt's shoulders.

I remembered that he had sworn to be the undoing of Finette. That he had, in fact, undone her I am now convinced. But my good taste has always prevented me from asking him whether it was by poison or stiletto. There was no blood. The point about some stilettos is, however, that they cause no extravasation.

It became known in the restaurant that Lord Dover had courageously seized the dog, and that the dog had expired in convulsions. The dining public returned. Lord Dover blossomed into a hero. He had to be presented to Selina, and Heaven knows what! It was Lord Dover, and nothing but Lord Dover, from end to end of the restaurant. I was nowhere, simply nowhere. And he didn't present us to his pretty little friend, as he might have done.

'In the midst of this great chastening sorrow,' said my great-aunt in the foyer, afterwards–Finette, done up in brown paper, being under her arm– 'I can bear nobody ill-will. And perhaps, Jack may die before me, after all. Selina and Gerald, shake hands.'

The feud was ended.

I began a little homily suitable to the occasion, but Lord Dover and his charming companion happened to pass through the foyer just then. My ladies offered their backs to me and bowed him a gracious adieu, which he returned with just the slight hint of condescension that becomes a peer of the realm. Gerald had wandered off in search of a steadying brandy.

VI.

I arrived at my beautiful new flat at ten minutes past midnight. I had given Hatteras leave till midnight. I let myself in with my latch-key; but that incomparable valet came into the hall to meet me before I had had time to close the door. He was in his usual blue reefer suit.

'Hatteras,' I said, mildly, 'you might have warned me that

you also were going to the Louvre to-night.'

'A thousand apologies, sir,' said Hatteras, hastily. 'I was not aware that you had selected the Louvre for your dinner party. As a matter of fact, it was not I who selected the Louvre for *my* dinner party, sir; but had I known that you would be there, of course, nothing would have induced me to incommode you by my presence. I have to thank you very heartily, sir, for your forbearance.'

'Don't mention it, Hatteras,' I replied, 'and remember that I have relieved you of the duty of addressing me as "sir". Sad about Finette, wasn't it?'

'Very,' said he. 'I felt deeply for Miss Stout.'

He looked me fairly in the face. I noticed again the quiver of his eyelid.

'By the way, Hatteras,' I remarked, casually, as he was putting me to bed, 'that was a devilish pretty woman who dined with you!'

'Was it, sir?' he said. 'Excuse me, sir, but I beg you to permit me to call you "sir".'

'As you wish,' I muttered. And, after a pause, I continued, muttering: 'Yes; a remarkably attractive woman!'

'It was Lady Lettice Dovedale, one of my cousins,' said Hatteras.

'Ah! Hatteras!' I said. 'A widow, if I mistake not?'

'Yes, sir.'

'I thought she looked like a widow,' I said.

'Did you, sir?'

'Of course, Hatteras,' I said, 'I needn't tell you that you are always at liberty to have your friends here at any time you like.'

VII.

The County Court Judge dismissed Stout vs. Ashway, on both the claim and the counterclaim, and he refused leave to appeal.

PART IV.
DERANGEMENT OF A MARRIAGE.

I.

Four days after the famous repast at the Louvre Restaurant, at about eleven o'clock of the forenoon, who should visit me in my new flat in St. James's Street, but my cousin Selina's husband!

'Halloo! Gerald!' I greeted him, as he was shown into the drawing-room by my beautiful, new, spruce parlor-maid, 'I thought you always spent the mornings in philosophic meditation at one of your clubs. Anything wrong?'

This was the first time that Gerald Ashway had visited me on his own account, although I had now been in London nearly two months. I guessed that he had not come without a definite and perhaps delicate purpose.

Instead of answering my question, he demanded, in a half-whisper, grinning:

'Is *he* here? I was hoping he would have let me in.'

'Is who here?'

'Your valet. I thought I'd just come and have a look at him.'

'My dear Ashway,' I asked coldly, 'what on earth do you mean?'

'Now, old chap,' he said insinuatingly, 'don't come it over me like that. You know what I mean.' (As a fact I did–of course.) 'The wife's great-aunt told us only last night that you'd got Lord Dover for a valet. I wouldn't believe at first that that gilded dook with that awful pretty woman who sat at the next table to us on Friday night, was your valet. But it seems there's no gammon about it, and he is. Got converted or something, hasn't he? So I thought I'd come along and have a look at him. You are a card, Jack, no mistake! Fancy having a lord for a valet!'

'Ashway,' I admonished him, 'sit down. No, not in that

thing–take the sofa. Light a cigarette. Help yourself to the whisky here. Don't spill the potass on the table. And listen to me. I have a few remarks to make.'

He smiled amiably, and obeyed, save in the matter of the potass.

'Well?' he sighed interrogatively.

'You know the history of Lord Dover,' I said. 'His brilliant, meteoric and not altogether Quakerish career! How he shone blindingly on the turf and in the card-room. How he cut a dazzling figure under the nose of the public. How he blew the bubble, and blew it and blew it and blew it, until it burst, and there was nothing at all left! You know that by the time he reached the age of thirty he had frittered and gambled away everything, including a town house in Berkeley Square and three country estates! Answer me.'

'Everybody knows that,' Gerald murmured.

'Exactly. And what did Lord Dover do then? Did he sponge on his relatives and his pals? Did he creep into the City and make a few vile hundreds by lending the prestige of his title to a swindle? Did he even go on the stage? No! He pulled himself together. He became a changed man. "I have wasted some of the best years of my life," he said to himself. "I will not waste the rest. I will become a useful member of society." And he became one. He had no profession, no trade. There was only one honest calling at which he could hope to be an adept, that of a valet. He was not ashamed to be a valet. By chance I heard his story. I engaged him. I am proud to have him for a valet.'

'Yes, I should think you were!' Gerald put in.

'And here you are,' I proceeded sternly, ignoring the interruption, 'wanting to stare the stare of idle vulgar curiosity at this noble fellow who has been strong enough even at the eleventh hour to resist temptation and to live the higher life. No, Gerald, *he* is *not* here. And even if he had been he would not have let you in. You ought to know that it is not part of the duty of a valet to attend to the front-door. Especially when he is living the higher life.'

'Oh! All right old chap, all right! Thundering good whisky this! Thanks, I will.'

'I need not urge you,' I continued, 'to keep Lord Dover's secret. If it once got about among the other servants that there was a lord in their midst, I don't know what would happen.'

'I'm corked tight,' said Ashway.

'You mentioned an awfully pretty woman just now, Gerald,' I began again. 'That was Lady Lettice Dovedale, his cousin. She's a widow. I'm violently in love with her.' I gave vent to the last statement brusquely, almost defiantly.

'The deuce you are! I wasn't aware you were in that set at all.'

'I am not in that set,' I said. 'I do not know Lady Lettice Dovedale. I saw her for the only time in my life on Friday night. But I tell you I am in love with her. I tell you because I must tell someone. Her image remains with me. I cannot get rid of it. It is a remarkable instance of love at first sight.'

'What are you going to take for it?' Gerald asked. 'If I were you, I should see a doctor.'

'Don't try to be funny,' I remonstrated. 'I don't quite know what I am to do. One can't very well tell one's valet that one is in love with one's valet's cousin, can one? Such things aren't done.'

'But seeing that he's a–'

'He is my valet, and nothing else. Therein lies the essence of his reform. No, Gerald. In this affair *you* can be of use to me. You must inquire at your clubs, get to know her friends, and get me introduced by some roundabout channel. See?'

'By the way,' said he, 'I saw her driving down St. James's Street as I came along.'

'Why the dickens didn't you tell me before?' I exclaimed savagely.

'The carriage went to the bottom–'

'Gerald,' I cried, 'don't talk of her carriage as if it was a tramp steamer!'

He never laughed. 'I'm not doing,' he said, with his immovably calm stupidity. 'I meant to say it went to the bottom of the street and then turned back up the street again.'

I rushed to the window. A carriage was just stopping in front of my flat, and she was in it, radiant as the morn.

'Look here, Gerald,' I said, 'do you mind going now? The fact is, I've got an appointment.'

II.

As soon as I had exterminated my cousin's husband, I ran out to reconnoitre for my valet's cousin. My flat was on the first floor of the mansion. The landing was unoccupied, but when I put my head over the bannisters, I saw the top of a lovely grey hat ascending. The hat stopped half way up the flight, meditated, and then retired several steps; then it meditated again and began to reascend. Near the summit the hat hesitated once more.

'Excuse me,' I said, 'are you in search of Lord Dover?'

The hat tilted backwards, and showed the adorable and piquant face of Lady Lettice. I had suspected as much.

'Yes, I am,' said Lady Lettice. And she blushed; even her delightful snub nose blushed.

'I don't think he's in,' I told her. 'But if you'll come upstairs–'

She came upstairs, and she came into my drawing-room, and I introduced myself, and informed her that I was aware of her identity.

'And I of yours,' she said.

('You've got her safely inside, my bold hero,' I meditated. 'But what are you going to do now? And suppose the valet appears on the scene.')

'Is your business with Lord Dover urgent?' I inquired.

'Extremely urgent,' she answered. 'You are a great friend

of his, aren't you?'

'Yes,' I said doubtfully.

'A very great friend? You and he share these rooms?'

'Yes,' rather more doubtfully.

'I thought so,' Lady Lettice exclaimed gaily. 'He told me he was your valet. But, of course, I knew that was his way of putting it—that you and he were on the most intimate terms.'

I tried to laugh as naturally as possible.

'Yes,' I said, 'we are.'

'Since he went—since he gave up racing and all that,' Lady Lettice smiled, 'Dover has become a very mysterious person, indeed. He said I could write to him here, under the name of Hatteras, but that I was on no account to call. So I've called.'

I bowed my joy.

'I don't know where he is exactly at the moment,' I said. 'He may have run over to Paris. But he's certain to be back soon.'

'If he's gone to Paris he can't be back so very soon, can he?'

'Not *very* soon,' I admitted. 'But perhaps it isn't Paris?'

'You've got some scheme on, haven't you, you and he?' asked Lady Lettice.

'Yes,' I said. 'You might call it a scheme.'

I could not find it in my heart to tell this exquisite and stylish creature, whose horses were stamping on St. James's Street, that her cousin was in fact my valet. I felt that it would not sound well, even though I added that he was living the higher life.

'I guessed you had some scheme in hand,' she said. 'And it's such a tremendous secret that Dover wouldn't tell even me. I shan't ask *you* to tell me. But you *would* tell me if I asked you, wouldn't you?'

'I should do anything you asked me to, Lady Lettice,' I replied.

'Well tell me, then, instantly.'

('They're all alike,' I reflected. 'But she's deliciousness nevertheless.')

'As soon as Lord Dover comes in,' I said, 'I will tell you as much as I think a pretty woman ought to know.'

'Oh!' she observed. 'It's *that* sort of thing, is it.'

'Not precisely,' I said. 'But anyhow you can wait a little, surely?'

'It's my business that can't wait,' she explained. 'Oh! Whatever's that?'

'Only the tape-machine,'[1] I said.

To save myself the trouble of reading newspapers I had a tape-machine installed in my drawing-room. It stood behind a screen, between the cigar cabinet and 'Fifty Years of Punch.'[2] It was ticking busily. I walked over to it.

'Nothing!' I said. 'African Incorporateds[3] have fallen a point, that's all!'

'All!' she cried. 'Poor Dover will be ruined. That's what I've come about. Something must be done immediately, immediately.'

'Let me do it,' I replied vaguely. 'Give me the honor of doing it.'

'On Friday night,' she spoke rapidly, 'I asked Dover if he had any spare cash. He said he had a little. I have never known him really fast for a few thousands. So I advised him to buy five thousand African Incorporateds on Saturday morning. I knew on the highest authority that the government was going to grant them their supplementary charter.'

'Well?'

'Now I know on the highest authority that the government isn't going to grant them their supplementary charter,' said Lady Lettice. 'And it seems as if a lot of other people are also aware of the fact. The shares were at 4 on Saturday. Yesterday at noon they were at $5^1/_4$, but they weakened a little at the close.'

'They are now at $4^1/_8$,' I said.

'And no doubt falling!'

'Possibly.'

'But, my dear Mr. Stout, what is to be done? Poor Dover bought 5,000 at 4. They may be at 3 to-night! And he isn't here! He isn't here! He's in Paris!'

'The procedure is perfectly simple,' I said. 'All we have to do is to telephone to my stockbrokers to sell 5,000, and your cousin is saved. The telephone is there, behind the door. Shall I attend to the matter?'

'Oh, please do!' she murmured.

In four minutes I had sold the shares at $4^{1}/_{32}$.

'The difference will just about cover the brokerage charges,' I said. 'So that our poor friend won't lose a penny.'

'Mr. Stout,' exclaimed Lady Lettice, 'do you know you are a wonderful man, with your tape-machine and your telephone? If only you had a pianola I would sit down and play "See the Conquering Hero Comes"!'

'I *have* a pianola,' I said. 'But wouldn't you prefer to play something else? Some nocturne of Chopin's? Something dreamy and passionate, dear lady?'

So she sat down and played the *Valse Bleu*.

It was amazing. I stood by her side, gazing at her tiny and yet perfect figure, while she rendered the music with a technical dexterity that Paderewski[4] himself could not hope to rival.

And just as she arrived at the most luscious crisis of the waltz, in came my valet Hatteras, known to the world as Lord Dover, and he was bearing in his arms three pairs of trousers stretched on stretchers, and a new pair of boot-trees.

'If you please, sir–'

Mercifully the luscious crisis of the waltz was *fortissimo*, and Lady Lettice did not hear that 'sir.' However, Hatteras, in his astonishment, dropped his burden on the floor, and she heard that.

There was a kind of a tableau. The waltz had ceased.

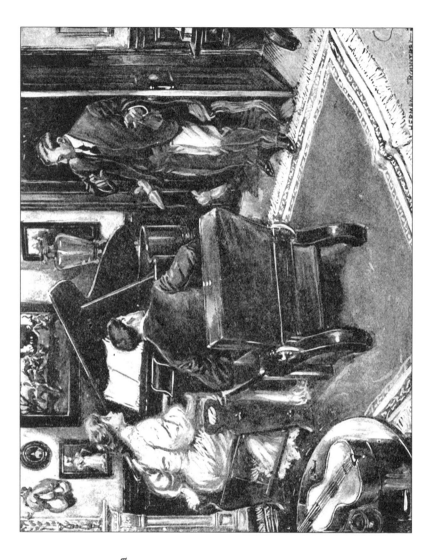

'There was a
kind of a
tableau.'

'He's not gone to Paris after all,' I stated.

'Le–ettice?' Hatteras whispered.

'The secret's out,' I exclaimed, looking at Hatteras. 'Shall I tell your cousin, old man?'

He nodded weakly.

'The fact is, Lady Lettice,' I turned to her, 'Lord Dover and I have taken out patents for some new sorts of stretchers for various articles of male attire. And we're just–just trying them, before launching out in a big scale. Suppose you take away those things, old chap!' I said to Hatteras. 'Lady Lettice had some business for you, but I've attended to it.'

And he gathered up his load, and disappeared without a word.

'So that's your secret, is it?' said Lady Lettice.

'There is a terrific demand for those articles,' I answered. 'You've no idea! The spread of education has increased the use of trouser-stretchers to such an extent–'

'I suppose Dover has told you that he and I are engaged to be married,' she burst out suddenly.

My heart stopped beating.

'No,' I muttered. 'That is, yes–he–'

At this moment there was the uproar of a colossal smash in the smoking-room.

'Excuse me,' I managed to say. 'I must see what that is. Do finish the *Valse Bleu*, won't you?'

And I fled from her presence.

So she was engaged to be married! My life was blasted at a blow.

III.

Lord Dover, in the midst of the smoking-room, stood staring at a pile of volumes of the Encyclopædia Britannica,[5] which had evidently just descended from the table to the floor.

'Hatteras,' I said, 'you told me that the Enc. Brit. was absolutely necessary to the well-being of an up-to-date flat.

Why have you cast this invaluable work of reference on to the carpet?'

'I did it simply to attract your attention, sir. I felt that I must speak to you at once. Happily my ruse has succeeded. Sir, I cannot thank you sufficiently for the manner in which you saved appearances a few moments ago in the other room. It was worthy of the finest tradition of the French stage. I regret that my state of mind was such as to unfit me for adding to your ingenious invention.'

'My dear Hatteras,' I said, 'have you thrown twenty-three volumes of the Enc. Brit. on the floor merely in order to enable you to express to me your gratitude and your regrets. Because, if so–'

'Pardon me, sir,' said Hatteras, 'my feelings. You seem to have established yourself in the esteem of Lady Lettice, sir. You had the appearance of being quite intimate with her.' He spoke with a peculiar intonation.

'Fairly, Hatteras, fairly!' I admitted. 'I did what I could to attend to her requirements in your absence. And in the course of my attention a certain friendliness grew up.'

'May I ask if my cousin has told you that we are going to be married?' he inquired timidly.

'Lady Lettice did mention the possibility of such an arrangement. Naturally our interview was based on the assumption that you and I were very intimate, Hatteras.'

'Naturally, sir, I ought to have told you of my contemplated marriage on Friday night, when it was arranged. It is a servant's duty to disclose such personal details to his employer. But I did not! I did not!'

'You don't seem excessively joyous at the prospect of this change in your existence, Hatteras.'

It occurred to me that since Friday his demeanor had been a shade on the side of sombre.

'Oh, yes, sir, I am full of joy,' he said sadly. 'Full of joy! You see, Lady Lettice is a very wealthy woman, and her vast fortune will enable us to restore the prestige of the family name. We shall probably buy back one or two of the estates.'

'And you love her?'

'Madly,' said he, sinking nervelessly into a chair. 'Madly,' he repeated, with a gloomy sigh.

'Ah!' I ejaculated.

I began to perceive that perhaps my life was not so blasted after all.

'Of course it will be a great change for me,' said Hatteras. 'I had started on an honorable career of usefulness. I was learning to despise the gewgaws of rank and wealth. I had cultivated a taste for Emerson.[6] I have not seen *The Sporting Life*[7] for many weeks. I knew the satisfactions of the simpler and the higher life. And now circumstances are to alter all that, and all that will be as though it had never been, and I shall be taken back to the place from where I came.'

The strains of the *Valse Bleu* came from the drawing-room.

'Hatteras,' I said, 'you should have thought of this aspect of the case before you proposed to your charming cousin.'

'Sir,' he replied, 'in duty to myself, and in order to prove to you that your good influence has not been wasted on me, I must tell you one thing. I did not propose to her. Lady Lettice invited me to dinner, and to share her life and fortune.'

'Are you sure?' I demanded.

'Why do you ask such a question?'

'Because,' I said, 'Lady Lettice has not mentioned this affair as definitely settled, but merely as one under discussion, as a suggestion for a *mariage de convenance*.'

The man was obviously dashed, but he could not contradict Lady Lettice.

'Just so,' he said, after a pause, 'just so. Of course, nothing is settled. But, assuming it to be settled, what a change for me!

However, I love her madly. My only fear is lest I might slip back–slip back–'

'On to the turf, and that sort of thing?'

He nodded.

'Have no fear,' I reassured him. 'Lady Lettice confided to me–you understand, my dear Hatteras, that we were discussing the weaknesses of your character with the loving freedom of intimate friends–Lady Lettice confided to me that, if the marriage was arranged, she should absolutely forbid racing and bridge, and that, moreover, in your highest interests, she meant to retain complete control of her fortune.'

'She said that, did she?' murmured Hatteras, obviously still more dashed.

He lapsed into meditation.

'Of course,' I added, 'you will not breathe a word of this to Lady Lettice. I have been indiscreet, perhaps, but it was done solely in order to cheer you up, and enable you to face the future with more confidence.'

'Thank you, sir,' he said.

'And now,' I finished, 'I must go back to Lady Lettice. Make yourself presentable, Hatteras, forget for an hour or two that you are my valet, and come and join me. I will ask Lady Lettice to stay to lunch.

IV.

'Pardon my rudeness,' I said to Lady Lettice when I returned to the drawing-room. 'I found poor Dover buried under a pile of the Encyclopædia Britannica.'

'Not hurt?' she enquired calmly, as she moved away from the pianola, where she had been playing Handel's 'Largo' at the speed of a drinking song.

'No,' I said. 'He will come in directly, as soon as he has cleansed the stains of this untimely sepulture.'

'So you have the Encyclopædia Britannica?' she observed.

'Do take this easy-chair,' I urged her.

She looked entrancing in it; she was so tiny and so perfect.

'Yes,' I replied, 'inventors like ourselves are constantly in need of miscellaneous knowledge. And the article on "Trouser

Stretchers" is a masterpiece from beginning to end.'

'I have only consulted the work once,' said Lady Lettice.

'I wanted to decide some point at Bridge, and there was no article on Bridge at all!' Her smile was adorable.

'Ah!' I said. That is one reason why I bought it.'

'Why?'

'Because of *him*.'

'Dover?'

'Yes. I did not want him to be reminded by the least thing of his former life. I might have bought a cheaper encyclopædia. I might have bought a lighter one. I might have bought a more amusing one. But I bought the Brit. for this negative excellence –it had no article on Bridge.'

'How good you are!' she murmured.

I shook my head.

'Dover says you are to be sure and stay for lunch,' I remarked. 'I needn't say how glad I shall be if you will.'

'But my carriage is waiting.'

'Let me send it away, then, dear lady. It will not require two sixteen-hand horses, two portly men, and an equipage weighing over a ton, to take you home after one of our simple lunches. My coupé shall be at your service.'

'You are funny!' she laughed.

'You only say that because I'm such a short man,' I told her.

'*Are* you short?' she replied. 'I hadn't noticed it. You're taller than I am.'

I was. The thing was admirably said.

'Dover is much too tall,' she remarked, after the carriage had been sent away. And she added, 'I suppose he has quite, quite settled down.'

'Oh! Quite, quite!' I answered. 'But, of course, he would be very likely to break out again if circumstances were favorable.'

'What do you mean?' she asked me abruptly.

'May I speak confidentially?'

'Please do, Mr. Stout.'

'Dover told me casually yesterday that it was his firm intention, provided the marriage between you actually took place, to resume his career as an owner of race-horses. And also that there would be no reason, *then*, why he shouldn't play cards again . . . Of course, all this is strictly between you and me, Lady Lettice.'

'Of course,' she said, blushing, and putting her lips together.

'You love him, Lady Lettice?' I went on impertinently. 'But need I ask? Our Dover, with all his charming qualities! And your love will be his salvation. Excuse my familiarity. I fear I presume.'

'We have known each other ever since we were six years old,' said Lady Lettice.

This was exactly what I had suspected.

'Then he has always been in love with you,' I said. 'That goes without saying.'

'Who knows?' she queried absently.

'And your first marriage must have desolated him.'

'In those days,' said she, 'Dover was not easily desolated.'

'I hope I may soon have the pleasure of congratulating you both on your engagement.'

'Our engagement! But we are–' she stopped.

'You are cousins, I know,' I said calmly. 'But that need not prevent an engagement. Dover has told me that the proposal for a *mariage de convenance* between you has been under consideration for some days, and that it will be decided one way or the other very shortly. But why he should have called it a *mariage de convenance* I cannot guess. Doubtless, his humorosness.'

'Oh, yes!' said Lady Lettice, putting her lips together still more tightly. 'It will be decided shortly, *very* shortly.'

'Of course, I understand,' I said, 'that in considering such an alliance as this, many aspects of the affair present themselves, and demand careful attention.'

'Very careful,' said she.

Then Dover appeared. He was pale, but self-possessed.

By the manner of their greeting I perceived still more hope for the unblasting of my career.

V.

I was compelled to go to an inordinate amount of trouble in the arrangement of the lunch. Any man who has tried to lunch with his own valet in his own house, without the knowledge of the other servants, will appreciate my position. I ordered a cold lunch so that the parlor-maid would not have to wait. Then I was confronted with the difficulty of ordering three covers when obviously there were only myself and one guest. However, I surmounted this by saying that a second guest might possibly arrive, and that it would be well to lay for him. Lady Lettice and I went to the dining-room, and as soon as the parlor-maid had left, Lord Dover followed us. We ate somewhat gloomily. But since I had deliberately brought this gloom about, with intent that joy might come later, I did not complain. Indeed, my heart sang.

Nothing occurred at the lunch. But something occurred immediately after.

My beautiful, new, spruce parlor-maid caught me alone in the corridor.

'I wish to give notice, sir,' she said.

'But why, Matilda. Why this sudden defection?'

'I can't stay in a place where the valet eats with the master, sir. I can't do it, and keep my self-respect. I always misdoubted there was something peculiar about Mr. Hatteras, sir; though I must say he's polite enough for ten men.'

'Matilda,' I replied, diplomatically, 'sooner than lose you I will tell you the whole truth. I admit that Mr. Hatteras lunched with Lady Lettice Dovedale and myself to-day. I meant to hide the fact from you and the other servants in order not to hurt your perfectly justifiable feelings. Now that you have found me out, you must have the explanation. It is quite simple. By a curious chance Mr. Hatteras happens to be Lady Lettice Dovedale's foster-brother. She discovered this, and she asked me as a special favor to allow him to lunch with us. Could I refuse such a request, Matilda?'

'Not very well, sir.'

'Thank you, Matilda. The thing shall not occur again, and this time I shall rely on you to look over it.'

I do flatter myself that I have a way with parlor-maids–

I rejoined the others, humming a gay tune.

The tape-machine was clicking.

'African Incorporateds are down to 3,' I said, scanning the message. 'Quite a panic. Dover, it's a good thing we sold your shares when we did.'

'What shares?' asked Hatteras.

Now, we had been so occupied and preoccupied with other affairs that the affair of the African Incorporated shares had never been mentioned.

'What shares!' I repeated. 'Why, *your* shares!'

He looked blank.

'Didn't you buy those shares that I advised you to, George?' asked Lady Lettice.

'No,' he said shortly.

'Why not?'

'Hadn't enough coin even for a five per cent. cover,' he said.

'George!' she exclaimed. I had no idea you were *really* hard up!'

'It appears to me,' I said, 'that I have sold 5,000 shares that I hadn't got. I must buy them.' And I went to the telephone and bought 5,000 A.I. shares at 3. 'Now,' I proceeded, 'I have bought on your behalf, Dover, 5,000 shares at 3, and sold 5,000 shares at $4^{1}/_{2}$. I have, therefore realized a profit of something over £5,000–on your behalf, Dover. Remind me of the matter next settling-day, will you?'

'But I can't accept–I can't-' he began protestingly.

'Yes, you can,' I cut him short. 'And if you make any fuss over it, I tell you I'll give the whole show away.'

And I looked at him meaningly.

Soon afterwards Lady Lettice left.

'May I call on you?' I entreated her.

She smiled her answer. 'The sooner the better,' she said.

On Thursday I gave Hatteras an extra evening off. And on Friday he informed me that the marriage had *not* been arranged. He said that he could not bring himself to demand such a sacrifice from Lady Lettice, and that anyhow he thought it wiser to continue his reformed and simple life in his present sphere of honourable usefulness.

That same afternoon I called on Lady Lettice. She was very cheerful, and charmingly hospitable.

The moral of all this is that there are occasions on which lying–cold, deliberate, calculated, slanderous lying–coupled with a trifle of bad manners, may be the highest virtue and sagacity. Had I not grossly misrepresented Lady Lettice and Hatteras to each other, they would have fallen into a horribly unhappy marriage. She had had a caprice of self-sacrifice, much as women often suffer from, and he would have been fool enough to accept it. They did not love each other; they only knew each other intimately. And further, I should have been deprived of the opportunity of trying my luck with that adorable dot of a widow.

Besides, I daresay that sometime I shall make a clean breast of it all to them.

PART V.
THE HOUSEBOAT EPISODE.

I.

The first curious thing that happened on that curious Sunday was that as I was proceeding westward on my way to Walton in my new 8 h.p. De Dion Bouton,[8] I narrowly escaped cutting into two equal parts Lady Lettice Dovedale's carriage, which was coming out of Hyde Park. Of course, I pretended that I had merely been showing off the wondrous capabilities of the car. (I did not seek to impose on my mechanic, only on Lady Lettice.)

'Where are you going to so early?' I asked. Her coachman had stopped.

'Waterloo, on my way to Walton. Your cousin Selina—'

'What!' I cried, full of sudden joy. 'Has Selina asked you, too? She never told me.'

'Perhaps she meant me to be a pleasant surprise,' said Lady Lettice.

And she said it so archly, so sweetly, so daringly, so challengingly, and she was so exquisitely dressed, all in white drill, and she was so tiny and perfect lying back there in the great carriage, that I said to myself: 'Jack, you shall propose to that woman before midnight. I swear to Aphrodite you shall.'

It had been coming on for about three months. I knew it and so did she.

'Won't you give me the pleasure of taking you to Walton in my new toy?' I asked her.

She referred to danger, dust, and other things, but I could see from the first moment that she meant to accept, and I merely waited for her to get out and get in. I can love a woman without having any illusions about her.

In a few moments her horses were returning to their stables, and Lady Lettice was sitting beside me in the back seats of the De Dion, while Biskett, my mechanic, drove. At first I thought that we would occupy the front seats and that I would drive, just to show her what a devil of a driver I was. And then I thought that the act of driving was not favorable to the progress of my passion, and further that if by any unlucky accident I ran over a perambulator and killed twins while informing Lady Lettice that, though I had known many women, I had never known any woman who affected me in the way that, etc., etc.–the results might cast a gloom over our idyll. So Biskett, in whose life was no Lady Lettice –at least he had assured me of his freedom from incumbrances, urged and guided the machine to Walton.

I didn't know how to begin the day's conversation. The fact is that, having taken the oath, I was nervous. No man could have had more material for small talk than I. I had now been in London for five months, after my long absence, and my impressions were assuming shape. I had been making a careful study of clubs, mixed clubs, golf, musical comedy, English billiards, English climate, the Sandow[9] system, cab fares, restaurants, cigarettes, hair restorers, motor cars, and Lady Lettice. My mind was a medley of interests . . . And I could not find a word to say, except banalities about the joy of speed!

'You *are* nervous,' she said.

'No, I'm not,' I said sharply. 'A person who knows he is nervous is not nervous. And don't imagine I'm nervous of *you*. Because I'm not. I understand you to the marrow of your bones. You are delicious, but you are a minx. Every young widow is a minx. You can't deny you are in love with me.'

'I! In love with you! My dear little Mr. Stout, nothing could be farther from the truth. I like you; but then I like scores of people.'

'It's not the slightest use you pretending. I tell you I *know*.'

'Well, if you're so certain–'

Perhaps it is scarcely necessary to state that we did not exchange these extremely personal remarks with our lips, but with our eyes.

Our lips were behaving primly, somewhat thus:

'We're doing quite eighteen now. Not bad for the Fulham Road!'

'Really. And it doesn't seem as if there would be much dust.'

'No. The rain in the night.'

'Did it rain? I never heard it.'

'Yes, about four o'clock.'

'How smoothly your car runs! Aren't you afraid of policemen?'

It was not until we were crossing Putney Bridge that Lady Lettice said something out of the common way. And then she certainly did contrive to avoid the ordinary.

'By the way,' she said, 'your cousin Selina tells me that they caught sight of Dover the other day up at Walton. He was in a canoe.'

Now, if there was one person in the world whom I was not anxious to encounter that Sunday up at Walton, it was Lord Dover.

'Oh!' I ejaculated.

I said nothing else, because to talk to a woman about a man to whom she was engaged only three months ago, is a little delicate, especially when you yourself have plotted and brought to pass the breaking of the engagement.

'You haven't seen poor Dover lately, have you?' she enquired.

'No,' I said, 'I have not.'

'He gave everybody to understand he was dead to the world, and we were to forget him.'

She spoke plaintively, with a certain chastened sorrow, a disturbing regret. (I mean that the regret disturbed *me*.)

'Lord Dover was the most peculiar and eccentric man I ever knew,' I remarked.

'Really!' she said, stiffly. '*I* never thought so.'

('Be careful, Jack Stout!' I said to myself. 'Remember

you've got to propose to her before midnight.')

'That is possibly because you have never known the whole truth about Dover, my dear lady,' I said gravely and deferentially.

'Well,' she said, 'I think you might tell me, and then I can judge.'

And all of a sudden I decided that I *would* tell her. I saw that that would be the best. I didn't care twopence what Dover would think. Besides, he would never know.

'Does it not strike you as eccentric and peculiar, on Lord Dover's part, after his dazzling social career and his equally dazzling downfall, to have chosen the profession of a valet?'

'A valet? What do you mean?'

I related to her how Lord Dover had come to me under the name of Hatteras, asked for a situation as my valet, and got it.

'Then that day when I called,' she exclaimed, 'he was really your valet all the time. I was engaged to a valet!'

'If you like to put it that way,' I said.

Then our eyes took a turn.

'You are a horrid thing!' her eyes said. 'You have only told me this to humiliate me. You've done it on purpose.'

'Not at all,' mine answered. 'You first mentioned Lord Dover, and you mentioned him out of pure coquetry, just to tease me. I told you the truth simply to punish you, to make you understand I am not to be trifled with, that I love you and will have you.'

'You are a horrid man–horrid, horrid, horrid!'

'I know I am. But I love you.'

'Of course he left you,' her lips said.

'Yes,' I replied. 'The situation–not *his*, but *the* situation– became impossible. And when he got that five thousand pounds for the African Incorporated shares he said he would disappear and live the simpler and higher life on the interest.'

'What is the simpler and higher life?' she demanded.

'I can't tell you,' I said. 'Perhaps it's Lord Dover's notion of a dramatic contrast, after his previous career.'

'How strange!' she murmured.

'You'll pardon my brutal candor,' I changed the key of the conversation, 'but that's a most awfully pretty dress you've got on, and it suits you down to the ground.'

'Not quite!' she smiled. 'The skirt is a good two inches off!'

I laughed.

Her eyes said:

'I'll be friends now, if you will.'

And mine said:

'Yes, rather. Let's.'

The affair went so well that I do believe that, in spite of the presence of Biskett's back, I should have fulfilled my oath, in a whisper, of course, on the way to Walton, but–

The worst of the De Dion Bouton cars is that they travel so fast and they never break down. The infernal contraption landed us in Walton far, far too soon.

II.

The Ashways, who had become acquainted with Lady Lettice through my agency and for my ends, had asked us to spend a day on the river with them in their new boat. Gerald and Selina had just acquired this craft, and they were extremely proud of it, as I had had ample opportunity of judging from their conversation. I did not know exactly what kind of a vessel it was, but I gathered that it was the best of its kind. They affected to make light of motors. Motors were artificial, perilous, noisy, undependable, unpleasant, costly and several other things. How could one possibly enjoy our beautiful rural England scorching across it at forty miles an hour with one's eyes glued to the centre of the road? Hence the boat.

When I drove up to within a few feet of the towpath, the boat was most obviously there, moored to the bank. It was a surprise to me. And it was a surprise to Lady Lettice.

'Is *that* it?' she exclaimed.

I presumed that that *was* it, since Gerald, attired in the innocency of white flannels, with a blue blazer, was aboard fiddling with a small flag and a rope.

'Halloo!' he cried loudly and breezily. 'I'm nailing the colors to the mast.'

'Why do people in boats invariably shout when they greet people on land?'

The mast was the most salient thing about that boat. It seemed to tower right up out of the river to about the height of Snowdon.[10] The flag went up and up and up till it was nearly out of sight, and then it stopped and fluttered like a feather in the windy sky. It is a most remarkable thing that I had not noticed the strength of the wind until I saw that high mast. Indeed, I had not observed the presence of a wind at all. I now observed that the wind amounted to what I should call half a gale. The trees were swaying in it; positively not a leaf was still.

'How-do, Lady Lettice!' cried Gerald from the boat. 'So glad you've come. Come with Jack, have you? In his car? I hope you had no accidents. Never know where you are with a motor, do you? What do you think of my punt?'

'A punt, is it?' said Lady Lettice.

'Yes. A sailing punt. Quickest and safest thing in existence.'

'And what's that funny blade sticking up out of the middle?' I ventured to enquire.

'That's the centre-board. You let it down and it keeps her steady. See?'

'How many sails are there?' asked Lady Lettice.

'Only one,' said Gerald, 'and it's enough!'

I judged he was right. The sail, tied to two long pieces of wood, lay along the length of his craft, and it reached from the mast, which was near the prow, to about two feet beyond the stern, where it hung suspended over the water.

'If that's its width,' I murmured to Lady Lettice, 'and it's as high as the mast is, it ought to be just about enough.'

Then Selina came down the towpath, carrying a bottle.

'Got the whisky, my little lass?' shouted Gerald cheerily. 'Chuck it aboard. Now, friends, Romans, countrymen,' he proceeded in a marine tone, 'lend me your eyes. We've got a fine luncheon in the forecastle. Jump aboard lively–give me your hand, Lady Lettice–and we will slip down to Sunbury Lock, go through, and have our snack at a spot I know just below there. Eh?'

'Look here, Gerald,' I said, 'it's after twelve. Suppose we have lunch here on the bank before we start. I've always had a fancy for dying on a full stomach.'

'Dining on a full–!' said Gerald.

'Dying!' I repeated.

'Oh! Come on, old chap. 'Don't talk rot.'

However, I had made up my mind to delay that departure as long as possible.

'I'm fearfully hungry,' I said, 'so is Lady Lettice.'

Lady Lettice smiled.

So we had lunch, partly on the bank and partly on the boat. And I have pleasure in testifying that a very good luncheon it was. Gerald is at his best in arranging an *al fresco* luncheon. He is not the sort of person who forgets the salt or the knives. He forgets nothing.

Afterwards I wanted to go for a walk with Lady Lettice, but Gerald wouldn't hear of perambulation. He said we could walk afterwards. And when I replied that I doubted it, he was the shadow of a shade cross.

So we got in–I mean, we went aboard. Gerald told us where to sit, and he and Selina began operations on the sail. The boat was made of mahogany with brass ornamentations. It was not more than a foot deep. I felt as if I was at sea in a plate. Lady Lettice seemed to think it tremendous fun.

'I should put a reef in the sail, if I were you, Jerry,' said Selina.

'Reef! What nonsense! There's nothing but a nice gentle breeze.'

'Yes, but–'

'We went out this morning without a reef,' said Gerald.

'I know we did. That's why I say–'

'Well, my pet,' Gerald finished the discussion, 'if you'll mind your business, I'll mind mine.'

'Certainly, dear,' said Selina.

But I noticed her lips twitched, and I knew she hadn't got red hair for nothing.

The sail went up, flapping horribly; it went right up to the top of the mast and much higher. It was colossal and terrifying. The boat rocked.

'Sit tight,' Gerald said excitedly, and he skipped to the stern, and seized the tiller and sat down opposite Lady Lettice and me.

'Cast her off,' he shouted to Selina, who was at the prow near the mast.

She did not move for a second.

'Cast her off!' shouted Gerald more loudly. 'Do you want the mast blown out of her?'

Upon this Selina sprang neatly ashore, undid the rope, and threw the end aboard.

'I'll *walk* down to the lock,' she said calmly. 'I'll join you there.'

And we were off!

The boat flew like an arrow from a bow, heeling over on Gerald's side, so much so that he hastily crept across to our side.

'Let her zip!' he exclaimed. 'Doesn't she travel?' He was a little cooler now.

She decidedly did travel.

The wind was blowing direct off the south bank: we had our backs to it, and the other side of the boat was within two inches of Father Thames.

We passed rowing boats as though they were standing

still. A small launch hooted at us. But we bore straight down on it, and in the nick of time it slipped out of our path. Our course was parallel with the south bank.

Presently we approached the canal leading to Sunbury Lock. We had done a mile in about a minute and a half. The weir was far away to our left, and for this I was thankful.

'Better slow down here, old man, hadn't we?' I suggested.

'Can't go slower than the wind takes us,' said Gerald. He was becoming excited again. 'There's a bit more breeze than I thought.'

'Well, we'd better stop altogether and row, then,' I said.

We had swept between two other craft to the imminent danger of everyone. Our pace was becoming hotter, and oaths followed us as seagulls follow a steamer. We had something like the pace of a steamer.

'Better stop her,' I said.

'My dear fellow, how can I stop her?' said Gerald through clenched teeth, and he smiled by force of will at Lady Lettice.

'There's no room to turn here, and I can't run her into the bank!'

'Can't you put a brake on?' I asked.

We were approaching the lock, amid a swirl of water. The mast was bent over like a fishing rod.

'Brake!' said he. 'We aren't in a motor car.'

'No,' I said, 'I almost wish we were.'

'Well, we aren't!'

'Can't you lower the sail?' I tried a new suggestion.

'And leave the tiller?'

'Can't I lower the sail?'

'Can you get to the mast?' he queried.

'Don't move, I implore you,' exclaimed Lady Lettice. 'You'll upset the balance.'

And she clung to me. It was a purely instinctive motion, no doubt. But I resolved that I liked it and that I would not move.

We were within twenty yards of the lock. The gates were opened, and the lock-keeper, brandishing a pole, appealed to us furiously to stop.

But we did not stop. We were not in a motor car. We had no brake. We couldn't compel the breeze to drop. We swept towards the lock with a magnificent and unparalleled sweep at the rate of twenty-five knots. I was reminded of a middle-aged friend of mine who boldly began to learn the bicycle, and who was unable to come in to dinner one summer evening because he had got on and could not get off: he could only keep on going.

The lock was already pretty full of craft, including a small steamer.

Gerald, clinging to the tiller, steered our T.B.D. accurately into the entrance of the lock. We entered, or, rather, we took the place by storm. In a fraction of a second we had rammed the stern of the little steamer with terrific force. Our mast snapped like a match. I wished it had snapped before. The boat glanced off the steamer somewhat and slid along her side. The next moment is indescribable. I do not know what occurred. But at the end of it I found that I had stepped acrobatically aboard the little steamer and that Lady Lettice was chiefly in my arms. That Gerald was struggling in the water of the lock, and that the lock was full of cries and curses.

A man in a canoe was offering the blade of his paddle to Gerald and Gerald seemed to be accepting it with thankfulness. The man in the canoe was Lord Dover.

'Oh! Where's Mr. Ashway?' sobbed Lady Lettice, still clinging to me. 'Oh, he's in the water! Oh! That's Dover, with a beard, and he's pulling Mr. Ashway out. How clever he is at it!'

('She's in my arms!' I said to myself. 'But I don't seem to be much nearer keeping my oath.')

'You must all come to my place,' said Lord Dover afterwards, when the shouting and excitations had subsided, and Gerald was wringing himself out on the shore of the lock.

III.

Lord Dover's 'place' proved to be a houseboat, moored on the north bank a little above Walton. It was a very severe thing in houseboats, painted a neutral grey, and it called itself *Nirvana*. It had no ornaments save seven pots of geraniums placed at regular intervals on what I should have termed the roof, but what I now know is called the deck of the ark. We had walked in a silent procession from the lock to a spot opposite *Nirvana*, Lord Dover making the pace in his canoe. As the canoe would only hold one and its lord and master, we had to be ferried over singly. I was taken last. We stepped out of the canoe into the drawing-room of the houseboat, an apartment with a polished carpetless floor.

'Really this is extremely kind of you, my lord,' began Selina, who had joined us.

'Mr. Hatteras, if you please,' said the Lord, 'I am plain Mr. Hatteras now, and this is my simple home, to which I welcome you all. I have no other. What can I offer you? You, Mr. Ashway, must accept my other suit of clothes. I have only two, two being enough. But you should have something to drink first. Happily the day is warm.'

'Well, Hatteras,' I said, being more accustomed to him than the rest, except perhaps Lady Lettice, 'what can you offer us to drink?'

'I live the simple life here,' was the reply. 'Would you prefer hot tea or cold tea, or hot water or cold water. I drink a good deal of hot water myself. Of course, I use the Pasteur filter.[11] No one need be under any apprehension.'

The ballot was strongly in favor of hot tea. The host prepared it himself, and he added, into the bargain, several Osborne biscuits[12] to the feast.

'My life here is a solitary one,' he told us as he daintily poured out the tea, 'but probably not an unhappy one. By dint of cold meals, which are surely more natural than hot, and with the aid of the stores, I can dispense with a cook. And all those other household duties which are so wrongly called menial I perform myself. I take a joy in performing them. In washing a saucer I am conscious of ecstasy. These things are completed by ten a.m. I have the remainder of the day, till seven p.m., for meditation and reading.'

'And what do you meditate upon?' asked Selina, characteristically curious about the habits of the upper classes.

'Upon the past and the future.'

'And you read?'

'Emerson, Suetonius[13] and Kelly's Directory.'[14]

'Kelly's –!'

'Yes. I find it soothes me. It helps me to attain Nirvana. I have tried other directories, but there is nothing equal to Kelly's.'

'And what do you do at seven p.m.?' asked the dauntless Selina.

'I water my seven geranium plants,' said Mr. Hatteras.

'And at night?'

'I play Patience.'

'And you see no one?'

'Yes. Every Monday morning at 9.30 my laundress voyages over. We count handkerchiefs, socks, etcetera, together.'

'But, Mr. Hatteras,' demanded Selina seriously, 'do you consider this a useful life? You consider you are doing your duty to humanity. Pardon my rudeness.'

'Your question is a proper one, Mrs. Ashway,' said Hatteras. 'Yes, I make myself useful to the human race on Sundays. I save lives in the lock. Up to the present I have saved seventeen and a half. The half was a boy under twelve.'

'Including Ashway?' I inquired.

'Including Mr. Ashway,' said Hatteras simply.

'I'm awfully obliged to you,' Gerald sputtered out. 'It was my fault, I'm afraid.'

'Not at all,' I said, 'it was the fault of the breeze that

wouldn't drop when you wanted to stop.'

Soon afterwards Gerald's coat, waistcoat, socks, collar and necktie were pegged out to dry between the geraniums on deck in that same disobedient breeze; the remainder of his attire was dried in a more discreet elsewhere. And Gerald was feeling proud in Lord Dover's other suit of flannels.

All this time Lady Lettice had been strangely quiet.

'What is the matter with you, bright star?' I asked her.

'My feet are wet through,' she answered mildly.

'Heavens!' I exclaimed. 'And I thought I had saved you! Will you come for a quick walk. Your feet will soon dry on a day like this.'

'My dear cousin,' said Hatteras, 'why did you not tell me this before? I can supply your wants.' And he opened a cupboard, and there were several tiny pairs of women's slippers, and even stockings rolled neatly up.

'George!' cried Lady Lettice, 'you said you lived alone here! And why have you grown that horrid beard?'

'I have grown a beard,' replied Hatteras, with undiminished suavity, 'in order that I might not waste moments of eternity in futile shaving. And I do live alone here. A certain proportion of the victims of the Thames are ladies, and I have deemed it part of my duty to humanity to obtain this small stock of feminine attire.'

'Oh!' said Lady Lettice.

And she, with Selina to support her, retired to the kitchen-let of *Nirvana*.

'Won't you come for a walk now?' I urged Lady Lettice when they returned.

'How can I go for a walk in felt slippers?' she said.

('Confound his felt slippers!' I said to myself. 'How am I going to propose to her on this disgusting hulk?')

'No, Jack,' said Selina, 'I wonder at you suggesting such a foolish thing! We had much better remain quietly here, as Lord Do–as Mr. Hatteras has so kindly invited us.'

'As you wish!' I sighed

In five minutes, Heaven is my witness, Hatteras was showing them a wonderful variety of Patience, and in a quarter of an hour Bridge had been established. Hatteras said he had no objection to Bridge provided we played for green peas. He said the rest of us could put the peas at any price we liked, and settle among ourselves afterwards, but that for him a pea upon the river's brim was a green pea and nothing more. He furnished us with a quart bottle of the best preserved French peas from Harrod's.[15] Gerald Ashway and I agreed that the peas should be worth a shilling each.

The late September afternoon began to draw in. I suggested departure. I had lost several pounds worth of peas. But Hatteras would not hear of it. We went upstairs on deck, where the light was stronger, and played Bridge for shilling peas among the geraniums and collars and neckties, while the traffic of the Thames passed to and fro. It grew dark, and Hatteras lighted a lantern. By this time it was definitely decided that we should stay for supper. And then Hatteras descended alone, and in ten minutes hailed us to supper, and supper consisted of everything that was preserved and pickled, and biscuits, with hot or cold water, according to taste.

The Ashways, having got themselves under the roof of a member of the House of Lords, seemed determined to stay there. And as for Lady Lettice, she had all the appearance of enjoying her cousin's society.

I said that my man and my car would be waiting for me, and that I must go, and that if Lady Lettice would again do me the honor–

Useless! Bridge was in the air. Hatteras had won over two hundred peas and was radiant and excited. Gerald had also won. So had Lady Lettice. Gerald told me that I could at a pinch take the entire party back to London in my car.

'In that case,' said Hatteras, 'you must stay till midnight. I will make more tea. The night is warm. I must go on deck to water my poor geraniums. You will join me there. We will continue our game by the light of lanterns.'

And he did.

('Midnight!' I said to myself. 'And my oath?')

I resolved that the game should end before midnight.

IV.

'Hatteras,' I said, between two and three hours later, 'you probably are not aware that there is something like half an inch of water on your polished drawing-room floor.'

I had retired temporarily from the Bridge party and had been wandering about below. I climbed up the ladder again to give this warning. The card-players, their faces reddish under the glow of the Chinese lanterns, turned suddenly to gaze at me.

'What?' demanded Gerald.

'Half an inch of water on the drawing-room floor,' I repeated.

'What do you mean?' Hatteras asked anxiously.

'I mean that this singular craft of yours is leaking, Hatteras. I should guess she is making about half an inch of water an hour.'

'I have been half drowned already to-day,' said Gerald. 'I do not want the operation completed.'

'And in sight of land!' murmured Selina.

'Had we not better look at it?' suggested Lady Lettice in a low tone. She had been strangely quiet and preoccupied all the afternoon and evening.

We ran or fell down the ladder, and inspected the condition of the drawing-room floor by means of matches. Ultimately Hatteras bravely paddled into the flood and lighted the lamp in the middle of the pond which a short time ago had been his best chamber. His boots splashed about.

'We must save ourselves, and quickly,' was Hatteras' verdict.

'Yes,' I said, 'and there must be no panic. Women and

children first. Captain last to leave the ship. No, captain, you can't leave last, because no one but you can navigate that canoe–our sole hope of safety. She's sinking by the head!'

It was agreed that Hatteras should ferry us one by one from the doomed vessel. There was a dispute as to whether Selina or Lettice should go first.

'You must go first, Selina,' I decided, 'because you're taller and heavier and older.'

She was cross, but she went.

Gerald, Lady Lettice and I watched the canoe slip away from the side of the fated two-decker into the gloom. The night had now turned chilly and a mist had formed in the river. We mumbled nothings to each other, and continually tested the dreadful progress of the water on the drawing-room floor.

Then the canoe came back again into the circle of the lamplight.

'Now, Letty,' cried Hatteras.

'Lady Lettice,' I said, 'you've forgotten your shoes and things. Come and show me where they are.'

'Look sharp. Please,' said Gerald.

She disappeared into the interior of the ship, and I followed.

'You must stay there till I come for you,' I whispered to her sternly. 'Our safety depends on it.'

I went back to the bulwarks.

'She's changing her shoes,' I said to Hatteras and Gerald. 'She won't be long, but she says you had better go first, Gerald, so as not to waste time. There's no real danger, you know.'

'Changing her shoes!' Gerald muttered. 'Women! Women!'

But he went. I watched the second boat-load vanish on the broad and misty bosom of the Thames. Lady Lettice and I were *enfin seuls* on that strange argosy. I went to the stern, and then to the prow, and after a suitable interval I sought my companion and engaged her in the most platitudinous conversation that I could invent. The two and eleven-penny alarm-clock in the drawing-room showed nearly eleven o'clock.

'What a long time the canoe is in coming back! The mist is thicker and thicker.'

'Yes,' I said.

'Why!' she cried, 'we're moving!'

'I am aware of it. *Nirvana* has broken loose from her moorings!'

'What is that noise?' she demanded.

'It is the weir,' I answered simply. 'We are approaching it.' I took her hand: she did not forbid.

Ages elapsed. Then there was a bump, a gentle bump. *Nirvana* had run against something. The noise of falling water was loud in our ears.

'We are against the weir,' I said. 'We can go no further.'

I got the lantern and held it out over the deep.

'And she is sinking!' sighed Lady Lettice.

We came to the taffrail.[16]

'There is no need for us to take to the rigging,' I said. 'I have stopped the leak.'

'You have–'

I raised the lantern above her eyes. 'Bright star,' I said, 'I made the leak, and I have unmade it. I cut the moorings. We are here because I wished to be alone with you and secure from interruption. I swore when I saw you this morning that before midnight I would tell you I loved you. With me an oath is an oath. I have kept mine. I am five feet nothing, but you are only four feet eleven. I have an income of five thousand a year, and should probably have no occasion to draw on your vast fortune. Lettice–'

She gave a little love sigh.

Two minutes later the weir heard, and the Chinese lantern saw, me kiss the most adorable and piquant little girl in the world.

'I raised the lantern above her eyes.'

PART VI.
THE WEDDING IN THE FOG.

I.

My man came discreetly into the bedroom while the night was yet dark. This was my new valet, with a mortal frame and an immortal soul therein very different from the unique Mr. Hatteras. His name was Jenkins, and he had been born in a mews in Mayfair, and was functionally incapable of pronouncing the vowel O. For him the five vowels were I, E, I, OW, YEW. He was a very tall man, aged perhaps fifty, with grey hair and an imposing and protruding stomach, and he had a fatherly and coughing manner. His real vocation in life was certainly that of a churchwarden.

He coughed under his hand.

'Is that you Jenkins?' I said.

'Yes, sir.'

'I told you to waken me at eight o'clock.'

'It is exactly eight o'clock.'

'But I told you to waken me.'

'Yes, sir.'

'Well, you haven't done it. I've not been to sleep all night.'

He smiled dutifully, and gave me my tea. 'Possibly the chestnut sauce, sir, if I may venture to say so.'

'It is not the chestnut sauce, Jenkins. I almost wish it was. No, I don't mean that.'

'Now, sir.'

'It's excitement, Jenkins.'

'Excitement, sir.'

'Yes. I've got a very important appointment at 2.30. And I don't want to be late for it. That's why I asked you to call me early. I would sooner be an hour too soon for that appointment than a minute late for it.'

'I howp you won't be, sir.'

'Draw the curtains aside, Jenkins. Brightly dawns my wedding day.'

'Matrimony, sir?' he said calmly. 'If I may venture to say so, I should never 'ave guessed it.'

'I thought you wouldn't, Jenkins. And that is why I have told you. I deemed it proper for you to know. A man of your experience ought to have some good tips to give on this occasion. Have you ever been married, Jenkins?'

'Yes, sir, I '*ave* ever been married. I'm married now, in a manner of speaking, thow I never sees her. In a manner of speaking I've been married twice. First I married my wife. And then I married my deceased wife's sister, in Holland, sir. My advice to any one would be, sir, don't marry your deceased wife's sister. They're terrible.'

'I shall endeavor not to do so, Jenkins.'

'Am I to go with you, sir?'

'No,' said I. 'Lady Lettice Dovedale and I are going alone on this particular trip.'

'Ow!' he said, 'Lydy Lettice Dovedile! May I congratulate you, sir, seeing as you mentioned the matter to me? Then I'm to stay here? And afterwards, sir?'

'After what?'

'After the 'oneymoon, sir.'

'You will come to me at No. 17 Queen's Gate.'

'You're giving the flat up, sir?'

'Not at present, Jenkins.'

'You're going to see how it goes on, like, first, sir, before burning your bowts, sir, in a manner of speaking.' He smiled his discreet smile.

'That is one way of putting it, Jenkins. Will you kindly draw the curtains?'

'But, sir–'

'Will you kindly draw the curtains? And turn the light off.'

'Yes, sir.'

He obeyed. The room became nearly dark.

'You see, sir,' he said, turning on the electric light again, 'it's the fog. It was pretty bad last night. And it's worse this morning. A London partickler,[1] sir,' he added.

'Oh!' I exclaimed, 'it will clear away. It will disappear. It's bound to.'

'Yes, sir.'

'Bring me that suit that came from Poole's[2] last night. I want to look at it. In fact I shall put it on.'

'It didn't come, sir.'

'But those are my wedding clothes, Jenkins! They *must* have come!'

'Doubtless owing to the fog, sir.'

I was on the point of bursting out in a paroxysm of annoyance. But I reflected and saw how futile this would be, and that I must try to be a man on my wedding-day.

'Never mind,' I said, 'there's plenty of time. The parcel will certainly come when the fog clears away.'

'Certainly, sir.'

'In the meantime, put out that dark grey suit. And make my bath rather hotter than usual.'

'The post, sir,' said Jenkins coming in a little later. 'Half an hour be'ind time owing to the fog, sir.'

The post consisted of one letter. And it was from my cousin Selina Ashway, to say that poor Gerald, my cousin Selina's husband, looked like having influenza and might not be able to support me at my wedding.

I may state that there was no question of a best man. My wedding was to be of the informal sort; no breakfast, no bridesmaids, no groomsman; nothing but bride, bridegroom, clergy and church, and the Ashways and my great-aunt Anne, who were to find themselves in the church at the moment of the knot as it were by accident. Neither Lettice nor I had the least taste for the usual West End wedding, such as she knew it and I had heard it described. Happily she possessed few relatives. A youngish uncle was about all she had to show. This uncle, the Reverend Mark Parker, happened to be a curate in the parish of St. Mary-le-Strand,[3] and he was to give her away, and we were to be married at that famous and unfashionable church, by the incumbent thereof. The residential formalities had been duly attended to.

'No clothes! No Gerald! And this fog!' I reflected. 'A superstitious man could imagine that ill-luck was dogging him.'

However, at ten o'clock or so the fog lifted somewhat. At any rate I could see the windows of the Devonshire Club[4] across St. James's Street. This cheered me. And at the same time it filled me with a desire to see Lettice. Could I wait four and a half hours to see her? I could not. Ought she not to know of Gerald's lamentable illness? She ought. And of the distressing absence of that wedding suit of mine? . . . Well, perhaps she ought, perhaps she oughtn't.

I called for my thickest overcoat, and I went out into the street and hailed a cab, and in ten minutes I was at Lettice's great house. The fog was always inconvenient, but it did not seriously impede traffic, and it had ceased to be a London particular.

With Lettice's butler I was a favorite, and he showed me up to the boudoir without any preliminaries. Lettice was seated at an Empire table[5] looking through letters.

'My dear,' I said, preparatorily.

She looked up sharply, and instantly I perceived that in visiting her I had done something wrong.

'You appalling creature!' she greeted me.

'I couldn't help it,' I said. 'I felt as if I must see you, Letty. Besides–'

'Do you know,' she went on sternly, 'that this is the very height and summit of indelicacy?'

'What?'

'If I had any female relations–'

'Which you haven't. You've only the Reverend Mark, and he isn't here.'

'I say *if* I had–'

'And I say *which* you haven't–'

'Never mind,' she said, 'it's a safe rule for unattached women always to behave as if they had female relations, whether they have any or not. My remark is that if I had any female relations they would be absolutely scandalized by this atrocious conduct of yours.'

'What have I done?' I demanded.

'Can you ask?' she said. 'Here you are and here am I. We are to be married to-day at 2.30. The ceremony has not taken place, and yet you are found on my premises. You must surely be aware that on the day of the wedding the parties–yes, the "parties," that is the word–should on no account see each other till they see each other in church?'

'Lettice,' I said, 'I was not aware of this rule. Remember that I have been out of England for seventeen years. And I have been married so seldom.'

'Evidently,' she ejaculated. 'Now you must go–no, don't come further into the room–and we'll pretend we haven't seen each other. *Au revoir.*'

'But I want to tell you about Gerald.'

'Never mind about Gerald,'

'But he's ill and perhaps he can't come.'

'Well,' said Lettice, 'he's your cousin, not mine.'

'I shouldn't be surprised if he's dying.'

'Really!' snapped the little minx, staring me full in the face.

'Aren't you glad the fog's gone?' I said.

'Yes,' she said, 'I am. Is that all?'

I left her, slamming the door. And never have I adored her more than I did in that moment of my discomfiture. I saw that I had done something extremely wicked and against all the rules. Before I regained my flat the fog had resumed its sway, more terribly than ever. I quitted the cab at the corner of St. James's Street, and I had considerable difficulty in finding my abode, though it was only a few yards away. The meteorological conditions were those of night joined to vapor from the River Styx.[6]

'Jenkins,' I said, 'has that parcel come?'

'No, sir.'

'Then you must go up to Savile Row[7] and fetch it. It isn't far. Keep to the kerb and to the northeast, and be as quick as you can.'

'I'll do my best, sir.'

And Jenkins went out into the night of eleven a.m.

At noon he had not returned.

I should have gone myself in search of him, but felt that such a course would not be prudent. Hence I sent my cook. My cook laughed at fogs, and with a hood round her head she, too, sallied forth. At 12.15 a telegraph-boy came. His message said: *'Gerald worse, not serious but I can't leave him best wishes you and dearest Letty Selina.'* I asked the boy how he found his way to my residence. He said it was only across the street and it had only taken him half an hour to do the journey. I informed him that there was a reply message, and I wrote out this: *'Reverend Parker, St. Mary-le-Strand Church. Coming as quick as I can please wait Stout.'* I sent this merely as a matter of precaution; it sprang out of my natural prudence. I wondered how Letty and her maid would contrive to reach that church, and I said to myself: 'Well, no matter what the fog, if I can't beat a couple of women in the race to St. Mary-le-Strand my name is not Jack Stout!'

At 12.40 neither Jenkins nor my cook had returned. And by way of a third and final effort I dispatched my parlor maid in search of the erring pair. I felt that it was like throwing good money after bad, but in the interest of suitable high-class raiment I did it.

I was alone in the electric-lighted flat.

A clock struck one. I dared wait no longer. An hour and a half to reach the church in that fog was not too generous an allowance. I went into the kitchen, and found an apple, an

orange, and some cucumber sandwiches. Armed with these–
for I had eaten nothing, having sacrificed my cook–I set out for
my wedding, dressed as I was. I put the apple in one pocket of
my big overcoat and the orange in the other. The sandwiches
were so small and thin that I ate them while brushing my hat.
I left the front door of the flat open and all lights burning, and
I wrote on a sheet of notepaper, which I laid down flat on the
hall-floor, these words: *'I have gone. Jenkins must see that my
luggage is at Charing Cross[8] at 3.15. J.S.'*

II.

The last surviving man left alone on this planet will not feel
more solitary than I felt as I stepped on the pavement of St.
James's Street. I assume it was the pavement, my reasoning
faculties told me it was the pavement; but I could not see it. I
could see my hand if I held it close to my chin; but for practical
purposes all that I could perceive of this mighty and splendid
universe was my own nose, and only the tip of that. I could
hear noises, consisting chiefly of obscene language, and the
collisions of vehicles. Occasionally, as I stood motionless,
daunted, aghast, something enormous and mysterious
loomed shadowily past me: it was a fellow creature.

'So this is a London fog,' I meditated. 'My first!

'No doubt a number of liars will tell me after it's over
that it was really nothing compared to the worst fogs that visit
London.

'I have got to get to St. Mary-le-Strand.

'I shall never get there.

'I must get there. If I am killed on the way, I must get there.

'Why did we fix our marriage for the end of November?

'My friends ought to have warned me.'

I walked across the pavement and touched something
with my hand. In the vicinity I could hear a fierce dragon or
something of that kind breathing stertorously. I felt the curves
of the object, running my hand over it high and low. At length

I came to a conclusion.

'This is a four-wheeler,' I said, 'and Providence is in it.'

Not meaning that Providence was in the four-wheeler, though I would not deny the possibility, but that Providence had had something to do with the four-wheeler being opposite my door at that moment. I felt in the four-wheeler for a passenger, but found none. Then I made two paces down the street, and aimed my mouth at the dragon-breathing.

'Are you engaged, cabby?' I cried into the void.

'Yes,' came a hoarse message from the void. 'I'm engaged in wondering how long this 'ere blighted fog's going to last.'

'Well,' I said, 'if you can worry along to St. Mary-le-Strand Church I'll give you a couple of sovereigns.'

'Oh!' was the response. 'St. Mary-le-Strand will wait. She'll be standing there all right to-morrow. I ain't much on church-going to-day, gov-nor.'

'I positively must be there by 2.30,' I said. 'I am to be married.'

'Married!' came an exclamation.

'Yes,' I said. 'You can understand my anxiety, can't you?'

'Cummere,' a command came down to me.

'Where?'

'Up here on the box. Put yer foot on the wheel. That's it. Come closer.'

I got up on to the seat, and edged a little way along it, and then I saw a vague dark, red wrinkled face, issuing from about thirteen mufflers, within a couple of inches of my face.

'Is that you?' bellowed the face.

'Yes,' I said.

'Listen,' said the face solemnly. 'This is good-luck, this is. It's a warning to you, this fog is. You got a chance to shunt that marriage, and it's yer last chance! Do yer mean to tell me as yer won't take it?'

'I know it's silly of me,' I said. 'I know I oughtn't to fly in the face of a warning like this fog. But I shall. I'm that sort. I determined to be married to-day.'

'Well,' said the face, 'get down and go inside. I'll take yer there if I bust up the blighted machine for it. You got a nerve, you have, guv'nor.'

'Good!' I exclaimed.

'But, guv'nor. It's worth a fiver, ain't it?'

I sighed. 'Yes,' I said. 'I daresay the crock is worth a fiver. And if he dies on the way I'll give you a fiver. Go down St. James's Street, and along Pall Mall, and cross Trafalgar Square by the top, and you can't lose yourself.'

'Right *oh!*' floated down to me.

We started. We plunged into the mid-night sea of St. James's Street. Before the cab turned at the bottom we had stopped twenty-four times, seventeen times with violence, and seven times of our own prudent accord. I felt like a cat in a bag being shaken up by a cruel boy. There we had a spell of uninterrupted frantic speed at the rate of about half a mile an hour. And then we came to an absolute and complete halt. We were in the grip of two omnibuses.[9]

It suddenly occurred to me that for some reason best known to the British Legislature, no marriage could take place after three o'clock, and that the law made no allowance for fogs. We had fixed the ceremony for half-past two in order that we might avoid the awful tedium of a wedding breakfast. Our intention was to go direct to Charing Cross. But now I would have given quite a considerable sum for even a wedding-breakfast. The apple and the orange had been as nothing to my hunger. And I perceived the fearful riskiness involved in arranging a marriage for half-past two. The margin was entirely too small. I resolved that if ever I married again I would marry at eight in the morning so as to make sure.

However, the vehicle began to move.

The sounds of concussions, collisions, and vituperative epithets became gradually louder and more confused in that world of darkness, but we continued to make progress. 'I shall do it yet,' I said to myself. And then the cab seemed without the slightest warning to be climbing a very steep hill. 'Surely,' I thought, 'we haven't passed the church and got to Ludgate Hill.' Then the ascent ceased. I heard the voice of my driver, and presently the vehicle moved sharply backwards down the hill again.

'The 'orse's mistake,' cried out my driver. 'He was going up the steps of Exeter 'All. It is nearly a church ain't it, sir?'

We resumed our course, and stopped and started for interminable minutes. And then without any preparation we ran straight out of the fog into sunshine. I gazed out of the window, and instantly perceived that we were on the Southside of Waterloo Bridge. How we had got to the Southside of Waterloo Bridge while making a bee line along the Strand, has never been explained and probably never will be.

All right, sir,' said the driver cheerfully. 'I'll do it yet.'

And he intrepidly turned back again into the fog.

But the hour was now 2.10. I gave up hope.

'I shan't be married to-day,' I said, 'that's evident.'

I felt gloomy and sad. But ultimately I brought philosophy to my aid. 'What can it matter,' I demanded of the circumambient fog, 'whether Letty and I are married to-day or to-morrow? What is a day more or less in the long vista of our future happiness. It is simply nothing, simply nothing, simply nothing. Besides, Letty herself will certainly not have reached the church. If I fail, with my indomitable pluck and my masculine intelligence, will not she?'

Thus I comforted myself.

But all the time another part of me was murmuring forlornly: 'She *may* get there, by a fluke. And I *do* want to be married to-day. A day makes all the difference in the world!'

Ages passed.

Then the driver came to the window. I could see him faintly. The fog was slightly less dense. 'Here you are, sir,' he said.

'What! The church?'

'The church, sir.'

It was only 2.40. I jumped out with glee and could dimly perceive the railings of the church, and an open gate. I penetrated into the yard, and put my hand on the church. It was there. Then I returned to the driver and gave him five sovereigns.[10] I had it in me to give him fifty.

III.

'I honestly never expected to do it,' I said to myself as I somewhat nervously opened the front door of St. Mary-le-Strand. 'Of course, Letty won't be here,' I added. 'No marriage to-day. That's a certainty. I must make the best of it.'

But no sooner had I opened the front doors than a sort of a beadle person[11] popped out from somewhere. He was fat and flurried.

'Are you the bridegroom?' he asked me.

'I am,' I said.

'They've been waiting for you three-quarters of an hour, sir, all of 'em. Better give me your coat and 'at sir, and slip in.'

'Three-quarters of an hour!' I exclaimed. 'I'm barely ten minutes late, and I've done marvels to get here.'

He merely hummed as he took my things. Then he opened the second pair of swing-doors, and I saw the interior of the church. It was very nearly as full of fog as the street outside. A gas chandelier was lighted at the other end, near the chancel, and beneath its darting rays I saw my wedding-party grouped, patiently waiting. I hesitated a moment, and then, summoning all my fortitude, I tried to walk up the aisle as though it belonged to me. I may say that I failed, failed miserably. I resembled more a heretic going to the Inquisition than an owner of churches.

'Are you the bridegroom?' asked a robed parson who stood with a book in his hand. And the tone of his voice said: 'You'd better mind your p's and q's, young man. Fog or no fog, we've waited too long for you. And what's the meaning of that grey lounge suit?'

'I am,' I whispered, bowing my head to the rebuke.

'Kindly take your place to the right of the bride.'

I obeyed.

Lettice was wearing a heavy veil, which I was surprised to see, as she had distinctly told me that she would not wear a veil. She was wearing clothes which I had never before seen, and I did not consider that they suited her very well, either. The curate stood by his superior officer, and I thought: 'That's a curious place for him to stand in, if he is to give her away.' My great-aunt Anne stood some distance to the left. She also was robed in strange finery. I said to myself: 'At a wedding all women are alike. You never know what they'll do.' Neither my bride nor my great-aunt raised her head to look at me. The occasion was too much for them.

The service began.

And just as the parson was getting into his stride, Letty sneezed, and then raised her veil. I glanced at her, and started back horror-struck. 'Pardon me,' I stopped the parson.

'Sir,' he protested angrily.

'Pardon me,' I said firmly, 'but I must put an end to this before it is too late. This is not my wedding, and this lady is not my bride. There is a mistake.'

My false bride screamed.

'Mistake!' cried the parson. 'Impossible! We have only one wedding here to-day, and it is yours.'

' What church is this?' I demanded.

'St. Clement Dane's,[12] of course,' said the parson.

'My dear sir, and all the congregation,' I said, 'I have just given a cabman five pounds under the fixed impression that it was St. Mary-le-Strand. Excuse my hurried departure.'

And I hurriedly departed, by way of the aisle, and met two young men just coming in who obviously were the real bridegroom and his best man. I stayed not to reason, nor to explain, nor to bandy politeness. I fled. The beadle person gave me my overcoat and hat (in exchange for a shilling) with an air which indicated his opinion that I was no better than I should be, and that if a policeman had bccn handy–

I vanished from his sight into the fog, and stood once more at the gate of St. Clement Dane's.

'No,' I murmured, 'the one thing that is clear in this fog is the fact that I shall not succeed in getting myself married.'

Providence decidedly played pitch-and-toss with me on that day, for on leaving St. Clement Dane's I walked straight into the ample bosom of a policeman.

'Officer,' I said to him, scanning his young countenance as well as I could in the gloom, 'here we are face to face alone in the midst of all the havoc and misery of this terrible fog, and in front on St. Clement Dane's Church. We ought to be standing in front of St. Mary-le-Strand. Take me there at once, and a sovereign is yours.'

'You want to go to St. Mary-le-Strand, sir?'

'If I am not there by three o'clock, officer, I shall kill myself.'

'Well, it's straight along, sir. You can't miss it.'

'Yes, I can,' I said, 'I am capable of missing anything. I am capable of finding myself in St. Paul's Cathedral or Westminster Abbey in mistake for St. Mary-le-Strand. Officer, take me. Lead me there. I am a British citizen.'

'Sorry I can't, sir,' said he, 'I'm on fixed point duty.'

'What does that matter?' I cried. 'Who's to know you're on fixed point duty. You might as well be in Timbuctoo for all the good you're doing here. Come along. Two sovereigns are yours. You can be back in five minutes.'

'And suppose the inspector cops me, sir?'

'Officer,' I said, 'if he does, I will allow you a hundred a year for life.'

He took me, but not directly. We arrived at Short's wine shop before he discovered that he was not in the path of righteousness.

When I touched the blessed doors of St. Mary-le-Strand it

was three minutes past three. I knew it was three minutes past three. However, I set back my watch to five minutes to three. And then the beadle of St. Mary-le-Strand appeared before me. 'Is there a wedding party here?' I asked, and he said there was. 'I'm part of it,' I said. 'What time is it?'

'Three minutes past three, sir.'

'No, it isn't,' I corrected him. ' It's five minutes to three. I daresay the fog has affected your watch. Alter it. Here's a sovereign. And if I appeal to you for the exact time against the clergyman–well, here's another sovereign. See?'

And there they were, in an interior exactly like St. Clement Dane's–my precious Letty, Great-aunt Anne, the Reverend Mark Parker, and the incumbent.

Altogether the affair cost me nine pounds in addition to the normal fees.

*   *   *   *   *   *   *   *   *   *

'But how did you get to the church in time?' I questioned my wife in the vestry.

'Great-aunt called for me,' was the reply.

'Of course, I did,' said Great-aunt Anne. 'As soon as the fog lifted at eleven o'clock, I took a cab and brought her right away. I knew it was her only chance. I knew the fog would come on again. We lunched at Short's.'

'At Short's!'

'Yes, because it was nearest to the church. And if *you*, Jack, had had any sense, you would have–'

'Great-auntie,' I said, 'I cannot stand much, so be careful. Only by the exercise of the utmost sangfroid and audacity have I escaped being married to the wrong person!'

As the fog lasted for several days, Letty and I spent our honeymoon at the Savoy Hotel.[13] We couldn't get any further. Afterwards we went to Algiers. I had passed seventeen years there, and I absolutely guaranteed to Letty that there would be no fog.

NOTES
PARTS I-III

1. *Gunter's Magazine.* 'Lord Dover' was serialised: Parts I-III in Volume 1, No.5, May 1905, pages 421-448. Parts IV-V in Volume 1, No.6, June 1905, pages 572-591. Part VI in Volume 1, No.7, July 1905, pages 677-685. Signed Arnold Bennett. Illustrations by Herman Rountree. Rountree, an accomplished illustrator, lived and worked in Rhode Island, U.S.A. The monthly magazine was published in New York by Gunter's Home Publishing Company at a cover price of 20 cents. It first appeared in February 1905 and continued appearing as *Gunter's Magazine* until September 1910. It was subsequently issued under various titles - *The New Gunter's Magazine, The New Magazine, New Story Magazine* - until November 1915. Archibald Clavering Gunter (1847-1907) was himself a playwright and prolific self-published novelist. Bennett reviewed Gunter's novel *The King's Stockbroker* in his 'Book Chat' column in *Woman* (11 July 1894).

2. This is one of Bennett's earliest published direct references to the notion of a 'card'.

3. After his father's death in January 1902, his mother's return to Burslem, and with the expiry of the lease on Trinity Hall Farm, Hockcliffe, Bedfordshire, Bennett made an unaccompanied visit to Algeria during January and February 1903. With no published *Journal* entries between 26 May 1901 and 28 September 1903, and no published correspondence between 12 January 1903 and 27 March 1903 (although there is a postcard sent from Algeria to his mother in the Potteries Museum & Art Gallery's Arnold Bennett Archive), Bennett's Algerian stay remains one of the least documented periods of his literary life.

The only published clue to Bennett's Algerian experience is his series of six stories called 'The Loot of Cities', published in *Windsor* magazine between June-November 1904, and in particular 'A Solution of the Algiers Mystery' (September 1904). These stories were reprinted in *The Loot of Cities* by Alston Rivers (1905) and in an expanded form by Thomas Nelson (1917).

4. Bennett's novel *The Grand Babylon Hotel* was published in 1902, although it had previously been serialised in *The Golden Penny* - a relatively short-lived periodical which appeared from 15 June 1895- 26 December 1903, and which also serialised Bennett's 'Teresa of Watling Street' in 1903 - between 2 February and 15 June 1901. Bennett features the hotel in many subsequent novels and stories. The most overt intertextual reference to the hotel as a fictional location occurs in the story 'Midnight at the Grand Babylon', included in the 1917 *The Loot of Cities*. In the course of researching 'Stella's

Journey' for this volume I also discovered a much earlier appearance of 'Midnight at the Grand Babylon' in the New Zealand *Star* newspaper for 24 March 1905.

5. 'Hugo's' is the name of the vast and impressive London department store that provides the setting for Bennett's 1906 novel *Hugo. A Fantasia on Modern Themes.* The novel had previously been serialised in 12 episodes in *To-Day*, Volume XLVII, between 3 May and 19 July, thus appearing at the same time as 'Lord Dover'.

6. Capital punishment for murder was not abolished in the U.K. until 1969 (1973 in Northern Ireland). The last execution took place in 1964.

7. During the Crimean War Harry Bessemer patented a process for the speedy conversion of molten pig-iron into steel. His Sheffield Steelworks was noted for its mass production of guns and steel rails, rather than paper-knives.

8. At the time of the story (1905) Sweden had assumed a global leadership in the match industry. In the early 1900s England and Germany provided its major export markets.

9. Used as a laxative in the early 1900s, the side-effects of castor oil may have been worse than the complaint. Children were often given a regular weekly dose irrespective of their needs.

10. A valet's duties were widely defined. Mrs. Beaton felt it necessary to describe them as part of the routine of household management:

> His day commences by seeing that his master's drawing-room is in order; that the housemaid has swept & dusted it properly; that the fire is lighted & burns cheerfully; & some time before his master is expected, he will do well to throw up the sash to admit fresh air, closing it, however, in time to recover the temperature which he knows his master prefers. It is now his duty to place the body-linen before the fire, to be aired properly; to lay the trousers intended to be worn, carefully brushed & cleaned, on the back of his master's chair; while the coat & waistcoat, carefully brushed & folded, & the collar cleaned, are laid in their places ready to be put on when required. All the articles of the toilet should be in their places, the razors properly set & stropped, & hot water ready for use. Mrs. Beaton, *The Book of Household Management,* 1881 edition, p.978

Chapter III of *The Regent*, 'Wilkins's', deals with Denry Machin's urgent necessity to acquire the services of a valet if he is to cast off the mantle of provincialism in dealing with London's *literati*. As in 'Lord Dover' the approbation of the aristocracy is important: 'In another five minutes Edward

Henry had engaged a skilled valet, aged twenty-four, name Joseph, with a testimonial of efficiency from Sir Nicholas Winkworth, Bart., at a salary of a pound a week and all found.' (p.79)

11. The *Morning Post* (1772-1937) was a conservative daily newspaper noted for its attention to the activities and interests of the wealthy and influential members of society. It merged with *The Daily Telegraph* in 1937. Bennett never wrote for the paper, although he was one of many illustrious signatories, including Thomas Hardy, Arthur Quiller-Couch and Josiah C. Wedgwood, whose letter upholding the freedom of the press in war-time was printed in the paper on 17 March 1917.

In Bennett's short story 'The White Feather' (1914), the industrialist Hawker Maffick amuses himself by inserting provocative messages, questioning the manhood of unenlisted men, in the Agony columns of the *Morning Post* (*Uncollected Short Stories 1892-1932*, p.354).

12. Count d'Orsay (1801-1852) was a French amateur artist and dandy. His flamboyant style of dress included a crimson velvet waistcoat across which he flaunted a profusion of jewellery.

13. The Turf Club, established in 1861, is regarded as the aristocratic bastion of London gentlemen's clubs.

14. White's, established in 1693, originally sold hot chocolate, a rare and expensive commodity at the time. It owes its name, 'Mrs. White's Chocolate House', to that of its first proprietor, Mrs. White.

15. The Carlton Club was founded in 1832 by Tory Peers, MPs and Conservative gentlemen, as a place to co-ordinate party activity after the party's defeat over the First Reform Act.

16. Newmarket, in Suffolk, is the headquarters of British horse racing.

17. *The Field*, published continuously since 1858, is the world's oldest country and field sports magazine.

18. *Queen* magazine is an illustrated society publication first published in 1801. Bennett contributed two short stories to the magazine, 'The Police Station' (15 September 1900) and 'The Farlls and a Woman ' (17 October 1908). The latter is published in *Arnold Bennett's Uncollected Short Stories 1892-1932*, pp.335-348.

19. The *Sporting Times* was a British newspaper (1865-1932) devoted mainly to sport, particularly horse racing, and informally known as the *Pink 'Un* as it was printed on pink paper.

20. Here Bennett's addition is incorrect by one penny (1d.) and given his close attention to financial details in his private life this may well be a deliberate error intended as a private joke.

21. Rocco features as the villain in Bennett's *Grand Babylon Hotel*, published in four consecutive monthly instalments in *Myra's Journal* (2 February 1901-15 June 1901) and as a novel on 9 January 1902. (He is also mentioned in the story 'The Farlls and a Woman' (see Note 18 above).

22. A reefer suit has a serviceable short coat or jacket of thick cloth, double-breasted with a double row of buttons, and with matching trousers.

23. This is a warning against meddling or approach.

24. For details of the *Pall Mall Gazette* see 'On Growing Old', Note 1.

25. The Tivoli provided a very different sort of social experience to Exeter Hall! The Tivoli Music Hall in the Strand opened in 1890. It was demolished in 1957 and replaced with an office building and shops. Exeter Hall, built on the north side of the Strand between 1829-1831, was used mainly for religious and philanthropic meetings. It was demolished in 1907 and the site is now occupied by the Strand Palace Hotel.

26. In his 'Preface' to *Nicholas Nickleby* (1839), Charles Dickens writes: '.... those who take an interest in this tale, will be glad to learn that the BROTHERS CHEERYBLE live; that their liberal charity, their singleness of heart, their noble nature, and their unbounded benevolence are no creations of the Author's brain; but are prompting every day (and often by stealth) some munificent and generous deed ....' The Cheeryble twins are presumed to be based on the philanthropic Manchester merchants David and William Grant. Dickens' assurance that they 'live' resulted in him receiving hundreds of begging letters addressed to these worthy gentlemen.

PARTS IV-V

1. By the 1880s there were some 1,000 tape-machines, or stock-tickers, installed in the offices and boardrooms of New York bankers and brokers. The machine printed a series of symbols - usually a shortened form of a specific company's name - followed by a brief up-date about the performance of the company's stock.

In his short story 'The Farlls and a Woman' (1903) Bennett writes of Godfrey Farll, 'a financier of the shrewdest sort to be found in the City' (p.355) who has a drawing-room with 'a tape-machine inclosed in a marvellously carved oaken case' (*Uncollected Short Stories* p.339).

2. *Punch, or the London Charivari,* founded in 1841, was an illustrated weekly magazine which gradually changed in emphasis from pursuing a radical agenda to one of humour. It stopped publishing for a period between 1992-1996.

Bennett never wrote for *Punch* although he featured on its pages, most notably perhaps on 8 April 1931 when the magazine published a valedictory poem, 'A Man From The North'. The poem includes one particular apposite verse:

'Here lies a jester with a sense of duty,
A master-craftsman in his art engrossed,
A steadfast friend, a worshipper of beauty,
A kindly critic and a perfect host.'
(quoted in Pound, p.368)

More typically, *Punch* greeted the news that Bennett had taken up dancing with a passion with the suggestion that his novel *Helen With the High Hand* should be renamed *Helen With the High Kick.*

3. Bennett makes the rapid fluctuation in the value of South African gold shares the central plot device in his short 1895 story 'A Little Deal in Kaffirs' (*Uncollected Short Stories*). In a similar vein, Denry Machin's speculations in London in *The Regent* (1912) are contingent upon stock-market fluctuations linked to colonial commodity production.

4. Ignacy Jan Paderewski (1860-1941) was not only a celebrated Polish concert pianist and composer, but also a diplomat and the second Prime Minister of the Republic of Poland.

In Bennett's short story 'The Dog' (*Tales of the Five Towns*, 1905), Paderewski became a metaphor for sartorial elegance: 'Now, Ellis [the fictional 'dog' of the title] was a great interpretive artist, and the tailor recognised the fact. When the tailor met Ellis on Duck Bank greatly wearing a new suit, the scene was impressive. It was as though Elgar had stopped to hear Paderewski play "Pomp and Circumstance" on the piano' (p.88).

5. The *Encyclopædia Britannica*, the oldest English language encyclopædia still in print, first appeared in 1768. Jack Stout would almost certainly have owned the ninth edition (1875-1889). Bennett considers the *Encyclopædia* in one of his 'Books and Persons' columns for the *New Age* periodical (23 March 1911), written under the *nom de plume* of Jacob Tonson. Today Bennett commands his own entry in the *Enclyclopædia*.

6. Ralph Waldo Emerson (1803-1882), American philosopher and poet, evolved the quasi-religious concept of Transcendentalism, a form of mystic idealism and reverence for nature.

Bennett recommended reading Emerson in Chapter VIII 'The Reflective Mood' in *How to Live on 24 Hours a Day* (1910): 'In the formation or modification of principles, and the practice of conduct, much help can be derived from printed books.... Pascal, La Bruyère, and Emerson' (p.42). Bennett also references Emerson in Chapter VIII, 'System in Reading' in his

1909 study *Literary Taste, How to Form It*, where he commends Emerson's distinction between 'the literature of "power" and the literature of "knowledge"' (p.66). Bennett retained his early admiration for Emerson: 'I had no tea, but read Emerson's essays instead. The essay on History is very noble' (*Journal* entry for 14 April 1920).

7. The *Sporting Life* was a British newspaper, published from 1859-1998, that was primarily known for its extensive coverage of horse racing.

8. De Dion-Bouton was a French automobile manufacturer, operating from 1883-1932, whose company was at one time the largest car manufacturer in the world. The 8 hp model appeared in 1902 and had a front-mounted engine under a coal-scuttle bonnet. It was noted for its outstanding record of reliability.

9. Eugen Sandow (1867-1925), a pioneering advocate of body building, became known as the 'father of modern body building'. Bennett may well have seen either the short 1894 film by the Edison Studios or that by Kinetoscope, showing him flexing his muscles. Sandow held the first ever major body building contest at the Royal Festival Hall (14 September 1901) where Sir Arthur Conan Doyle was one of the judges.

10. Snowdon is the highest mountain in Wales, and the highest point in the British Isles outside Scotland.

11. Charles Chamberland worked alongside Louis Pasteur to develop in 1884 a porcelain filter capable of removing micro-organisms from pressurised water. It filtered and purified water for drinking.

12. Osborne biscuits were first produced in 1860 and became one of the first semi-sweet varieties to appeal to public taste. Queen Victoria declined an invitation to lend her name to the commercially produced biscuit, but nevertheless suggested naming it after her favourite home, Osborne House, on the Isle of Wight.

13. Suetonius (ca. 69/75-after 130) was a Roman historian whose most important surviving work is a set of biographies of twelve successive Roman rulers. Bennett's *Journal* records his purchase of 'the hundred books which Bells allow you to select from the 600 volumes of Bohn's Libraries .... I cut several of them and looked through Juvenal, Suetonius, and da Vinci' (3 July 1899).

14. *Kelly's Directory* was a U.K. trade directory, listing the businesses and tradespeople in named towns and cities. It also served as a general directory of postal addresses for important individuals and organisations. An item from the *Directory* on the North Staffordshire Infirmary at Hartshill (Bennett's Pirehill Infirmary) can be found at www.thepotteries.org.

15. Harrods is a luxury department store on the Brompton Road (Borough of

Kensington and Chelsea). Hatteras's purchase of a 'quart bottle of the best preserved French peas from Harrod's' is, therefore, hardly the act of a man devoted to the simple life and following the precepts of Emersonian philosophy.

Bennett refused an invitation to write publicity material for the store, saying that to do so would 'lose caste' (*Golden Book*, IX, May 1929, p.46).

16. The taffrail is found round the stern of the vessel.

PART VI

1. In the early 19th century the phenomenon of London's frequent and dense fogs came to be known as 'London particulars'. Charles Dickens's *Bleak House* (1853) is metaphorically shrouded in fog: '.... I asked him whether there was a great fire anywhere? For the streets were so full of dense brown smoke that scarcely anything was to be seen. "Oh dear no, miss," he said. "This is a London particular"' (p.76).

2. Poole's, founded in 1806, is a renowned gentlemen's bespoke tailor, credited with creating the dinner suit. Among its many distinguished clients today is the Lord Chamberlain's office, which it provides with court dress.

3. Consecrated in 1723, St. Mary-le-Strand was one of fifty churches built in London under the auspices of the Commission For Building New Churches. It avoided demolition in the 20th century, thanks to a conservation campaign led by the artist Walter Crane, and later survived the blitz despite nearby damage.

4. The Devonshire Club (1874-1976) was originally founded to accommodate the growing number of Liberal voters in the wake of the extended franchise created by the 1832 Reform Act. In many ways it was an adjunct to the senior Reform Club. It was named after its first Chairman, the Duke of Devonshire.

5. Empire furniture owes its designation to a style made popular during the first French Empire (1804-1815) under Napoleon Bonaparte. It is characterised by massiveness and lavish bronze and brass ornamentation.

6. In Greek mythology the River Styx encircles the underworld (Hades) over which the boatman Charon ferries the souls of the dead.

7. Savile Row in London's Mayfair is famous for the quality of its traditional men's bespoke tailoring.

8. Charing Cross railway station is a central London terminus, and the fifth busiest in the capital.

In 'The Gates of Empire' (*Manchester Daily Dispatch*, 11 January 1908) Bennett extols the luxuries of the station, particularly its electric lights and lavatories, after a return journey from Paris.

9. The London General Omnibus Company was founded in 1855 to amalgamate and regulate the large number of independent operators. Motorised omnibuses, or buses, first appeared in 1902, although horse-drawn vehicles were still to be seen until as late as 1911.

10. A sovereign is a British gold coin with a nominal face value of £1 sterling but which today serves as a bullion coin.

When Denry Machin, Jack Stout's fictional 'card' descendant, returns from a successful business venture in Llandudno, sovereigns flow like champagne. Telling his mother that he had collected beach pebbles in a hat-box, she opens it and 'then there was a scream from Mrs. Machin, and the hat-box rolled with a terrific crash to the tiled floor, and she was ankle-deep in sovereigns. She could see sovereigns running about all over the parlour' (p.127).

11. The 'sort of beadle person' is a lay official of the church who may, as here, act as an usher. He could also be expected to keep order and to assist in religious functions.

12. St. Clement Danes is mentioned in the Domesday Book (1086). It escaped damage in the Great Fire of London (1666) but was virtually destroyed by German incendiary bombs in May 1941, leaving only the wall and tower intact. It was completely restored and re-consecrated in 1958 to become the capital's central church of the Royal Air Force.

A memorial service for Bennett was held at St. Clement Danes. Reginald Pound, writing in 1952, before the restoration project, makes the point that '[t]his was the church which had been faithfully and fearfully attended for twenty years by another celebrated Staffordshire man, Dr. Samuel Johnson, whose statue stands unscathed amid the ruin which later came to the church' (p.367).

13. The Savoy Hotel, London, opened in 1889. Built by Richard D'Oyly Carte, owner of the neighbouring Savoy Theatre, it could claim to be the capital's first true luxury hotel. Among its innovations were the use of electric lighting and the provision of en suite bathroom facilities in most of its rooms.

Bennett took the Savoy Hotel for his model in both *The Grand Babylon Hotel* (1902) and *Imperial Palace* (1930). He stayed at the Savoy in September 1929, making extensive notes on its operations.

& OTHER LOST STORIES

A young Arnold Bennett in Burslem before his move to London.

WHAT'S BRED IN THE BONE.[1]
A CONDENSATION IN SIX PORTIONS OF MR. GRANT ALLEN'S
£1,000 PRIZE NOVEL.

I. – A CAUTION TO SNAKES.

Once upon a time a pony was carrying a young lady to the railway station. If that pony hadn't jibbed you would never have experienced this happy moment.

But it did, and the young lady nearly missed the train. If she had, the world would have lost a great book (and, we must also add, a most diverting condensation thereof). But she didn't. A porter managed to insert her sylph-like form in a second-class carriage just as the train commenced its mad career, and she found herself 'alone–with an artist.'

Thus, at the very beginning, the hero and heroine were brought together, Cyril Waring and Elma Clifford.

Cyril was an artist (an admirable trait in a hero). Elma was the daughter of Mr. Reginald Clifford, C.M.G., a man who had written his name in his country's history as governor of some comical little speck of a sugary niggery West Indian Island. Description of her is useless. Heroines always baffle it.

Briefly, she was charming–and dark. Cyril and Elma were together, but there was no one to introduce them. The course of true love never *did* run smooth.

However, Elma betrayed a natural anxiety to sit down, and it happened that Cyril was travelling with a snake of considerable magnitude, which he was putting into a picture. She was on the point of converting this snake into a pulp, when Cyril, apologizing for its presence, snatched the animal from a fearful fate. They began to talk, and in a few minutes a keen ear might have caught the whistle of Cupid's arrows in that carriage.

She knew at once that he was an artist. Not by his raiment (for he was not arrayed like one of these), but by her woman's intuition. She had that badly.

The same reader will also note that Elma immediately became chummy with the snake.

They chattered on. He half offended her, and she was about to stand on her dignity, when the train rushed into a tunnel. There was a low, dull thud, and a quick blank stoppage, and Elma found herself deposited in Cyril's arms.

The clever reader has foreseen a collision, no doubt. Ah! Well, it just wasn't a collision. No! the tunnel had fallen in. Cyril and Elma extricated themselves from the remains of the carriage, and attempted to run back. But fate frowned, and the tunnel gave way in the rear of the train also. They were locked in.

II. – NOT QUITE SIAMESE.

From the darkness of the tunnel Cyril and Elma came out, not in weekly parts, as might have been expected, but complete in two volumes.

They were rescued after being buried alive for fifteen hours. Elma's father called it incarceration.

In his manly bosom and her tender breast love smouldered, and they knew it not.

They met again, at a garden party. The opportunities for a *tête-à-tête* were not so frequent and free as at their last interview, yet they managed to suck romance from a glance, a blush, a smile, a squeeze of the hand.

Now Cyril was one of twins. The other was Guy. And the physiology of these twain was so similar that they had the toothache together.

But whether or no they used the same soap is not recorded.

The problem, which was most like the other, was a life-study to many. And the origin of the twins, even as the origin of sausage, was veiled in mystery and doubt. None knew it, save one.

At the garden party, where Cyril and Elma learned to love, was Colonel Kelmscott, of Tilgate.

The Colonel, upon being suddenly introduced to Guy, was, appropriately enough, knocked into a cocked hat. He thought he had covered his emotion, but he knew not that Elma and her mother were afflicted with hereditary intuition, which is the worst sort.

The fact was, and we state it without reserve, that the Colonel himself was the origin of the twins.

III. – NIGHT THOUGHTS.

On the night of the horticultural gathering, as Elma sat in her bedroom, thinking upon the Manly Bosom, she felt herself gradually seized by a power which compelled her to arise and make a violent excursion around the room, whirling and dancing. What the power was she could not describe. She thought she was mad.

But it was not so. She was merely the descendant of gipsy snake-charmers. The polite said that she had Roumanian blood.

It came to the same thing.

When, after this, the Manly Bosom, bursting with love, proposed for her hand, Elma spoke to him kindly but firmly. The reason of her refusal she kept secret.

Of course the explanation was that she was too conscientious to become the wife of the husband of a lunatic. Now Cyril thought that her objection related to himself.

On the night previously referred to, the origin of the twins had a worse time of it even than Elma. Snakes and boas certainly consist chiefly of tail, but they have no entail. The Colonel enjoyed an entail, and it simply played *Hamlet* with his night's sleep. The sight of the twins had awakened remorse in this way.

Before his present marriage he had, in strictest privacy,

tied the knot with a poor girl who died in becoming the mother of the twins. Disguised as a gay bachelor, he then, under the paternal orders, walked off with the affections of the Lady Emily, who was his second wife. The fruit of this second venture was Granville Kelmscott, who was brought up as the heir of the entail, a rôle which he adorned.

The peculiarity of an entail is that it will break but not bend. The Colonel decided to break it. Without descending to unnecessary family details he informed Granville of his intentions.

That young gentleman was astute enough to guess that the Colonel had known family cares for a longer period than he had been led to believe.

He had secretly exchanged hearts with Gwendoline, daughter of Gilbert Gildersleeve, Q.C.

As a younger son, he could not ask her to carry things to the bitter end. He vaguely told her that all was over, and set sail for the Cape.

IV. –OUR FRIEND THE ENEMY.

Now the twins had a friend who stuck closer than court plaster, and he lent lustre to the name of Nevitt. He was a bank clerk and a villain. They knew he was the former.

And when he had assimilated £6,000 of their money they knew he was the latter; but not till then. Which was an indiscretion, and showed lack of insight.

He speculated. And his capital was large, for he traded on Guy's innocence. Naturally, he put Guy in the way of making his fortune.

But the company went the way of other companies, and the liquidator stood to win £3,000 each from Guy and Nevitt in the way of calls. And neither of them had such a thing about him.

Now, we must tell you that the Origin, in order to get a night's sleep, had anonymously placed £6,ooo to the credit of

Cyril at his bank, and the twins knew not who had done this thing. Cyril was away on the Continent, and Nevitt induced Guy to write out a cheque in his brother's name for this amount. It was merely a matter of convenience, he said, and could be explained afterwards.

Ordinary people call it forgery; but, then, ordinary people are so atrociously prosaic.

Nevitt took charge of the money (he was ever kind), paid his own calls, and proceeded to put himself into another county. He wanted a change of air.

It was here that he met Gilbert Gildersleeve, Q.C., aforementioned. The barrister was strong and fat–much fatter than a certain skeleton which he kept in his cupboard. He thought Nevitt was trying to get a private view of this skeleton. Words ruled high in the market, and they so far forgot themselves as to come to blows.

The Q.C. had large hands, and he, quite unintentionally, choked the bank clerk. End of Nevitt. And thus he got his change of air.

V. – AFRIC'S CORAL STRAND.

When Guy realised that he had been relieved of that £6,000 he developed a healthy appetite for Nevitt's gore, and went after him. Entirely ignorant of his late friend's sudden exit from a weary world, he managed to get himself suspected of the murder.

He heard that the hearts of the police ached for one fond look at his face, and, thinking only of the forgery, he decided that South Africa was the best place for him.

On board the steamer he met Granville Kelmscott. They were half-brothers and knew it not, but before they returned they were *half brothers* and knew it.

Cyril was arrested for the crime. On such occasions it is highly inconvenient to be exactly like someone else who is wanted.

Gildersleeve offered himself for the defence, and being in truth a great *criminal* barrister, he won his case. Elma attended the trial, and it had been better for Gilderslccve if she had never been born. During the hearing she had a severe attack of intuition.

She looked at Gildersleeve, and from that hour he never had a moment's happiness, although shortly afterwards he was promoted to the Bench.

She knew who was the murderer of Montague Nevitt.

And he knew that she knew.

And she knew that he knew that she knew.

VI. – KNOTS CUT AND TIED.

Time passed on–it seems to be about all he is capable of doing–and Guy and Granville had adventures in South Africa. They startled the natives, and the natives startled them. It was a new and strange kind of business.

But they made it pay, which is everything.

And they came back, heralded by cablegrams, and Granville found peace in the arms of Gwendoline Gildersleeve.

Guy intended to give himself up for forgery, but the police weren't having any. They said that murder was about his size, and Guy felt doubly injured.

The great Sir Gilbert Gildersleeve presided at the trial. He was pale, and we don't blame him.

When the jury returned a verdict of 'Guilty', Judge Gildersleeve arrived at the conclusion that he was in one of the smallest-sized corners ever constructed.

After all, he wasn't a bad sort. He told the jury that he was sorry to disagree with them, but he himself had assisted at the despatch of Nevitt to another clime.

He continued to behave sensibly and died.

Cyril, now that he could marry without making his wife the sister-in-law of a supposed murderer was anxious to join the charming descendant of snake-charmers in an attempt to solve the problem whether marriage really was a failure.

Moreover, the Origin had expired, and he enjoyed great riches.

And Elma had discovered from a relative that her terpsichorean and boa-constrictor tendencies were not a form of madness, and would gradually wither to their primeval atoms.

And so they lived happy ever afterwards.

At least, we suppose so.

NOTES

1. *Tit-Bits.* 19 December 1891, page 192. Grant Allen (1848-1899) was already an established author before his 1891 serial, *What's Bred in the Bone*, won the *Tit-Bits* £1,000 prize. Bennett, at the time a young clerk in London, subsequently entered and won the twenty guinea (£21) prize for the best condensation of Allen's serial. The parody was printed under the heading 'TWENTY GUINEA CONDENSATION PRIZE. Awarded to -Mr. Arnold Bennett, 6, Victoria Grove, Chelsea, S.W.'

A Charming Mantle. Design No. 3,010.

*(Cut-to-measure and stock size patterns supplied. See page 10.
Price of stock-size pattern 3¼d., post free.)*

This mantle is very easy to make. It looks well in velours du
Nord, velveteen, or cloth. Cloth should be used merely with silk;
velvet and velveteen need an interlining of domet. The mantle
consists of a back and two draped fronts, which hook down the
centre. These pieces are attached to a lined waistbelt, to which
the added flaps are secured. There are two long flaps in front, two
shorter ones at the back. Wing sleeve (one piece) lined with
domet and silk. Edge the garment with fur; two-piece collar,
stiffened, faced with the mantle material, edged with fur. Quantity
of 24-inch velveteen required, 6 yards. If single-width material be
used, added corners must be seamed on the straight to make the
material wide enough for the sleeve-pattern. If 2s. 11d. be given
for the velveteen and 1s. for the "Nearsilk" lining, the cost of
materials (apart from fur) will work out at about 28s.

This advertisement appears alongside an article by Bennett advising
husbands on ways to limit their wives personal expenditure.
(*Woman.* 28 December, 1898)

THE ADVANCED WOMAN.[1]
SOME DOCUMENTS.

The harmless bibliophile, ferreting among the costers' book-barrows which line Farringdon-road, occasionally makes a curious find.[2] It was my fortune the other day to come across, in a particularly dirty barrow, a privately-printed book, entitled 'The Future of Marriage.' It bore the ex-libris of a famous man, but the contents appeared to be mediocre, and I should certainly not have bought it had there not been some papers carefully jammed inside its cover. These were headed 'Human documents bearing upon this question.' They interested me, and I set them out here exactly as they stand, in the hope that they may interest others. They need no editing.

Hotel d'Albion, Cannes, Sunday.

My dearest Constance,–Your letter alarmed me; you always were deliciously alive you know, even when you were an active member of the League. And I find you as sweetly innocent as ever. But, seriously, I fear that all my trouble in teaching you the principles of Theosophy[3] and the true mission of Woman has been absolutely wasted. I feel sure you will obey your husband and go to church and work for bazaars and establish soup-kitchens with all the energy which you *pretended* to throw into the study of 'Isis Unveiled.'[4]

Ah! it is you 'good women' who are the most formidable obstacle to the real emancipation of Woman. I read the newspaper accounts of your wedding which you sent me. Shocking, my dear girl! Carriages from Eaton-square to Sloane-street! Full choral service. Four officiating clergymen including a bishop. Is this the way you assist the Cause? I tell you, dearest Constance, and I tell the world, that every woman who consents to go through the religious ceremony of marriage simply forges another link in the horrible chain by which we are already bound. Why, the marriage service is a wanton insult to any self-respecting woman, or would be if only her eyes were opened. And you, you, from whom we all expected something, have not only kissed the rod, but made a public exhibition of your ignominy.

I know what you are going to say. It is scarcely a year ago that I myself went through the same ceremony. It was a mistake, I see it now. But I only yielded after great pressure. Richard assured me that the Misses Grundy[5] would cease to buy his novels, if it came to be known that he and I had not conformed to conventional usage in the matter of wedlock. Not that this alone would have moved me. I yielded on account of the pressure of relatives. One must consider the feelings of one's family. And we did it as quietly as possible, went away to Bournemouth, and got the affair over with the least necessary fuss.

If I had the time to live through again, I would act differently. No cause can prosper without martyrs. And I ought to have been ready to sacrifice myself. I know Richard would have been ready to defy convention, had I asked him to do so, even though it had cost him his livelihood. And I had money enough for us both. We would doubtless have been 'cut' by most people, but not by all, for the League has not existed for ten years in vain. The world has ceased to laugh at us.

*   *   *

Baby is astonishingly well, but I am afraid the air of Cannes is not quite suitable for him. Nurse is carrying him up and down the garden, and I have one eye on them and one on my writing.

Richard is still in London, but will rejoin us shortly. His new novel is to be sent to press in a few days. It is called 'A Window in Heaven.' I wish I could get him to write seriously, to embody our philosophy in artistic form. But he says it is so much easier to write what the public wants. Sometimes I suspect he only half believes in our theories, although he is, as far as domestic affairs go, strictly conscientious in the practice of them.

My recent articles in the *Woman's Monthly* will be published in book form in the spring. I think I shall call the book 'The Woman of the Twentieth Century.'

And here I must stop. No doubt you are sufficiently bored. Kindest regards to your husband.–Believe me, your affectionate friend, CLARA CLAYTON.

Authors' Club, London, May 27.

My darling Clara,–One line before the mail goes, with some curious information culled from to-day's paper. The cutting herewith explains itself.

I hope you will now be satisfied. For the sake of your friends, you have once offered yourself up a sacrifice on the matrimonial altar, and they cannot reasonably ask you to do the hated thing again, simply because the all-important parson turns out not to have been a parson at all, and the ceremony of no effect. I, at any rate, shall not press you.

If the wicked Lovibond has solemnised other marriages I am afraid the people concerned will not receive the news so equably as ourselves. Your revolutionary theories have not, I fancy, yet permeated the populace.

I congratulate you on your wonderful luck. Do you take it for a sign that the New Era approaches?

Shall be with you in ten days.–Thine, Dick.

(Newspaper cutting, enclosed.)

'Considerable sensation has been caused at Bournemouth by the arrest of a man named Lovibond on a charge of falsely pretending to be a duly-ordained clergyman of the Church of England. The fraud was most ingeniously managed, and the pseudo-curate had actually achieved immense popularity in his parish. The rector, on learning the news, was taken seriously ill, and is confined to his bed.'

(Letter undated.)

My dear Husband,--I scarcely know what to say. I believe you tried to be as horrid as you could in your letter. I feel very much upset. I am not sure, now, that it is wise to defy the conventions. What can one woman do against the whole strength of society? I shall be laughed at, and probably worse, unless something is done. Besides, it may do the League grave harm.

Dear Richard.–Something must be done. Pray make all inquiries and telegraph to me. I suppose it is not certain yet that Lovibond is not a clergyman after all.

–Your loving wife, CLARA.

P.S.–Think of the horrible position of dear baby, without even a name! Even if we were re-married, he will still be–what he is. I believe that in France the marriage of parents legitimatises previously-born children. Oh, Dick, cannot we settle down in France, and become French citizens? We must be willing to make any sacrifice for the child's sake.–C.

Authors' Club,[6] London, June 4.

My own Clara,– I could not think of taking out French papers. You forget the conscription. It would be impossible for me as a member of the Peace Society,[7] to serve as a soldier. Besides, I should not care for it. I believe the hardships of barrack life, and especially the rations, would cause my speedy decease.

But it is wicked thus to trifle with you. I rejoice to say that the babe will be able to hold up his head once more. I have been down to Bournemouth, and ascertained that we were not married by Lovibond (as we both thought), but by another curate who, owing to some contretemps, had to take his place at the last moment.

Can you after this refuse to believe in Providence? I shall tell you all when we meet.

Your loving husband, DICK.

P.S.–Your letter was a sad shock to my faith in the 'advanced woman'.

NOTES

1. *The Sun*. 29 July 1893, page 1. Signed A.B. T.P. O'Connor, Irish Nationalist M.P. and radical journalist, founded what is generally regarded as the first modern newspaper, *The Star,* in 1887, followed by *The Sun* in 1893.

2. When Bennett first moved to London to work as a clerk his spare-time hobby was to scour London's bookstalls, compiling his own bibliographic catalogue.

3. Theosophy is a set of occult beliefs, popular in late-Victorian Britain, rejecting Judeo-Christian theology, and incorporating elements of Buddhism and Hinduism. Bennett read and recommended Annie Besant's book on Theosophists' teachings, *Thought Power*. Chapter XIII of his *The Human Machine* looks at her writing in the context of Marcus Aurelius and Epictetus: 'In the matter of concentration, I hesitate to recommend Mrs. Annie Besant's *Thought Power* and yet I should be possibly unjust if I did not recommend it, having regard to its immense influence on myself.... It contains an appreciable quantity of what strikes me as feeble sentimentalism, and also a lot of sheer dogma. But it is the least unsatisfactory manual of the brain that I have met with' (p.121).

4. *Isis Unveiled* (1877) by Helena Petrovna Blavatsky is a two-volume book of esoteric philosophy suggesting that in order to reach spiritual perfection each person has to pass through a series of (re)incarnations. She was also the Corresponding Secretary of the Theosophical Society.

5. Mrs. Grundy is the figurative name for an extremely priggish person ready to take offence at any challenge to social orthodoxy. The character herself began fictional life as a minor character in Thomas Morton's play *Speed the Plough* (1798).

6. The Authors' Club was founded in 1891 by novelist and critic Walter Besant, (Annie Besant's brother-in-law), as a place for writers to meet and talk. Its first president was George Meredith.

7. The Peace Society was founded in 1816 to promote disarmament and to establish the principle of arbitration to solve international disputes.

The Sun expanded traditional newspaper coverage to include everyday concerns, political debate, interviews, campaigning issues, celebrity gossip, alongside fictional contributions such as 'Restaurant Spooks'.

RESTAURANT SPOOKS.[1]
AN INTERVIEW.

It was my first interview, and I mounted the marble steps of M. Bonnebouche's superb mansion at Boxhill with considerable trepidation. Fourteen magnificent menials conducted me through a series of noble corridors and lofty halls, till at length I found myself in an apartment, simply but comfortably furnished, which was evidently the great man's 'den'.

He came in presently and greeted me with true French politeness, but in perfect English.

'I am expecting a visit from Mr. Raymond Blathwayt,' he said, 'and for a moment I thought you might be he.'

'Sir,' said I, 'I am not that great man. He has now, indeed, become a lion-tamer, and scorns his former pursuits.'

'But you wish to interview me?'

'I do. I want you to tell me everything—everything, that is, that I can crowd into a column.'

'About my restaurants?'

'If you please.'

'Well, you see, I used, years ago, to be a clerk in London, and I made the discovery that the vast majority of clerks, of whom there are scores of thousands between Lincoln's-inn-fields and Eastcheap, wanted a light dinner in the middle of the day—not a heavy meal, for it is impossible to work after it; nor yet a mere 'snack,' for that is insufficient to sustain them till seven or eight o'clock when they take a hearty tea. I further made the discovery that there was absolutely no restaurant in the town which offered just what they wanted at a price which they could afford.'[2]

'The humble shilling, I suppose.'

'Exactly, the humble shilling.'[3]

'But, even before your time there were a number of places where a "cut from the joint, two vegetables, and bread and cheese" could be had for that sum.'

'Yes,' he replied. 'And what did they give you? In the first place the meat was suspicious, and the vegetables were trifling in quantity and of no quality at all. Then the surroundings, the cutlery, glass, and linen, were unsatisfactory, and the waiting atrocious.'

'True, true,' I murmured. 'But what about the vegetarian restaurants?'

'A few of them are admirable, but among the great body of clerks there seems to be an insuperable objection to a vegetarian diet. They must have flesh.'

'And you proposed to yourself to solve the difficulty, with what result everyone knows?'

'I did. I knew that in France, and also in Soho here, you could get a four-course déjeuner, beautifully served, consisting of soup, fish, an entrée, and bread, butter and cheese for a franc and a half, or 1s. 2d. And I determined to improve even on that. I studied gastronomy, and the prices of all the different foods, and at length I saw my way clear. As you may remember, I opened my first restaurant in Chancery-lane.'

'I shall never forget the first meal I took there,' I put in.

He bowed, and continued:–

'I gave particular attention to a host of minor details, each, perhaps, of little importance alone, but not to be despised in the sum. For instance, I said to myself that it was as cheap in these days to decorate a dining-room artistically as to make it a horror to any person of taste. Accordingly, I bought wall papers designed by well-known men–Morris,[4] Crane,[5] Voysey,[6] Marriott[7]–and I hung up a few good prints in plain oak frames; I spent the money usually lavished on advertising in buying linen of the best quality and good cutlery, and I carefully avoided cheap earthenware and glass. I had my tables of ample width and my chairs ditto. I dressed my waitresses in dark blue, with caps and aprons of lighter tint. I took care that my kitchen should not adjoin the dining-room, and so did away with unnecessary odours.'

'But the food, the food, Mr. Bonnebouche?'

'Well, you know the quality of it. The fixed price for dinners is one shilling.'

'And a penny for the waitress?'

'No; that is forbidden. They are paid a reasonable wage. I usually give four courses–soup, fish, according to the season, meat and cheese. Of course none of the dishes is overwhelming in quantity, but when one has four courses in the middle of the day one doesn't want much of each.'

'And about drinks?'

'Water is freely supplied, and in this hot weather it is iced. A glass of lemonade may be had for one penny, and a half pint of beer or stout for twopence. If he prefers it, however, the diner may have beer, &c., instead of soup, or lemonade instead of cheese.'

'And you find this pays marvellously?'

Mr. Bonnebouche shrugged his shoulders, as if to intimate that that was a matter of common knowledge.

'I have 60 establishments in London now,' he said, 'and next month I shall open two more. Of course it pays. The wonder is that no one thought of doing what I have done before. It is obvious that if little specks of restaurants in Soho can set before their customers a certain meal for 1s. 2d. and make a profit, I, carrying on a vast business, and therefore, buying in much cheaper markets, can do the same thing for 1s; and also make a profit, perhaps a larger profit.'

I assented, and asked him if he was about to turn himself into a company.

'Yes,' he replied, 'the capital will be based on an annual profit of £50,000 per annum. Anything else you want to know?'

'That is all, and I must thank you very much for what you have told me.'

I rose to shake hands, but his figure seemed to fade away.

* * * *

'Chop, shilling; 'taters, threepence; bread, penny; one and four. Thank ye, sir.'

As I walked out of the stuffy little restaurant it came upon me that I must have been dreaming. Perhaps it was the effect of the 'chop, shilling.'

The shaded thermometer at the Law Courts stood at 82, and I thought of a certain little village by the sea where no restaurants are.

NOTES

1. *The Sun.* 25 August 1893, page 1. Signed Enoch Arnold Bennett.

2. When he first came to London, Bennett was employed as a clerk with Messrs. Le Brasseur & Oakley, New Court, Lincoln's Inn at a salary of twenty-five shillings a week. In his anonymously published autobiographical *The Truth About An Author* (1903) Bennett writes: 'This young man had invaded the town as a clerk at twenty-five shillings a week for a bed-sitting room, threepence for his breakfast, and sixpence for his vegetarian dinner' (p.194). In her *Arnold Bennett. A Biography* (1974) Margaret Drabble provides the additional information that '[h]e was quite comfortably off; he was soon given a rise, to £200 a year, which went a long way in those days .... He was able to go to theatres, to buy a book a day, to visit the music halls' (p.49).

3. Before decimalisation in February 1971 there were 20 shillings in one pound, and 12 pence in a shilling. With decimalisation the shilling was replaced by a new five-pence coin, which was initially of identical size and weight, and had the same value.

4. William Morris (1834-1896) is one of the most influential designers of the 19th century. He was instrumental in persuading Dante Gabriel Rossetti, Edward Burne-Jones, Philip Webb, Ford Maddox Brown and others to found the firm of Morris, Marshall, Faulkner and Co. in 1861, and which grew into a flourishing and fashionable decorating firm renowned for its wallpapers and textiles.

5. Walter Crane (1845-1915) is most well-known for his coloured picture books for children and for his flower books. Deeply influenced by William Morris, he played a major role in the Arts and Crafts Movement, becoming the first President of the Arts and Crafts Exhibition Society. He began designing wallpaper in 1874 and was soon recognised as the leading imaginative designer of children's wallpaper.

6.   Charles Francis Annesley Voysey (1857-1941) was an architect and furniture and textile designer. His early work, at the time Bennett cites him, embraced the design of wallpapers, fabrics and furnishings in a simple Arts and Crafts style. Bennett may have admired Voysey's 'Bird and Berries' wallpaper (circa 1893) with his signature heart motif outlined by salmon coloured berries.

7. Frederick Marriott (1860-1941) was born in Stoke-on-Trent. He was a tile painter in Shropshire before becoming art master at Goldsmith's College, London. In his early years in London Bennett lodged with the Marriotts in Victoria Grove, Chelsea, and they became lifelong friends. Any link with a professional interest in wallpaper appears tenuous, although when he arrived at Marriott's house the 'pattern of the frieze of the newly papered wall; the frieze itself astonishes [Bennett].... He can hardly believe that a grown man can take such an interest in the appearance of his wallpaper' (Drabble, p.52). Bennett dedicated his 1904 novel *A Great Man. A Frolic:* 'To My Dear Friend Frederick Marriott and to the Imperishable Memory of Old Times'.

THE RENAISSANCE OF THE ROMP.[1]

SCENE: *A box at Daly's Theatre:*[2] *performance of 'Twelfth Night':
during the interval between Acts II and III.*

ROSALYS.--How finely Viola gives the words, 'I'm the man!'
Do you know, I always think that *Twelfth Night*, and *As You
Like It*, and *Cymbeline* are so suggestive, so helpfully
suggestive, to the women of to-day.

SIR RICHARD.--??

ROSALYS.--I look upon these plays as exquisite prophetic
allegories, showing us how we may break through all
conventional barriers of sex, and take our proper place with
men in the real life and struggle of the world, without losing
one gracious quality of womanhood.

SIR RICHARD.--Pretty enough for a sonnet! The idea is, then,
that the spectacle of Ada Rehan,[3] breeched but bewitching,
will help the modern woman to smoke a cigar, command a
county council, or ride a bicycle without looking ridiculous.
Eh?

ROSALYS.--Are you ever serious, Sir Richard?

SIR RICHARD.--No, never, except when I'm hungry. It's an
indiscretion. The risk of being taken for an Apostle of
something or another is too great.

ROSALYS.--And you have no sympathy with the great sex
movement which marks the twilight of the century? You
don't wish to see woman freed from the false trammels which
have hitherto bound her? (*Leaning forward*). Frankly, Sir
Richard, you disappoint me.

SIR RICHARD.--Of course I'm old and narrow and
prejudiced--

ROSALYS.--I didn't--

SIR RICHARD.--No, I admire your self-control. I say I am old and prejudiced, but if there *is* any great sex movement, or any false trammels, then I am with you. Only--I have failed to observe any great sex movement, and as to the trammels--

ROSALYS (*pityingly*).--But surely you can see it around you. Why, at least one member of the Government is absolutely pledged to women's suffrage.[4]

SIR RICHARD.--Truly a memorable triumph for the great sex movement!

ROSALYS (*fanning herself gently*).--Of course, I was only giving an illustration, to show how far things have moved in one direction, at any rate. *Le secret d'ennuyer est celui de tout dire.*[5] But you have nothing but a sneer for the noblest aspirations, and the sincerest desires of the best of our sex.

SIR RICHARD.--Believe me, my dear young lady, you wrong me. A sneer is a sure sign of respect, and I need all my respect for myself. I should never think of lavishing it on other people's mere aspirations, however noble, even if they existed. I remember, when you were a little girl--long, long ago in the far-off--

ROSALYS.--Thanks!

SIR RICHARD.--In the far-off eighties, you would now and again have a spell of--shall I say--excessive womanishness. You used to be shocked if I stole a kiss, and your brother was a horrid *boy*, and you hated romping because it messed your frock. But after these little fits there always followed a period of violent reaction, during which you gave yourself up to leapfrog, ripped your dresses, fought, wrecked the furniture, and cried bitterly when you were not allowed to do exactly what Bob did. True, isn't it?

ROSALYS (*shrugging her shoulders*).--Exaggerated.

SIR RICHARD.--Not much. Now my idea is that your delicious sex is just at present engaged in waking up and shaking itself after a bad attack of femininity. Frocks are being torn and furniture wrecked. The man's ideal of woman--

ROSALYS.--A pretty thing that is! All you ask of us is indirect flattery and the faculty of shutting our eyes to your unspeakable wickedness.

SIR RICHARD.--I was about to say that the man's ideal of woman used to be too rife in the land. There was too much clinging drapery, shaded light, perfumed air, and anæmic innocence about your existence. The Misses Grundy--at our instigation, I admit--made for themselves, out of bread-and-butter softened by weak tea, a little god, which they called Propriety; and all who didn't bow down were branded as unsexed, and not asked to the Misses Grundy's croquet-parties. Naturally there came a reaction. Someone smashed the little bread-and-butter god with a mallet, and the usual war-dance round the mangled remains is taking place. I perceive that the metaphor is getting too hot to hold; I must drop it. In plain language, the tomboy spirit has re-appeared - it is never absent for long--and the renaissance of the romp is an accomplished fact.

ROSALYS.--And so there has been no real advance in the position of woman--only a renaissance of the romp. A comfortable doctrine, truly!

SIR RICHARD.--I don't say that. Nothing marks time, except an occasional clock, and of course there has been an advance. But you must beware of measuring the distance travelled by the amount of dust raised. A few women, working unostenta-tiously, may be, and probably are, doing something of real progressive value, but nine-tenths of the aggressive feminine activity which just now surrounds us, springs from the old, old desire of being mannish. It shows itself in different ways.

It may spend itself in hard, loyal work on a school board, or in free perspiration over a tennis tournament; or it may flower in the fatuous devilry of a Dodo--

ROSALYS.--Sir Richard!

SIR RICHARD.--I mean it. But there it is; it comes and it goes. And at the present moment it happens to have come.

ROSALYS.--My dear Sir Richard, I think you are quite wrong - and weren't you getting actually serious?

SIR RICHARD.--Was I? How particularly unwise! Ah! We must return to Shakspere.

The curtain rises on Olivia's garden.

NOTES

1. *Woman*. 28 February 1894, page 16. Signed Sarah Volatile (one of Bennett's many *noms de plume* when writing for *Woman* and other periodicals). The periodical was a penny illustrated weekly which appeared from 3 January 1890 to 9 August 1912. Bennett, with his father's financial backing, became Assistant Editor in late December 1893, and two years later, the Editor. He remained with *Woman* until September 1901. His first article for the weekly, 'Wrinkles. Supper for a Children's Party', appeared on 3 January 1894. The dramatic sketch 'Renaissance of the Romp' appeared alongside 'The Silken Serpent', his first story for *Woman.*

2. Daly's Theatre, in Leicester Square, London, opened in June 1893 (demolished in 1937). It was purpose built for the American theatrical producer Augustin Daly. Given Bennett's frequent criticism of the poor design of British theatres, particularly their bad sight-lines, he must have found Daly's Theatre a welcome change: 'The auditorium will seat upwards of twelve hundred persons, and it has been so arrayed that the public will be able to obtain a good view of the stage from all parts of the house' (The *Daily Graphic*, 28 June 1893).

3. Ada Rehan (1859-1916) was born in Ireland but when she was six was taken to the United States and began her acting career. She joined Augustin Daly's company in New York in 1878 and worked with him until his death twenty years later. She was widely admired in Europe, was the model for the statue of Justice at the 1893 Chicago World Trade Fair, and had her portrait

painted by John Singer Sargent in 1894.

At the time of Bennett's story Ada Rehan was playing the part of Viola for 119 performances at Daly's Theatre. George Bernard Shaw strongly deprecated Daly's textual cutting, but praised Ada's performance for bringing the play to life with a sense of theatrical magic.

Bennett reviewed Augustin Daly's *The Countess Gucki*, with Ada Rehan in the lead role, in his 'Music and Mummery' column (*Woman*, 15 July 1896, p.7).

4. This may be a reference to Jacob Bright MP (1821-1899), a Liberal politician who campaigned for women's rights, introducing the Second Reading of the Women's Suffrage Bill in May 1871. He was seen as a radical MP because of his support for women's suffrage.

5. 'The secret of being a bore is to tell everything': Voltaire (1694-1778), *Sept Discours en Vers sur l'Homme* (1738).

LITTLE POPOW.[1]

From the French of
GEORGES D'ESPARBES.[2]

The little *moujik*[3] Stazzewsko stretches himself and gets up.

It is early morning.

The pigeons are cooing and pecking at the thatch - the cottage is thatched with the straw of Indian corn. The horses, uneasy and wakeful, are snorting in the stable. Stazzewsko begins to dress himself; he strides hastily into his *Lesghis*[4] pantaloons, carefully envelopes his feet in *onoutchi*–four bands of red wool, crossed–and lastly puts on his *shouba*,[5] that superb *shouba* which cost two roubles and a year's harvest of honey.

His wife Kiwkine falls asleep again. He rubs her nose with his finger and tickles her on both cheeks, wakening her up.

'I'm off to town,' he says, 'to grandfather's, to get those things you asked for, a flute that will play higher than cousin Serkow's, and the fat sheep that you are going to broil for Lent.'

Kiwkine smiles sleepily.

'I shall take Popow with me; the air is fresh; and the trip will do the little fellow good. I'll wake him. Popow! Popow! I'll rouse him up.'

And the little *moujik* begins to laugh boisterously.

The *moujik* is a good fellow. He is a shoemaker by trade. He goes regularly to church, and never uses bad language. He makes the sign of the cross when he sees a funeral, says a prayer every night, and well knows that if his hand harnesses the horse, it is the Lord who guides him.

He wakes his son, and little Popow rubs his eyes at the gentle blows. Then the *moujik* puts on a big, rough voice:

'I'm off to town to find a flute and a sheep,' he says. 'Who wants to go with me?'

'I do,' cries little Popow.

He lifts the child out of bed, perches him on his shoulders, and descends to the stable. Then he gets the carriage out and harnesses the horses to the leathern shafts. Look at the dawn; a fresh lilac tint spreads itself over the Eastern sky!

Stazzewkso and little Popow are in the carriage comfortably seated and well wrapped up. The *moujik* starts the horses with a touch, and throws a kiss to his wife:--

'Dove of my dwelling,' his voice comes to her on the breeze, 'Dear Snowdrop, Kiwkine! I will bring thee the flute and the sheep to-night.' And so they disappear.

*　　*　　*　　*　　*

They are gone. The wife feels uneasy as she watches them fly down the road. 'Heaven send they are not frost-bitten on the way, and the horses are nimble.' She goes into the house, lights a taper before the *icona*, kneels down, and says these verses:--

The Lord will protect them that fear Him.

The breath of the Lord is a divine lamp, which uncovereth the wickedness in Man's bosom.

Let us prepare our souls, let us govern our tongue.

Let us observe the law.

Father and son traverse fields and plains. The carriage rolls swiftly along. Popow questions the *moujik*; he is eight years old, and a good little chap.

'Father, what art thou getting the sheep for?'

'For the festival of Lent. We must take care to find the family plenty to eat.'

'And the flute, father?'

'The flute is for the bees. The bees are like ordinary people, they like music.'

That satisfies Popow. He is a curious child, given to reflection. Underneath that beautiful head of hair hover some sober thoughts, but they are happy ones, and the child smiles gravely.

'I shall pick the sheep's bones,' he sings out presently, 'and I shall play on the flute.'

The *moujik* whips up his black horses.

'Come, my little papa; come, my little pigeon!'

And the horses fly on their way. They leave behind roads, ditches, banks, streams. And suddenly they come out upon the steppe which spreads in front of them like a sea.

They gallop! They gallop! The axle seems equal to every strain, whether they jolt through ruts or over stones. The lilac tint ascends higher and higher into the sky, and the sun appears. Popow claps his hands.

'Good, it is day!'

To amuse the child, Stazzewsko sings him a Siberian exile song, all about the police and the *pomeschtchik*.[6]

The *pomeschtchik* has a green eye,

Aï, aï, tra-ra-raï, aï!

Holy Virgin! He has a green eye.

'Against whom art thou singing?' asks little Popow, aghast.

'Against the lords, the masters of the soil.'

'The soil, what is that?'

'The land, the earth.'

Popow does not understand.

'The earth has masters, then?' he asks innocently.

But the *moujik* does not answer at first. He whips up the horses again, and shouts in a furious voice:

'Kss. Kss. Little demons!'

Then he turns to his son:

'The poor speak only by supplications; the rich respond only with hard words.'

'And we, father, are we rich or poor?'

'We are a little of both,' says the *moujik* simply.

* * * *

Noon. They have reached the great town. Grandfather is quite pleased to see them; he laughs with little shakes; he makes them drink a bottle of tea, offers them cake, gives the *moujik* a pipe, and Popow an earthenware Cossack which puts out its tongue. He asks how the shoes are selling, if honey is plentiful, and whether Kiwkine is quite well.

When the *moujik* can get in a word, he says:–

'I have come for a fat sheep.'

'No use; the last was sold this morning.'

'Also a shrill flute.'

'Ah! I've got three beauties.'

The *moujik* plays on all three flutes, and chooses the one that makes the most noise.

Then they go for a stroll through the town. They gaze at the pretty barinias[7] lounging on cushions, at the shops, and at the people in the street who are talking French. And when they have feasted their eyes, the *moujik* decides:

'Time's up. We must set out.'

'Go, my son,' says grandfather; 'and God keep thee.'

And now father and son are flying homewards over the fields and plains. And just as in the morning, Popow questions his father.

'Father, thou hast the flute?'

'Yes.'

'And the bees love music, really?'

'Like ordinary people,' replies Stazzewsko. And he gives the reins a shake. 'Get on, my little papa; get on, my little pigeon!'

The two horses fly on their way. They leave behind roads, ditches, banks, streams. And suddenly they come out upon the steppe, which spreads in front of them like a sea.

They gallop! They gallop! The axle seems equal to any strain, whether they jolt through ruts or over stones. The hyacinth tint of evening ascends from the horizon, and the moon appears. Popow claps his hands.

'Good, the night!'

Once more the *moujik* murmurs the Siberian exile song:–

The *pomeschtchik* has a green eye,

Aï, aï, tra-ra-raï, aï!

Holy Virgin! He has a green eye!

For two hours they gallop along. The crescent moon

shines bright. The steam from the horses ascends in wreaths of mist. Their eight hoofs beat the ground together like one stroke.

'Kss! Kss! On! On! my butterflies!' cries the *moujik*.

But down below, near the wheel, two white specks suddenly light up, and these dots of fire follow the flying horses. The *moujik* shivers slightly, a little shiver that runs down his back. But he is a brave man, this Stazzewsko, and he lashes the wolf across the eyes with his whip. The animal drops behind, and reappears on the other side of the vehicle. And even while the *moujik* is cutting at him with the whip other dots of fire light up in the darkness, and now two wolves are in pursuit. They leap up out of the mist, and gaze at the *moujik* hungrily, silently.

Stazzewsko is afraid. He looks round the dark landscape, and then he sees, not four, but ten fiery specks, skipping along with the carriage.

'Ho! ho! Little pigeon; little papa! Quicker, quicker.'

And the excited animals lift their feet and stretch their necks, gasping. They move so fast that they look like serpents.

'Ho! Ho! Kss! Kss!' yells Stazzewsko.

The *moujik* stands erect, the reins tightened, his cap at the back of his head, and his eyes wide open, like circles, staring into the night. Ah! this is not a mere pack, it is a multitude at his heels. You can hear them running at top speed, their paws striking the ground like the passing of a herd.

'Ho! Ho! Little pigeon, little papa! On! On! Quicker!'

The carriage flies.

It is like a running shadow. Stazzewsko straightens himself, a mournful postillion with gleaming eyes! He is afraid, afraid. He fancies the wolves are about to leap upon him, to grip his jacket, to wrench his arm, to spring at the horses, to sever the reins, to tear his child to pieces. Popow is quite happy. Sitting on the floor of the carriage, he is ignorant of the danger. Now and then he blows a note on the flute, his eyes turned towards the stars.

'Ho! Ho! Kss! Kss!'

Poor Stazzewsko. He thinks of his wife, pretty and blonde, who awaits them; of the pearl barley broth which is steaming on the dresser; of the account he should give of the journey. But here are wolves, wolves, wolves, enraged, implacable, increasing by twenties and by hundreds, hungry to see a horse stumble. The fierce wind strikes the *moujik* full in the face, and every mouthful of the sharpened air freezes him to the bone.

'Clic! Clac! Ho! Ho! Kss! Kss!'

A wolf has leaped onto the seat and bitten his boot. Stazzewkso utters a cry, and seizing the animal by the hair of his jaw, dashes it to the ground. But a sudden access of terror overcomes him. He jumps on the crupper of one of the horses, and weeps over his faithful beasts.

'Quicker, my lamb! Quicker, my pigeon! It is for Popow!'

Flight. Terror. Darkness.

'Holy Virgin!' howls Stazzewsko, suddenly.

A wolf is clinging to the shafts. Stazzewkso slides from the horse back into the carriage. He raises the tilt, and looks....

There are a hundred, three hundred, five hundred, a thousand. They have the appearance of a huge, uneasy shadow, a sea of stars–the firmament of hell reflected in the steppe.

And all the time the *moujik* shouts:–

'Ho! ho! Kss! Kss!'

But he has lost hope. He is panting! Popow has dropped the flute, the pretty flute which the bees love.

'Popow!' the *moujik* cries, suddenly.

'What father?' murmurs the child.

'Popow!' sobs the *moujik*.

'Father, father, what is it?'

'Popow, thou seest the wolves!'

'Yes, father, yes!'

'How can we stop them?'

'Father, the flute–'

'They will kill us.'

'No, father. If the bees like music, the wolves–'

But Popow does not finish. The *moujik* seizes the child by the throat, blaspheming God, and brays to his horses in the darkness–

And with a terrific, despairing effort, he throws Popow to the wolves!

The black crowd stops, then . . . . It stays to divide the prey, and the carriage continues on its route.

Now it has passed the steppe. Look! The horses slacken their pace; they enter the yard; lights are out, but the wife, Kiwkine, the mother of little Popow, pretty and blonde, stands waiting on the threshold.

'Well, Stazz, my beloved Stazz, have you had a quiet journey? Was Popow cold? Have the horses run well?'

But the little *moujik* does not answer. He laughs. He whistles on the flute....

He is mad.

NOTES

1. *Woman*. 21 March 1894, pages 14-15. Signed E.A.B.

A month earlier, 29 February 1894, Bennett had published his version of Rémy de Gourmont's 'The Silken Serpent' in *Woman*. (*Uncollected Short Stories*, pages 56-59.) This and 'Little Popow' appear to be his only story translations, both published very early in his writing career.

Bennett readily acknowledged the influence of French writers on his own work, claiming that his long-lasting career as a literary critic began in the early 1890s when he sent an unsolicited review of a French book to the *Illustrated London News:*

> Forty years ago, when I was free-lancing, I wrote a review of a book by an obscure French author and sent it in to the *Illustrated London News*. Nothing more ignorantly foolish than such a journalistic proceeding could be conceived. As if editors of great papers accepted from outsiders reviews of books of no importance whatever! Still, the review was accepted. It did not appear for many weeks, and I spent a large part of my remuneration (15s.) in vainly buying issues of the paper week

after week at sixpence a time; but it did at last appear.('I Am Not An
Amateur Reviewer', 10 July 1930,
reprinted in *Evening Standard Years*, p.391)

Whilst Bennett's Francophile sentiment is evident, his recall of events may be
confused since the review that did 'at last appear' in the *Illustrated London
News* was of works by Andrew Lang (18 November 1893) and Heinrich Heine
(24 March 1894), the latter only three days after 'Little Popow' appeared.

Bennett published 'Little Popow' under his own initials, although the story
seems to have first appeared in an English translation by Mrs George F.
Duysters in two Australian newspapers some two years earlier. Both *The
Argus* (Melbourne, Victoria, 1848-1956, 28 May 1892, p. 4) and the *Western Mail*
(Perth, Western Australia, 1885-1954, 25 June 1892, p. 29) printed the story
under the title 'Stazzemsko, The Moujik [From the French of D'Esparbes]'.

Whilst the plot remains the same, there are significant differences in the
translation. Mrs. Duyster's opening reads:

It is morning. The little moujik Stazzemsko arises, very drowsy yet.
The pigeons, cooing, brush their wings lightly against the roof of yellow
straw. The horses are snorting impatiently over their mangers. The
moujik pulls a pair of trousers of Lesghis cloth, wraps his feet with the
onoutchi, four bands of red wool folded crosswise, and to complete his
costume puts on the schouba, the comfortable schouba, very long and
very warm, which cost two roubles and a year's harvesting of money.

She concludes her story:

'Well! Stazz, dear Stazz, hast thou had a peaceful journey? Was Popow
cold? Did the horses go well?'
But the moujik answers not. He plays upon the flute, laughing long
and loud, a strange shuddering laugh, for his mind is dead to all things.

2. Georges Auguste Esparbès (1863-1944) was a popular French writer, many
of whose stories appeared in *La Plume,* a magazine devoted to promoting a
wide range of artistic talent. Under its motto 'For Art' it published work by
Paul Verlaine and Stéphane Mallarmé, together with illustrations by Henri de
Toulouse-Lautrec, Paul Gaugin and Camille Pissarro.

3. The term refers to a Russian peasant and suggests a degree of poverty.

4. A tribe in the Caucasus who were eventually subjugated and brought
under Russian rule.

5. A wide sleeved long fur robe, open down the front with waist length sleeves.

6. Feudal landlords.

7. Well-to-do female landowners.

VARNISH AND VANITY AT THE R.A.[1]

Once hung, twice sky.
-- Whistler.[2]

In the world where one exhibits one gets up early on Varnishing Day, especially if one is a woman. And one generally *is* a woman–everybody knows that the Royal Academy Exhibition is painted chiefly by R.A.'s, Associates, and women; and the two former classes total a bare seventy together. It is an understood thing that on that great day the woman who paints, for pelf or pastime, goes forth arrayed by Worth[3] (on the other 364 days she is usually dowdy), arrives early, and stays till she is turned out.

And however early one arrives, there is surely a rude, pushing, excited crowd round the table on which the catalogue lies. And until one has, by physical force or clever stratagem, got sight of that catalogue, and ascertained one's numbers, one throws to the winds all rules of politeness, all thought of consideration for others.

'Am I skied or am I not skied?' That is the question.

Then the rush, or the studiedly calm walk, into the rooms, the wild glance round, the divine ecstasy of seeing one's canvas well placed! Who can describe the thrill of thrills?

There is pleasure in the shine
Of your picture on the line
At the Royal Acade-my,

says Rudyard Kipling,[4] but even he, who doesn't know what literary fear is, has never dared to put that pleasure on paper. Only Shakspeare could have done it, and in his day Academies were not, neither art-critics. And if one's picture *is* in the clouds, a sort of ceiling decoration, even then one feels that a work of such conspicuous merit cannot fail to be noticed by all discerning persons. And as for the ruck of Philistines–a fig for them!

At length one stealthily glances round to see if anyone else is looking at *the* picture, and one finds that its existence is positively ignored.

'Good morning, Miss Crosshatch,' one says, seeing an acquaintance. 'So glad to see you. What have you here? Are you well hung?'

'Two on the line. Have you *many* in?'

('Many!' Horrid thing! But one must smile.)

'Only one; not *quite* on the line. Over there, see?'

'Ah, yes,' says Miss Crosshatch. 'It's *rather* high, don't you think? Very pretty little thing. *Cows*, is it?'

'No. Er–it's called "Maiden meditation fancy free," study of a girl's head. *Au revoir*. See you again later.'

The galleries are just comfortably full. Everybody is excited, and everybody is talking to everybody. The place looks much as it does on an ordinary day, except that steps are scattered about, and that some of the very, very important works are carefully veiled from the common artistic eye. They say that that large affair on the left will be the picture of the year. It is by Simeon Stylites, A.R.A., the renowned painter of 'Baby's Tub,' and represents a child feeding a pussy cat with strawberry jam. One hears that the *Graphic*[5] people have bought it for two thousand guineas.

Ah! There is Mr. Stylites himself, and, as one has the inexpressible honour of his acquaintance, one bows. He is talking to Mr. John Parker, the American portrait painter. 'L. S. D.,' an etcher and the critic of the *Tatler*, says that Mr. Parker is perhaps the greatest *painter* (the italics are L. S. D.'s) since Velasquez, and he certainly gets five hundred guineas for a portrait. He is, in fact, a great artist, but if he didn't charge so much he wouldn't get a single commission.

'James, dear,' says Mrs. Nouveau-Riche to her beloved. 'I'm told that Mr. Parker, the American, charges five hundred guineas for a portrait. You positively must ask him to paint mine, and I'll wear my diamonds.'

'Very well, love.'

It is only when the portrait is finished that the trouble begins. For Mr. Parker is what is called a painter's painter. Ordinary persons don't quite see the point of his work. Sometimes the ordinary person indignantly refuses to accept a commissioned portrait. Then Mr. Parker introduces a few accessories, and calls it 'The Reading Girl,' or 'Portrait of a Man,' and the French Government or the Corporation of Liverpool buys it, and the dilettanti travel hundreds of miles to see it.

But to return to one's varnishing. It is curious that the creators of all the pictures which happen to be on the line are assiduously at work, either touching up or varnishing. They never leave them. They hold miniature receptions and consume sandwiches in the immediate vicinity, but they never desert those immortal works. While on the other hand, although steps are provided for the especial purpose of reaching them, the skied canvases are left alone in all the height of their glory. One does not like to acknowledge publicly that one is skied.

The day wears on, and at length even the most diligent and inventive have done everything to their pictures that possibly can be done. As for the aquarellists, the pastellists, the etchers, the sculptors, the architects, and the black-and-white people generally, they naturally don't come to varnish, even in theory. They come simply to gaze and to gossip. So do the oil painters, for the matter of that. One's enthusiasm for one's own work grows less absorbing, and one asks the question which everyone has asked at least a dozen times during the day: 'Is it a good Academy?'

'Pretty fair,' says Mr. Simeon Stylites.

'There isn't a single square inch of real *painting* in it,' says 'L.S.D.,' etcher and critic.

And the general verdict is, indeed, somewhat pessimistic. One hears that the President has done nothing remarkable this year, that Duck, the new A.R.A., from whom so much was expected, has sent all his stuff to the New, and that that terrible Stipplefinick, R.A., has had the impudence to send six canvases of vast acreage.

'Stipplefinick ought to have been a scene painter,' says 'L.S.D.,' etcher and critic.

Going out, one meets Miss Bella Siffleuse,[6] whose large picture has the place of honour.

'My *dear*!' she says in her patronising way, 'I didn't know *you* exhibited.'

'Oh! yes, I've been sending pictures here for ten years.'

'Really now–'

'But they were always rejected.'

NOTES

1. *Woman*. 9 May 1894, pages 3-4. Signed Sarah Volatile.

2. James Abbott McNeill Whistler (1834-1903) was an American born, British based artist. His troubled relationship with the conservatively-biased Royal Academy dates back to 1861 when his first famous work, *Symphony in White, No.1: The White Girl*, was refused exhibition space. Whistler remained frustrated over both the irregular acceptance and poor hanging of his paintings for exhibition. When he was later invited to exhibit with the British contingent at the 1893 World's Columbian Exposition in Chicago he recalled past grudges at being 'skied' - hung well above eye level, making viewing difficult and carrying a suggestion of lesser artistic work - in replying to the Royal Academy's Secretary J.M.Beck: 'Pray convey my distinguished consideration to the President [Sir Frederick Leighton], and say that I have an undefined sense of something ominously flattering occurring - but that no previous desire on his part ever to deal with work of mine, has prepared me with the proper sort of acknowledgment. No! no Mr. Beck - "Once hung - twice Sky!"' (July 1892)

One of Bennett's earliest stories, 'The Artist's Model' (*Tit-Bits*, 6 May 1893), featured an artist who suffered from being 'skied': 'Unless he could in some way arrest the attention of the public he would probably remain all his life an ill-paid designer. True, by some freak of fortune, one of his pictures had once been exhibited at the Royal Academy. But it was 'skied', - not a single critic noticed it and it was reproduced in none of the illustrated catalogues.' (*Uncollected Stories*, p.35).

3. Charles Frederick Worth (1826-1895), widely regarded as the father of haute couture, was an English fashion designer who rose to fame after moving to Paris in 1846.

Published in the *Woman Literary Supplement* just one week before 'Varnish and Vanity at the R.A.', Bennett's story 'Five o'Clock at the Heroines' Club. A Fantasia' also made reference to Worth: 'I obsessed that although few of these were dressed according to the latest modes, yet none of them seemed old fashioned, while some of the youngest girls, gowned by Worth... were already beginning to look out of date.' (*Uncollected Stories*, p.72).

4. Rudyard Kipling (1865-1936), 'The Naulahka' (excerpt):

> There is pleasure in the wet, wet clay
> When the artist's hand is potting it.
> There is pleasure in the wet, wet lay
> When the poet's pad is blotting it.
> There is pleasure in the shine of your picture on the line
> At the Royal Acade-my,
> But the pleasure felt in these is chalk to Cheddar cheese
> When it comes to a well made Lie.

The Naulahka, A Story of West and East, written partly in collaboration with Walcott Balestier, was serialised in the *Century Magazine* from November 1891 to July 1892. The story originally appeared without chapter headings - a pamphlet, 'Rhymed Chapter Headings', was printed in 1892 to establish copyright and these verse headings were then included in subsequent book editions.

5. *The Graphic* was an illustrated weekly newspaper, published under this title from December 1869 to April 1932. Bennett's sole contribution to the journal was a three-part serialisation of 'From the Log of the Velsa' in July-August 1914.

6. A typical example of Bennett's knowing humour, since Miss Bella Siffleuse translates literally as Miss Beautiful Whistler.

ON GROWING OLD.[1]

I did not know her name, but she had large eyes, and I do so
hate an afternoon call. Mrs. Vivian had seated herself in a
way which I well know indicated an hour of leisure; and the
girl was my nearest neighbour. Moreover, it was a retired
little nook. I had not been to the theatre, I had not seen Duse;[2]
since I went to a dance my hair has grown grey; and on Sir
Henry Irving[3] and Sir Walter Besant's[4] productions I hold no
opinion whatever. Finally, I have not put my head inside
Burlington House[5] for years. So I had seized the bull by the
horns; it was the only thing to do.

'I--I don't think I quite understand,' said she. 'Let us put
it in this way,' said I. 'Happiness is the stuff of our dreams;
pleasure is the phantom we pursue; and life is the little
course between two goals. Do you follow me?' 'Two goals!'
she said with some perplexity. 'Certainly,' I answered
gravely. 'We make a hurried entrance into life, but it is death
we seek most. Surely you have not lived so far without
discovering that.' 'But I don't--but you seem--I don't think
people want to die,' she protested at length. 'And why not?'
I asked severely. 'Oh, because--.' She looked about her. 'Oh, I
think people are quite happy as a rule, you know.' 'You
speak,' said I, 'out of your personal feelings, I suppose. Who
are you to judge for others? Do you think that the elderly
lady in the grey dress yonder–the one with the glasses, I
mean--is not fulfilled with the desire of death? Better for her,
far better, a quiet corner in the grave than this withered,
querulous existence under skies that freckle beauty and rains
that spoil silk dresses.' The lady in question turned a serene
glance upon us and smiled at my companion. 'Oh, but you
are quite mistaken,' said she eagerly; 'that is my aunt.' I was
a little taken aback, but I dared not face silence, and I could
not remember the name of any novel, so I pushed forward
desperately.

'Well, then, take yourself,' said I sternly; 'you are quite happy, you say. Perhaps you have a lover.' My young lady blushed, and shook her head; she suddenly displayed a restless desire to leave me. 'No, no,' said I. 'This is not idle curiosity; the philosophic mind takes no account of personalities. Let us discuss the matter freely and with proper solemnity.' She looked at me timorously. 'If you have no lover you will have one soon. Is not that so?' 'You ask such strange things,' she murmured. 'Let us say then that for the next five years of your life you will continue in your supposititious state of content,' I went on with logical calm. 'Granted. And after that?' She shifted uneasily on her seat. 'Oh, I'm sure I don't–perhaps I shall–I suppose I shall be– married,' she murmured. 'Very well,' said I cheerfully. 'Let us suppose that too. And then?' She moved with more uneasiness; a colour struck into her cheeks. 'Come, come,' said I peremptorily, 'and then?' 'Really,' she said, 'you are so–I'm sure I don't know.' 'Oh, well I think we may take it for granted,' said I. This time I believe she would really have made a bolt for it, but I had no desire to be left stranded, and so I took an heroic course. I put my hand on her arm. 'I'm sure,' said I, with kind gravity, 'that you are too sensible a girl to wish to shirk a great moral problem like this. It is our duty to understand these things.' She regarded me doubtfully and timidly. 'You–think it is?' she asked. I bowed my head. 'Now then, let us continue. We will add to the hypothesis that the new–er–condition of–'. My young lady coughed. 'Well, the new surroundings and responsibilities will maintain the lump sum of your happiness a few more years–what after that?' 'I don't see,' faltered she, with rising colour, 'that it need be-that it is necessary to leave off caring so soon for–for–' 'Husband and children?' I ended for her. 'Yes,' she murmured faintly. I looked at her, critically. 'You are a vigorous woman of intelligence,' I said dispassionately. 'Can you conceive yourself satisfied, say, in ten years' time with a husband who grumbles and gambles, and a pack of children who eat the heart from your life and confine and wear away your individuality? Would you view without emotion the process of your own conversion into a vegetable, bound by its roots and decaying on its stalk?' 'You–I think you are very cynical,' said she in some confusion. 'Or take it at the best,' I resumed. 'See, your beauty fades,'--she blushed again–'your straight young figure goes,'--the blush was still there–'and you settle down with grey hairs to a placid indifference, for all the world like–that dear lady over there,' said I, indicating a stout woman who was at that moment engaging in a lively conversation with Mrs. Vivian.

'But that is my mother,' said she quickly. I wondered why Mrs. Vivian did not move. Really it was intolerable, and afternoon calls are always abominable. After that, of course, I dared not continue, and I was racking my brains for some quite remote and innocent topic. I vaguely wondered if the weather would suit. But to my surprise it was she who resumed the conversation. She did not seem offended; she only looked troubled. 'I think,' she said, 'that you are a little hard on elderly people. They–they have their consolations.' 'Indeed,' said I, grateful for her toleration, 'that I should know very well myself. But youth, youth!' There was a slight contraction in her forehead. 'I–I don't think all people grow old the same way,' she ventured. That was quite true, and I said so. She seemed relieved. 'There is the dignity of age, you know,' she said. 'Certainly,' I remarked, drawing myself up. 'And then you get to know so much,' she added quite cheerfully. 'Oh, yes, we get to know a great deal,' I agreed affably. 'I think it would be quite nice to be old,' she asserted boldly. 'It is not pretty,' said I, reviewing my face in the mirror. She shuffled a little and was silent. 'But some people may keep their looks,' she said hesitatingly. 'Oh, yes,' I cried, and feeling called upon to make some amends for my blunder I referred politely to her mother. Strange to say she did not take the compliment as I had expected. I added to it. 'Few people,' said I, 'retain their looks as well as she has done.' 'Do you think so?' she asked, with some disappointment. 'Now I come to think of it,' I said, 'I do not remember any one who–. You can see, too, that she must have had a very fine figure when she was young, much the same as–.' I looked at my companion. I think she winced, but I will swear that till that moment I had no idea what had put her out. There was quite a long pause, and then, 'Do you think,' she observed with an air of great indifference and philosophy, 'that children always take after their parents in– physically, you know?' I could not help it. 'Almost always,' I said, decidedly and after reflection. Her face certainly fell. She sighed. 'It is nice to be young,' she said. I suppose she had given it up.

NOTES

1. *Pall Mall Gazette*. 29 June 1895, page 3. Unsigned. (Anita Miller explains in her *Annotated Bibliography*, pp. xviii-xix, that she identifies anonymous contributions through Bennett's letters, journals and reminiscences, and wherever possible by additionally confirming them against reminiscences of those who could speak with the greatest authority about his work - for example, Lewis Hind, the editor of the *Academy* during the Bennett years). Founded in 1865 with the crusading journalist W. T. Stead as editor, the *Gazette* was acquired in 1892 by the American millionaire William Waldorf Astor, who converted it from a radical to a conservative paper. It eventually merged with the *Evening Standard*.

Bennett contributed four articles to the *Gazette* (between 1894-1911) of which 'On Growing Old' was the only fictional piece.

2. Eleonora Duse (1858-1924) was an Italian actress often known, as in Bennett's story, simply as Duse. Born in Vigevano, Lombardy, she began acting in the family troupe at the age of four. She gained her first major success in Europe before touring in South America, Russia and the United States. John Singer Sargent painted her portrait in 1893 and she later became the first woman (and Italian) to feature on the cover of *Time* magazine (1923).

Bennett reviewed her appearances at the London Lyceum Theatre in 'At the Play', *Hearth and Home*, (24 May 1900, p.132).

3. Sir Henry Irving (1838-1905) was an English actor-manager who played the leading classical roles for many seasons at the Lyceum between 1878 and 1902. He was the first actor to be awarded a knighthood.

Bennett reviewed five of Irving's performances at the Lyceum between September 1896 and April 1899 in *Woman*.

4. Sir Walter Besant (1836-1921) was a novelist, historian and philanthropist. Bennett reviewed several of his books between March 1895 and October 1902. (See also Note 6 'The Advanced Woman'.)

5. Burlington House, originally a private Palladian mansion in Piccadilly, became home to the Royal Academy in 1867.

THE TRAIN.[1]

ARTHUR - - - aged 22 } affianced.
ROSE - - - - aged 20 }
BILL - - - - any age.

*A diminutive railway station, where the signal is always down,
ready for the next train; single line; porter sort of person
supporting himself against the station shanty; late September
evening; lovely sunset; sound of the sea in the distance.*

I.

ARTHUR (*rushing into the station panting; he wears
flannels and is trailing a lady's macintosh and a banjo*).–I say,
what time is it?

BILL - Don't know, sir. Station clock stopped.

ROSE - (*gasping two seconds after*). Has the 5.50 gone,
anyway?

BILL - No, it ain't.

ARTHUR - That's all right, then. How long will it be?

BILL - Don't know.

ARTHUR - Where's the stationmaster?

BILL - I'm the stationmaster.

ROSE - Oh!

BILL - *And* the ticket clerk, *and* the signalman, *and* the
foreman porter, *and* the inspector.

Arnold Bennett's Christmas entertainment.
(*Woman*. December 1897.)

ARTHUR - Well, if you happen to be the traffic superintendent of this division also, would you mind telling us how long you *think* the 5.50 will be?

BILL (*surveying the entire landscape as if in search of inspiration*) - I should say, judging by the sun, 'alf a hour, or 'ardly–that is, taking a average like. It's always from five minutes to a hour late.

ROSE - Thank you *so* much.

ARTHUR (*watching Bill as he fades away into the recesses of the shanty*) - A character, that! Now, miss, what shall we do?

ROSE - We shall sit down and rest. I don't know why we ran so hard. We might have known the train would be late.

ARTHUR - Never mind; if you had brought your watch . . .

ROSE - If you had brought yours . . .

ARTHUR - No sensible man carries a watch when he wears flannels.

ROSE - Oh, doesn't he?

ARTHUR - No, he doesn't . . . (*Seeing a look on Rose's face he stops, and then takes measures to cure it.*)

ROSE (*angelic*) - Where shall we sit?

ARTHUR (*glancing round*) - There positively isn't a seat.

ROSE (*with woman's wit*) - Yes, there is! (*She plumps down on the edge of the platform, her feet overhanging the rails. Arthur does likewise, evidently determined that they shall occupy as little of the platform as possible.*)

"*Well, if you happen to be the traffic superintendent of this division also, would you mind telling us how long you think the 5.50 will be?*"

ARTHUR (*sighing*). - Ah! What a holiday it has been!

ROSE (*sighing in unison*). - And to-morrow it is over.

ARTHUR - Yes, to-morrow I shall be back in Gray's Inn.[2]

ROSE - And to-morrow I shall be back in Leeds.

They comfort each other.

ARTHUR (*cheerfully kicking his feet against the stonework*). - But I shall see you again at Christmas; and by that time I shall be a real live barrister.

ROSE - But there are so many barristers.

ARTHUR - Just so. That's what relieves my mind. One more or less–what does it matter? I shall be raking the dollars together in no time. Then there will be a certain wedding.

ROSE (*in maiden meditation*). - Ah!

ARTHUR - How long have we been engaged?

ROSE (*promptly*). - Forty-six hours.

ARTHUR - It seems years.

The sun sinks lingeringly; the ceaseless chant of the unseen waves bears its own message to the lovers, who, yielding to the delicious influences of the scene and of the moment, begin to occupy even less of the platform than before. Pause. Statuesque immobility. Twilight gently supervenes. Bill, singing to himself within the shanty, breaks and dissolves the beauteous dream.

ARTHUR - I wonder how long we've sat here?

ROSE - It seems rather a long time.

"' Ah ! what a holiday it has been !'"

ARTHUR - I fancy I shall soon be hungry.

ROSE (*maternally; fumbling in her pocket*). - Was it hungry then?

ARTHUR - Yes, it was, it was.

ROSE - Then it shan't be. (*She produces two small apples and a paper of sandwiches.*) Now, sandwiches first, apples for dessert.

After the repast, Arthur jumps down on to the line, and stands facing Rose, his eyes mischievous.

ROSE (*contemplating him*). - Well, Mr. Pet.

ARTHUR (*giant refreshed*). - Mr. Pet give Mrs. Pet a nice big ride?

ROSE - No, no.

But he picks her up and is walking down the line with her in his arms, when Bill appears. Rose wriggles hurriedly to her feet. They endeavour not to look like school children, and don't succeed.

BILL (*unmoved*). - Telegram from the junction . . . . There won't be no 5.50 to-night.

ARTHUR (*indignantly*). - Why won't there be a 5.50 to-night?

BILL - Because there won't. Because there's been a bit of an accident, and the line's blocked.

ROSE - Will there be *any* train to-night?

BILL - No, there won't. (*He re-enters the shanty.*)

ARTHUR - This is disgusting, these railways . . .

ROSE - Whatever will papa and mamma think? We can't walk back, I suppose?

ARTHUR - Walk back! Sixteen miles! *You* can't. You must stay at the nearest hotel, and I'll walk home and relieve the anxious parents. (*Calling to the stationmaster-porter.*) I say!

ROSE - If we only had our bicycles.

ARTHUR - Oh, shut up. (*Bawling.*) I say!

BILL (*reappearing*) - Sir?

ARTHUR - Where is the nearest hotel?

BILL - There ain't no nearest hotel . . . only a few cottages, overcrowded, as you might say, already. There's nothink within ten miles of this 'ere station as 'll shelter *you*.

ARTHUR - Oh, but there must be.

BILL - Must there? Better go and find it then. I don't know on it.

ROSE - Well, then, what's the station for?

BILL - Don't know.

ARTHUR - Where do you sleep?

BILL (*pointing to the attic window of the station shanty*) - I sleep there.

ROSE - What a pretty window.

> *Long silence, during which they stare at one another.*

BILL (*extremely confused*). - You're welcome to my room, miss.

ARTHUR - The very thing! And I'll get off home . . .

ROSE - What! And leave poor me alone? Arthur!

ARTHUR - !!!

Bill slips away.

ROSE - Of course if you *wish* to go . . .

ARTHUR - I have it (*timidly*), I've often wanted to do it. I will stay under your window–serenade sort of thing–moonlight, love songs, you know.

ROSE (*clapping her hands*). - Oh, how lovely! But won't you be bored?

ARTHUR (*with ineffable scorn*). - Bored! Under *your* window! My dear . . .

II.

ARTHUR (*gazing at the upper window*). - Comfy up there?

ROSE - Yes, thanks. It's quite remarkably clean. (*Whispers*) Where's the porter?

ARTHUR - Oh! He's asleep in what I suppose they call the ticket office, snoring.

Silence. Twilight deepens.

ROSE - I can see a star.

ARTHUR (*meaningly*). - So can I.

Silence. Night falls. Arthur fingers the banjo.

ROSE - Darlingest.

ARTHUR - Yes, darlingest.

ROSE - Are you going to sing?

ARTHUR - Of course . . . But you know, I can't play while you are looking out. You must go inside.

ROSE (*with sweet surrender*). - Nighty nighty!

ARTHUR - Night night. Leave the window open.

The evening breeze wanders wilfully through the adjacent foliage, and lifts Arthur's straw hat off. He jams it on tightly, and arranges himself with the banjo.

THE BANJO (*feeling its way*). -
   Ponk-pink, pink, ponk,
   Ponk-pink, pink, ponk,
    Pink, pink, pink, pink, pink, pink, ponk-pink.

ARTHUR (melodious) -
   I arise from dreams of thee,[3]
    In the first sweet sleep of night,
   When the winds are breathing low,
    And the stars are shining bright:
   I arise from dreams of thee,
    And a spirit in my feet
   Hath led me-who knows how?
    To thy chamber window, sweet!

SOFT WHISPER (*from within*) - It's awfully pretty, Artie dear.

THE BANJO (*elated*) -
   Tump, timp-tump, timp,

Tu-u-u-u-mp, timp,
Tump.

Pause. The earth stands still in anticipation.

ARTHUR (*a pent volcano*). -
The wandering airs they faint
On the dark, the silent stream
(and so on)
The nightingale's complaint,
It dies upon her heart.
(Arthur bursts forth like a flame)
As I must on thine,
O! beloved as thou art!
(with an ineffable pianissimo)
O lift me from the grass
I die! I faint! I fall!
(and so on)
(self-pityingly)
My cheek is cold and white, alas!
My heart beats loud and fast;
Oh! Press it close to thine again,
Where it will break at last.

THE BANJO (*conclusive*).–
Pawnk–
Ponk.

*Arthur listens for the Soft Whisper, but hears nothing except the
waves and the rising wind.
He coughs. No sound.*

ARTHUR - Rosie.

Only the sea answers.

ARTHUR - Rosie.

VOICE (*from within, rather loud and startled*). - Yes, yes.

ARTHUR - Did Mrs. Pet like it?

VOICE (*dreamily*). - Rather. Very, very much. Do sing again, darlingest.

He sings again.

III.

Darkness. The banjo lies apart on the cruel ground. It realises that the world is hard and forgetful. Arthur is sitting crunched up under the window. He wonders vaguely where the moon is, and how in September the weather contrives to be so hot in the daytime and so cold, even unimpassioned, at night. He suspects the air of frostiness. There is now a recurrent note of anger in the sea's monotonous chant. A creaking noise above. He looks up, and observes in the darkness that the window is being stealthily closed. He moves; the window is instantly motionless.

ARTHUR - Rosie.

ROSE (*within*). - Yes, dear.

ARTHUR - Are you all right in that stuffy little place?

ROSE - Oh, yes, thanks.

ARTHUR - I thought you might be feeling chilly, perhaps.

ROSE - I'm *perfectly* happy.

ARTHUR - I had a sort of notion you were closing the window.

ROSE (*positively*) - Dearest! I think you must have been dreaming just a wee wee bit. Why, if I shut the window I couldn't hear you *half* so well. *You* all right?

ARTHUR - Oh, *I'm* all right, of course.

ROSE - What a beautiful night!

ARTHUR - Ye–es . . . Nice breeze.

ROSE - Don't you think this is a lovely adventure?

ARTHUR - Ripping.

ROSE - I shall remember it all my life. Just listen to the waves.

They both listen.

ARTHUR - I say!

ROSE - Well, Mr. Pet!

ARTHUR - What time do you think it is?

ROSE - Don't know. It must be *awfully* late.

ARTHUR - Yes. Not far off dawn, I should imagine.

ROSE - Really?

ARTHUR - Well, *can't* be far off. Look here, you must get a little rest.

ROSE (*with an endearing acquiescence*). - If you wish it, darling.

Solemn stillness, in which Arthur awaits the dawn. Indefinite time elapses. Then Arthur cautiously picks up the banjo and thrums a chord.

ARTHUR - Rosie, darling!

Again the solemn stillness.

THE BANJO -
   Pratt, prett,
   Pratt, prett-pratt

ARTHUR - Roh-sie!

VOICE - Is that you, Arthur?

ARTHUR - Hope I didn't disturb you?

VOICE - I was thinking of you.

ARTHUR - Got a macintosh up there, haven't you?

VOICE (*faint*) - Eh?

ARTHUR - Have you got a macintosh up there?

VOICE - Yes, it's quite safe.

ARTHUR - Well, you might throw it down.

ROSE (*at the window*) - Is 'oo cold?

ARTHUR (*sharply*). - No, but it might rain. In fact, it looks rather like rain. And I shouldn't want to disturb you for it in the middle of your sleep.

Descent of the macintosh.

ROSE - Catch!

ARTHUR - Ta, darling. Now go to feepy.

ROSE - But what shall you do?

ARTHUR - Oh, just walk about. I feel as fresh as paint.

*He puts the macintosh round his shoulders and squirms into a
   corner. Pause. He gets up again, anxiously examines the sky for
   any sign of dawn, but cannot find the least. Then he re-settles
   himself.*

VOICE - Sing me to sleep.

ARTHUR (*bracing himself*) - Certainly, darling. I was just
going to.

VOICE - Sing that first song you sang.

THE BANJO (curtly and bored) -
                 Tum,
                 Tom.

ARTHUR (huskily lyrical) -
    I arise from dreams of thee
      In the first sweet sleep of night.
    When the winds are -
    Asleep, darling?
    (*poco-a-poco diminuendo*)
                        - breathing low
      And the stars are shining bright
    And–a–spirit–in–my–feet
    Hath . . . . led . . . . . .

A long hush.

BILL (*coming out from his lair, fortissimo*). - Here's the train,
sir. They've got the line clear and she's coming on. She'll be
here in a couple of minutes.

IV.

Interior of second-class carriage, dimly lighted. The engine whistles.

ROSE - We're off.

ARTHUR - Yes, sooner than we expected.

ROSE (*aside, patting the cushion*). - You dear train!

ARTHUR (*sticking his head out of the window*). - I say, guard, what time is it?

VOICE OF THE GUARD (*from somewhere near a flashing lamp*). - Half-past eight, sir.

ARTHUR - What!!

ROSE - What time did he say?

ARTHUR - Er - I didn't catch.

He puts up the window.

NOTES

1. *Woman.* 8 December 1897, pages 11-13. Signed Sarah Volatile. Illustrations by M.E. Thompson.

2. Gray's Inn is the smallest of the four Inns of Court (professional associations for barristers and judges) in London, on a site dating back to the 14th century.

3. Bennett's choice of Percy Bysshe Shelley's (1792-1822) 'The Indian Serenade' ('Song Written from an Indian Air') is entirely apposite. In December 1819 life for Shelley 'became more social and frivolous at Palazzo Marini [Florence] under the influence of a charming young English girl, Miss Sophia Stacey....' (Richard Holmes, *Shelley the Pursuit*, p.564). Shelley not only helped with her Italian but also taught her the words of a Carbonari ballad and a local love-story. 'The Indian Serenade' was one of several short love-lyrics which he wrote especially for Sophia Stacey. They were intended to be sung to a musical accompaniment, although it is doubtful if Shelley had the banjo in mind!

HOW PERCY GOES TO THE OFFICE.[1]
BY HIS SISTER.

We have breakfast at eight o'clock. That is, father and mother and I have breakfast at eight o'clock. Percy has his usually between 8.10 and 8.15; sometimes it is 8.20. Once, when he happened to be down at 8 o'clock sharp, Percy tried to excuse his punctuality. One night we arranged to have breakfast next day half an hour later than ordinary. But Percy contrived to be late as usual. When I remarked in a general sort of way that if we breakfasted at noon, he would come down at 12.15, he said quite angrily, 'Well, it's only 8.34.' He didn't seem to see that he was being funny, not even when both father and I burst out laughing.

That is the worst of Percy, he is so silly; he never appears to have the slightest notion of the ridiculous side of himself. I suppose it is because he is so awfully handsome. As his elder sister, I must admit his beauty. He is twenty-two, very fair, and with a lovely aquiline nose, and a pretty moustache over simply perfect teeth. A dear old lady who remembered him as a child, once said to me:–'Ah, Miss Ronalds, he used to look like a little angel.' I told this to Percy, and he blushed and was obviously very annoyed. Yet he well knows how handsome he is, and, as a matter of fact, he is absurdly proud of his good looks. Such is the curiousness of the male youth.

You can guess how he fancies himself, by the way he enters the breakfast-room. It is like a triumph. You can also guess how mother fancies him. 'Good morning, my dear,' she says. 'How are you, this morning?' just as if it was he and not she who was the invalid. 'Oh, all right, mater,' he says, nonchalantly, and then, in a kind of royal style, he permits her to give him a good kiss. He never inquires after mother's health, unless she is frightfully ill, nor does she dream of expecting him to do so. I am convinced that this peculiar state of affairs is attributable to Percy's extraordinary manly beauty. Then begins the customary dialogue between mother and Percy as to what Percy shall eat. Percy must be tempted. (His appetite is that of an ox.) 'I'm afraid the bacon is cold, dear,' mother will say, as if that was her fault. Or, 'Just open that egg, my love, and see if it is boiled right for you.'

'Don't worry yourself, my little pigeon,' says Percy. This is how he gets round her. Now if I called father 'my little pigeon,' we should both expire with laughter. Yet Percy can use the phrase with impunity. It is strange how the household of four is divided into two camps–purely amicable camps, by the way– namely, father and I, and mother and Percy. Father, I may mention, is a rather popular novelist, and I am getting on fairly well in journalism.[2] We are both somewhat grim and silent. We look at each other, and exchange jokes with the eyes which the other two never catch. The other two are distinctly un-literary. Mother doesn't pretend to understand literary matters. Percy scorns them. I know young men who would give their heads to be allowed to eat familiarly at the same table with father (and me), and to see his study and the table on which he writes, and all that sort of thing. Yet Percy betrays not the slightest interest in father as an author. He is only interested in father as father. Percy is afraid of father. He is also afraid of me, though he tries desperately to hide that. The explanation of his fear is that we are both inclined to be sarcastic, and to extract fun from Percy in ways he doesn't understand.

At breakfast, however - and I must return to my subject– father and I are usually taciturn. (Literary people, I believe, seldom talk at breakfast.) It is mother who talks, and always on the same subject–Percy.

'Your cough seems rather bad this morning, dear.'

Percy had typhoid fever six years ago, and ever since then this cough has returned at intervals. It is a most useful cough to Percy sometimes–but not always.

'Oh, no mater,' he replies, looking to see how far his

handkerchief is sticking out of his pocket.

'I think you must have taken cold last night,' she says. 'In this hot weather it is very easy to take cold.'

'What time did you come in last night?' I ask him pointedly. Percy has a latch-key, though he is only twenty-two.

'Oh, about eleven.'

'And the rest,' I say, while casting a glance at father, who is reading the paper.

'Had any returned manuscripts this morning, Eva?' Percy asks me, innocently. This is his manner of turning the tables and annoying me. (He is rather acute, occasionally.) But I am not to be put off, and I continue:

'I suppose you were playing billiards at that wretched little tobacconist's?'

'Well, and what if I was?' His chin goes up.

'It's coming out of that stuffy room into the open air that makes you cough,' I add.

'Percy, I wish you wouldn't play billiards. You know father doesn't like it.' This from mother.

Percy emphatically does know that father doesn't like it.

Yet father has never said so. However, Percy braves it out.

'Well, mater, I *must* learn, you know.'

At this point, father unexpectedly looks up from his paper. I retire from the field.

'What stakes do you play for?' he inquires over his eyeglasses.

'Just the table money,' Percy replies meekly.

'What was your highest break last night?'

'Oh, I was a bit off.'

'What was your highest break last night?'

'Well, four.'

'What's the highest break you've ever made?'

'I can't remember.'

'Do you think it's above ten? Honour bright?'

'N–no.'

**A Foulard Blouse. Design No.
3,372.**

Percy's sister might well have bought this blouse pattern, which appeared as
a large advertisement in the central column of Bennett's story.

'Let me see, when's your exam?'

'October.'

'Humph!'

That is all. Both father and I feel that we have talked more than literary people should at breakfast. Mother tries to dispel the slight gloom which has thickened the atmosphere of the breakfast-table. But the attempt is useless. Percy has nearly finished his breakfast, and towards the end of the meal he invariably grows subdued and quiet. Apparently he becomes obsessed by the business cares which await him at the office. Whenever the office is referred to, he puts on a look of jaded anxiety. He is an articled clerk with a firm of solicitors in Broad Street, and will be 'out of his time' in a few months. The examination to which father referred was his Final. I firmly believe that, in actual truth, he does little or nothing at the office. But he persuades himself that his importance there is terrific. The last morsel of marmalade eaten, the last drop of coffee drunk, he pushes away his plate with a resigned air, and a sigh which says as plain as words: 'Now I must address myself to my daily task of keeping my employers from ruin.'

But before he begins to keep his employers from ruin, there is the cigarette. Percy has smoked for over a year now. He is getting used to it, and it isn't so funny as it used to be, though it is moderately funny still. He takes out of the left-hand trouser-pocket his silver cigarette case, which is firmly attached to his person by means of a long steel chain. Percy has several chains. His latch-key is attached to another long steel chain. To see him take that latch-key from his hip-pocket is as good as seeing a ship weigh anchor. Then there is his gold watch-chain, which goes through the second button of his waistcoat, and after stretching right across him ends in a matchbox in the opposite pocket.

Well, he takes a cigarette from the case, and looks at it meditatively, as though he had never seen a cigarette before. Then he dances it end-up on the table, and inserts the extreme tip of it between his ruby lips. Then, very slowly, he strikes a match and applies it to the cigarette. You see no smoke; you only see that the end of the cigarette is red. He drops the match into the slop basin, where it hisses. He leans back; looks at the ceiling; takes the cigarette from his mouth. Lastly, after an interval of seconds, he opens his mouth and blows a huge blast of smoke across the table, while still investigating the ceiling. You have opportunity to perceive his beautiful teeth.

Suddenly he looks at his watch.

'By Jove! I must be off. Got three summonses in Chambers this morning. By-bye, mater.'

'Good-bye, my love. Be home as early as you can.'

He is gone. Mother used to accompany him to the front door, but he stopped that. He didn't like it. Sometimes, however, I surreptitiously observe him from the window. He poises his Panama straw at a trifling angle on his curly locks. In one hand is his stick; in the other a pair of suède gloves, which he never wears. As he leaves the gate, he seldom fails to feel whether his collar is perfectly safe. Then he pulls at his wrist-bands till they emerge from his coat sleeves by precisely half an inch. Then he twirls his stick to signify that all is accomplished, save buying *The Sportsman*[3]from the boy at the corner. Finally a 'bus swallows him up, and mother has to exist without him till 6.30 in the evening.

NOTES

1. *Woman.* 23 August 1899, pages 17-18. Signed Sarah Volatile.

2. Bennett subtitles his sketch 'By His Sister', who is 'getting on fairly well in journalism'. He published his *Journalism For Women. A Practical Guide* in 1898, in which he advises aspiring female journalists to submit articles on precisely such topics as 'How Percy Goes to the Office'. She should look to the 'occurrences of one's everyday life' such as 'Queer ways of sleeping .... How to economise space in a small bedroom .... Where some Queens sleep .... Is breakfast in bed enjoyable .... Papa at breakfast' (pp. 64-65).

3. The first British newspaper titled *The Sportsman* began publishing in 1865 and ran until 1924. One of its many competitors, *The Sporting Times,* (otherwise known as *'The Pink 'Un'*), began publication in the same year.

THE INNER CIRCLE EXPRESS.[1]

It is not good for the public to know everything. This is an axiom of all high officials, especially the high officials of railway companies, whose strangest secrets are well kept from the world. Therefore a Central News reporter who had got wind of the affair whose true inwardness I am about to disclose, was put off with an ingeniously-wrought distortion which robbed startling facts of their piquancy and reduced a fine sensation to the level of flatness, resulting in a mere peaceful and innocent-faced paragraph. My readers may, perhaps, remember the paragraph. It appeared in one or two Sunday papers last June but one, and referred in a very mild manner to the singular career of an Inner Circle train on the previous night. It spoke vaguely of a temporary failure of telegraphic communication between signal-boxes, and the consequent diversion of the train on to a wrong line. You might call it a flaccid paragraph, the sort of stuff that, when perused in large quantities, makes the average man assert strenuously, 'There's nothing *in* the paper,' and feel a desire to go down into Fleet Street[2] and show Fleet Street how newspapers ought to be edited. Seemingly it was of no genuine interest. A 'Rash Act' or a 'Humour on the Bench' would have crowded it out, but on that Sunday there happened to be a paucity of news and so the paragraph got itself born into print.

Although the paragraph was gorgeously false, I do not blame the high official. He acted in the interest of shareholders, for the immediate publication of the true version of the incident would most assuredly have affected traffic, and traffic variations have a way of affecting dividends. But of this, since a year and more has passed and secrecy is no longer advisable, you shall now judge.

I have called the affair sensational. So it was–the actual affair, but the beginning of it, the prologue, was quietude itself. As thus:–

At 7.30 p.m. on that Saturday night Robert Twemlow, engine-driver in the employ of the Metropolitan Railway,[3] was waiting with his engine in the western bay under the bridge at South Kensington Station to back on to the circle train due out at 7.36. All outer rail circle trains change engines at South Kensington; inner rail trains change engines at High Street, Kensington: it is the law.

While his youthful stoker was conscientiously tickling the recesses of the engine with a long-nosed oil-can, Twemlow leaned motionless against the rail of the cab, his gaze directed along the platform. He was a firmly built, square-shouldered man of about thirty-five, with gleaming eyes, set stolid lips that meant business, and that air of aloofness and of reserve force which all engine-drivers acquire. He was usually gentle enough, but his mates took pains never to rouse him into a quarrel. To-night, towards the end of a day's work, he looked anxious and overstrained. Beneath the grime of his occupation you could detect a pallor, and the features were a little sharp, as after an illness. He had in fact only that morning returned to duty after a severe and obstinate attack of influenza which had lasted over a month.

A girl hurried down the platform towards the waiting engine. If you could have seen the faces of those two, the girl and the engine-driver, as they caught sight of each other, you would have instantly guessed that they were in love. The girl was accompanied by a man, with whom she was talking and laughing. Leaving this companion, she half ran forward sending forth bright glances in front of her. The engine-driver moved uneasily, nodded to the girl, and then gave a swift backward look at his stoker.

'Well, Bob,' the girl said in a kind, pleasant voice, as she stood by the side of the engine, 'feeling pretty well?'

'Middlin',' he answered, without answering her smile.

He examined her with his eyes. Mary Adderley was a pretty girl, tall and well developed, and dressed in a grey linsey[4] frock, which buttoned down the back with about a hundred and one buttons: a distinctly desirable girl, with strong ungloved hands, a brown honest face, and a most agreeable June straw hat at the top of all. She had been engaged to Robert Twemlow nearly a year, and as she lived with her father quite close to South Kensington, it had become customary for her to descend daily into the station in order to have a minute with her lover while he waited to pick up his train. To-day she had come twice to see him, but to-day was special–she regarded him yet as an invalid.

'What's *he* doin' here?' Robert Twemlow put the question to her curtly, jerking out his elbow to indicate the short man in corduroys and a blue cotton coat whom she had just left and who was now approaching.

'He's got to sign on for Parson's Green at eight o'clock, and he just came along with me,' Mary replied, and then the other man joined the group.

'How do, Twemlow?'

'How do, Twemlow?'

The two men were neither brothers nor cousins, but merely friends of the same name, Twemlow being a popular cognomen in their county of Staffordshire[5]–a county which they had simultaneously abandoned to come to London. Arthur Twemlow, the man on the platform, was a little younger than his namesake, and very much slighter of frame and merrier of face. He was now a foreman platelayer on the Wimbledon section of the Metropolitan District Railway. He and the engine-driver had lived in lodgings together in Chelsea until six months ago, when the exigencies of his work made it necessary for the latter to migrate to the region of King's Cross. The two men had not seen each other since Robert's illness, but 'Well, Twemlow,' was all they said at the moment–they did not even shake hands. They were both very Staffordshire, and down Staffordshire way it is not customary to waste words in phrases of politeness.

'Getting strong again, Bob?' Arthur said at length.

'Middlin',' replied the engine-driver again, and there was a pause, in which both Arthur Twemlow and Mary silently made allowances for the moodiness natural to a convalescent.

'Mary,' the engine-driver said suddenly, 'come round with me, if you've got th' time. Will ye?'

'To-night?' she questioned, deprecatingly.

'Ay,' he said, insistent.

'If you like,' she smiled to humour him.

Sometimes Mary would make the circle with her lover, sitting in the compartment nearest to the engine and popping out to him here and there at stations for ten seconds. There are seven thousand ways of being in love: this was one, and both Mary and Robert found pleasure in it.

'Go and get a ticket,' the engine-driver said, giving an eye to the signal, which had just been pulled off, 'and be slippy.'

'I'll go and book for her,' said Arthur Twemlow, the foreman platelayer.

'Thee stay here. I've summat to say to thee,' the engine-driver said, falling into the Staffordshire dialect, which these two always used when talking together by themselves. 'Off with ye, Mary.'

'What's up?' asked Arthur lightly, when the girl was gone.

'Thou seems a bit sweet on my girl, Twemlow, talkin' and laughin' wi' her,' said the engine-driver, fiercely, and he bent a little lower over the rail to the man on the platform. 'I've suspected thee ever sin' I went to bide at King's Cross. Hast been tampering wi' her while I've been ailing?' His face was dark, sinister.

'Get out wi' thee, Twemlow,' the platelayer said, firmly. 'Thou'rt ailing yet, or thou wouldna say such a thing.'

'Thou wast always sweet on her. I believe thou has tampered wi' her affections.'

'Thou knows I have 'na.'

'I say I believe thou hast.' The engine-driver almost spat the words at his friend.

'Well, believe it then,' burst out Arthur Twemlow, and thereupon left him, his own time being now short. Mary returned with her ticket, and Arthur, meeting her in full sight of her lover, stopped and joked with her, and shook hands. Then the train clattered in, the other engine uncoupled, Robert Twemlow backed on, and in a quarter of a minute drew out of the station, with Mary among his handful of passengers.

And that, according to Arthur Twemlow, who told me as I tell you, was absolutely the whole of the prologue. As for Robert's suspicion, the platelayer assured me positively that it was entirely without foundation.

* * * * *

About an hour and a-half later Arthur Twemlow was superintending a small gang of platelayers just outside the Parson's Green box, on the Putney and Wimbledon line, when he heard the electric bell go.

One stroke– pause–five strokes–pause–five strokes.

That was a highly unusual signal. It meant, 'Vehicles running away on wrong line.' Arthur Twemlow jumped at once to the box and warned his men. Then he heard the receiver furiously ticking.

'What's up, mate?' he called, and the signalman after a moment put his hand out of the open window of the box. It was a warm summer's evening. The light was just beginning

"THEE STAY HERE—I'VE SUMMAT
TO SAY TO THEE!"

to fail, and signal lamps shone out here and there in the dusk.

'We're going to have an Inner Circle along here for a change,' said the signalman calmly. Then the receiver started to tick again, and the signalman whipped his head back into the cabin. From time to time he sent out news to Arthur Twemlow as instructions reached him.

The Inner Circle train thus heralded at Parson's Green had first attracted attention to itself at Victoria. It drew up with correctness at that station, but no sooner had the guard and one of his passengers jumped out, than the driver, opening his whistle to an ear-splitting scream, started again. A lady, who was dismounting, fell on to the platform, and several would-be travellers were disappointed. Even the guard was left behind, and stood stock-still in astonishment at beholding his own tail-lamp.

The station officials shared the guard's speechless amazement, for this incredible driver had done that which cannot possibly *be* done. He had started before the guard had flagged him, and--a thousand times worse--he had openly defied the signal, which had not been pulled off and still showed a flaring red for all to see and tremble thereat. The signalman came to his door and spoke for an instant to the station inspector, who happened to be on the platform; then he telegraphed on to Sloane Square that the train had left Victoria without the guard and against the signal. The Sloane Square man put his signals against the train, called to a porter, and waited. He had not to wait long. In less than two minutes 'The Inner Circle Express' (as the staff have ever since called it) went through Sloane Square in grand style, with several doors swinging and a general air of untidiness and haste--went through quite heedless of signals and the shouts of the solitary porter.

It was magnificent, but it was not the block system.

The block system, admirable as it is, suffers from one defect. Its efficiency chiefly depends upon the engine-driver being a consenting party to it. A signal won't stop a train; it is shutting off steam and the application of brakes that stop a train; and if the driver says, 'I shan't play,' then this elaborate game by which between the Mansion House and Gloucester Road four trains can run to the mile, tumbles at once to bits, and chaos and collisions supervene. Happily they do not run four trains to the mile at nine o'clock on a Saturday night, that being a very quiet time, when the citizens are neither going to amusements nor returning from labour. Nevertheless the situation was serious, nearly as serious as it could be. Imagine the perturbation of the official mind when it realised that an unchartered and disobedient express was running amok through the thickest of its system! Messages of warning flew westward along the wires, and signalmen, closing their eyes, tried to see maps of moving trains, in order to find out where the inevitable smash would occur.

I should mention here that a few seconds after the express left Victoria, a lamed and battered stoker crawled on to the platform from the East Tunnel, and with what strength was left to him explained that his driver, just before they entered Victoria, had taken him unawares by the neck and the trouser-band and pitched him clean into the six-foot way. Asked what the driver meant by such conduct, he could offer no suggestion. He was young, had only just been promoted from the position of cleaner in the sheds, and his brains were fully employed in getting used to the idea that to the other disadvantages of locomotive-firing must be added the liability to be thrown off the footplate by your own driver.

As the express approached South Kensington, an Ealing up train was leaving the station, and in doing so necessarily crossed the metals on which, had it bided its time, the express should have travelled; for it is at this point that the Inner and Outer Circles join and become one. Had the two trains met, my story would have ended just here, but fortunately in certain respects the block system can rise superior even to a mutinous driver. The signal being in favour of the Outer Circle up train, the west-bound express was automatically switched on to the Outer Circle down rails, and a collision avoided. Therefore the express now found itself jerked on to a pair of rails which it had never seen before, and it sailed through South Kensington on the south side, while the station staff beheld it with awe. The few passengers had had the wit to close the doors of the compartments, and they could be seen vainly gesticulating as the train went by.

So far no mishap had occurred, but an accident within the next five minutes seemed fairly certain. Half way between South Kensington and Gloucester Road, a North-Western (Willesden and Broad Street) train was ambling leisurely westward, innocent of the Nemesis in its rear. At Gloucester Road the driver of the train had not drawn up before he received instructions from the excited station inspector, in person, to make instantly for Earl's Court, at his best speed. Twenty seconds after he had left Gloucester Road, the express thundered through, all flags flying, as it were, and the station inspector declares that the driver leaned out from the cab in passing, and deliberately smiled in answer to his angry shout. And indeed, that station-master futilely shouting is a symbol of the utter helplessness of the authorities to deal with the affair. For this was not a mere runaway engine, which might be steered to a convenient spot and then tripped up by means of points set half over; it was a train with passengers, and a rebel on the footplate–a rebel who knew his power and used it.

The question was whether the North-Western would reach Earl's Court in sufficient time to enable the points to be shifted over after it and before the express arrived. The signalman at Earl's Court East had his instructions, and he performed the feat with a margin of only five seconds, for the express had gained on the heavier North-Western. The latter had scarcely come to a standstill on the north side of the island platform, when its pursuer swept with grand impudence along the south side.

The Inner Circle express now had a choice of three routes. It might go to Addison Road (for Willesden and other places), or to Hammersmith (for Ealing and Richmond), or to Putney (for Wimbledon). The signalman at Earl's Court West, with commendable sagacity, set its head-light towards Putney, which was much the safest route of the three for a train with the bit between its teeth. Its pace was some twenty-five miles an hour, and this was about the best it could do, for the suburban tank-engine is not built for swiftness, but chiefly to be able to get up its full speed within about its own length. It had a clear run before it to Wimbledon; an empty train waiting on the down line at Putney Bridge had been moved to the up line, an operation which delayed an up Wimbledon train nearly fifteen minutes on the bridge over the Thames. The express swaggered through Brompton Road, and flew noisily down the incline of the cutting which carries the District under the West London Junction Railway. Here begins the remarkable series of gradients for which the section between Earl's Court and East Putney is notable. There is a gradient of one in sixty-three, both ways, at the lowest part of the cutting, and even at Walham Green the rise is one in a hundred and twenty-five. The express breathed heavily up these steeps, and having passed Walham Green and another set of amazed railway men, it continued its climb towards Putney Bridge. And now it was gazed upon by the back windows of hundreds of suburban houses, not one of which suspected anything unusual. So easily may the incredible occur, and people know nothing of it.

It happens that the stiffest part of this stiff ascent from Walham Green to the river is precisely at Parson's Green station, where the gradient is one in sixty-four. Here something of a shock awaited the express. Arthur Twemlow, foreman platelayer, being a man of logic and a man of resource, and having gathered from the signalman all necessary particulars, had decided that something had gone wrong with the driver of this much heralded express, and further, that prompt measures must be taken. He conceived the measures and took them. Even as the rebel, bearing brazenly its 'Inner Circle' board, and without the two lamps, one above another, on the off side which every engine in this section is obliged to carry, rounded the curve into the station, two of Arthur's men might be seen carefully pouring oil on the down metals; as the train approached, they skipped aside. Arthur Twemlow, keen, braced, alert, and looking curiously small in his light corduroys and blue cotton coat, stood at the extreme west end of the down platform, and waited. The express was doing a smooth twenty miles an hour, but when its driving wheels got on to the oiled metals there were strange jarring noises, a sudden whiz, and the speed dropped as it were by a miracle to about ten miles an hour. As the engine passed him, at this rate, Arthur Twemlow, setting his teeth, swung himself neatly on to the footplate, and instantly the indomitable suburban tank-engine, having left the oil behind, began to put on pace again.

He was not quite surprised to find that the driver was Robert Twemlow. Ever since the first message had reached him the suspicion that Robert was in the strange business had been at the back of his mind. For a second the two men stared blankly at each other, and then Arthur Twemlow, the platelayer, thought it was time to act. He did not possess a profound technical knowledge of locomotives, but he was aware of the lever and the short stumpy handle of the vacuum brake, and for these he instinctively made a dart. With a deep inarticulate growl Robert pushed him violently away, and Arthur knew by the feel of the man's arm that trouble lay in the immediate future.

'Thee dare,' the engine-driver exclaimed, his eyes blazing, his frame shaking with passion, 'and I'll murder thee!'

And then he stooped and picked up a heavy iron stoking

tool with his disengaged hand, and held it menacingly ready for emergencies.

Arthur Twemlow saw that he had a lunatic to deal with. The engine-driver, he observed, had the wild and shifty look, the uncontrolled play of facial muscles, the unsteady voice, and the other symptoms typical of the dangerously insane. Then it was that the platelayer suddenly remembered that, within his own knowledge, influenza sometimes left the physically-restored patient in a temporary condition of lunacy. This had not been Robert's first severe attack of influenza, and on the previous occasion, after he had recovered his strength, he had been a little out of his mind for several weeks. The doctor then had said that the mental aberration would pass, and it did pass and was duly forgotten. Now apparently the symptoms had repeated themselves in a more violent form.

The platelayer, scarcely yet used to the swaying of the engine as it doggedly mounted the incline towards Putney Bridge station, rapidly considered his position, and decided to go off on a new tack.

'What's the game?' he asked lightly. 'What art tha' doing this for?'

'Thee shan't have the wench, Arthur, and so I tell thee,' the engine driver said, his hand firm on the lever.

'What wench?'

'My Mary. She's aboard this train, and I'm takkin' her away. It's no good thee climbing on to my engine. Thee sha't na' have her.'

Arthur began to perceive the nature of his friend's delusion.

'Who wants her?' he asked, still trying the effect of a jocular tone.

'Thee wants her.'

'Not I.'

The engine-driver leaned towards him and roared with clinching emphasis:

"'THEE DARE, AND I'LL
MURDER THEE!'"

'Then what art tha' doing aboard my engine? Tell me that.'

Arthur laughed.

'I wanted for to get to know how thee cam'st on the Wimbledon Line, lad. Thee knows thee's Inner Circle.'

'It's the will o' the Lord,' the engine-driver answered solemnly. 'It's the will o' the Lord. I'm takkin' the wench away, and we're in th' hands o' God.'

Then he was silent.

The train was now passing over the river. Arthur pondered afresh. He was as cool as ever, with all his wits handy for use. He desired particularly not to irritate the lunatic, because he well knew that if it came to a struggle between them the lunatic would win hands down. There was still a run of about three miles to Wimbledon, and a clear line before them, and Arthur trusted that before they got within collision-distance of the terminus something favourable would happen. For a second he hoped that the stokerless engine would come to a stop of its own accord, but a glance at the gauge showed him that the steam-pressure was still at least normal, and he recollected the interesting fact that when the fire burns down clear and bright, to within a few inches of the furnace bars, the amount of steam generated increases, at any rate for a time.

Presently the engine-driver began to speak, half-shouting, so that his companion might hear him distinctly above the rattle of the engine as it strained round the stiff curve outside East Putney Station, and plunged under West Hill.

'Her got out at St. James's Park, and told me her should leave me at South Kensington and go home. But I guessed if her went home thee 'ud meet her, and tak' her from me. Two can play at that game, says I. So what did I do? I chucked Jimmy off i' th' tunnel, and I left th' guard behind at Victoria so as there'd be no one to meddle with th' brakes, and I just com'd away. Damn the signals, says I–I'm takkin' my girl away.'

He gave a cackling laugh.

'The'll get into serious trouble for this, Twemlow,' said Arthur.

'I shall none come back. Me and Mary's goin' away. Thee sha't na' have her, Twemlow, so thee mi't as well jump off.'

Arthur sprang at the proposal. They were approaching Southfields.

'Stop for me, and I'll get off then. I'll leave her to thee, Bob. Pull th' lever over, there's a lad, and I'll get off.'

But the engine-driver was far too cunning.

'Not if I knows it,' he said. 'Thou gotst on as thou couldst, and thou shalt get off as thou canst. Jump, lad, and tak' thy luck.' He waved the iron playfully.

Again the platelayer was baffled. They passed Southfields. The signalman flagged them furiously, and Arthur waved him a hand. Then, almost in a twinkling, as it seemed to Arthur, they were at Wimbledon Park. Two more minutes would see them at Wimbledon, and though the speed had decreased slightly within the last mile, it was still near upon twenty miles an hour. Arthur was conscious of an uncomfortable thrill. It was in his mind to wish fervently that he had not meddled with the Inner Circle express. He trembled to think what would occur at Wimbledon. The officials would know everything, but the officials would be helpless. To turn an irresponsible and ungovernable express on to the crowded South-Western main line would be sheer idiocy, and their only alternative would be to allow the train to crash through the station wall and wreck itself in the cab yard beyond.

'Twemlow,' he said, pulling himself together, 'thee'll be at Wimbledon in a minute, and what shalt do then?'

The engine-driver was entirely unperturbed.

'The Lord knows,' he said, 'the Lord will provide.'

'Thee'll overrun th' platform, and fall on thy side in th' street, my lad, and some people'll get killed, and there'll be an inquest, and thee'll be had up for manslaughter, if thee's alive.'

'I'm i' God's hands. I'm takkin' her away.'

'She'll be killed.'

'We're i' His hands. Not a sparrow falls but He knows on it.'[6]

Then there was a pause. The train swiftly approached the terminus. Arthur saw the station in the distance, and could descry a little crowd of men on the look-out for them. He raised his hands for a desperate onslaught; simultaneously the engine-driver raised his iron bar, and Arthur stopped to consider.

'Look here, Twemlow,' he said.

'Well, what sayst thou now?'

'I *do* want her, and I'll fight thee for her. That's fair.'

The engine-driver was clearly touched.

'Ay!' he said, slowly. 'That's fair. Come on.'

'Nay, not here,' retorted Arthur. 'Dost think I'm such a fool as to fight a driver on his own foot-plate? I'm not on even terms wi' thee, lad. Us'll fight on th' six-foot way.'

'Damned if I'll stop!'

'Thee darena' stop, Ben Twemlow. Thee darena' fight me on level ground.'

'Thee knows I dare.'

'Thee darena', Arthur insisted with elaborate scorching contempt–and now he could see the buffers at the end of the platform. 'Thee darena'. Thou'rt a coward, and what's more, *her* knows it, Mary knows it.'

'I'll show thee.'

Robert dropped the iron bar, jerked the lever over, and put on the brake. Suddenly Arthur could feel his heart beating –beating for wild joy of the music of the brake. The train stopped half way up the platform.

'Come on, and I'll fight thee,' shouted the engine-driver, jumping on to the platform and squaring his elbows. But at a sign two porters seized him from behind and Arthur attacked in front. The run of the Inner Circle express was over.

*   *   *   *   *

The most delicate part of the subsequent proceedings was

of course the explanation to the passengers. The truth was absolutely impossible. It would have worked more harm to the underground traffic than even six weeks of ninety-in-the-shade weather. There were thirteen passengers. One of them, a lady of middle-age, had actually a ticket for Wimbledon, and had observed nothing extraordinary on the journey; indeed, she was rather pleased with the quickness of it. The other twelve had to be content with vague talk of confusion between their train and a special from a southern line which was due to travel over the route about the same time. It was horribly lame (the officials tried to improve on it later), but it had to serve. The passengers were at once returned to Gloucester Road and the realms of the Inner Circle. They had lost an hour out of their valuable lives.

The most curious thing of all is that Mary did not hear of the affair till later, when Arthur himself told her. She had jumped out at Victoria to speak to her lover again, and had been left behind.

Robert recovered his reason in a few weeks, and Mary is now his wife. But she is not the wife of an engine-driver. The Metropolitan Railway Company have no use for drivers of the pattern of Robert Twemlow, and Mary's husband is now proprietor of a tobacconist's shop in King's Road, Chelsea, and doing sufficiently well. As for Arthur, he was promoted, and the directors also voted him a *douceur*[7] of twenty guineas, which does not appear in the published accounts.

And the moral of everything is that a secret can be known to scores of people, and yet remain a secret. Not an employé on the Underground but could have told you this story. For months it was *the* topic in lamp-rooms, signal-boxes, and ticket-offices. But it didn't get about, and it might never have been published if I, a journalist, had not by pure chance formed an acquaintanceship with Arthur Twemlow, the platelayer. For the world exists in many sections, and each has a way of keeping itself to itself.

NOTES

1. *Hearth and Home*. 29 November 1900, pages 159-162. Signed E.A. Bennett. Illustrated by Lance Thackeray. The journal began publication in May 1891, and ran until January 1914, before merging with *Vanity Fair*. Bennett wrote for it from September 1897 until November 1903. In a letter to his friend George Sturt (1863-1927), written on 11 May 1898, he records having written 12,000 words for *Hearth and Home* since the beginning of March that year.

Lance Thackeray (1869-1916) was a British-born artist best known for his comic sporting illustrations, especially golf and billiards, and his comic portraits. He co-founded the London Sketch Club in 1898. Thackeray was the illustrator for Bennett's story 'A Millionaire's Wife' (*Woman*, 6 December 1899, and reprinted in *Uncollected Short Stories*). Working during what is now widely regarded as the Golden Age of Postcards he produced more than 950 designs which sold world-wide. He died in 1916 while serving with the Artists' Rifles Regiment.

2. Fleet Street, in Central London, was the headquarters of the British press until the 1980s. It takes its name from the old Fleet river which flowed into the Thames at Blackfriars, passing under the Fleet Bridge at what today is Ludgate Circus.

3. The Metropolitan Railway was originally incorporated as the Bayswater, Paddington and Holborn Bridge Railway in January 1853. An agreement between the District Railway and the Metropolitan, which eventually merged, led to the extension of both lines between Aldgate and Mansion House. This completed the route encircling central London and was known as the Inner Circle. Services began in October 1884. The complete thirteen mile trip took 70 minutes.

4. A linsey dress is made from a course inferior cloth of linen and wool, or cotton and wool.

5. The cognomen (or family name), Twemlow, also features in Bennett's *Leonora* (1903).

6. 'Are not two sparrows sold for a farthing? And one of them shall not fall on the ground without your Father.' *King James Bible*, 'St. Matthew,' Chapter 11, verse 29.

7. Technically in this case a *douceur* is a gratuity, but in the context of the Company wishing to hush up the affair it might also be seen as a bribe.

STELLA'S JOURNEY.[1]

Stella Marston was showing her young sister round the picture gallery in the quaint and marvellous old town of Bruges, when the idea first took possession of her that she must return home at once, without the least delay. They happened to be looking at a classical landscape entitled 'Nero fiddling.'[2] You could see Rome burning with much vermilion in the distance, while the foreground was occupied by a figure of Nero so comical that both the sisters burst out laughing at it.

Yet suddenly, for no apparent reason, Stella grew serious. 'I think we must go home to-morrow, Agnes dear,' she said.

'Go home, Stella!' the little girl pouted. 'But you said we should go to Brussels and Antwerp and Cologne and all those places. I do so want to see the Zoo at Antwerp. And you promised, you know.'

'Yes, dear. But if I ask you to let me off–'

'But why?'

'I think we must.'

She gave no reason because she had none to give.

They walked in a rather mournful silence through the curious cobble-paved streets to their hotel. Arrived there, Stella rang for her maid.

'We shall go home to-morrow, Claire. The Ostend boat express leaves at nine o'clock. Pack everything to-night.'

'Yes, mademoiselle. Has mademoiselle had bad news, perhaps?'

'Yes,' Stella answered absently, gazing out of the window at the great Belfry Tower which flanked the other end of the Square.

'Have you, Stella?' Agnes put in, astonished and a little hurt. 'You never told me.'

Stella recovered her wandering wits with a start.

'No, I have had no bad news, Claire, since you are curious

on the point. I wasn't thinking what I said. Nevertheless we will go home to-morrow.'

Then Agnes knew that the dreadful thing was settled, and she followed Claire out of the room to hide her tears from Stella.

It was a pretty and distinguished woman who reclined in an easy chair fronting the French window, absorbed in vague and uneasy apprehension. Aged just twenty-five, with an exquisitely clear olive-pale complexion, brown flashing eyes, and abundant red-brown hair which hid her ears, Stella Marston could never have been mistaken for the average vapid girl whom one meets in such numbers at the table d'hote of continental hotels. Her half mourning dress of grey and white was obviously the creation of an artist, and she wore it unusually well. There was in her resolute, calm countenance a mysterious charm–the melancholy charm which sorrow alone can give to a woman's face. For, though Stella happened to be rich, she had known sorrow.

She was the daughter of John Marston, late senior partner in the great earthenware firm of Marston, Baines and Co., of Bursley, famous throughout the Staffordshire potteries. Her mother had died when she was eleven. After four years Mr Marston had married again, and, quite contrary to all rule, Stella and her stepmother instantly became fast friends. But the second Mrs Marston had also died when Agnes was born, and Stella and her father sought distraction from their grief by devoting themselves to baby Agnes. Stella, who was sixteen, suddenly became a woman, and tried to bring up Agnes as Agnes's mother would have brought her up. Eight years passed thus, and then John Marston died unexpectedly at the age of fifty-five. That was a year ago.

Stella, bereaved for the third time, found herself with a hundred thousand pounds, a sister, and a partner, Charlie Baines, ten years older than herself. Her father, perceiving that she possessed sagacity and a good head for figures, had left her his share in the earthenware business, either to sell or to hold, and, as he had foreseen, she decided to hold it. A month after John Marston's death she had gone to the works and interviewed her partner, of whom previously, from various causes, she had seen little.

'Good morning, Miss Marston, what can I do for you?'

She liked him at once. His eyes were brown as her own, and he had a smile which said more than words could.

'I have come to take my share of the toil and worry,' she replied, 'I can spare three hours a day from Agnes, and you are going to let me assist you in the business.'

Some men would have objected, obstinately, furiously. But not Charlie Baines. He divined the sense of duty from which her action had sprung, and it appealed to him.

'I shall be glad of your assistance,' he said.

'And when may I start?'

'Now.'

And so she had taken off her hat and started; and that was the beginning of a firm understanding, and a mutual respect, between the partners. Baines was astonished at her aptitude, her pertinacity, her quick grasp of detail. The business had always prospered; now it prospered doubly. A friendship grew up between them. When Agnes fell ill Baines's solicitude and anxiety had touched Stella deeply. It was he who, on Agnes's convalescence, had suggested that the sisters should take this continental trip, so that the child might benefit by change and variety of scene. They had now been away rather more than a week, and Stella had received a letter from him, a simple, short letter, telling of business, and ending with good wishes.

This letter was so simple and matter-of-fact that it seemed scarcely necessary for her to read it more than once. Yet the next day, when they were on the homeward steamer, and Agnes was inspecting some far corner of the deck, she took it out of her pocket, and read it several times, just for the pleasure of doing so.

They reached Bursley about ten in the evening, having travelled continuously for twelve hours, with half-an-hour's rest in London. The cabs at Bursley Station are not very desirable vehicles, but, as Stella had forgotten to telegraph for the carriage, there was no alternative but to take one.

'Shawport House,'[3] she said to the driver, and the driver, who knew that name, touched his hat respectfully. Agnes and Claire, the maid, got in, and Stella was just following them, when suddenly she stopped, and remaining outside, closed the door.

'Aren't you coming, Stella?' Agnes inquired plaintively.

'No, dear, I will walk down to the works first. Claire, you will see that Miss Agnes has a good supper.'

'Why can't the works wait till to-morrow?' Agnes cried, as the cab moved away.

Stella shook her head, smiled, blew a kiss, and then set off for the works, which were at the other end of the town by the canal side.

Bursley is perhaps not more ugly than the average manufacturing town, but it is very ugly. On every side are large manufactories with their long monotonous frontages and tall chimneys and squat ovens throwing up columns of smoke day and night. At that hour the streets near the station were deserted, and everything was grim and sinister. Stella could not help contrasting the place with the beautiful city which she had left only that morning. She walked quickly, almost ran, and something within her seemed to say 'Quicker, quicker.' She had passed through the Market Square and was at the top of the steep Oldcastle Street, when, far away in front, down in the valley where the canal is, she perceived a mighty yellow glare. Waking from her absorbed reverie she noticed at the same moment that other people besides herself were hastening down Oldcastle Street.[4] She stopped two men who passed her, talking excitedly together.

'Is there a fire?' she asked.

'Yes, miss, and the biggest there's been i' this town for thirty year, so they say.'

'Where is it?'

'At Marston's works, miss.'

'Thank you.'

She spoke with apparently perfect composure, but there was that in her agitated heart which had never been there before. She ran after the men, and as she neared the works the streets began to be alive with men, women and children, all making for one goal.

Another five minutes and she was at the edge of a huge crowd in a short street, which, lying parallel to the canal, gives entrance to the works. The air was full of smoke and wandering sparks, and from somewhere in the distance came the deep pulsation of a fire-engine. She forced her way forward, breathlessly pushing, and was suddenly stopped by a cordon of police.

'Can't pass, miss.'

'My name is Marston.'

'Beg pardon.'

The constable saluted. The next minute she was in Marston's great yard, an irregular quadrangle flanked on three sides by the works buildings, and on the fourth by a ten-foot brick wall. The full spectacle of the fire was now before her tingling eyes. The huge warehouses, which lay in front, were ablaze from roof to ground, flame issuing from every window. The counting house and offices on the left seemed to be enveloped in smoke, but showed no light, while the workshops on the right hand were untouched. The fire-engine, dropping a continuous shower of white-hot cinders, panted in a far corner; lines of hose stretched across the yard, and the firemen in their brass helmets ran to and fro, aiming the water-jets now here, now there. The roar of the fire mingled with the hissing of the water and the hoarse calls of the firemen, was a scene of the highest excitement, and for a second Stella stood dazed. Then an old, white-haired man drifted towards her. It was Ben Shaw, the watchman, who had been with Marston's for forty years, ever since the time of Stella's grandfather.

'Ben,' she cried.

'Eh?' he murmured wildly. 'Who be ye?'

'I'm Stella Marston, you know me perfectly well, Ben. Pull yourself together.' She took him by the coat collar and shook him. 'Where is Mr Baines?'

'He's round on the canal front, Miss,' the old man quavered. 'They've just been getting th' account-books out o' th' office. Mr Baines saved them himself, he did. Th' books are safe in my lodge yonder, now.'

She ran forward and met other men.

'Where is Mr Baines?'

'On the canal front, Miss.' They told her the same tale, shouting it above the commotion of the fire.

Under an archway on the right, up a passage, along which a hose-pipe ran–and Stella was on the canal front, where the heat was terrific. The waters of the canal were red with reflected flame. Two firemen were perched on a fire escape, and from its summit they poured water in the building. She could see no sign of her partner.

'Where is Mr Baines?' she shouted.

'That you, Miss Marston?' It was the head warehouseman who approached her. 'Mr Baines was here a minute ago. I don't know where he is now. A sad sight, this, for you, Miss Marston. But Mr Baines says the insurance is ample. Thank God for that.'

'Yes,' she replied, mechanically, and ran off, urged by some impulse which she could neither explain nor control. Back she hurried to the yard and went to the door which led to the counting-house. Smoke came from it in stifling clouds, but, absolutely heedless of this, she rushed forward. She had not taken two steps within the doorway when she tripped over something. She bent down and felt with her fingers. It was the body of a man. Exerting all her strength, she dragged the man out of the passage into the fresh air of the yard.

It was Charlie Baines. Tight clasped in his hands was a long, thin account book.

In a few minutes he had recovered consciousness, and was able to explain that he had gone back to the counting-house for the customers' order-book, which it occurred to him had been forgotten.

'The smoke had been too much for me,' he said, looking up at her. 'You saved my life.'

'Did I?' she answered simply, with swimming eyes, and her hand rested in his. In that instant, without speech, each knew the other's dear secret.

'What brought you here, darling?'

'It must have been Love that spoke to me,' she said. 'Ever since yesterday I knew in my heart that you would be in danger, and that I should save you.'

And perhaps that was the best explanation of the mysterious prompting which led to Stella's journey.

They are partners now in more than business, and Agnes is very proud of having a brother-in-law.

Not every little girl of ten can boast such a valuable possession.

NOTES

1. *Star* (New Zealand). 9 December 1901, page 4. Signed E. A. Bennett. The *Star* began publication as the evening edition of the *Lyttelton Times* on 14 May 1868. It was regarded as a reliable source of local information, but was otherwise undistinguished. In 1935 the *Star* merged with the *Sun*, modelled on the London *Daily Mail*, to become the *Christchurch Star-Sun*. After several name changes it eventually ceased publication in 1991.

2. The painting's title is an allusion to Nero's reputed behaviour while Rome burned in AD 64, when he is supposed to have sung to his lyre whilst enjoying the spectacle.

3. Shawport House is also the fictional home of the Stanway family in Bennett's 1903 novel *Leonora*. The house may still be identified today as Moreton House, standing on the edge of Wolstanton Marsh on the road to Newcastle-under-Lyme. Only the façade remains to indicate its former fine architecture.

4. Oldcastle Street is Bennett's name for Newcastle Street, and the crowd's movement down it towards the fire suggests that Marston, Baines and Co. may well have been based on the Burgess & Leigh Pottery situated nearby on the canal-side. Burgess & Leigh is also the model for Henry Mynor's pottery in *Anna of the Five Towns* (1902) in which Anna Tellwright's sister is named Agnes.

Advertisement in the New Zealand *Star* for a popular silent film adaptation of a Bennett novel.

♪ THE CLOCK* ♪
BY ARNOLD BENNETT

THE CLOCK.¹

I.

It was not until my Aunt Susan had banged the door, and I stood solitary in the hall of her modest dwelling, that I realised that never before during my varied bachelor's existence of thirty-five years had I spent a night entirely alone in a house. Through the half-open door of the parlour came two sounds– the fizz or hiss of the incandescent light, and the slow ticking of my Aunt Susan's grandfather's clock. And these two sounds, one fussy and capricious, the other solemn and infinitely regular, seemed each in its own way to bear some secret and awe-inspiring significance; seemed to compel me to think of all the other dark and deserted rooms in the little house–of the tiled kitchen, and the coal-cellar, and my aunt's large and prim bedroom (just the sort of bedroom that an energetic widow with pronounced views about jam-making and the catechism would inhabit), and the small spare-bedroom where I was to sleep, and the extraordinary bathroom up in the attic. And it occurred to me for the first time in my life what a curious, creepy, mysterious, inexplicably alive sort of thing a human house really was.

Then I thought suddenly and boldly: 'What rot!' and went into the parlour and sat down.

I had come to spend a couple of nights under the austere roof of my Aunt Susan, partly from a sense of duty, partly from a genuine desire to renew the sensations of my early youth in the neighbourhood where I was born, and partly perhaps because of the fact (notorious in the bar mess) that the principal hotel in the next town, where the assizes were being held, was a bad hotel. My aunt's cooking (she kept no servant, being poor) was plain but perfect, and she had often suggested that I was too proud to stay with her. So at last I came. And she welcomed me sincerely in her Midland manner, and fed me to the full with rare Midland dishes that I had not tasted for many years. To all appearance we had little in common–she the widow of a small jobbing builder, and I the successful barrister–we certainly did not find much to talk about. Nevertheless, the same blood was in our veins; she admired me; she was intensely flattered by my presence. I respected her, and I rather liked, after many years in London, years of frock-coats and late dinners and evening-dress and clubs and theatres, to be back again amid the social customs of my obscure origin–where one dined at 12.30 and had high-tea at six and a snack of bread-and-cheese at nine, and removed one's boots in the parlour and didn't converse unless one had something to say. In fact, I enjoyed my evening.

And then, at half-past nine, had come the message that the first child of my Aunt Susan's eldest niece by marriage (my cousin) had just been successfully born, in the next town, and would my Aunt Susan care to go over at once? It was a hard struggle, in my aunt's mind, between that baby and me; of course, the baby won. My aunt sagaciously remarked that we couldn't talk all night, she and I, and that she would return to prepare breakfast, on the early workmen's car, and thus we should lose nothing by her expedition to the bedside of her eldest niece by marriage. And so she had banged the door and departed.

II.

As I sat in the parlour, glancing casually at a brief, there was a sudden tap in the corner of the room (I started, and thought of mice behind the ancient oak panelling of immemorial castles–but this was a cottage of eighteen shillings a month), then a smothered groan, then a long, uneasy, presaging whirr, and then the grandfather's clock burst into song and announced ten on its brass gong with a kind of impassioned clangour. The strike of that clock was simply terrific; it caused the room to vibrate; it also caused me to imagine that I was shut up alone in the house with an inhuman monster. But the clock was a beautiful clock, with a case of carved oak and a most exquisite dial. I envied my aunt that clock. I would have offered to buy it from her at a liberal figure, had I not been sure that she would have regarded the suggestion as an insult to her self-respect. It was her poverty (comparative poverty, that is to say–she had enough to live on decently) that was the cause of my Aunt Susan's touch-me-not pride. She constantly complained of her hard and penurious lot; but if any relative had proposed, however delicately, to make her an allowance, she would have flounced him out of the house in no time.

When the clock had quite finished striking ten, I decided on a courageous course of action; I decided to go to bed. I call it courageous, because I was beginning to feel afraid of the nocturnal solitude. No one who has not slept alone in a house will appreciate my feelings; but everyone who indeed has slept alone in a house, just an ordinary house, will appreciate them fully. I was afraid of the interior of the house, and of the silence and the emptiness and the solitude, and of dark corners, and of everything and of nothing. I heard sounds when there was no sound, and I had sensations like caterpillars gliding down my spine. However, being brave and determined and a successful barrister, I rose from my chair, gathered up my briefs, extinguished the gas in the parlour, went out, shut the room door, bolted the front door, lit a candle, extinguished the gas in the hall, climbed the stairs (ugh! the shadows), entered my bedroom, shut the bedroom door, and retired to rest.

I always read my briefs in bed, when on circuit, and I tried to read them then. But my eyes wandered over the page, struggling vainly for the sense. I was thinking all the time of all the other rooms in the little house, and of burglars, ghosts, strange apparitions and sudden deaths–in short, I went through the usual experiences. I thought I could hear something creeping about in the bathroom overhead, and then I thought I could hear the clock ticking. And I whispered: 'Suppose....' (Suppose what? I couldn't tell you.) At length I dropped the briefs, and blew out the candle and resolved not to be a silly ass, but to go to sleep. The next house was scarcely fifty yards off, and two respectably large towns were within a mile on east and west.

I really believe I was succeeding, when my sensitive ear caught the vibration of a dreadful thud–thud beneath the floor. It was the clock striking eleven, merely that. I could not hear the ring of the gong, but the heavy impact of the hammer on the metal affected all my body. 'That confounded machine will wake me up every hour,' I reflected. 'I must stop it.' And, lighting the candle again, I adventurously descended and faced the clock, which was ticking as calmly and leisurely as though nothing had happened. Instead of stopping it, I merely detached the right-hand weight (and a mighty piece of lead it was!) so that the clock would continue to show the time without striking. I tried to deposit the weight in the bottom of the case, but there was an obstruction, a box or something, and so I laid it on the floor against the skirting, behind my aunt's hassock. I said I would get up early and replace it before her arrival. Then I went to bed again, a little reassured by own bravery, and essayed to sleep.

But I could not sleep. At least I could only doze, unpleasantly. And when (after about a century and a half) the doze was merging into a sleep, I was jerked into a perfect and excruciating wakefulness by a most distinct knock–knock–

knock, a long way off. I did the natural thing; I pulled the clothes over my ear (my heart was beating like an engine), but I could still hear the knock–knock–knock. I was determined to take no notice. 'No power, earthly or unearthly,' I said 'shall draw me outside this room again.' But I could still hear the knock–knock–knock.

'The front door! My aunt returned!' This idea seized me suddenly, as in a vice, and then I knew that I should be compelled to rise and go to the front door.

And, having donned some clothes, I did go to the front door, and the knocking went on with gentle regularity as I descended the stairs, and I set the candle on the hall table, and I opened the front door with the courage worthy of a barrister. And a policeman and a young woman stood on the white step; the policeman was supporting the woman.

III.

The subsequent episode passed with the rapidity of a dream.

'She's in a fainting condition,' said the policeman. 'Can you give her some brandy?' Before speaking he had stared at me.

In a moment he had pushed the young woman into the hall.

'Come in,' I said, lamely, and I helped her into the parlour, taking the candle. The front door closed, leaving the policeman outside.

I perceived, as I allowed her to sink from my arms into a chair, that the young woman was a very pretty young woman, though plainly dressed. She sighed, and shut her eyes.

'The brandy, now,' I exclaimed. 'Where can it be?'

The presence of the pretty young woman interested me enormously, and piqued my curiosity. I felt that my night, after being fearsome, had become picturesquely strange.

'In these parts they often keep the spirits in the clock-case.' It was the young woman who spoke, or rather breathed out the words in a charming fatigued whisper.

'Of course,' I agreed.

And surely enough, the obstruction which I had previously discovered in the bottom of the clock-case proved to be a small spirit cabinet. I lifted it out.

'Now a glass and some water,' I said, and ran into the kitchen.

When I returned to the parlour the pretty young woman had vanished utterly. Can she be insane? I wondered. And I searched the house, but in vain. I opened the front door, and looked up and down the street, but there was no sign of her. Presently a heavy tread on the opposite side of the dark road indicated a policeman. 'Where's that girl you brought in just now?' I cried in the night.

'What girl?' came the reply. Then a pause. Then: 'Better go to bed, sir.'

The mystifying affair occupied all my thoughts for the remainder of the night, and I had no sleep whatever. I was thirty-five and staid, and not too fanciful; but the young woman was really so very pretty, and the circumstances of her appearance and disappearance were so romantic that.... well!

IV.

I told my aunt the next morning, told her before she had even been able to get in a word about the baby.

She jumped up, and opened the clock-case.

'Gracious powers above!' she cried. 'It's gone.'

Whereupon she swooned all in a heap on the floor.

'What's gone?' I asked, when I had restored her.

'The weight!'

'Not in the least,' I said. 'The weight is here,' and I produced it from behind the hassock.

She took the heavy thing feverishly from my hand, pulled out a plug from the under side, and drew forth from the cavity banknotes to the tune of more than a thousand pounds; and then she wept gently in her joy and relief.

'You wicked aunt,' I said. 'You're a perfect miser!'

She was in fact a miser, my Aunt Susan; and her poverty was simply a legend of her own invention!

Inquiries proved that the first policeman was a sham policeman. My wonderful episode was just a rather novel experiment in burglary on the part of expert thieves who had pried out Aunt Susan's secret and gone to work in an original manner. On discovering the absence of the weight, the young woman, already disconcerted by my unexpected presence, must have fled. I have felt sorry ever since that she was so pretty; it seemed a shame. And at every assize I tremble lest she and her sham policeman should turn up in the dock one fine morning. My aunt still sturdily survives. I have made her will for her. The banknotes are to go to the infant of my aunt's niece by marriage, and I am trustee and executor.

NOTES

1. *Black & White*. 2 September 1905, page 322. Signed Arnold Bennett. The illustrated weekly ran from February 1891 to January 1912, when it merged with *The Sphere.* A high quality, large format magazine with a token newspaper coverage of current affairs, its main emphasis was on art and literature. James Hepburn writes that '[during] the first years of its existence, *Black & White* was a notable addition to the literary scene, printing articles and stories by Thomas Hardy, Robert Louis Stevenson, and Henry James. Among the members of its staff were M.H. Spielmann, the art critic, W.A. MacKenzie, the author of *Rowton House Rhymes*, Eden Phillpotts, Violet Hunt, and Mrs. Belloc Lowndes' (*Letters Vol. I*, pp. 22-23).

Bennett's *Journal* entry for 23 February 1898 records a meeting with his friend and collaborator Eden Phillpotts (1862-1960) at the magazine's office: 'Sitting with me in his dark little office at *Black & White* after lunch, Eden Phillpotts, heavily wrapped up and pale after a long attack of influenza, told me something of his life.... He left the insurance office, married, and lived by his pen comfortably till *Black & White* offered him, through his agent, the post of assistant editor. As this meant an assured revenue, he accepted it. He works 3 days a week, machine-writing, free from responsibility, and the rest of his time he gives to novels and short stories.'

THE FORTRESS.[1]
A Drawing-Room Duologue.

CHARACTERS.

JUNIA COMFREY, a widow, aged 30.
OCTAVIUS PLATT, a bachelor, aged 40.

The scene represents Mrs. Comfrey's drawing room.
Time—evening.

MRS. COMFREY, *in a distinguished but somewhat informal toilette, is reading.*

Enter Octavius Platt.

MRS. C.: Mr. Platt!

MR. P. (*advancing to shake hands*): The same. How are you, my dear lady?

MRS. C. (*putting down book*): Your dear lady is in a state of high nervous tension.

MR. P.: Caused by?

MRS. C.: Caused by the effort to conceal her feelings.

MR. P.: The effort to produce a false impression on the exterior universe?

MRS. C.: Exactly.

MR. P.: I thought that women did nothing else. What can I do to relieve the situation?

MRS. C.: You can sit down and wear a soothing expression.

MR. P. (*obeying*): Will that do? (*Mrs. C. pouts.*) Come now, tell me *all* about it.

MRS. C.: I haven't lived four years alone in the world for nothing. I wouldn't tell anybody *all* about anything. It's a most dangerous proceeding.

MR. P.: But I am your oldest friend.

MRS. C.: You are my oldest enemy.

MR. P.: An enemy is one with whom one can be sincere. Tell me all about it.

MRS. C. (*shaking her head*): I'll see. And while I'm making up my mind, let us talk of trivial, unimportant things. How are you?

MR. P.: I'm hurrying towards eternity in much my usual way. I was forty last week, and such is my self-control that I have already recovered from the shock. (*Looking about the room.*)

MRS. C.: What are you looking for? Your lost youth? No, it isn't behind that curtain.

MR. P.: I was just wondering whether I *was* the first. I'm generally so late for your charming dinner-parties that this time I decided I would be very early. I hope I haven't come *too* early.

MRS. C.: Oh, no.

MR. P.: Your tone fills me with a horrid suspicion. I once arrived at a dinner party precisely twenty-four hours too soon. Most distressing! Don't tell me I've gone and done that trick again.

MRS. C. (*smiling*): Be perfectly calm. You have not.

MR. P.: Ah! Good! (*Glancing at book.*) What's the latest novel?

MRS. C. (*acidly*): The latest novel is Herbert Spencer's 'First Principles.'[2]

MR. P.: Sorry! I apologise.

MRS. C.: Why did you decide to come so early?

MR. P.: Oh! Just for a change. So you are reading Herbert–

MRS. C. (*interrupting him*): Now I can see you've got something on your mind. Don't pretend you're interested in the doings of a lone widow when you know very well you're only interested in yourself. You didn't come early just for a change. You came early because you wanted to have a few words with me in private.

MR. P.: Can it be that my skull is made of glass? Well, I did want to have a few words with you.

MRS. C.: I knew it.

MR. P.: I'm glad.

MRS. C.: Why?

MR. P.: Because now that you've proved yourself right, your nervous tension will slacken. In other words, you'll be in a better temper.

MRS. C.: Thank you. I'm waiting.

MR. P. (*leaning towards her with a caring manner*): Let's be serious. You've invited Jane, haven't you?

MRS. C.: Jane Foster?

MR. P.: Naturally. Did you think I meant Jane Cakebread?

MRS. C.: Yes. I invited Miss Foster.

MR. P. (*abruptly*): May I take her in?

(*A pause.*)

Mrs. C. rises and rings the bell. Enter servant.

MRS. C. (*to servant*): Coffee please. Bring an extra cup. (*Exit servant.*)

MR. P. (*also rising*): Is this the latest dieting dodge–coffee before dinner?

MRS. C.: No. It's a little device of my own for giving originality to the repast. (*Enter servant with coffee.*) Sugar? There! (*Handing cup to Platt.*) You see, one begins the dinner at the end. After you've drunk that, if you're good, you shall have some fruit. We shall get to the hors d'œuvres about ten o'clock. (*Exit servant.*)

MR. P. (*nonplussed*): But–

MRS. C.: My good man! Doesn't it occur to you? I have already dined. When I'm by myself I always dine at seven. My party was last night. Your praiseworthy effort to be early has only resulted in your being a day or so late. Now you have the cause of my high nervous tension. (*His cup rattles.*) Here! Don't attempt to rival Cinquevalli[3] like that. Give me the cup. (*She takes it from his trembling hand.*) Be seated, my poor friend. (*She persuades him into a chair, and, having put his cup on a table, sits down near him, and calmly stirs her own coffee.*)

MR. P. (*gasping*): It's incredible.

MRS. C.: What is?

MR. P.: That I could have been so stupid.

MRS. C.: My dear man, it isn't a bit incredible. You underrate your own powers.

MR. P.: Of course, you were furious.

MRS. C.: I was furious.

MR. P.: And still are?

MRS. C.: And still am.

MR. P.: It would be absurd to offer excuses.

MRS. C.: Wealthy as you are, you can't offer what you haven't got.

MR. P.: I ruined your dinner.

MRS. C.: No. My dinner perfectly survived the ordeal of your absence. The ortolans[4] in particular were an immense success. It was my pride alone that suffered.

MR. P.: But surely you must be aware that the loss was mine, that it was an accident. A confusion in dates–

MRS. C.: When one is really looking forward to a dinner, one does not confuse dates. What *did* you do last night?

MR. P.: I–er–

MRS. C.: Now don't prevaricate. The least you owe me is the horrible truth.

MR. P.: I dined at the Cock-and-Hen in Albemarle Street.

MRS. C.: Alone?

MR. P.: Alone, I swear it.

MRS. C.: And afterwards? You needn't blush. I shan't.

MR. P.: I–I called at the Fosters'. She wasn't in–I mean, Miss Jane.

MRS. C.: That is not surprising. She was here. Was that all you did?

MR. P.: No. After that I went to bed.

MRS. C. (*ringing bell*): You're recovering from your shame already, I see. (*Enter servant.*) Bring some grapes, please. (*Exit servant.*)

MR. P.: I assure you I am not recovering. I'm shrivelled up and aged with shame. I shall never be the same again.

(Enter servant with grapes.)

MRS. C.: Take some soup–I mean grapes. (*Exit servant.*)

MR. P.: I obey. (*Eating grapes greedily.*) You see how I obey, though I have no appetite whatever.

MRS. C.: Now discourse to me on the subject of Jane Foster.

MR. P.: Oh, no! Though I am weak in dates, I have a certain sense of tact.

MRS. C.: But you *must* discourse to me on the subject of Jane Foster. That is your penance. She seemed to miss you dreadfully last night.

MR. P. (*drily*): Did she?

MRS. C.: Yes. And so you came early specially in order to ask me to let you take her in to dinner?

MR. P. (*in a confidential tone*): Do you forgive me for my–er–defective chronology?

MRS. C.: No.

MR. P.: Then I don't eat another grape. I die of inanition. And you will have to telephone for an ambulance.

MRS. C.: Very well, then. I forgive you.

MR. P.: Honest Injun?

MRS. C.: Yes.

MR. P. (*with an air of relief*): Ah! The ground being cleared, let me execute the penance. Yes, I wanted to take the adorable Jane in to dinner. Delightful girl, isn't she? (*With enthusiasm.*)

MRS. C. (*with enthusiasm*): Quite!

MR. P.: Pretty.

MRS. C.: She's so sensible.

MR. P.: Intelligent.

MRS. C.: She does her hair beautifully.

MR. P.: Knows the world.

MRS. C.: She reads a lot.

MR. P.: You and she are great friends.

MRS. C.: Oh; we tell each other everything.

MR. P.: Then I shall be careful. What has she said about me?

MRS. C.: About you? Nothing. Of course, if I may put it so, everyone has noticed that lately you haven't been indifferent to her charms.

MR. P.: I can speak to you frankly?

MRS. C. (*entreatingly*): Do!

MR. P.: Do you think she and I would suit each other?

MRS. C.: I don't know where you would find a better wife.

MR. P. (*rising, and adopting a decisive and rather brutal manner*): What an awful untruth! What an awful untruth!

MRS. C.: Mr. Platt!

MR. P.: You said a minute ago you shouldn't blush. (*Drawing his chair nearer to hers and sitting down.*) Don't. And don't faint, cry, scream, rise in haughty anger, or attempt to rival Cinquevalli with your cup. Permit me. (*Takes the cup from her trembling hand and puts it on the table.*) I repeat now, in a calm, respectful, but inexorable voice that you have uttered the thing which is not. You *do* know where I should find a better wife.

MRS. C. (*with timid protest*): Then why didn't you ask me to give you this precious information long ago?

MR. P.: Because I didn't know that you knew.

MRS. C.: And when, may I inquire, did you learn that I knew?

MR. P.: I will tell you the exact moment. When I said to you to-night, 'May I take her in?'

MRS. C.: But I made no remark whatever in reply to that request.

MR. P.: Excuse me. You made all sorts of remarks with your eyes, your hands, your whole body–that adorable frame that it has pleased heaven to give you.

MRS. C.: I –

MR. P. (*standing up*): I'm desperately serious now, desperately. I'm not a youth, and you must try not to be a girl.

If you didn't guess, you ought to have guessed, that my one object in mildly running after Jane Foster has been to see if I could make you jealous. Did I succeed?

MRS. C. (*after a pause*): Yes.

MR. P. (*gazing at her, and then sitting down and taking her hand*): You would not be jealous if you did not care for me.

MRS. C. (*smiling*): How horridly logical you are with your masculine superiority!

MR. P.: You *do* care for me?

MRS. C.: See here, my dear friend. (*Withdrawing her hand.*) Don't you think you are rather reversing the customary order of things? You want to make me express my feelings before you express yours.

MR. P. (*passionately*): I love you.

MRS. C.: Well, if I said I didn't love you I should not be *quite* sure that I was not telling a falsehood.

MR. P. (*meditatively*): You love me, and yet three months ago you kept me at arm's length. You wouldn't give me the slightest chance to–

MRS. C.: If you actually were forty last week, don't be a boy again this week.

MR. P.: How a boy?

MRS. C.: A man would know that a woman is a fortress.

MR. P.: Well?

MRS. C.: And has to be stormed. When a general attacks a fortress he doesn't usually say to the besieged garrison: 'I've blown my trumpets, and if you don't walk out instantly I shall just go away and storm some other fortress. So there!'

MR. P. (*taking her in his arms and kissing her violently*): You are stormed, my fortress, and there will be no quarter.

MRS. C.: Have I cried for quarter? (*Disengaging herself and ringing bell.*)

MR. P.: What are you going to do, dearest child?

MRS. C.: Feed the conquering force. (*Enter servant.*) Will you please bring in the cold fowl and a bottle of Chablis?

Curtain

NOTES

1. *T.P.'s Weekly*. 14 December 1906, pages 771-772. Signed Arnold Bennett. The paper's founder, T.P. O'Connor (1848-1929), was a radical journalist who saw the paper as a vehicle for his reformist ambitions. He later became an Irish Nationalist Member of Parliament.

In his *How to Become an Author* (1903) Bennett refers to *T.P.'s Weekly* as appealing 'to a slightly higher order of intelligence than the *Tit-Bits* class' (p.69) and publishing 'short stories of a rather superior class' (p.105). Besides regular book reviews, the paper included serials and short stories from such well-known writers as Henry Rider Haggard, Joseph Conrad, George Gissing and Jack London.

2. Herbert Spencer (1820-1903) was a British engineer, editor, philosopher and sociologist. He was one of the early exponents of evolutionary theory. His *First Principles* (1860) provided an outline of universal knowledge. Widely read in Britain and America in his life-time, he was very much regarded as the common man's philosopher. Bennett published several articles referring to Spencer between 1903 and 1928. His *Journal* entry for 15 September 1910 records: 'When I think how *First Principles*, by filling me up with the sense of causation everywhere, has altered my whole view of life, and undoubtedly immensely improved it, I am confirmed in my opinion of that book. You can see *First Principles* in nearly every line I write!' For an illuminating account of Spencer's influence on Bennett, see Chapter 3, 'High Modernity' in Robert Squillace's *Modernism, Modernity, and Arnold Bennett* (1997).

3. Paul Cinquevalli (1859-1918) was a famous juggler. He first performed in England in 1885 and such was his immediate success, he made London his touring base until his death. Junia Comfrey's reference to Cinquevalli as she removes a tea-cup from Octavius Platt's shaking hand is entirely appropriate as his trade-mark speciality was to juggle with everyday objects such as cups, bottles, plates, glasses and umbrellas. Bennett's *Journal* entry for 24 October 1897 records a visit to the Folies-Bergère, where the 'main part of the performance was a weak imitation of the Empire, with two well-known Empire stars, Loïe Fuller and Cinquevalli, to give distinction'. Bennett is still remembering and referring to Cinquevalli in his *Journal* as late as 6 October 1923.

4. The ortolan, a small bird, was long considered to be the pinnacle of gastronomic delight. It is now a protected species after being hunted almost to extinction.

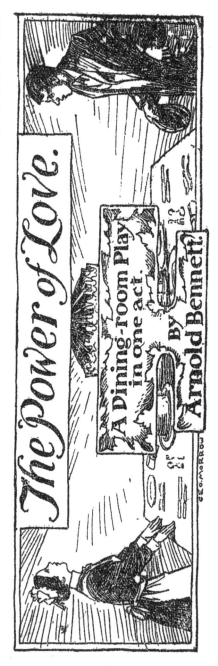

The Power of Love.

A Dining-Room Play in one act.

By Arnold Bennett.

GEO. MORROW

T. P.'s Weekly. Christmas 1906.

THE POWER OF LOVE.[1]
A Dining-room Play in one act.

CHARACTERS.

SYLVIA (aged 20).

JANE TWYCER, her mistress (aged 24).

PHILIP TWYCER, her master (aged 25).

CUTHBERT, the fruiterer's boy (aged 19).

The scene represents a small dining-room in a West London flat. Table set for dinner for two. A raised dessert dish, empty, stands prominent in the centre of the table. Doors back-centre and left.

Time: Evening in December.

Enter Sylvia (C.), followed by Cuthbert bearing a large basket on his arm. Sylvia is the incarnation of neatness; Cuthbert is not at all a dandy.

SYLVIA (*whose gestures, while modest, show that there is something in Cuthbert which has enslaved her*): Come in, come in.

CUTHBERT: In here?

SYLVIA: Why, of course! It's warm here. Now, give me your basket, and sit down. It's better here than out in that fog, isn't it? (*Coaxes him.*) There!

CUTHBERT: That's all very well, but what price my customers?

SYLVIA: Are you afraid of losing your Christmas boxes?[2]

CUTHBERT: Not much. I got 'em all in yesterday.

SYLVIA (*smoothing his coat*): And yet you can't bear to be late on your rounds! You're a regular hero, that's what you are!

CUTHBERT: I say, I often wanted to ask you–

SYLVIA: Ask me anything, *anything*.

CUTHBERT: Why do you sort of like me, in a way of speaking?

SYLVIA: Shall I tell you what first made me–? It was your

name–Cuthbert.

CUTHBERT (*disappointed*): Oh! I thought it was the pattern of my apron.

SYLVIA: I like your apron, too. I love it. But Cuthbert–it's such a *nice* name. I adore nice names. Mine's rather nice, isn't it?

CUTHBERT: Yes.

SYLVIA: Say it, and then you'll hear how it sounds.

CUTHBERT: Sylvia.

SYLVIA (*sighs, and controls herself*): What have you brought for us?

CUTHBERT: Pound o' grapes.

SYLVIA: You don't say! Well, my dinner's wasted, and that's all about it!

CUTHBERT: All along of a pound o'grapes?

SYLVIA: I'll tell you something; I love telling you things (*sighs*). Master and mistress quarrel.

CUTHBERT: Why?

SYLVIA (*hesitating*): I suppose it's because they're so much in love with each other. It gets on their nerves; only been married six months, you know.

CUTHBERT: Quarrel because they're in love? What rot!

SYLVIA: You don't understand love. I do. Love makes you do things. It's a queer–. Well; I was telling you. They quarrel. They have no secrets from me. They both say I'm a very superior girl, and I am! At least, I was. They've been quarrelling lately about whether they should have fruit or cake after dinner. Mistress wants grapes; master wants cake.

CUTHBERT: And he's right, by gum! If he knew as much about fruit as I do. But cake–I could eat *it* till I bust.

SYLVIA: It came to a head to-day.

CUTHBERT: What did?

SYLVIA: The quarrel. Master said if mistress didn't buy cake–

CUTHBERT: Why don't they have both?

SYLVIA: How silly you are! That wouldn't *do*. You don't

understand real love. One of them's got to give way. Well, as I was telling you, master said this afternoon if mistress didn't buy cake he should go upstairs and dine with his parents. And mistress said she should buy fruit, and if he *did* dine upstairs with his parents she should dine downstairs with *hers*.

CUTHBERT: All the family in one house. That's funny.

SYLVIA: No, it isn't. It began like that. Master and mistress first met in the lift.

CUTHBERT: Nice and cosy for 'em.

SYLVIA (*starting at this remark*): I believe you *do* understand love a bit.

CUTHBERT (*lifts his chin*): So your dinner's going to be wasted?

SYLVIA: Oh! Sure!

CUTHBERT (*sniffing*): Goose? (*Sylvia nods.*) Pity! I could shift a goose.

SYLVIA (*eagerly*): You shall–

A noise of latchkey, &c., outside. Sylvia springs up and pushes Cuthbert and his basket through the door (L).

Enter Mrs. Twycer, in furs, carrying a round parcel.

MRS. T.: Sylvia–
Sylvia puts her finger to her lips and points to the door (L).
MRS. T. (*whispering*): Has he come back?

SYLVIA (*whispering*): Yes, ma'am.

MRS. T. (*still whispering*): Has he brought any cigarettes?

SYLVIA: No, ma'am.

MRS. T. (*confidentially*): Look here, Sylvia. You are a superior girl. I can ask you. Is he in a good temper?

SYLVIA: No, ma'am–that is–I hardly like–

MRS. T.: That will do. He soon *will* be in a good temper. I changed my mind and brought him a cake. (*Unwraps cake, and puts it on dessert dish.*) Has the fruiterer sent?

SYLVIA (*unmoved, still whispering*): No, ma'am.

MRS. T.: Well, when the boy comes tell him to take back

the grapes I've ordered. I'm going to dress now.

SYLVIA: Yes, ma'am.

Exit Mrs. Twycer (C).

SYLVIA (*opening door L, in her ordinary tone of voice*): You can come back now.

Enter Cuthbert.

CUTHBERT (*timid*): By gum! (*gazing round cautiously*). All right?

SYLVIA: All right, except that she's gone and bought a cake.

CUTHBERT: Then they'll eat your dinner?

SYLVIA (*sadly*): Yes.

CUTHBERT: By gum! That gave me a start, that did. I'd better hook it afore worse happens.

SYLVIA (*in a new tone*): No hurry. She's dressing. She'll be half-an-hour. You look faint. Have some cake. Eat it till you bust. (*She cuts a good slice out of the cake with a fish knife, and presents it to his lips. He takes it, overcome by the temptation*). There! Great baby!

CUTHBERT (*with his mouth full, staring at hole in cake*): And what'll they say about *that*?

SYLVIA (*also staring at the wounded cake*): Oh, that! That's easy enough. (*She seizes fish knife again, and cuts the entire cake up into slices, and then quickly arranges the slices with a small gap between each, so as to conceal the fact that one slice has disappeared. Smiling*) There!

CUTHBERT: You are clever, no mistake!

SYLVIA: I hadn't used to be so clever. That's what love does, that is! It makes you kind of do things. I–. Have another slice?

A noise of latchkey, &c., outside.

SYLVIA: Master! (*whispering*): Where's them grapes? (*She pitches the whole cake on to the floor in a corner of the room, and puts the grapes on the dessert dish instead. Then she pushes Cuthbert and his basket through the door L).*

Enter Mr. Twycer, in a thick overcoat.

MR. T.: I say, Sylvia.

SYLVIA (*putting her finger to her lips and pointing to the door, L*): Hush.

MR. T. (*whispering*): My wife in there?

SYLVIA (*whispering*): Yes, sir.

MR. T. (*taking a small parcel from his pocket*): Look here, Sylvia. You're a decent girl. Take her these cigarettes, will you–from me. She isn't still–er–vexed, is she?

SYLVIA (*indicating grapes on dish, and making a discreet gesture*): It's not my place, sir, to–

MR. T. (*furious, no longer whispering*): She bought them, then, did she, after all! Very well! Very well! Kindly tell your mistress that I'm going to dine upstairs with father and mother.

Exit. Loud bang of door. Off.

Sylvia meditatively unties the box of cigarettes. She is just about to open the door (L) when enters Mrs. T., dressed for dinner. Sylvia just has time to whisk the grapes off the plate. She holds both them and the box of cigarettes behind her.

MRS. T.: Who was that? Not your master?

SYLVIA (*primly*): Yes, ma'am.

MRS. T.: What did he say? Where's he gone?

SYLVIA: He came in here, ma'am, out of the drawing-room (*pointing to the door, L*), and he looks at the cake–

MRS. T. (*interrupting*): Where is the cake?

SYLVIA (*unmoved, continuing*): He looks at that cake and he cuts it in two with a fish knife–yes'm, the fish knife. You can see for yourself (*holds up fish knife for inspection*).

MRS. T: What did he say?

SYLVIA (*as if imitating*): 'Um,' he says, 'Sultana! And she knows that's just the cake I don't like.' Then he hacks the cake all to pieces, ma'am, and pitches it into the corner. And there it is, ma'am (*pointing*). 'Kindly tell your mistress,' he says, ma'am, 'that I'm going to dine upstairs with father and mother.'

A pause.

MRS. T. (*breathing hard*): Kindly tell your master, Sylvia, that I'm going *down*-stairs to dine with *my* father and mother.

SYLVIA: But he's gone, ma'am.

Mrs.T., ignoring the remark, sweeps out.

Exit. Violent bang of door. Off.

Sylvia slowly and reflectively puts the grapes on a chair, takes a cigarette out of the box, picks up a match-box, and then opens door (L), inviting Cuthbert, with a smile, to enter.

Enter Cuthbert.

CUTHBERT: By gum! Coast clear? I'm going to hook it.

SYLVIA: You needn't (*offering a cigarette*). Would it like one? (*She puts the cigarette into his mouth, strikes a match, and lights it. She then picks up cake from floor.*)

CUTHBERT: So long. (*Puffing.*)

SYLVIA (*approaching him*): Cuthbert!

CUTHBERT: What oh?

She gently takes his basket from him, forces him into a chair at the table, and puts a piece of cake into his mouth.

SYLVIA: We're all alone. They're both gone. Wait there.

Exit Sylvia (C). Cuthbert expresses in silence his noncomprehension of events and his weakness in the hands of a woman. Re-enter Sylvia, bearing a goose, which she puts on table.

CUTHBERT: But what about my customers?

SYLVIA: What about this goose that you said you could shift?

CUTHBERT (*trying to eat cake and smoke simultaneously*): It's my guv'ner that'll shift me.

SYLVIA (*sitting down and beginning to carve*): Leg or wing?

CUTHBERT: But I say–

SYLVIA: Listen to me, you nice boy. They're both gone,

and they won't be back for ages. And my dinner hasn't got to be wasted. It would be a sin. Leg or wing?

CUTHBERT: Breast.

SYLVIA: How sensible you are (*carving*).

CUTHBERT: I'm not. I shall get the sack.

SYLVIA: No you won't.

CUTHBERT: How do you know I shan't? I'm jolly well sure I shall.

SYLVIA (*knife in air, cogitating; then suddenly*): Foggy night! Thieves about! They always are on foggy nights. You are attacked by Hooligans, who rob you of your basket, and run away. You search in vain. Then you find the basket, empty, of course, and you go back to the shop and tell your master. I shall eat the fruit. I adore fruit, oranges particularly.

CUTHBERT (*accepting goose*): You are about the smartest little thing–

SYLVIA: It's love.

CUTHBERT: It's awfully–well, *wrong*, ain't it?

SYLVIA: No, it's love. I hadn't used to be like that. I used to be just the ordinary superior girl.

CUTHBERT (*eating*): And what'll *you* say?

SYLVIA: When?

CUTHBERT: To-morrow, when they find as the goose is eaten.

SYLVIA: Oh, that's nothing! The goose is *nothing*. I've told them such awful stories to get them out. But I don't care. They won't sack *me*.

CUTHBERT: Why won't they?

SYLVIA: Sack a general servant! Did you ever hear of such a thing? Where would they get the next one from? Besides, I shall–. Well, I don't know *what* I shall do–so long as you like the goose, Cuthbert. Do you?

CUTHBERT (*with his mouth full, nodding*) Mm–mm!

SYLVIA (*rising, and picking a few grapes*): What lovely grapes! (*She puts the remainder of the bunch back on the dish. Then*

255

she selects an orange from the basket).

CUTHBERT: Jaffa!

SYLVIA (*with a little shriek*): Oh, you nice boy! You've forgotten your serviette! (*She ties a serviette lovingly round his neck*).

CUTHBERT (*still eating*): Why did you do that?

SYLVIA (*standing by his side*): Say 'Sylvia'. How can I tell who you're talking to if you don't say 'Sylvia'?

CUTHBERT: Sylvia.

SYLVIA (*to herself*): Love is the curiousest thing.

CUTHBERT: I could do a bit more o' that goose.

(Curtain)

NOTES

1. *T.P.'s Weekly*. Christmas 1906, pages 39-40. Signed Arnold Bennett. Illustration by George Morrow. Morrow (1870-1955) was born in Belfast. Four of his seven brothers were also cartoonists and illustrators. He studied in Paris and exhibited in London, including the Royal Academy, between 1897 and 1904. He first worked for *Punch* in 1906, later becoming its Art Editor.

2. A Christmas box was money given to workers, such as delivery boys and postmen, in recognition of good service provided throughout the year.

MISS SCROOGE[1]
Or the Story of a Christmas Day Curmudgeon.

Never before has the truth been realistically set down concerning the attitude towards Christmas of a certain type of mind—a mind unbending, unsentimental, egotistic, and philosophic with the cruel philosophy of the superman. Every December a vast conspiracy is hatched by the writers of Great Britain (and Ireland) to pretend that the sweet influences of Christmas mollify all hearts without exception, and that during at least twenty-four hours there exists not in these islands a human being unactuated by goodwill and peaceful desires.

Dickens initiated the conspiracy. He found pleasure in inventing the most satanic persons, and then popping them into Christmas, as a conjuror pops a carrot into a hat, and bringing them forth sudden angels, as a conjuror brings forth white doves out of a hat. A pretty entertainment, but grossly misleading!

Now *I* will faithfully describe for you the actual Christmas Day of a curmudgeon, as I myself saw it lived. I am determined to describe it, for valuable lessons are to be gathered from the recital. I must warn you, however, that the details are very disagreeable, and those who are afraid of uncompromising realism should not read any further. They should read 'A Christmas Carol'[2] over again.

Embittered by Experience.

She—yes, I regret to say it was a she. Scrooge in the masculine is bad enough, but Scrooge in the feminine is too bad. A female curmudgeon has always excited the disgust and horror of mankind. Nevertheless, I cannot change her sex in order to spare your nice feelings. The creature was of the sex which does not distinguish between a Havana and a Sumatra.[3]

She was almost toothless, and her hair was inclined to be thin–a peculiar trial for a woman. And it must be admitted that within the previous six months unexpected experiences had considerably aged her and embittered her.

Herein lies the sole excuse for her conduct. Ugly she was, and she was obese, but these characteristics do not palliate such behaviour as hers; especially as she was rich, and had everything she wanted, including a poor martyr of a personal attendant, who was at her beck and call from six o'clock in the morning to six o'clock in the morning, seven days a week.

She would not listen to Christmas; she would hear naught of it, nor of presents, nor of greetings, nor of any seasonableness.

There were three other people in the house–a large one–Thomas, aged nine, and his father and mother.

Dreams of Dinner.

When he woke up, Thomas, after untying and unwrapping a score of presents, including a 60 watch-spring motor car, and after whooping, immediately began to think upon how much he could eat during the day. His ideal was half a goose, four mince pies, trifle, four hot pikelets[4] (at tea), about a third of a turkey, three helpings of Christmas pudding, five mince pies, seventy and seven oranges, with sundries to make weight. He meant, if possible, to beat his own record of last year.

Thomas's father, on waking up, immediately began to think upon how little he could eat. 'Last year,' said Thomas's father, 'it was certainly the sage and onions that upset me. And, of course, for a man with my delicate digestion, sausage is simply ridiculous, and mince is the very deuce. I really must control myself at table.' Thomas's mother, on waking up, immediately began to think of her new evening dress; she then reminded her husband that it was quarter day,[5] and that there was a burst spout over the kitchen window; and she got him down into the hall and kissed him under mistletoe.

In short, the genuine Christmas feeling was in the air.

'Christians, Awake!'

Auntie (as they all flatteringly called the curmudgeon) was still asleep. Her relatives collected their gifts for her– simple things, but unshakable evidence of affection for a being buffeted by the world; they then waited for her to rouse up; it was still early. A prize brass band came along the street in the snow (for there was a little feeble snow), and, while inducing chilblains and other maladies in its extremities, commenced by means of blue, mittened fingers on cold metal to salute the happy morn. This picturesque salutation of the happy morn had the unfortunate effect of waking auntie. She ought to have been glad to be galvanised into consciousness by the pleasing Christmas spectacle and sound; she ought to have been proud that fifteen men with icy feet had combined to draw her attention to the fact of Christmas; but she was not. The effect on their relative of the prize brass band can be gathered from the phrase which Thomas's mother whispered to Thomas's father:

'She's upset for the day.'

Perhaps she was. Anyhow, she accepted their well-meant gifts in silence, scarcely examining them. She sent nothing out to the band, not even an orange apiece. She regarded the band simply as an organism for depriving her of sleep. She allowed it to be understood that she did not see the fun of paying fifteen men, either in money or fruit, for waking her up when she had no wish to be wakened up. She visited her displeasure on the relatives, and particularly on her attendant. Not that she grumbled or nagged. She maintained a cold, philosophic calm, after the first spasm of resentment. She thought neither of special evening dresses, nor of how much or how little she could eat. The notion of varying her diet (she was a vegetarian) because it was Christmas Day never even occurred to her. She had no craving to eat either more, or less, or differently. In short, she outraged the most sacred traditions of Christmas. Further, she spent not a halfpenny in presents. No one got anything at all. They left her; the attendant said it would be better so.

Living to Eat.

During the whole day she practised the philosophy which life had taught her, namely: first, that there is no satisfaction in this world equal to the satisfaction of eating regularly according to a scientific diet, which cannot disagree with you; second, that it is absurd to do anything yourself when you can force anyone else to do it for you; third, that you can always get what you want if you make yourself sufficiently unpleasant; fourth, that if you resolutely regard yourself as the centre and excuse for the universe you will succeed in persuading others to regard you in the same light.

She ignored the frantic but futile efforts of Thomas to eat as much as he wished to eat. She had no sympathy with Thomas. She said not a word in appreciation of the really exquisite frock which Thomas's mother donned towards evening. And when the guests for the Christmas dinner began to arrive, bursting with good-will, good wishes, and jollity, she merely went to bed. She had lived for herself throughout the day, thinking only of herself and her own aggrandisement and the satisfaction of her own desires; and she was happy in this achievement! Therefore she went to bed. Nobody asked her to remain downstairs to dinner, for she would only have spoilt the dinner by steadily continuing the ruthless practice of her philosophy. And while Thomas's father was sniffing at sage and onions, and falling a victim to the enchantments of sausage, the toothless superwoman calmly slept. Conscience never troubled her.

Such was her Christmas.

The Angel of the House.

On Boxing Day she woke up, refreshed, calm, in perfect health; it might have been any other morning. Thomas was very ill indeed. Thomas's father was in half-mourning for his digestion. Thomas's mother had her hands full of sick men and disillusions. It was a draggled, jaundiced crowd that went in to pay respects to an Auntie placid and self-absorbed as ever.

'Hello, Auntie!' exclaimed Thomas's father, with a pitiful attempt to be joyous.

'I won't have her called Auntie any more!' said Thomas's mother crossly.

'Don't be silly!' said Thomas's father, secretly rather glad of an opportunity to be cross also.

'I'm not silly!' said Thomas's mother. 'But it might bring her bad luck in marriage. Nurse, did she take her bottle properly? The little angel is just six months old to-day!'

There you are! An unmitigated and relentless egotist–and yet she could find people to call her a little angel. This is real life.

NOTES

1. *Daily Dispatch.* 24 December 1907, page 4. Signed Arnold Bennett. In 1900 Ned Hulton started the *Daily Dispatch* as a Manchester based newspaper to compete with the bigger daily newspapers. His premises in Withy Grove - an area sometimes referred to as 'the other Fleet Street' - became the biggest printing house in Europe, continuing to operate until the late 1980s.

'Miss Scrooge' was Bennett's first contribution to the paper, followed by a series of articles over the following two years.

2. Charles Dickens's *A Christmas Carol* (1843) tells the story of Scrooge, an old curmudgeon, who mends his ways as the result of a series of visions of his past life. At the moment of his spiritual rebirth Scrooge has lost count of time and compares his state to that of a baby: '"I don't know what day of the month it is! .... I don't know anything. I'm quite a baby. Never mind. I don't care. I'd rather be a baby"' (p.128).

3. The Havana and the Sumatra are types of cigars.

4. Pikelets are a type of pancake made with a mixture of plain and self-raising flour with currants, sultanas and raisins. Potteries' writer and artist Arthur Berry (1925-1994) provides, perhaps, the best definition:

> The Pikelet you ask what's that?
> It's a sort of female Oatcake
> Smaller thicker, sweeter
> More immediately seductive
> Sometimes with currants in it
> A muffin for the Lumpen working class
> Best eaten soaked in butter or marge.
>
> 'Homage to the Oatcake',
> *Dandelions. Poems.* p.25.

Pikelets appear on the literary menu in several Bennett stories and novels, forming, for example, part of the wedding breakfast in the Five Towns story 'The Long Lost Uncle' (*The Matador of the Five Towns*, p.211) and appearing for sale alongside the fruit and vegetables in Bursley market in *The Old Wives' Tale* (p.49).

5. Quarter Days in England, Scotland and Wales refer to the four dates in the year on which servants were hired, and, in this story, when rents were paid one quarter in advance. Less significant today when modern transport facilitates ease of movement, nevertheless some leasehold payments and property rents still fall due on: 25 March (Lady Day), 24 June (Midsummer Day), 29 September (Michaelmas), 25 December (Christmas Day).

THE LURE OF LIFE.[1]
GETTING AWAY FROM THE OFFICE.

Charles Florius was a man of letters in the widest sense of the term, in full working order and activity, and in the full flower of his maturity. His friends, who were men of business, envied him a little because his name was always in the papers, and a great deal because his existence was so free and so easy. This man, they said, had never to be on a particular spot of the earth's surface at a particular moment of terrestrial time–such as Chancery-lane at a quarter-past nine a.m. He could perform his work anywhere. All he had to do was to sit down and write the things that came into his head–because he was born like that. The friends of Charles Florius said: 'This man really lives. His life amounts to one long holiday.'

Now Charles Florius was saying to himself: 'I haven't had a holiday for fifteen years. Every year for at least ten I have resolved to take a complete holiday, and I have never done it. This year I will do it. During one month I will do no work whatever.'

And with his keen, trained, professional imagination he imagined himself setting off on a bicycle one morning (for he was a simple man), and leaving everything behind him except his address.

* * *

He felt most acutely the call of life. He knew better than anybody that he had never had time to live, and that the years were passing under his feet at a terrific rate. He knew that the life of his business friends was an infantile diversion compared to his complicated and anxious and crowded existence. Their day began at nine or ten, or even ten-thirty; his at six a.m. Theirs ended at six p.m.; his ended when he dropped off to sleep, and often recommenced in the middle of the night. They had week-ends, every week-end; he never had a week-end. They went away for periods, long or short, and left their offices behind. The walls of his office were always around him. See him on the Leas at Folkstone. You think he is on the Leas, idling. No, he is in his office, too busy to live. He said to himself: 'I will positively walk out of my office.'

It was a difficult thing to manage. Charles Florius wrote a novel, sometimes two, a play, and a number of short stories every year; and one or two articles every week. The commercial side of his career was very complex, and an agent attended to this for him; but he had to attend to the agent, and they were always in correspondence, about copyright in Canada, or a German translation, or the prices offered by a monthly review, or some such thing. Then he had to keep a journal, because a journal is useful, in the end saving much trouble. If a good notion struck him, he had no secret peace till it was safe in writing, for the best notions forget themselves; generally the good notion proved to be worthless. And if notions did not arrive of their own free will, he had to go out with a net and catch them. A constant supply of notions was essential to the prosecution of his career. The charming old scheme of 'waiting for inspiration' would have ruined Charles Florius in six months. Newspapers, reviews, and publishers don't wait for inspiration; they won't. They want contracts, and precise dates in these contracts.

* * *

The program of Charles Florius was definitely fixed long in advance. On such a day the first of a series of twelve articles had to be delivered; on such a day a story; on or before such a day the complete MS. of a novel, not less than so many thousand words; on or before such a day the scenario of a play. And so it was always. Thus, the extreme difficulty of getting out of his office may be judged; the feat had to be arranged for months in advance. Indeed, it was generally known in Fleet-st. and similar spots in the middle of winter, that between two given dates in the summer Charles Florius meant to be out of his office. Editors and colleagues laughed.

But there were other and equally serious difficulties, perhaps more serious. He had a continual extensive correspondence to deal with. One of his Sunday relaxations was to clear off its arrears. He was always saying that he would cut most of it, and that letters answered themselves if you left them alone, etc. But in practice the idea would not work. His correspondence defeated him; he was never quite even with it. Then he had to read newspapers of all colors, and he had to think about what he read, and put two and two together, and do other tiresome things that happier persons never have to do. For his active and voracious brain required constant nourishment. Besides, people said that he reflected his age. How could he reflect his age unless he was always staring at it?

* * *

Moreover, he had no speciality; he could not confine himself to one department; the entire age was his province. And to understand his age he had to read about other ages, a most tedious affair. And of course he had to keep abreast with new literature, literature also being a part of his age. And he had to travel and see the world, otherwise he would have remained narrow and insular. And then at least three days a week he had to read his Press-cuttings, just to see how his reputation was getting on, and what the impudent younger generation was saying about him. In odd moments he thought about posterity. And far more important than his reputation was his bodily health. His was the unhealthiest of all vocations, and the most dependent upon good health. A headache–a simple headache–and all Charles Florius's machinery was stopped dead, and programs twisted and correspondence multiplied!

Finally, if he did have an odd moment, be sure that he was obliged to devote it to expressing his opinion about something–something serious. There are about fifty thousand excellent 'movements' afoot in England, all of which call aloud to be encouraged by a good out-and-out Radical; and some forty-nine thousand of these movements spent postage in writing letters to Charles Florius–letters which usually ended, 'Your name will be of service to us.'

* * *

Well, he did what he had sworn to do. He emerged from his office. It cost him an immense effort, but he did it. He had imagined himself setting off on a bicycle one morning, free, untrammelled, in search of life. The event came to pass. And it was quite exquisitely enjoyable as he had anticipated. As he coasted down hills, and as he pushed the package-laden bicycle up hills, he experienced such sensations as he had never experienced. He said to himself that he had spent forty years odd in preparing to live, and had never lived; he had only written about life; and he wondered that he could have been so stupid, he who was accounted so clever and so wise. Life itself! He rushed forward as if to savor it –especially when the gradient was easy.

This felicitous mood lasted for a couple of days. Then it began to weaken. Then it expired, and Charles Florius was aware of ennui. It was not that he had not found Life. He had not expected to find it. He was stupid, but not so stupid as that. What disconcerted him was that he had no assurance of getting nearer to Life; indeed the contrary.

One evening (after less than a week), looking at a map as he lolled on the verandah of an agreeable hotel, he made a wonderful discovery. He saw on the map exactly where Life was. He had left Life behind in his office, and it was calling to him like anything! He had arranged to be out of his office for a month; and he was a man who would suffer tortures rather than alter an arrangement. So he did not instantly fly back. But he modified his route, and, turning his face a little towards Life the next day, he approached it circuitously, like a Red Indian stalking his unsuspecting prey.

NOTES

1. *Morning Leader.* 3 August 1910, page 4. Signed Arnold Bennett. The paper was published in London from 1892 until 1912, when it merged with the *Daily News.* Although published in London, 'colors' and 'savor' appear in their American spelling.

'The Lure of Life' is Bennett's sole contribution to the paper, although the merged *Daily News and Leader* later serialised his novel *The Price of Love* (1914), together with a number of wartime articles.

THE ALARM.[1]
a futurist play[2] in one act and five minutes

CHARACTERS

A Militant Suffragette[3]   (Aged about 30. Rather chic and sprightly. Middle-class matter-of-factness beneath a veneer of upper-class modernity.)

An Archbishop   (Any age over 50. Impressive, but now and then sprightly, and with a good sense of humour.)

A fireman

A policeman

SCENE   Horse Guards Parade. In the middle of the stage is a Fire Alarm. Nothing else is visible. The Fire Alarm is of a grotesque shape, exaggerating the peculiarities of a fire-alarm. A single ray of light falls on it from above. The costumes of all the characters are also slightly grotesque. The noise of the approaching fire engines, at the end of the play, must be a grotesque imitation of the real thing, made vocally by people in the wings. The fire-hose too must be grotesque.
In all these details realism is to be avoided.

TIME   Night

The Militant is staring at the Fire Alarm.
Enter the Archbishop, rather jauntily.

ARCHBISHOP
My good woman, what are you gazing at with such vehemence?

MILITANT

(<u>After examining him</u>) This fire alarm,–my good man.

ARCHBISHOP

Ah! So here we have a fire alarm. I have often heard of this clever little–if I may say so–dodge. Madam, we live in a wonderful age, do we not? But (<u>suddenly bending to the alarm</u>) the example under our consideration scarcely coincides with my conception of the sane, healthy, English fire alarm. Surely there is something abnormal about it?

MILITANT

(<u>gravely</u>) It must be the essence of the fire alarm. Truth, as distinguished from mere realism.

ARCHBISHOP

(<u>surprised at her vocabulary</u>) Madam! .... But surely the glass is broken!

MILITANT

Yes. I've just broken it. (<u>pulls the handle</u>) And now I've pulled the handle.

ARCHBISHOP

Where is the conflagration?

MILITANT

There is none, just at present. But there will be in less than a minute (<u>shows a great box of matches</u>).

ARCHBISHOP

(<u>sternly</u>) Madam, what are you?

MILITANT

(<u>saucily</u>) What are you, first?

ARCHBISHOP

I am an archbishop.

MILITANT

That's funny now. I was just thinking you looked as if you might be interested in cathedrals. Can I trust you?

ARCHBISHOP

(spreading himself) Madam, do I not inspire confidence? What is your secret?

MILITANT

I'm a militant. The Prime Minister is giving a party at No 10 Downing Street, just round the corner. The entire Cabinet is there. My orders are to lock the doors and set fire to the house.

ARCHBISHOP

(wonderstruck and admiring) What a marvellous idea! What a conclusive answer to their arid arguments! Strange that no one ever thought of it before!

MILITANT

(startled) Then you approve?

ARCHBISHOP

No–No! For an instant I allowed myself to be carried away. But upon calmer reflection I perceive that every archiepiscopal convention compels me to forbid this scheme. Answer me only one question,–why do you give the alarm first and light the fire afterwards? Is the procedure quite, quite logical, sane, –in a word normal?

MILITANT

Because I don't approve of the idea, either. Poison's one thing –burning alive's quite another. I've sworn to do my duty, and do it I shall, but I'm taking precautions. Well, I must run off. (fingering match box)

ARCHBISHOP

Stop: how did you become a militant?

MILITANT

(<u>staccato</u>) Lone widow! Ratepayer![4] Rates twelve shillings in pound! Forgot to pay 'em! Summons! Bumbailiffs![5]

ARCHBISHOP

(<u>scared</u>) What mean you, madam? Are you out of breath?

MILITANT

(<u>rapidly</u>) Play has to finish in a minute.

ARCHBISHOP

Play? Has to finish?

MILITANT

What am I saying? I mean the fire-engine will be here in a minute. (<u>speaking very quickly</u>) You see I don't pay my rates prompt, and I should think not, indeed, me rated at thirty two pounds and rates twelve and three, and next year it'll be twelve and six you may be sure. Well, they summoned me, and I made a mistake in the date of the summons, and before I knew where I was they'd put the bumbailiffs in, and all the street knew. So when I'd paid 'em out I said to myself if I'm good enough to be summoned for my rates I'm good enough to vote, that's what I am, and off I went straight to the W.S.P.U.[6] And they taught me to make speeches standing on chairs in squares, and improved my accent,–only I forget it sometimes–and paid for my clothes, and little by little .... (<u>nearly breaking down, but controlling herself</u>) Well, never mind! I shall now be a cat-and-mouser![7] Hurrah!

ARCHBISHOP

Woman, be warned. Are you sure you have the strength of will necessary to become a–er–cat–and–mouser. Can you continue to refuse solid or light refreshments for long periods?

MILITANT

There's only one thing I can't refuse, and I'm quite sure they'll never offer me that at Holloway.[8]

ARCHBISHOP

And what is it?

MILITANT

Turkish Delight. Been a slave to it since birth! (<u>archly</u>) Well, bye bye. Come and see me in Holloway.

ARCHBISHOP

(<u>solemnly, raising a hand</u>) Pause, I say! If you make one single step further in the direction of Downing Street I shall drive straight to Holloway and inform the Governor that he can–if I may employ an unarchiepiscopal expression–do you in the eye with Turkish Delight. You will be covered with ignominy. Your cause, which has my sympathy, will be killed by ridicule, and civilisation may be thrown back for half a century!

MILITANT

You're not serious!

ARCHBISHOP

(<u>protesting</u>) Madam, I am an archbishop!

MILITANT

You're taking advantage of me.

ARCHBISHOP

(<u>protesting</u>) Madam! Me, an archbishop!

MILITANT

You're horribly mean. (<u>turns in opposite direction, and throws matchbox away; pettishly</u>)

ARCHBISHOP

(<u>softly</u>) My poor creature, go home to your children.

MILITANT

Haven't got any!

ARCHBISHOP

(sternly) Why not?

MILITANT

Well, if you must know, it's after ten o'clock, and magistrates won't grant licences for children nowadays.

ARCHBISHOP

(aside) She raves! (to Militant) Here! Take this half-crown. (gives her coin)

MILITANT

For the cause?

ARCHBISHOP

No. For Turkish Delight.

MILITANT

You're a dear, after all!

ARCHBISHOP

(protesting) Go! I hear the fire-engine.

MILITANT

The firemen will be angry if there is no fire for them.

ARCHBISHOP

Rely upon me to deal with the brigade.

MILITANT

(lightly) Oh very well! (Exit)

Noise of fire-engines approaching. Deafening climax. Clouds of steam, etc.

Enter firemen each dragging a long hose. They surround fire-alarm and Archbishop.

ARCHBISHOP

Calm yourselves, my good men. We are nearly in the middle of the Horse Guards Parade. I myself am the only combustible object in sight, and I can assure you that I am not on fire.

FIREMAN

Where is the houtbreak?

ARCHBISHOP

There is no outbreak. There was going to be an outbreak, and the alarm was sounded as a precautionary measure. However, I succeeded, I may say, in making other arrangements.

FIREMAN

Drunk as a blooming cook! One more false alarm–and me dozing so beautiful! Bill, run for a bobby.[9] (exit a fireman–Archbishop moves uneasily) You stand still. Who are you?

ARCHBISHOP

I am an archbishop.

FIREMAN

Which?

ARCHBISHOP

I decline to give the name of my province. I decline absolutely. If the police are to be brought in, I simply will not disclose my identity. An archbishop! Nothing more!

FIREMAN

Archbishop, eh? Well, while we're on the subject, who d'ye think I am? I'm the Tetrarch.[10] Archbishop! (sneers). You've been to Covent Garden Fancy Dress Ball and you've mixed your drinks. You ain't real for two d.

274

ARCHBISHOP

If it comes to that you are not a real fireman. Just look at yourself! And this moonlight isn't real, either. And this isn't real hose! And that isn't a real fire-alarm!

POLICEMAN

(<u>approaching from behind, and clapping him on the shoulder</u>) Perhaps not! But I'm a real policeman. (<u>Slips handcuffs on Archbishop</u>) Call these unreal if you like. <u>I</u> don't mind. Only come along. And quick!

ARCHBISHOP

(<u>stopping for an instant at wings. Mildly</u>) I confess I had not envisaged this result.

CURTAIN

NOTES

1. *Designer.* January 1915, page 5. Signed Arnold Bennett. The version reproduced here is transcribed from Bennett's original typescript dated 31 May 1914, with 'Comarques Thorpe-le-Soken' handwritten on the title page. Bennett moved to 'Comarques', his country house in Essex, on 25 February 1913.

2. In using the term 'futurist play' Bennett may have been alluding to Filippo Tommaso Marinetti (1876-1944), the Italian dramatist who launched Futurism in 1909, although there is no record of his ever having referred to him by name. Certainly 'The Alarm' meets the Futurist dramatic criteria of 'abandon[ing] verisimilitude and traditional methods of characterisation and plot development' (*Oxford Companion to English Literature*, p.642).

3. The militant suffragette movement, the WSPU, (Women's Social and Political Union), was founded by Emmeline and Christabel Pankhurst in 1903 in opposition to the non-militant National Union of Women's Suffrage Societies. In Manchester, where it began, the WSPU members were-like Bennett's character-'educated middle class women, often university trained school teachers, neither very rich nor very poor' (Jill Liddington and Jill Norris *One Hand Tied Behind Us. The Rise of the Women's Suffrage Movement*, p.226).

4. Rates were an annual tax on property.

5. Bumbailiff is a scatological deprecatory slang term for an officer employed to collect debts and arrest debtors for non-payment. An early form of the term occurs in Shakespeare's *Twelfth Night* when Sir Toby Belch urges Sir Andrew Aguecheek to accost Malvolio: 'Go, Sir Andrew; scout me for him at the corner of the orchard, like a bum-bailey' (Act III, Scene IV). Bennett also uses the term in *Anna of the Five Towns* (1902) when Ephraim Tellwright tells Willie Price that he doubts his father's business acumen: 'Dunna tell me as Titus Price's never heard of a bumbailiff afore.' (p.7)

6. The WSPU's central concern was to acquire the vote. Their campaign escalated to encompass arson, including the partial destruction of the home of the Chancellor, David Lloyd George.

7. The 'Cat and Mouse Act' was the Liberal Government's response to the growing number of women prisoners going on hunger strike in protest against their treatment. Rather than risk the death of a hunger striker, the Act permitted prisoners to be temporarily discharged to recover their health and then readmitted to prison.

8. The practice of suffragette hunger strikes began in Holloway prison in June 1909 when Marion Wallace-Dunlop was sent there for refusing to pay a fine for damaging the stone-work of St. Stephen's Hall. She refused food for several days and, with the very real possibility that her death might create a martyr for the cause, she was released. Soon afterwards other suffragettes in Holloway adopted a similar strategy with similar success. The 'Cat and Mouse Act' was the Government's callous response.

9. As Chief Secretary in Dublin in 1818, Robert Peel (1788-1850) proposed setting up a modern police force. As Home Secretary under Lord Liverpool he was able to create a new, and somewhat controversial, Metropolitan Police Force. Bobbies (or 'Peelers' in Ireland) are named after him.

10. Clearly an ultra-sophisticated fireman, understanding sufficient Ancient Greek to call himself the Tetrarch (one of the four co-emperors of the Roman Empire).

WHAT MEN WANT.[1]

I.

They stood arguing on the crowded Paris pavement between a waiting taxi and the imposing façade of the establishment of Mme. Lecœur, one of the ten great French dressmakers.

The lovely widow, Lydia, said: 'But surely you can come in for a minute or two, my dear Andrew. I want you fo . . . And it's rather your affair,' she added, smiling. 'We shall be married before I get the bill.'

'It's three-fifteen. My appointment's for three-thirty. The fellow's leaving for Brussels at four o'clock.'

Andrew's appointment, he being a London solicitor of some importance, was with one of those Anglo-Saxon international lawyers latent in Paris who, by reason of having miraculously passed legal examinations in various countries, charge what they like to clients who have got themselves into any sort of international mess. Andrew himself could not have said whether, if Lydia had not happened to be in Paris just then, he would not have sent a clerk to Paris instead of coming over from London in person.

'Oh, you're always such an awful worrier!' exclaimed Lydia petulantly.

He paid off the taxi.

'You are a dear,' Lydia murmured.

Lydia was as much at home in the vast establishment of Lecœur as Andrew in the Law Courts, Strand. The aged janissary at the foot of the grand staircase saluted her with a smile. The stout, white-faced, black-robed lady at the entrance to the salons shook hands with her in passing.

'That's the head saleswoman,' Lydia murmured. 'She makes 160,000 francs a year.'

There were three large salons, intercommunicating. On chairs ranged round the walls of the lofty rooms sat potential customers, waiting. Some were hags; but they had just the same desire as the young and the pretty ones to make the very best of themselves. All the customers were women; all the hovering staff were women; and Andrew had the sensation also of innumerable women in the rooms behind, where oddments such as scent and earrings were sold and frocks tried on. He was the only male in the place.

'How late they always are here!' said Lydia, tapping with her foot impatiently. Yet a few moments earlier she had been lamenting that she would not be in time to see the first costumes shown. Interminably, exasperating minutes elapsed.

A mannequin entered the salon in a three-piece sports dress. Everybody became sternly attentive. Lydia was a different woman–as preoccupied, ruthless, and watchful as a soldier entering into battle. Spanish in style, with midnight hair and an exquisite fair skin, the slim mannequin tripped through the salons, advancing, receding, turning, mincing on her high, trembling heels, showing off her attire in every respect. She was a mere employee, but also she was a beautiful creature and knew her power.

'She too,' thought Andrew, 'has some man in the background.'

A WORLD OF WOMEN.

Another mannequin appeared–several; there must have been six or eight. They came and went, continually reappearing in new clothes which they changed with astonishing quickness.

'What the deuce am I doing in a place like this?' Andrew asked himself.

It was a world of women. It was a highly costly world, which men were paying for. Yes, all the salaries, all the silks and stuffs, all the rent, all the brains were being paid for by men. Andrew heard figures such as 2,000 francs, 3,500 francs,

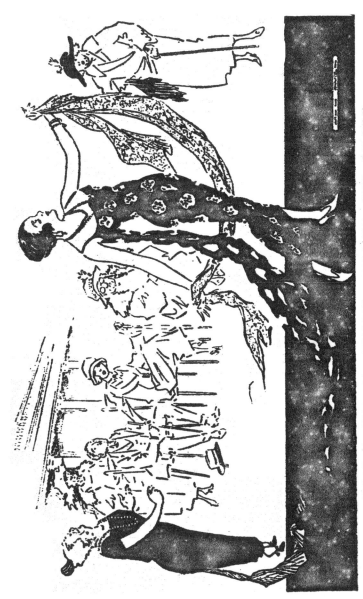

"THE MANNEQUIN TRIPPED THROUGH THE SALON."

5,000 francs. It was a world with one object–the beautifying of women to please men. And there were many such places in Paris; and many such places in every large capital. And this one had to do only with dresses. There were similar places for lingerie, shoes, hair, jewellery, what not.

And all these women could not have been more completely in earnest if the fate of Europe had depended upon their decisions.

LOVE.

Andrew knew why he was in this world. He was in it because he loved Lydia. And he knew he was in love, not because he was happy in her society, but because he was unhappy out of her society, and because she was gradually absorbing all his old interests into herself. When he thought of golf, he thought of her playing golf; when he read, he wondered if she would like the book; when he walked the streets he looked into all the shops devoted to women and into no others. He was as interested as she herself in the thousand problems connected with her adornment. And he was passionately curious about her mind, which he admired; for she managed somehow to talk intelligently upon all current topics. That section of his own mind which he never unlocked was half aware that she did not really understand the topics; but she had the air of understanding–like a journalist–and this sufficed.

'I really must go,' he said at length, gravely disturbed by his professional conscience.

'Mademoiselle!' said Lydia sharply, ignoring him. One of the saleswomen stopped obsequiously in front of her. 'What number is that dress?'

'What number is that dress?' the saleswoman asked the mannequin, who also halted.

'No.32,' said the mannequin, with a triumphant gesture.

'The dress interests you, madam?' asked the saleswoman.

'Do you like it, dear?' Lydia asked Andrew earnestly, with

a touching, enchanting smile.

'Very much,' he answered, perceiving that she wanted an affirmative.

Saying no more, except 'Wait half a second,' she then vanished from the salons with the saleswoman.

Andrew waited, tormented, broken in two by the claims of his business and of his fiancée. Then, after an age, suddenly, desperately, he rose, grasped his stick and gloves, and departed, like a criminal.

He was still, in spite of himself, feeling like a criminal when he called at the Hôtel du Rhin to take her out to dinner. Positively he was afraid to enter the private sitting-room. Her cousin Annette was there, a rather plain girl of twenty-five, simply dressed, as always. Annette was neither stylish nor intellectual. But she had affectionate eyes, and did fine needlework. She acted as Lydia's companion, and, having no pretensions, was always ready either to go out or to stay at home, according to Lydia's plans. Andrew talked nervously to her about her needlework–not a word about Lydia.

THE STORM.

Lydia entered, a perfect marvel of a confection from tiara to toes, each fingernail a work of applied art; and the storm broke. Lydia did not care twopence that Annette was present.

'Why did you run off like that?' Her cold voice was like an ultimatum. Her brow was transformed.

'Well, I had to, my dear. I simply had to. I was late as it was. Five past four.'

'Then you might as well have stayed, if you didn't see the lawyer. I specially asked you to stay. I was choosing a dress for you.'

'I did see him. He had had a telegram from Brussels saying that he needn't go there till to-morrow. So I had over an hour with him–fortunately.'

'I knew it would be all right!' said Lydia harshly. 'You're

always worrying about nothing. You see, you might just as well have stayed for me.'

BACK IN LONDON.

'"Half a second,"' said Andrew. 'And I waited at least ten minutes!. . . No notion of time whatever! And why should I have waited?' But he did not say this aloud. He, the important, clever, hard solicitor dared not.

She continued in the same ruthless vein. Annette bent her head and blushed.

Then Lydia's brow smoothed itself out.

'No use spoiling our evening,' she said, and laughed charmingly; and out they went to dinner, leaving Annette behind.

The next day Andrew returned to London. And London seemed to be nothing but a gigantic congeries of resplendent shops given up to the beautifying of women. It was amazing; it was overwhelming. The whole round earth revolved in order to perfect the lure of feminine elegance and charm.[2]

'Curse them!' breathed Andrew. 'They look as though they were conferring a great favour on us by being alive at all. Anyhow, she does! Why?'

And he began to doubt whether such divine creatures as Lydia, so lovely, so marvellous, so finished, so fragile, so complex, so exacting, could be quite a suitable diet for the human male's daily food.

II.

Two months later.

It was a Saturday, and Lydia had a luncheon appointment with Andrew at the Arlington Hotel, Piccadilly, for one-thirty. She arrived at one-forty-three, after a heavy morning. She had been dancing till 2 a.m. (extension night at the Legation Club) with Andrew and others; and so quite naturally and properly she had wakened later. Then there was the visit of her new

Swedish masseur, who was doing her good, but who had annoyed her by warning her against aspirin, brandy, rouge, powder, cocktails, and other matters, saying firmly in an impressive foreign accent that they would each and all age her. Then, of course, she had to read a little about the construction of the atom, about the effect of birth-control on the welfare of the nation, and about the most recent phenomena of spirit communications with another world. Further, her Sealyham was indisposed. Then she had a lot of telephoning–appointments with her crystal-gazer or soothsayer, three appointments in Bond-street, about her face, her brassieres, and her instep. But perhaps the chief telephoning was to make arrangements with a high legal functionary for a seat at the great murder trial in the following week. It was indeed rather marvellous that after such a morning (a not unusual sort of morning for her) she should arrive at the Arlington at all. She was only thirteen minutes late (call it ten), and she had arrived lovely; she had arrived perfect, with both her mind and her body wonderfully attired and beautified so that she might ravish Andrew. All her hard labour was for his sake–and a little also for the sake of the male sex at large.

She had a terrible, a unique shock on entering the crystal foyer of the Arlington. Andrew was not waiting for her! She could scarcely believe it. Still, he was not there. She was always late for appointments herself (except with the soothsayer, who would stand no nonsense from anybody); and she excused herself therefore; but she held that a man's vilest sin was to keep a woman waiting in a public resort. She sat down, deeply annoyed, and put all her exasperation into a little fluttering movement of her toes. She had done simply everything to please Andrew, and he was not there to receive her! It was monstrous. She was very fond of Andrew. Andrew was something of a personage in his own funny world, but scarcely a personage in hers. Indeed, her friends thought, and she did not quite disagree with them, that in accepting his offer of marriage she had bestowed a benefit on him, with her position, her beauty, her youth, her style, her chic, her intelligence, and her money. (She had had the money under her late husband's will; but exactly how her financial affairs then stood she did not know.)

However, she was very fond of Andrew. Sometimes she was quite silly about him. She liked him perhaps best when they were sitting together in a corner of the empty smoking-room of the country club, and he wore a tweed suit and smoked a pipe and threw his tweed cap down on the table in front of them. She could not keep her fingers from toying with that cap–so masculine was it, more masculine even than the lovely coarse odour of pipe tobacco, and the faint 'tweedy' odour of his loose jacket. Now and then she had a desire to steal the cap and keep it in a drawer in her bedroom among fluffy and filmy things. That was Lydia!

WAITING . . . .

But Andrew had been getting a bit out of hand lately, getting a bit morose, dry, combative, though never failing in utter politeness. To-day he had failed in politeness, unmentionably and totally failed.

'Something drastic will have to be done about this business,' she said to herself grimly, as she watched the incredible clock creeping on towards the hour of two. The clock reached the hour of two, passed it. Should she go into the restaurant and eat alone? . . . A pretty figure he would cut when he did come! Or should she go home?

Three dandical men and two stylish women entered, talking rather loudly. Lydia knew them all.

'Why, my dear Lydia!' the oldest of the men greeted her. 'Are you doing the patience stunt on a monument?'[3]

Lydia laughed, covering her chagrin with a chiffon of gaiety.

'My prospective host,' she said, 'has either forgotten me, or he's inexcusably late. Which is worse? . . . I don't know what to do.'

'Yes, you do know. Come and lunch with us.'

'I will! How perfectly sweet of you!'

And she began to arrange her ideas for bright, discursive, intellectual conversation.

ANDREW DEPARTS.

That afternoon Andrew called on Lydia. Her resentment had had time to develop blossoms of fire.

'I waited at the Piccadilly entrance till a quarter past two,' Andrew explained. 'I'm so sorry.'

'But you knew there were two entrances to the Arlington,' she retorted, blazing. 'Either you aren't really keen on me–or you are a fool. Take your choice. Anyway, I've finished with you. Good-bye.'

'Very good. Good-bye!' Andrew replied, and turned to leave. Then he turned back and added:–

'I was really keen on you. And I'm not a fool. And naturally I knew there are two entrances to the Arlington. And I thought I'd just try you for once, and see whether you had the sense and the decency and the humility to say to yourself that you might have come to the wrong entrance–and go to the other to look for me. You hadn't the sense and the decency and the humility to do this.'

And he departed.

III.

When a man who has felt solitude breaks a betrothal it is a hundred to one that he will become engaged again within a year. Andrew married Annette. Annette had sense, decency, humility–enough for two wives. She adored. He was affectionate. They were happy. Annette tried hard to be all in all to him.

Yet after a few months of the soft idyll he was saying to her:–

'My dear, can't you pay a little more attention to your clothes, your appearance—be a bit smarter? And if you could keep an eye on the papers and see what's going on . . .'

But a man can't have everything in one woman.

NOTES

1. *Harper's Bazar.* February 1924, pages 40-41. Signed Arnold Bennett. Illustrations by Everett Shinn. *Harper's Bazar* was first published in New York in December 1867, (eventually changing its spelling to *Harper's Bazaar)*, as a weekly magazine showing European fashion and aimed at an upper-middle and upper class readership. It moved from a weekly newspaper design format to monthly publication in 1901. Founded by Harper Brothers, it was purchased by William Randolph Hearst in 1912. Bennett published twelve articles/stories for the magazine between 1920 and 1927.

'What Men Want' appears again two months later in *The Sunday Express,* 18 April 1924, page 11, but with a single illustration by Will Owen (1869-1957). Owen is probably best remembered today for his iconic 'Bisto Kids' advertisement. Typically, as in this picture, he signed his name in a cartouche (a scroll with rolled-up ends).

The Sunday Express was founded by Lord Beaverbrook in December 1918, soon after his close war-time association with Bennett had ended. (Beaverbrook appointed Bennett Director of British Propaganda in France in May 1918.) The instant close nature of their enduring friendship is captured in Bennett's *Journal* entry for 18 November 1917:

> I made the acquaintance of Lord Beaverbrook Thursday week. He and Ross lunched with me on Friday. At this second meeting he asked me to take him to Leicester Gallery, where I had mentioned there was a good etching of Rops. I did so, with Ross. He asked which was the etching, bought it (20 guineas), and gave it me on the spot.

Bennett contributed 15 articles/stories to the paper from 1922 to 1929.

2. As if to confirm the story's verisimilitude, the American printing aligns it with a half page advertisement for 'Reads' Fabrics' promising 'lovely new shades and weaves for Spring' which will allow the readers' 'taste for beauty to find its full expression.' Following straight on from the story is the announcement: 'As indicated in this issue of Harper's Bazar, hats stay small; but there is something else besides the cloche. In next month's Bazar the new hats will be considered in relation to the costume as a whole.'

3. Shakespeare. *Twelfth Night,* Act III, scene iv. Viola; 'She sat like Patience on a monument', referring to the allegorical figure of Patience often found on Renaissance tombstones.